The Knockoff

LUCY SYKES AND JO PIAZZA

* * *

Lucy Sykes has worked in the fashion world as a stylist, fashion editor, and fashion director. For six years Lucy was the fashion director at *Marie Claire* magazine, and was most recently fashion director for Rent the Runway. Her own children's clothing line, Lucy Sykes New York, was sold in more than a hundred department stores worldwide, including Saks Fifth Avenue, Barneys, Bergdorf Goodman, and Nordstrom. Together with her twin sister Plum, Lucy moved from London to New York City in 1997, where she now lives with her husband and two children.

Jo Piazza is the managing editor of Yahoo Travel and a regular contributor to *The Wall Street Journal*. Her work has appeared in *The New York Times, New York* magazine, *Glamour, Gotham, The Daily Beast,* and *Slate*. She is the author of *Celebrity, Inc.: How Famous People Make Money* and a novel, *Love Rehab: A Novel in 12 Steps* and *If Nuns Ruled the World: Ten Sisters on a Mission*. She lives in New York City with her giant dog.

⟨⟨⟨ *The Knockoff* ⟩⟩⟩

The Knockoff

<<< A NOVEL >>>

LUCY SYKES AND JO PIAZZA

* * *

ANCHOR BOOKS
A Division of Penguin Random House LLC
New York

12-15

FIRST ANCHOR BOOKS INTERNATIONAL EDITION, JUNE 2015

Copyright © 2015 by Lucy Sykes

Anchor International Edition ISBN: 978-1-101-87390-8

www.anchorbooks.com

Printed in the United States of America
10 9 8 7 6 5 4 3 2 1

For the boys, Euan, Heathcliff and Titus

For John and Tracey

For all the Imogen Tates

"Always forgive your enemies; nothing annoys them so much."

—OSCAR WILDE

* * *

"In order to be irreplaceable one must always be different."

—COCO CHANEL

‹ ‹ ‹   *The Knockoff*   › › ›

SEPTEMBER 5, 1999

The pretty young associate editor crossed her bare legs nervously, allowing her right foot to bounce up and down. She worried her black bouclé pencil skirt might be a touch too short for sitting in the front row. By most measures she was perfectly ordinary in this crowd of black-clad men and women in fine Italian fabrics cut in French lines made with an American sensibility. She looked the part. Still, she couldn't believe she was actually there. Never in a million years could she have imagined she would be sitting in the front row of a New York City fashion show during Fashion Week. She flipped the heavy vellum invitation over one more time to read the embossed gold writing. There was no mistake. Her seat was 11A. She was in the right place at the right time.

At twenty-six, Imogen Tate had already been poring over the photographs from these fashion shows with her bosses at *Moda* magazine for five years, but she had never seen one in the flesh.

This plum assignment for the Oscar de la Renta show only came her way because the senior editors were overscheduled. Bridgett Hart, a striking black model and one of Imogen's three roommates, was walking in this show. Imogen glanced at her watch. Five thirty.

It was scheduled to start at five, but the seats weren't even close to being filled. Despite Bridgett promising her that nothing ever began on time during Fashion Week, Imogen arrived promptly at four forty-five. Best to be early. She considered getting up to say hello to her friend Audrey, a publicist for Bergdorf Goodman who was chatting with a reporter from the *Trib* about ten seats away, but Imogen worried someone would steal her assigned seat. She'd been warned about one particularly vigilant new-money socialite who could never secure front row and would hover along the periphery waiting for her chance to pounce if someone didn't show up.

A piece of hair fell into Imogen's face and she quickly tucked it back behind her ear. Only last week she let her new colorist persuade her to return to her natural blond after a series of more dramatic darker shades. It was understated. "Chic" was the right word to describe her new life in America. "Ouch!" Imogen lifted her foot and scowled at the paparazzo who had trampled on her exposed little toe in the very best (and only) strappy snakeskin sandals that she owned.

"You're in the way," he sneered.

"I'm in *my* seat," Imogen countered in her most distinguished British accent. She added an emphasis on "my." It was indeed her seat and her name on the invitation. That meant something. The fashion industry was an insular community of designers, editors, retail buyers and select heiresses. Access to these kinds of events was allotted stingily, and could easily be taken away.

"Well, your seat is in my way," the ornery photographer said before darting across the plastic-covered runway to take a picture of Anna Wintour, the editor in chief of *Vogue,* as she gracefully took her own place across the runway from Imogen. With Anna seated the show could finally begin. Security men in bulky black turtlenecks, carrying large walkie-talkies, ushered the photographers into a holding pen at the end of the runway. All photos from the show were under strict embargo, pending approval from the designer. Imogen had a little point-and-shoot camera in her bag, but she didn't dare take it out. She had taken plenty of pictures outside the tents in Bryant Park and planned to drop the film at one of those one-hour developing places on her way back to work. From inside her purse she removed a small black notebook.

Assistants in head-to-toe black stripped the industrial plastic from the runway, revealing a pristine white surface. The lights dimmed and the house grew silent. The crowd respectfully slipped their purses and briefcases under their chairs. So attentive was the audience of what was happening on the runway that they refrained from whispering to one another or even shuffling papers on their laps once the lights went down.

Out of the silence, a dance beat boomed "Livin' La Vida Loca" by Ricky Martin as white light bathed the room. Models, never breaking their gaze, strode down the catwalk one after the other. Imogen hardly had time to take notes on each of the looks. This really would be an excellent time to use that camera, but she didn't dare.

Across from her, Imogen noticed Jacques Santos. Dressed in his signature white jeans, the photographer turned creative director for one of the big magazines whipped out his Nikon and furiously began shooting the models as they walked past him. Out of the corner of her eye, Imogen could see security begin to twitch from their posts at the end of the runway. It wasn't until Jacques actually stood and hoisted the camera over his head to take an aerial shot that they made their move. Perfectly timed between models, one guard approached Jacques from either side, and before the Frenchman knew what was happening they tackled him and confiscated his camera. He lay stunned on the runway.

Bridgett, Imogen's statuesque friend, didn't even blink as she calmly stepped over the man in her thigh-high leather boots and continued her journey down the runway with the elegance of a panther, her right toe slightly pointed as it rose off the ground. The camera in one hand, the security guard pulled Jacques to his feet, dusted him off and gestured for him to sit back down. He removed the film from the Nikon and handed the camera back before returning to his post at the end of the aisle.

The show went on.

CHAPTER ONE

AUGUST 2015

At first, Imogen didn't recognize the girl twirling around in her chair taking a picture of her own magenta Tory Burch flats and matching fingernails. One hand clutched her white-and-gold iPhone, while the other extended toward her shoes, manicured fingers splayed in front of the screen.

Imogen smoothed her fine blond hair behind her ears and gave a confident click with her right heel so the girl, now pouting into the phone's camera to take a selfie, would know she wasn't alone in the corner office.

"Oh." Eve Morton, Imogen's former assistant, snapped to attention, startled. The phone clattered to the floor. A note of surprise rose in Eve's husky voice as she glanced over Imogen's shoulder to see if anyone else was behind her. "You're back?" The girl's coltish legs covered the space between them in a few seconds before she wrapped Imogen in a hug that felt too familiar. Eve looked different now. Her auburn curls were blown out, some sort of keratin treatment, most likely. The shiny pin-straight hair framed a flawlessly made-up face with a slightly newer, cuter nose than Imogen remembered.

Why was Eve sitting at the desk of the editor in chief? Imogen's desk.

Imogen racked her brain to find any reason Eve would be in this building at all so early in the morning. She no longer worked here. She had been Imogen's assistant two years ago and hadn't been back since.

Eve had been an extraordinarily competent assistant and, for all intents and purposes, a friend, but this was an irritating distraction on her first day back at work. All Imogen wanted was to get settled before the rest of the staff arrived, call down for a cappuccino and have someone help her wade through the inevitable swamp of her email.

"Eve? Darling, why are you here? I thought you were off at Harvard Business School?" Imogen sidestepped her to settle into her chair. Sinking into the leather seat after so much time away felt good.

The girl folded her long legs beneath her instead of crossing them when she sat facing Imogen. "I finished in January actually. I went to a start-up incubator in Palo Alto for a few months. Then I came back here in July."

What was a start-up incubator? Imogen wondered. She imagined it had something to do with chickens, but didn't have the inclination or the interest to ask.

"Back to New York? That's lovely. I'm sure some monstrous investment bank has snatched you up now that you have an MBA," Imogen replied evenly, pressing the power button on her computer.

Eve threw her head back with a throaty laugh that surprised Imogen in its maturity and depth. Her old laugh was sweet and lilting. This laugh belonged to a stranger. "No. I came back to New York and back to *Glossy*! I sent my résumé to Mr. Worthington in January. We talked just before you went off on sick leave. In July I moved back to New York and I came here. I mean . . . it's like a dream job. He told me he was going to tell you. I didn't even think you would be in until your usual time . . . about ten. I figured you would have a meeting with Worthington and he could fill you in on my new role."

Old assistant. New role. Eve, twenty-six years old, her eyes heavy with aubergine liner and naked ambition, sitting in Imogen's office.

Imogen had communicated with Carter Worthington, the publisher and her boss, exactly two times during her six-month hiatus from work. For the first time since she walked through the doors of *Glossy* that morning, she took a hard look around the floor and noticed small differences. Most of the lights were still dim, accentuating the buttery morning sun pouring in through the windows beyond the elevator bank. But the traditionally sparse-by-design floor felt more crowded. When she left, the floor had contained roomy cubicles with low partitions, each desk having enough space for a keyboard and a computer monitor. Now the partitions were gone and a snug collection of tables formed a continuous row across the room with laptops so close they kissed one another like dominos preparing to topple. Her favorite photograph, Mario Testino's close-up of Kate Moss's face, was missing from the wall. In its place was a broad whiteboard drawn over with numbered lists and doodles in every color of marker. Elsewhere on the soft gray walls were signs printed in cursive letters and matted in juvenile colors: "Taking risks gives you energy!" "What would you do if you weren't afraid?" "What would Beyoncé do?" "Good, Great, Gorgeous, *GLOSSY*!" Inside Imogen's office one major thing was missing: her cork inspiration board, usually covered over with scraps of magazines, tear sheets from shoots, pieces of fabric, old photographs and anything else that caught her fancy and inspired her. *Who the hell thought they could remove my board?*

An irrational anxiety swelled in Imogen's stomach. Something was different and whatever was different felt wrong. All she could think was, *Get out of my office,* but instead, after a tiny pause, she asked politely, "What exactly is your new job here, Eve?" At that moment she noticed that a large ballerina-pink beanbag chair occupied the corner of the room.

"I'm in charge of digital content for Glossy-dot-com." Eve smiled briefly, but unconvincingly, as she picked at her nail polish.

Imogen maintained her poker face and breathed an internal sigh of relief. Okay. Eve was only in charge of Internet content. For a second she'd panicked and thought Eve was there in some kind of senior role that she hadn't been told about. Of course it was 2015 and of course the magazine had a website and sure, all of that meant something. But the website was just a necessary appendage of the actual pages of the magazine, used mainly as a dumping ground for favors for advertisers and leftover stories. Right? The girl was in charge of something relatively inconsequential. Still, why hadn't anyone consulted Imogen before they hired her old assistant for a new position? It was poor form.

Eve rushed on. "I can't wait to talk about all the new changes. The site has never been stronger. I just think you're going to love the relaunch."

A headache threatened to spring from the base of Imogen's skull. "I think it is great that they finally gave the website a redesign. And I really am happy that you're back. I would love to have lunch with you once I'm all caught up." She nodded, hoping the girl would just blog off already so that Imogen could start her day.

Perhaps cracking a joke would speed the process along. "As long as the redesign has nothing to do with my magazine and"—she hoped to make a point—"as long as they haven't given away my office."

Eve blinked in confusion, eyelash extensions flickering like hummingbird wings.

"I think you need to talk to Carter, Imogen." It was strange to hear a vaguely authoritative tone in Eve's twenty-six-year-old voice, and odder still for her to address their boss, Carter Worthington, by his first name. All at once, Imogen could feel her heart begin to beat faster again. She had been right the first time. Eve was not just working on the website. Imogen worried for a moment that Eve, who had once been so good at anticipating her every need, could read her mind right now. She stood.

"I actually have a meeting with him anyway," Imogen lied. "First thing this morning. I should head up there now."

Shifting her weight from one heel onto the other, she turned to walk away from Eve, past several young women she didn't recognize who were starting to trickle in. Her hand shook. Her face revealed nothing but a static smile as she pressed the elevator button for the lobby. In a building this large you had to go back down to go farther up.

Gus, at the lobby coffee stand, practically leaped over the counter, doing a two-step in her direction as she hurried between the building's two elevator banks.

"I thought you never be coming back!" he exclaimed, smelling sweetly of cinnamon and steamed milk. His sandy mustache bounced with each syllable. "How has that magazine survived for six months without an editor in chief? They must have missed you so, so much!" He squeezed her hand with care. Of course he knew why she had been gone. They had tried to keep it out of the press, but these days there wasn't much you could hide from the gossip columns.

In February, half a year earlier, Imogen was diagnosed with stage II breast cancer in her left breast, the same disease that had taken her grandmother and two aunts. In March she'd opted for a double mastectomy and reconstruction to both eradicate the cancer and prevent it from spreading. She'd spent the next six months in chemo and recovery.

"Here I am." Imogen forced herself to deliver a warm smile. This was all too much before nine a.m. But at least Gus carried with him kindness and the promise of caffeine. He led her over to the coffee counter and, without having to say anything, busied himself making her drink, topping the foam off with an affectionate heart. He waved her away as she pulled four crisp dollar bills out of her wallet and pushed the cup into her hand.

"My treat. A very special day! If I known this was going to be your first day back I would have had the missus make you something special . . . some of her baklava . . . with the honey that you like. You be here tomorrow? She make it tonight. I bring it to you tomorrow. With the honey." She nodded and thanked him, savoring the jolt of caffeine as she made her way to the elevator. Workers streamed into the lobby now. A handsome middle-aged man with salt-and-pepper hair and a pocket square in his immaculate suit gave Imogen's legs an approving glance as he joined her in the lift.

On the ride up, her head still swimming, Imogen remembered clearly the moment Eve Morton walked into her life five years earlier. She had only just been promoted to be editor in chief of *Glossy* and was exhausted from weeks of interviewing candidates to be her assistant. Human Resources sent her practically the entire senior class of

Le Rosey (that Swiss finishing school where rich Americans sent their spoiled children to meet other rich Americans), all of them bored and privileged. None of them had the kind of ineffable drive Imogen knew would make them hungry enough to excel at *Glossy*. Imogen understood better than anyone how important it was for someone to be hungry for a job like this one. She had once been an assistant herself, to her very first boss and mentor, Molly Watson, editor in chief of *Moda* magazine, the most inspiring person Imogen had known in her entire life.

The day Eve Morton walked into the *Glossy* offices for the first time she was a single class shy of graduating from New York University. Wearing a rumpled trench coat, she'd been sopping wet, hair strung around her face, giving her the appearance of a bedraggled kitten. Outside it was the kind of rainy April day that transforms even hardened New Yorkers into timid tourists in their own city, reluctant to venture out without the promise of a car ready to whisk them off to their next destination.

While tall and broad, Eve was mousy and shy. Yet there was a gleam in her eye that sparkled all the more as she pulled out her laptop to reveal a PowerPoint presentation with slides featuring magazine pages from the early nineties to the present.

"I've read every magazine you have worked on," she let spill from her slightly lopsided, but not altogether unpretty, mouth. "This is the most exciting moment of my entire life, just sitting here in this office. You're seriously one of the best magazine editors in the world. I think I have read every single story about you, too. I just love all the parties you throw with the designers during Fashion Week and the way you expressly asked *not* to be seated near Kim Kardashian at the London shows. I love all the changes you've made to *Glossy*. You're the reason I want to work in magazines."

Imogen wasn't immune to flattery, but she did have a finely tuned bullshit detector. Still, she didn't think she had ever met anyone who had read every single issue of *Glossy* for the past three years, *Harper's Bazaar* for the two years before that and *Elle* for two prior. She wasn't even sure if she could say with a straight face that she herself had read all of those issues cover to cover. Imogen peered at the girl with a measure of incredulity, the edge of her J.Crew skirt still dripping onto the white hardwood floors of her office.

"Well, thank you, but you seem much too young to have been reading my magazines for that long."

"Oh, I've been reading fashion books since I could *read.* When you shot the couture collections on window-washing scaffolding seventy floors above Times Square, I mean, I literally died."

Eve was referring to a shoot later described in the press as "Do or Die," where Imogen envisioned the models in place of window washers, with photographers as spectators on different floors. Iconic supermodels dangled like insects from ledges, their hemlines catching expertly on the breeze. The magazine's insurance premiums skyrocketed. That didn't stop Imogen from taking over an entire subway station for the following month's shoot, and a supermarket in Queens for the one after. They'd brought in Chanel-branded ham for that one.

"When I saw that—it completely altered the course of my whole life," Eve said, bringing Imogen back to the present with words she didn't entirely believe could be true.

"I did? It did? My God, how?"

"I couldn't get those images out of my mind. They stuck with me. It was an out-of-this-world experience. The clothes came alive for me then. From that moment I knew there was one thing that I was meant to do in the entire world. From that moment I knew I was destined to come to New York, where these magazines were made. I applied to New York University and FIT. I was accepted to both and I chose NYU so I could design my own major focusing on marketing, management and the history of fashion. From then on all I ever wanted was to come here and work with you. The innovations you have made in fashion magazines have been the most exciting thing to happen to editorial content in decades."

Eve's shoulders finally shrugged a bit, as if a weight had been lifted now that she had delivered a monologue practiced many times in front of a dorm-room mirror covered in fingerprints and Windex smudges.

Imogen smiled at her. She was good at accepting praise, but this was difficult for even the most seasoned egotist to swallow. "Well, now that you've been here and seen all of this up close, what do you think?"

Eve looked around the room with her saucer-sized green eyes. "It is even better than I expected. I just know that I can learn so much from you and I'll do whatever it takes to make your life run as smoothly as possible."

She added, "Give me a chance. I'll change your life." That line should have sent chills up Imogen's spine, but she was no Cassandra, and she was desperate for someone hardworking and eager who could start right away.

Eve Morton did exactly what she promised. She was on the ball. She was prompt. She was a fast learner and an overachiever who proved her worth in matters large and small. All day long they talked to each other through Imogen's open door. Imogen's baby son, Johnny, had pneumonia for weeks on end soon after Eve took the position. Together they crafted a furtive system that kept the rest of the magazine in the dark about Imogen leaving for hours to take care of him. Eve sat guard outside her office, routing all calls to Imogen's cell phone and assuring visitors that she was hard at work and must not be disturbed. Eve would print new versions of the layouts and bring them to Imogen's town house after everyone else had gone home for the evening. Imogen would make her changes by hand and Eve would whip them into impressive mock-ups before the next morning's meeting. Her help was invaluable.

From the very beginning Imogen had been struck by how desperate Eve was to conform and please. If someone mentioned they needed a restaurant reservation, Eve would send them five options. If they said they liked her bracelet, she would buy them one for their birthday. When Imogen added new honey-colored highlights to her hair, Eve did the same.

The girl's wardrobe graduated from basic J.Crew to much more aspirational designers, funded mainly by a string of older gentlemen suitors who consistently picked her up from the office in their Town Cars late at night. Eve kept her ambition tucked inside her like a set of those Russian nesting dolls. Each time she shed a layer, she appeared more confident, more self-assured.

Just as Imogen was seriously considering promoting her to assistant editor, after two and a half years of dedicated service, Eve knocked on Imogen's door with red rings around her eyes. To please her father, a hard-nosed high school football coach with the most state championship wins in Wisconsin, a man who wished he had a son who would be a big-time banker and not a daughter who worked in fashion, Eve had taken the GMAT and applied to business school. She'd never expected to get in, but Harvard offered her a scholarship to get her MBA. Eve couldn't say no to her dad.

And so Imogen lost the best assistant she ever had. As a parting gift, Imogen presented Eve with a red vintage Hermès twill silk scarf.

Eve sent flowers twice when she learned Imogen was sick. One of the bouquets came with a card that said "Get Well Soon," with a picture of a sad kitten nudging an older and chubbier orange tabby cat. The other, a vase of ivory magnolias, Imogen's favorite flower, came with no real card at all. Just a piece of paper with "Eve" scrawled large across it.

Before the elevator doors opened into the executive suite that housed Worthington's office, Imogen gave herself a small pep talk. She was Imogen Tate, successful editor in chief, the woman responsible for breathing new life into *Glossy* and turning it around when everyone said it couldn't be done. She had won awards and wooed advertisers. On her brief ride up, Imogen had decided to play the next moments as dispassionately as she possibly could with Worthington. Her boss liked and respected her because she was always so level-headed. Imogen considered her ability to read both people and a room to be one of her best qualities.

Her shoulders thrust back, she coolly strode past Worthington's two homely assistants. The publisher's fourth wife, a former beauty queen and one of his old assistants (while he was married to his third wife), mandated their plainness because she knew exactly what her husband was capable of doing with ambitious young women. One of the young assistants moved to block Imogen, but—too late—was tripped up by an unflattering floor-length skirt. When Imogen broke through the imposing oak doors, Worthington, always an early riser, and especially more so now that the company was doing so much business with Asia, was standing parallel to a wall of windows over-looking downtown Manhattan. The office was a mixture of steel, glass and dark wood—cruise ship Art Deco—with German brass sconces that had once graced the ballroom of a Cunard ocean liner. With his puffy fingers looped lazily around the top of his putter, he resembled a Hirschfeld sketch of a well-fed executive. He was an ugly man, made handsome by virtue of being wealthy. With his bulbous nose and tiny pink ears he was Piggy from *Lord of the Flies*, all grown up as an alpha male. She'd heard him described as hilarious, eccentric, a genius and a lunatic, all by women who had once been married to him.

"Imogen," he boomed. "You look incredible. Have you lost weight?" His eyes cruised up and down her frame, resting too long at her breasts. Was he trying to figure out if these breasts were an improve-ment? *Yes, Carter, these breasts are about ten years younger, perkier and firmer. Perhaps a tad rounder. Thank you for noticing,* Imogen couldn't help but think. When a mechanic replaced an engine, he always gave it a little tune-up.

Determined to maintain an air of quiet control, she smiled, easing into the buttery leather of the couch to the right of the putting green, and got straight to the point. "I am delighted to see that you have rehired Eve Morton." Copies of Worthington's new memoir were placed at right angles on the steel Gemelli coffee table. His jowls, air-brushed into a jawline, sat above the bold title letters on the bottom of the cover—WORTH.

"Yes. Yes. Smart girl, that Eve. She has an MBA from Harvard, you know . . . and legs that go on for miles . . . like a young Susan Sarandon. Man, that broad could party back in the day." He winked to no one in particular. Imogen had long ago grown accustomed to the fact that women, including Susan Sarandon, in Worthington's lexicon were broads, chicks and gals, all an assemblage of beautiful or not beautiful parts, rather than a competent whole. He spoke in the language more befitting an Atlantic City cardsharp than a Man-hattan publisher. Her boss was never interested in idle chatter, but still Imogen wondered if he had any clue that today was her first day back in the office. And what having an MBA from Harvard and legs that went on for miles had to do with working on a website of a magazine, Imogen hadn't a clue. Imogen had friends who had gone off to business school in the late nineties and early 2000s. She had no idea what it was like when Eve went, but for many of those friends, MBAs meant two years of adult summer camp with keg parties and field trips: delayed adulthood that indiscriminately catapulted them into the next tax bracket.

She could tell that Worthington had a measure of goodwill toward Eve, so she played along.

"Top of her class, apparently. I am so excited that we have her back," Imogen said with a perfectly calibrated smile. "The website can always use good people."

"It's going to be much more than a website, Imogen. To be honest, I don't entirely get what it is going to be myself, but I think it will make us a shitload of money!" Worthington paused as if to consider the benefits of once again making the company an enormous amount of money. It wasn't too long ago that the consulting firm of McKittrick, McKittrick and Dressler set up shop at Mannering to try to figure out why the company, particularly the magazine division, was bleeding cash. It didn't take a $500-an-hour consultant to figure out where the money was going. There was the editor at large who kept an apartment in the first arrondissement in Paris for weekend trips with a revolving door of young male suitors. There was a permanent suite at the Four Seasons in Milan available for senior staff to enjoy during the fashion shows and other alternating weekends. There were the riders installed in editor in chief contracts (Imogen's included) for cars, clothes and dry cleaning. Worthington released a sigh for the good old days as he knocked his golf ball a couple of inches into the hole of the putting green.

He continued: "I'm happy you are excited about it. I was worried that you wouldn't take the news well. I know how devoted you are to the glossy pages. I was worried you wouldn't like the switch over to a digital magazine. In fact, I was worried you might just leave us for good. But we all know it's time for this company to put digital first."

What was a digital magazine? Nothing coming out of his fishlike mouth made any sense. Of course she was devoted to those glossy pages of the magazine. It was her job. Did he mean that they would be putting more of the magazine on the Internet? Was that why they brought in Eve? Maybe today's MBA programs taught you how to finally make money from putting a magazine on the Internet, something Imogen hadn't really thought was possible. In just the past few years there had been so much change. Publishing was a different world now. She knew that. Blogs, websites, tweets, linking and crossposting. These were all things people cared about.

Worthington pulled a shiny new ball from his pocket and continued, "The new business model that Eve came up with is unlike anything I have ever seen. It is Amazon meets Net-a-Porter on steroids. And to think . . . we get a cut of every single item we sell. This is what will save the company. Not to mention the money we are saving on printing and shipping."

As the weight of this new information sank in, Imogen felt the office walls move inward. The muscles behind her eyes tightened and twitched. Her head pounded and her stomach twisted. She dug her fingernails into the fleshy parts of her palms. *Pull yourself together.* She'd been a fool to think she could leave her job for months and expect everything to be just as she left it.

Imogen strained for another smile.

"Carter, what are you trying to tell me? What is happening to my magazine?"

He looked at her, very matter-of-factly, and then said in a tone he typically reserved for his five-year-old twins, "Your magazine is now an app."

<<< CHAPTER TWO. >>>

By the time she made it back down to the *Glossy* floor from
Worthington's office, a sea of new faces had gathered in
the conference room for the morning meeting. Imogen
had expected to have more time to prepare to see her
staff. Over the past week she'd practiced the speech she would make
during this very meeting on her first day back. Looking through the
glass walls, she didn't recognize anyone sitting around the table or
slouched against the wall at the back of the room. Her managing
editor, Jenny Packer, and creative director, Maxwell Todd, were con-
spicuously missing. Imogen's eyes searched for a familiar face as she
walked in and took a seat at the head of the long white table. Now she
recognized a couple of people from sales and marketing, but she still
didn't see any of her editors.

A young woman across the room smiled giddily at her. As soon as
she made eye contact Imogen knew it was a mistake.

"Imogen Tate!!!!" the girl squealed. "I just love you. I am so happy
that you are back! You're like a fashion goddess. A goddess. I just
tweeted that you were sitting here in our meeting and I got, like, fifteen retweets already. All of my friends are completely jealous of me
for getting to sit here in this room and breathe the air you are breathing." She reached her hand—nails painted a neon pink and decorated

on the tips with what looked like vanilla cake frosting—across the table. As she clasped it with her own, Imogen spied a chunky black rubber bracelet on the girl's wrist with pink writing: "Good, Great, Gorgeous, *GLOSSY.com*!"

"I'm Ashley. I'm your assistant. I'm also the community manager for the site?" Ashley's voice was childlike and twinkly and she ended the last sentence like it was a question even though Imogen was sure she hadn't meant it as one. Imogen had been looking for a new assistant when she left, so it would be helpful not to waste energy trying to find a new girl, but she was skeptical of this packaged deal. How was this girl going to be both her assistant and do whatever it was the community manager did?

"Which community exactly are you managing, darling?" Imogen asked as she took in Ashley's long corn-silk hair and huge pale blue eyes with absurdly long eyelashes that might have even been real. Her bee-stung lips were coated in a dark red lipstick that shouldn't have worked, but somehow just made her look more intense and beautiful. She was certainly an original in this room of girls who otherwise all looked the same.

Ashley laughed and jumped out of her seat with the energy of a Labrador puppy, her hair rippling in a silky wave. "*The* community. I manage all the social media. Twitter, Crackle, Facebook, Pinterest, Screamr, YouTube, Bloglogue, Instagram, Snapchat and ChatSnap. We're actually outsourcing the Tumblr right now to a digital agency, but I'm still working with them on it."

Imogen nodded, hoping to convey that she understood more than half of those words.

Just then, Eve walked into the room balancing her laptop in one hand and an iPad in the other. Eve shot daggers toward Ashley and reprimanded her. "This isn't a sorority meeting, girls."

Imogen had no university degree. Molly Watson had scooped her up as a shopgirl back in London when she was just seventeen and she had been hard at work ever since. Still, Imogen had immediate uncomfortable associations with sorority girls, imagining them as a prelude to the Real Housewives of New York, beautiful bitchy bullies.

She surveyed the gang of new women gathered around the table, most of them in their early twenties. Where was *her* staff? The fashion sense of these girls was of two flavors, hooker or gym bunny—too-tight dresses or coordinated track pants and hoodies.

No one here in this room followed the unwritten rules of how the fashion industry dressed. Sure, magazines were filled with bright colors and over-the-top accessories, a cast of characters in elaborate designs all bedecked in taffeta, techno leather and, more than once, an entire rainbow of furs. But the people who created fashion were, for the most part, simple and bare in their personal style. You could tell who belonged from the interlopers who snuck past security at Fashion Week because the fashion editor typically wore something effortlessly thrown together—a Céline look, perhaps a YSL blouse with a vintage Hermès trench. Their clothes maintained a sense of uniform and calm in a chaotic world. There was a reason Grace Coddington still wore black every single day. Most of the top editors and designers never even wore nail polish. Imogen had never seen a speck of color on Anna Wintour's nails—perhaps her toes, but never on her hands.

Everyone in the room pecked away at the small screens of iPhones and tablets. Imogen felt strangely naked and lacking without her own device, which she had left idle at her desk. She had never once brought a phone into a meeting. It was rude.

The *tip-tapping* slowed but did not come to a complete stop when Eve clapped her hands together.

"Let's do this! As all of you can see we have a new addition to the meeting today." Eve smiled over at her. "Some of you know Imogen Tate, our editor in chief, but many of you don't. She has been out on sick leave for the last six months." Imogen winced at those words. "Sick leave." That wasn't what she wanted to call it. She'd been on sabbatical, or hiatus. "Now she is back just in time for the launch of *Glossy*'s amazing new website and app. Let's all make sure to give her a warm Glossy.com welcome this week!" Before Imogen could even rise out of her seat to make her speech to the staff, the meeting moved forward at a rapid clip. This was a completely new Eve from the one who had sat outside her office and answered phones. This one fired on all cylinders. She appeared more clever, brighter and funnier than Imogen remembered.

A woman Imogen recognized as a booking assistant gave a brief rundown of a photo shoot scheduled for later in the week. Eve went through a complicated series of statistics: unique page views, organic traffic, referral traffic, cross-channel insight. Imogen wasn't quite sure what to make of any of it. She wrote the numbers down on the first blank page of her Smythson notebook along with the few words she was able to decipher, keeping a smile on her face throughout the entire ordeal. She was Imogen Tate. She was still the editor in chief. She had been one of the first fashion magazine editors to lobby for her magazine to have its own website, but she had never actually worked on it. Who was going to teach her how all this worked?

The moment Eve finished talking about something called the conversion rate, she let loose another clap and yelled with intense urgency:

"Go, go, go!"

Everyone pushed clear of the table in tandem and, in silence, darted back to their desks balancing their MacBook Airs on one hand like waitresses carrying trays. Imogen walked over to Eve, but too late realized that Eve was already speaking into earbuds plugged into her phone. Eve pointed at her wrist, which had no watch, and mouthed the words "just a minute" to Imogen.

She would just nip into the loo for a second to get her bearings. Sitting in the stall, Imogen rubbed her temples. What the hell was going on? This was an entirely new office from the one she'd left behind. Eve didn't seem to know her place in the pecking order of this magazine anymore. Where was the respect? Imogen's staff was nowhere to be found.

From twenty feet away Imogen could see a crowd in her office. Now, that was a nice touch. A small welcome back party, perhaps?

Drawing closer, she could see the new girls perched on every available surface in the room while Eve furiously drew a grid in purple marker on a whiteboard behind Imogen's desk.

She cleared her throat loudly, but it did nothing to slow the momentum of the meeting.

"Eve!" Imogen said, even louder than she had expected.

"Imogen, hey. Join us. We are just jamming on some new ideas in here."

Jamming on ideas? "Do you usually jam here in my office?"

Eve nodded earnestly. "We do. The engineers were up all night. They're napping in the conference room." She shrugged her broad shoulders. "You weren't here so we've been using the space."

Who just waltzes into someone's office and begins doodling on a wall?

"How about we jam later, ladies? Let me get up to speed a little?"

The young women in the room swiveled their heads between Imogen and Eve, unsure who had the authority in this situation. Eve raised an eyebrow, perhaps considering putting up a fight before thinking better of it.

"Sure thing." She snapped her fingers three times into the air. "Let's huddle by my desk." She looked over her shoulder as the staff fell in a line behind her. "Come over if you want, Imogen."

"Eve," Imogen called out. "Please take this with you." She hoisted the pink monstrosity of a beanbag chair out of the corner and into Eve's arms. It was heavier than it looked. "It doesn't belong in here, darling," Imogen said firmly.

When Imogen made it into to her seat she saw her lonely iPhone was still perched at the top of her handbag. It squawked at her as if it knew that all of the other devices had been invited to the meeting. Sitting on the keyboard was a black bracelet like Ashley's: "Good, Great, Gorgeous, *GLOSSY.com*!" Assuming it was some freebie from the marketing department, Imogen tossed it in the bin. Her computer screen was a mess of blinking notifications. She right-clicked her mouse and let out a small gasp. The monitor lit up like an arcade game, icons on the bottom bounced excitedly up and down and notification messages dotted the upper left side of the display, one after another. Her email in-box was at capacity. Imogen felt a distinct loss of control. Her eyes didn't know where to look first. How could she reach Ashley, her new assistant? She needed someone to clear her inbox. There was no longer an assistant's desk outside her office, and the exuberant girl was nowhere to be found.

Quickly scrolling through the most recent ten messages, Imogen realized that everyone had worked through that morning meeting. During a time when she thought she was supposed to detach from her electronics, brainstorm with her colleagues and plan their day, everyone else had been sending "Reply All" emails.

It felt as if Imogen had been in one meeting and the rest of the staff had been in another. An entire subtext was missing from her experience of the conversation in the conference room.

The photo shoot they discussed was already scheduled. A photographer, not the one she recommended, had been booked. Hair and makeup were still outstanding.

Wait.

No.

She scrolled up.

Hair and makeup had been booked. The cost for catering was too high.

This was déjà vu in reverse.

She picked up the phone sitting on the desk and dialed Eve's extension. It went to the voice mail of a man with a gruff Long Island accent. Of course Eve didn't have the same extension she had when she worked for Imogen. Did Eve even have a phone on her desk? Where was Eve's desk?

Imogen depressed the receiver with her index finger, hit zero for reception and was immediately diverted to an automated system requiring her to enter the first four letters of a person's first or last name. She typed in three-eight-three.

"To reach Eve Morton, please press three or dial six-nine-six."

No answer. Imogen hung up and tried again.

When she finally picked up, Eve's voice on the other end of the line was cautious, surprised and laden with a hint of suspicion.

"Hello?"

"Eve. It's Imogen. I wanted to ask you a few questions."

"Why are you calling me?"

Was the girl daft? She repeated herself, slower and slightly louder this time. "I wanted to ask you a few questions."

"I can heeeeeeaaaar you. Why didn't you just email me?"

"It's faster just to pick up the phone."

"No one talks on the phone. Email me. Text me. I am in the middle of, like, fifty things. Please don't call." The line went dead. No one talks on the phone? Eve behaved as though Imogen had just done something truly anachronistic, like send her a smoke signal or a fax.

A blinking red dot on the upper quadrant of the monitor distracted her. She clicked. It was a notification that she had one of the company's internal instant messages.

Oh good. Her assistant, Ashley, had sent a message to check in.

"You're so cutez! ROFL!" That wasn't exactly an offer of assistance. The message was followed by a short link to a site called Bitly. Bitly, Imogen reasoned by virtue of the adorable suffix, must be some kind of new kissing cousin to Etsy, the handmade crafts site that the other moms in her school salivated over on their iPhones during drop-off, comparing notes on the latest macramé plant hanger they had shipped from an artisan in Santa Fe who was more than one-half Cherokee.

Bitly was perhaps something similar, but for smaller wares— miniature macramé plant hangers?

But the link didn't take her to a site called Bitly. She was redirected to something called Keek.com. Imogen looked left and then right. Keek.com sounded vaguely like the pelvic floor exercises Imogen had learned in her prenatal classes. What exactly had Ashley sent her?

Underneath the neon-green Keek logo was a video. Imogen made sure to turn the volume down on the computer before hitting play.

She gasped again and held her breath.

The video was of her.

Oh no. There she was, yawning in the meeting. Yawning not once, but twice in quick succession. On the screen her eyes closed for a brief instant.

Ashley had taken a video of her without her knowledge. In a meeting. And then posted it on the Internet. What a grand invasion of her privacy! *Who just films someone without asking? Who just films*

someone when they are doing nothing at all but sitting in a meeting?
She looked tired. Her sharp black crepe dress from The Row looked
dull and old against the bright yellow hoodie of the woman sitting
next to her. Ashley's camera must have millions of megapixels. Imogen could see each and every last wrinkle fanning around her eyes
as she opened her mouth wide. She couldn't even remember yawning once, much less twice. There was a caption on the video: THE
RETURN OF IMOGEN TATE to @Glossy. #Hurrah #Love #Bosslady
#Shesback.

She looked at the right-hand column on the Keek site. There were
other videos. Imogen clicked the one at the top. It was Perry from the
Marketing Department, the one wearing the short skirt, blazer and
odd T-shirt with a cat on it, in the same meeting mere minutes later,
looking right at Ashley and sticking out her tongue.

The one below that was Adam in Accounting as he ran through
potential costs for the shoot. He expertly rattled off the expenditures,
but in between equipment and tailoring he ever so slightly glanced
directly into the camera, winked and delivered an ironic thumbs-up.

Everyone else in the meeting was very aware Ashley was documenting them and that after she took the video she would be sharing
bits and pieces of their meeting. That meant Imogen's yawns had
certainly been shared with the entire office.

Confirmation that all Imogen's co-workers had seen the video
arrived no less than thirty seconds later.

Incoming message from Eve: "Are you sleepy? Let me know if you
think you need to head home. We can regroup over a Google Hang-
out later if you want." Imogen hit delete and looked up to see Ashley
standing outside her office, a bundle of nervous energy, rocking back
and forth between her toes and heels.

"Do you like the keek?"

Imogen vacillated between wanting to give the girl a stern warning about playing around during meetings and wanting to seem like
she was a part of it. She opted for the latter.

"I just wish I had been ready for my close-up. Let me know next
time you are putting me on film." Relief flooded over the girl.

"Of course. One hundred percent. I'll let you know next time."

"Ashley, where is Eve's office?"

"Eve doesn't have an office. She doesn't believe in 'em. You know how at Facebook no one has an office, like, not even Sheryl Sandberg?" Imogen had not been aware of that fact. "Everyone sits at desks on the floor. Everyone is the same." Ashley looked around and lowered her voice. "Eve wants to turn your office into a nap room."

"A what?"

"A nap room."

Imogen shook her head. What the hell was a nap room? "That's not happening."

* * *

Imogen was exhausted, but giving Eve the satisfaction of leaving early would be the equivalent of JFK showing his belly to Castro. Instead, she worked through the day, clearing her in-box, taking control of the photo shoot and ensuring they hired the right photographer, one who would make absolutely all the difference.

Eve didn't have an office, but she did have an area all her own carved out of a corner surrounded by windows. She worked standing up at a desk raised to chest height.

At the end of the workday, Imogen compelled herself to visit Eve's work area. "Do you want a stand-up desk, Imogen? I can ask Carter to order you one. Everyone at Google has them. Human beings are 79 percent more effective standing than when sitting. We make decisions faster, we keep meetings shorter. I love it. I feel like I'm burning calories all day long," Eve said.

"That's okay, Eve. I feel like I am on my feet all the time when I am home with the kids." *What kind of badge of honor did one gain by standing all day long?*

Eve rolled her eyes, something she wouldn't have dared to do years earlier. "I forgot about your kids." *She's kidding, right? There is no way Eve could have forgotten my children.*

Imogen tried to remember back to her twenties, when having a child seemed like a handicap. Now Johnny was four, no longer a baby. At ten, Annabel did almost everything on her own, which made Imogen want to do more things for her, like braid her hair, help with a zipper she couldn't reach, explain complicated math problems involving fractions.

It pained her to think about the day Annabel would walk out the door without needing her at all every morning.

Imogen forced herself to keep it light. "The kids are actually doing great. You wouldn't believe how tall Johnny is getting. He is positively delicious right now."

Eve mustered a small smile. "I'm sure. . . . Sooo, what's up?"

"I just wanted to check in about the editors. Are they on a new rotating schedule? I didn't see a lot of them in today. And there were so many faces I didn't recognize. I want to meet some of the new girls."

Without even looking up from her screen, Eve explained to Imogen that staff head count had doubled while she was on medical leave. She didn't have to add that the median age had also dropped by twelve years. Imogen could see that for herself.

"We got rid of soooo much excess baggage," Eve went on. It took a minute for Imogen to realize that Eve was referring to human beings, human beings she had hired, as wasteful luggage.

"There were so many redundant staffers who had been on board since the seventies doing God knows what," Eve said.

With the salaries of the old staff now at her disposal, Eve had hired thirty content producers who could craft "traffic-driving" articles for the website (and soon-to-launch new app!) all day, all night and through the weekend, ratcheting up their numbers to get them the big digital advertising dollars and consumers who would click on the products.

"Make sense?" she said in a clipped tone. She didn't let Imogen answer. "It will. Let it marinate for a few days. You'll get it."

Was that condescension in her voice? Who was Eve Morton to be patronizing to her?

"I've been doing this a long time, Eve. It's not rocket science."

* * *

As with any transition of power, Imogen saw that allegiances had shifted to Eve the way ants swarmed a fallen piece of doughnut on the sidewalk.

Managing editor Jenny Packer, a half-Japanese, half-Jewish beauty with a thick Texas accent who had ruled the roost long before Imogen was hired, had been annexed to what looked like a supply closet in a far-off windowless corner behind the kitchen. She hadn't attended the morning meeting.

Imogen stumbled upon Jenny by accident while looking for a new set of pads and pencils, which she was beginning to suspect she would never find in this new office of tablets, phablets and other smart devices. Her beloved colleague's hair was disheveled and circles like two overinflated tires burrowed beneath her eyes. Imogen immediately hugged her in relief, noting that she could feel Jenny's ribs beneath her silk Tucker button-down.

"Welcome to my new digs." Jenny spread out her arms, nearly touching each of the opposite walls in the tiny space. Her old office had been just a couple of doors down from Imogen's, not quite as large, but still spacious and with a view of downtown. They engaged in the requisite small talk. How was Imogen feeling? What was Jenny's husband, Steve, the architect responsible for making Williamsburg in Brooklyn hip and expensive, working on now? Was Alex buried in the McAlwyn case? The answer to that question was indisputably yes. Imogen thought she would have heard something by now from her husband on her first day back at work, but Alex Marretti, assistant U.S. attorney, had been in his own office since six a.m. working on what was quickly becoming one of the more high-profile Ponzi scheme crackdowns in the past twenty years. Marty "Meatball" McAlwyn, the defendant, had been a stockbroker to the stars until the United States Attorney's Office finally got a whistle-blower to reveal that his entire investment portfolio was a fraud. According to the indictment against McAlwyn, he created false trading reports, back-dated trades, manipulated account statements and ultimately used other people's money to pay out false returns. If Alex won the case it would mean big things for his career.

Imogen looked around. Her hips had no choice but to brush against Jenny's as they stood chatting in the small space. "Why are you all the way back here? Did she turn your office into a nap room too?"

"Yup." Jenny nodded as Imogen's smile faded. She had been joking. "She has them working around the clock, but the girls need to sleep. I think they should sleep in beds at home! But, since she never lets them leave, they need somewhere to get some rest. It's fine really." There was a distinct resignation in her voice. "I don't plan on sticking around much longer." The "she" was very clearly Eve.

With no pages left to plan out and then produce, the job of a managing editor, what Jenny did was now obsolete.

"You need to learn how to code." Jenny expertly mimicked Eve's newly affected accent, a cross between Boston and old New York with a lot of soft vowels and condescension, as she recounted to Imogen what Eve told her when she had asked what her new responsibilities were at the website. " 'You're drowning in the ocean and I am throwing you a life jacket to pull you into the digital future' is what she said to me."

"So fucking patronizing!" Imogen shook her head. "What code does she want you to learn? Morse code?" That was the only kind of code Imogen could think of. She knew it was wrong the second it came out of her mouth. If she were being honest with herself, she would admit she had buried her head in the sand these past few years when it came to the Internet. "It's not my problem" and "It's not what I do" were the phrases that came to mind. Other people had simply taken care of it.

Jenny gave a wry smile and moved her hand across the few inches between them to pat her on the arm. "HTML, Ruby on Rails, the things that make a website. Don't feel bad. I didn't know what the hell the stupid little cow was talking about either, but I've been doing some research. Here is the thing—I just don't think that's where my heart is. I'm no engineer and I don't want to be. Steve and I may take some time and live in the house in Hudson Valley. I might finish my novel. I used to be someone important in this office and she's made me feel like an unwelcome guest. She never asks my opinion, never tells me when meetings are. She's just waiting for me to quit."

"Let me talk to her," Imogen said. "I can fix this."

Was Jenny looking at her with something akin to pity?

"Thank you, and I appreciate it. Truly. But I think I've already made up my mind. Mannering is offering buyouts, you know. They want to get rid of all of us old-timers and our inflated salaries." Jenny made a disgusted face and air quotes around the word "inflated." I don't see any reason I shouldn't take it."

For the next two hours Imogen's only goal was to keep an anxiety attack at bay.

As the clock struck six, her eyes blurring from working without her reading glasses, Imogen let herself stray to the website of *Women's Wear Daily* to peruse a bit of industry gossip. She came across news that made her heart sink. Molly Watson, the woman responsible for her entire career in magazines, had been fired after forty years at *Moda* magazine, according to an article by the media columnist Addison Cao.

"Ms. Watson will be replaced with a group of 'pop-up editors,' a rotating cast of iconic designers, stylists and former editors, who will each play the part of editor in chief for a month before passing the baton to the next boldfaced name."

Imogen's big title, the one she'd coveted for so many years, no longer felt like such a big deal at all. Editor in chief was apparently something anyone could do for a month at a time.

She spun her chair around to face the windows behind her desk in an effort to hide the swell of emotion brought on by the news of Molly's termination. Molly, who always did the right thing. Molly, who always took the high road in an industry known for low blows. Molly was the reason she was here at all.

Her mentor first spotted Imogen while she was working at the R.Soles cowboy boot shop on King's Road in Chelsea, London, in the early nineties.

Slightly gangly from a late adolescence, Imogen had dyed black hair then, back-combed into a beehive supported by heaps of hairspray. She didn't walk out of the house without her black liquid-liner cat eyes and Spice lip liner. Weighing nearly nothing, she hardly filled out a teeny-weeny vintage blue gingham minidress. White cowgirl boots over black fishnet stockings completed the look.

Rusty, who owned the shop, gave Imogen the freedom to style it however she wanted. One cold January morning she dragged a red leather sofa in from the street. Rusty painted the floor black and made a nook in the corner to sell well-worn leather biker jackets, the really beaten-up, James Dean kind. She fashioned a collage of Elvis Presley photos—the little boy to the hound dog, all in black and white—no pictures after thirty allowed. Imogen sold truckloads of R.Soles cowboy boots to boarding-school brats with Mockney accents and beatnik uniforms. They walked in packs up and down the King's Road during the summer holidays chain-smoking Marlboro Lights when they weren't vacationing in Barbados. They adored Imogen's real South London accent and would bring her single ciggies and cups of tea from Chelsea Kitchen down the street.

Rusty was generally off his head and always dressed in Day-Glo sportswear with black high-tops. He danced around the shop listening to Paul Oakenfold trance music on his Discman, his arms waving wildly in front of him. That was how he nearly clocked Molly Watson when she walked in one sunny Saturday in July. She was American, cool and rich, and had her two young, handsome English nephews with her.

"I'll take two pairs for each of them, size two and three, and here's my card," she said to Imogen, all in one breath. "Who put the store together? I love it. Was it you?"

From then on Imogen was under Molly's wing. But where was Molly now?

CHAPTER THREE

Most of the young women were already in the office when Imogen arrived at nine the next day, hunched over their laptops and pecking away at keyboards while wearing giant headphones in varying colors of the rainbow like doughnut-shaped earmuffs. Aside from the tapping, the room was silent. Imogen wandered over to a setup of food that resembled a movie set's craft services in the corner of the room. Her eye was first drawn to a Pepto-pink sign reading WE ARE WHAT WE EAT! Next she noticed the bowls of fresh fruit and translucent cylinders filled with nuts, seeds and granola that sat on the counter.

"It means we never have to leave." Ashley snuck behind her without making a sound, like the ghost-faced children in Japanese horror movies. After making herself known, she bounced eagerly around Imogen in a pair of black leather leggings that hugged her lithe figure, and pointed to the chia pudding and Greek yogurt at eye-level in the glass-doored refrigerator next to eight different kinds of kombucha. "All of the healthy things are up here, but the good stuff is down here." Ashley knelt on the floor and pulled open cabinets adjacent to the fridge to reveal Popchips, gummy candies, Snickers bars and Reese's Peanut Butter Cups.

"It's positive psychology. You have to work for the stuff that makes you fat so they keep it out of sight. Out of sight, out of mind. Eve modeled it on Google. We also just got a service that brings in breakfast each morning plus dinner at seven. On Tuesdays we get vegan tacos. Taco Tuesday!" The girl smiled at the alliteration. Imogen knew the days of the two-martini lunch had ended with the second Bush presidency, but the idea of eating every meal in the office seemed horrific.

Back at her desk, Imogen typed "Glossy.com" into her Internet browser. Lists and quizzes dominated the right rail of the page. Imogen was intrigued by "5 Things You Must Buy at This Hermès Pop-up Store," and less pleased about "Take This Quiz: What Shoe R U?" and "10 Ridiculously Hot Celebrities with Adorable Cats Wearing Fall Booties." Splashed across the top half of the site was a carousel of rotating photos from a shoot Imogen had styled just before leaving for her surgery. It was sexy and provocative and looked almost as provocative on her screen as it did on the pages of her magazine. Small tabs at the bottom of the screen told her that 12,315 people had liked the photograph and 5,535 shoppers had bought something featured in the shoot. She clicked on an indelicate pair of Wolford tights and was presented with the original pair, retailing for just under $100. As she scrolled down the price decreased, all the way to a $2.99 pair of sheer black L'eggs.

* * *

Surprisingly, quickly, it was five p.m. and Imogen was happy the snack food was there. She was starving and actually felt uncomfortable asking Ashley to order her something.

The company had issued her a new laptop and she had no idea how it worked. In the past her assistants had printed most of her emails. Ashley came in to try to show her the basics of cloud computing. After ten years of having the exact same system in place, *Glossy* employees no longer saved anything on their actual computers.

"This way you can work on anything from anywhere," Ashley explained, carefully going through everything Imogen needed to know with the patience of a kindergarten teacher.

There were four different passwords to get through what Ashley described as four different "firewalls." Imogen wrote them in her notebook.

"You should probably memorize them," Ashley said. "Eve is bonkers about security."

Why did Imogen have to learn any of this? That is exactly what assistants were for. Right? All of this felt like a giant waste of her time. She should be thinking big picture, not staring at a bloody screen all day. She couldn't wrap her head around the new, allegedly "intuitive" database that existed only on the Internet. She kept saving things only to have them disappear into the ether of the web. Each click brought an error message and a sense of frustration.

God, this was infantilizing. "Okay. I've got it," Imogen said and clicked on one of the file folders. "No, wait. I don't have it."

"It takes some getting used to," Ashley said sympathetically. "We can try again tomorrow."

Imogen reached out to grab the girl's arm. "One more thing. Help me set up my printer. I don't want you to have to print all of my emails out for me."

"How about I do that first thing in the morning," Ashley replied cheerily. "Join us for cocktails after work. Eve is leaving early today for the first time in *months*. We think we can sneak out behind her."

Imogen always loved hanging out with the younger girls in her office. Nurturing young talent was one of her favorite parts of her job. She wished she could bottle their energy.

"Let me call my nanny."

* * *

There is something delightful but also terrifying about drinking with twenty-two-year-olds. First comes the sense of freedom when no one pointedly looks at her watch, making offhand comments about how the nanny is passive-aggressive after nine p.m. Then there is the sheer panic of abandoning adult drinking rules one sets at the age of thirty: say no to shots, never drink anything blue, drink one glass of water for every alcoholic beverage. Those rules exist for a reason, and yet Imogen took her first tequila shot of the evening standing at the bar while their group waited for a table. This was the kind of place people in their twenties gravitated to after work, all fit bodies pressing up against one another, knowing a few drinks could get you into bed with someone new for the night. The difference between this scene and similar ones Imogen encountered when she was in her own twenties was that everyone was deeply absorbed in their phones instead of scoping the crowd. They texted, they tweeted and they checked Facebook, oblivious to the world around them. Was there even a point to being in the same room as one another anymore? Their entire lives were condensed in the palms of their hands.

As the temperature in the crowded bar rose, the girls from the office all removed their high-cropped leather motorcycle jackets in various shades of taupe to reveal perfectly tanned shoulders.

They were very excited about a new mobile app called "Yo."

"What does it do?" Imogen asked.

"It just lets you say 'yo' to someone," Mandi said.

"What does that even mean?"

Mandi giggled a little. "It just means yo." She wiggled her head and waved her hand in the universal signal for hello.

"That's ridiculous!" Imogen said, with the certainty that it was absolutely ridiculous. Mandi shrugged and Ali nodded her head vigorously.

"I mean. I can't even. Ridiculous or not," Ali said, "they just got a million dollars in funding. There's another app that lets you just text pictures of tacos. I think they got funded too."

Spending time with her junior editors in the past consisted mainly of coffees and the occasional cocktail party. This was incredibly intimate. The lines of propriety were erased. Yet these girls still treated her with respect. She noticed they were all wearing that black bracelet.

When it came time to order wine, the girls deferred to Imogen. Perry from Marketing shyly handed her the not terribly extensive wine list.

"You probably know way more about wine than we do," Perry deferred. That was true, Imogen did know something about picking a good wine, the kind of wine that wouldn't break a twentysomething's bank account but didn't need to be swallowed quickly to bypass the taste buds either. She ordered two bottles of the Borsao rosé for the group. As they waited for it to arrive at the table, the buzz of Patrón wearing away, Ashley groaned about how her mother was driving her insane.

"Menopause," she carped. Imogen chose to ignore the sideways glances cast her way. Did these girls really believe menopause was something that happened the second you turned forty? She had a four-year-old at home and a menstrual cycle like clockwork. But she decided to cut them some slack. When she was twenty-two she too had thought everyone over thirty was the same age—old. Imogen *had* been nervous when she turned forty and noticed that waiters began calling her ma'am in an unironic way. One of her friends, who was closer to fifty than forty (if you stole a peek at her driver's license), referred to forty as the "rush hour of life." Victor Hugo called it the "old age of youth." Imogen still felt reasonably young, but beyond that she was certain that she was in the prime of her life.

"It used to drive me crazy too, when my mother popped across the pond unexpectedly," Imogen chimed in. "My mum always arrived bearing some kind of English gift—Waitrose tea bags, sacks of lavender or a hot water bottle. She would never knock before coming into the apartment since she managed to get a key from the super, so I was always in some embarrassing state when she arrived."

She recounted to the group of gathered co-workers how, when she was their age, she once worked a celebrity shoot for four days straight in Los Angeles. She returned to New York City on the night of her birthday, having smuggled a silver sequined Versace minidress from the set. She donned it, along with a pair of strappy silver dancing shoes, in the cab, putting a sheer pashmina between her and the cabbie as she stripped down in the backseat. All the other assistants from *Moda* met her at a smoky lounge in the Village, the name of which she could no longer recall. At the end of the evening Imogen stumbled home with a Hugh Grant look-alike. When her mum walked through the door carrying scones and a handmade patchwork quilt the next morning, the floppy-haired gentleman had his very white backside poking up toward the ceiling.

The group of women at the table laughed appreciatively at her story but Imogen could tell they were not entirely sure who Hugh Grant was.

"Where are your parents from?" Imogen asked Ashley, bring the conversation back to the irritating mother.

"We're on Eighty-Fifth and Park," the girl replied. "At least you had an ocean between you and your mom. Try being with your parents all the time."

Ashley lived with her parents? Imogen tried to conceal a look of surprise.

"Are you staying with them until you find your own place?"

"Yeah, I figure I'll be there a couple more years." Ashley spoke around a bit of asparagus wrapped in a thin layer of prosciutto she had selected from the appetizers the waiter brought out, along with several plates stacked high with arugula covered in finely shaved Parmesan. "The building is getting a new gym next summer."

As the other girls at the table nodded in unison, Imogen grew more confused.

"You don't want your own place sooner than that?"

"Why would I? We all live with our parents." The others nodded again. "Well, Mandi doesn't, but that's because her parents live in, like, Idaho."

"Virginia," Mandi interjected.

"Or something," Ashley finished her sentence. "Your parents still pay for your loft in Williamsburg. Why would we get our own apartments when we get everything we need at our parents' places? They have all the right food. There is laundry service. Besides. Who can afford to live in Manhattan on our salaries?"

The jumbo, matching Chanel 2.55 bags the girls all slung over their shoulders made sense now. Imogen herself had survived on $35,000 a year when she first came to the city, living with two young women in a railroad apartment on the Upper East Side she'd found in the back-page listings of *The Village Voice*. The walls had been painted a prominent purple and the stairs always smelled vaguely of illicit sex. The place was so small that if someone took a hot shower in the narrow bathroom, the window in the kitchen on the apartment's far side would fog up with steam.

"We wouldn't be able to afford anything with a doorman," Perry said. "And who wants to have to walk up stairs?"

Imogen found their conversation fascinating. They were not unlike the Spaniards she had met one summer in Madrid who flocked to public parks and crowded subways to make out and sometimes more because they lived with their parents until marriage. She also felt sad for them. These women would never know the joys of sharing a tiny space with two other girls, all in the same boat, all trying to make ends meet over Pringles and bits snuck home from a fancy store opening. One time her roommate Bridgett snuck an entire bottle of Dom Pérignon down the front of her Calvin Klein shift dress. They bought strawberries on the street and melted a Hershey's bar over their always-present yellow Bic lighters to make chocolate-covered treats as they sipped the golden liquid with the most delicate bubbles that had ever touched their tongues. Then they stayed up that night talking until dawn about the women they wanted to be when they were finished being the girls who stole champagne and smoked a pack of Marlboros in a day. It was during that conversation that Imogen first declared she wanted to be the editor in chief of a women's fashion magazine. No one laughed. All of them had equally serious and lofty ambitions, most of which had now come to fruition in their forties.

Their fridge in those days was filled with beauty products and the kitchen shelves were laden with vintage sweaters. Rails and rails of clothing racks on wheels lined the walls. It was little more than a one-bedroom closet with small nooks carved out for sleeping.

Had it not been for that apartment and that sense of ambition that can only be born out of struggle, she wouldn't be who she was today.

Before Imogen could write the new breed of *Glossy* girls off as flighty nitwits, they revealed their own elaborate business plans, each one more violently ambitious than the next. In her spare time one created a website that allowed women all over the world to shop from one another's closets, borrowing items for short or long amounts of time, based on a barter system. Another was determined to build a social network that expressly focused on shoe-shopping. They didn't speak about positions like editor in chief or even CEO. They spoke in terms of equity, customer acquisition and fund-raising rounds. They spoke about billions of dollars.

"Success to me is doing something you're passionate about. It's kind of my goal one day to have my own company, to be part of something that is going to do something meaningful and make the world a better place. That's why I'm in tech," Mandi said.

Was tech the industry they worked in now? They seemed so innocent. They still lived at home and yet they juggled all these projects at once. They *were* hardworking. She felt a certain energy, but couldn't explain what it was. Imogen had no idea how her magazine could exist only online. She could tell that these girls couldn't imagine a future in which it existed anywhere but.

By the end of the night, three glasses of wine nipping the neurons in her brain, Imogen felt threatened again. The way the girls lived might be childish, but their ideas were adult. They were personally stunted but brilliant with business acumen. Their technological prowess and self-awareness were intimidating. One thing she was learning about this generation was how secure they were in the knowledge that they were all very special snowflakes.

She was almost relieved when an email from Eve gave her a reason to make her excuses and leave.

From: Eve Morton (EMorton@Glossy.com)
To: Imogen Tate (ITate@Glossy.com)

Im,

You're probably SO overwhelmed. Breakfast tomorrow morning, 8:00? We'll talk about everything. You don't hate me or anything now? I sure hope not. LOL. I need you on board for this. The new site is going to be SO AWESOME. WE ARE GOING TO DISRUPT THE FASHION INDUSTRY!!!!!! ♥♥♥X★👒👜

xo
E.

With that Imogen ordered a glass of water instead of another wine and politely said her good-byes.

From: Imogen Tate (ITate@Glossy.com)
To: Eve Morton (EMorton@Glossy.com)

E.

8:30. The Four Seasons. See you there.

Best,
Imogen

Perry piped up as Imogen drew a crisp hundred-dollar bill out of her wallet.

"I am going to get the bill with my Amex so I can get the points. Does everyone want to just Venmo me?"

Imogen handed over the bill. "Do I want to what? I have cash. I'll give you a hundred."

"It would be so much easier if you could Venmo me," Perry insisted. Not for the first time that day, Imogen didn't understand the verb coming out of someone's mouth. She worried for a moment that she was acquiring a rare neurological disease, the kind that made you forget the meanings of simple things you had known for years.

"It's an app," Perry said. "Venmo. It transfers the money right from your bank account to my bank account."

"But I could also just give you money," Imogen said plainly. Perry looked at the hundred-dollar bill like it had a disease.

"I hate carrying cash. This is soooooo much easier."

"It really does seem easier if I just hand you actual money," Imogen said, too tired to argue with the girl, practically forcing the hundred-dollar bill into her hand.

Ashley grabbed the hundred from Imogen and gave Perry a look. "I'll Venmo from my account. It can be glitchy sometimes. Share a cab with me?"

They were finally able to hail a taxi after walking a block over to

Madison Avenue. "Do you mind just dropping me on the east side?" Ashley smiled generously before she began furiously moving her thumbs on the keyboard of her iPhone. Imogen nodded and turned her eyes to her own device as the cabbie clicked the meter on. Alex relieved Tilly, the nanny, an hour ago and was waiting in bed for her; his emails had a tinge of attitude about her not being home when he had obviously made an effort to see her before going to sleep.

Imogen felt uncomfortable sitting in silence. "What are you working on?" she asked Ashley.

She was startled by the small talk. "Oh, I'm not working now. I'll work more when I get home, of course. I was just doing Seamless to make sure my Thai food arrives right when I walk in the door." Imogen nodded.

Perhaps it was the wine that made Imogen more curious about the persistent typing.

"Are you still ordering food?"

Ashley laughed. "No. Now I am ordering men. I'm on my Fixd."

"Your what?"

"Fixd. It takes your Facebook and Twitter and Instagram friends and then matches you up with the hottest ones based on location and key words in your captions, tweets and profiles to find men you would be compatible with who are within a one-mile radius.

"I mean, I'm not looking for one right now." Ashley blushed. "I'm not that kind of Fixd person. I don't order men to my door. I'm just kind of looking for someone to maybe hang out with this weekend."

"Well, that seems convenient" was all Imogen could think to say. Ashley shrugged as the cab pulled to a stop to let her out. "You go on a lot of dates . . . but you know it really weighs on the soul when you have to, like, break up with one or two guys via text every week." They awkwardly exchanged a fashionable kiss on each cheek as Ashley got out of the taxi to the promise of pad Thai and perhaps a weekend date.

Imogen was no stranger to late nights. Her and Alex's busy professional lives demanded they attend a certain number of social events a week, from cocktail parties to benefits to impromptu dinners with investors and advertisers on her end and attorneys and politicians on

Alex's. But somehow this evening exhausted her. The girls from the office had this limitless energy, fueled no doubt partly by the slim blue tablets of Adderall many of them had on hand.

Her stomach tightened and from Forty-Second Street to Fourteenth she allowed herself twenty-eight blocks of self-pity. What the hell was she doing? As if he knew she was burrowing into a den of despair, the only person she wanted to talk to at that very moment rang her cell phone.

"Ciao, bella."

"Ciao, bello."

Four years ago, Massimo Frazzano, then a fashion editor at *Moda* magazine and one of Imogen's former interns, had just finished a half-marathon in Montauk. Doctors would later say that he might have been slightly disoriented and dehydrated from the race because instead of diving into the deep end of his pool, he plunged headfirst into the shallow end, clipping his chin on the bottom and shattering his C4 vertebrae. He was floating facedown when his partner, Scott, found him less than a minute later. They managed to revive him on the scene and helicoptered him to Manhattan, but after eighteen hours of surgery the doctors told the assembled crowd, including Imogen, then massively pregnant with Johnny, that Massimo would never walk again. They warned that he might not even regain use of his arms. Massimo didn't speak to anyone for days. Scott worried he would do something drastic to harm himself. Four days later Massimo invited everyone back to his hospital room.

He was propped up in bed, a bandage around the top of his skull, his head completely shaven. Imogen bit her bottom lip so that the pain would keep her from crying.

"I'll walk again," Massimo said smoothly, without any doubt in his voice. "I'll walk again." That was that. From that day on Imogen never felt sad for him when they were together. He wouldn't allow it. He was just too much fun. She left their frequent dinner and shopping dates feeling renewed and inspired. His nervous system was impaired in a way that made it difficult for him to sweat. With Scott's help, he developed a line of organic salves to soothe and moisturize his damaged skin. It turned out there was a market for exactly that. His products soon graced the shelves of Barneys and Fred Segal. Massimo was still in a wheelchair, but through grit, determination and reconstructive nerve surgery he regained the use of his arms and wrists. Last year he began feeling sensation in his stomach and his lower back. The day Imogen went in for her own surgery he told her he was starting to feel the difference between hot and cold in his upper legs.

Massimo was right beside Alex in that drab cancer ward when she opened her eyes after her own procedure. He was the one who taped a photograph of her dancing on the beach with the kids to the hard plastic footboard of the bed. It kept falling off no matter how many pieces of Scotch tape she stuck to its back. He didn't allow her even a minute to feel sorry for herself.

"Alex, let me have a peek beneath the sheets. This set of boobs is definitely an upgrade," he said with his typical humor, reaching for her bandages with a well-manicured hand. Selfishly, Imogen often thought of him as a gift. Massimo was the reason she could never let her own fears for her health allow her to wallow too long in the shallow pool of self-pity.

Riding in the cab, she recounted her first day back to her friend. He grew silent for a beat.

"You know what I love about you as an editor, Im?"

"How my legs look in Manolos?"

"That too. I love that you're always willing to step outside the box. You've never shied away from a challenge. Now might be the time that you decide to take on something new. Something really hard and really different that could totally change your life."

He always said the right thing, the thing that coming from anyone else would read like a saying from a stale fortune cookie, but from him worked wonders on a wounded soul.

"When will I see you, my dear? First day of Fashion Week?" he asked her.

Massimo had stayed on as a contributing editor to *Moda* after his accident and would often joke that the wheelchair was the best thing that had ever happened to him because it got him front-row.

"You will, darling. I simply can't wait to get back to something I know! Do you need me for anything? Will Priscilla be with you?" Massimo loved beautiful women, as evidenced by Priscilla, his assistant and nurse, who was a dead ringer for a young Naomi Watts with the shiniest hair Imogen had ever seen.

"She will. We need to find her a good man, or a good woman, whichever she prefers. She needs something more than pushing an invalid around town all day." They bantered for one more minute, until the taxi pulled in front of Imogen's redbrick town house. Only after she hung up the phone did Imogen realize she'd forgotten to ask Massimo what happened to Molly. She tipped the driver well for putting up with her chatter in the backseat.

Alex obviously had made a valiant effort to stay awake, but he was slack-jawed and gently snoring while sitting up in bed, his wire-frame glasses still covering closed lids and long lashes. Imogen kissed both of the children good night before gently urging Alex's body into a prone position without waking him and wrapping her arms around his taut middle. His middle relaxed into hers. She relished the feel of the soft flannel pajama bottoms he had worn for the past ten years. His skin peeked through at the backs of the thighs where the material had worn thin. Alex hated throwing anything away and Imogen would at some point need to secretly plot how to replace these with an identical pair of pajama pants. He stirred when she buried her head between his shoulder blades.

"I adore the fact that my wife still comes home smelling like tequila after twelve devoted years of marriage to me," he mumbled, rolling to face her and pulling her hand up to his lips. "Have you had a day?" he mumbled through her fingers. Ever since the surgery Alex had stopped asking her "How was your day?"

"I'm so tired, Al," she whispered, with the weight of the next twenty-four hours already crushing her.

"I know, baby. I know. I want to tell you that it will get better tomorrow, but I don't want to lie to you."

"No, really, lie. Please, do lie."

He smiled and she took off his glasses. She kissed him before rolling over and letting him hold her. Sleep took time, but finally came.

* * *

Ashley Arnsdale kept tapping away on her phone as she walked through the lobby of 740 Park Avenue, the very same building her parents brought her home to twenty-four years earlier, two days after she had been born. She stopped briefly at the front desk, where JP, the night doorman, handed her a brown paper delivery bag of gluten-free pad Thai from Golden Lotus on Eighty-Fourth Street.

In the elevator she switched applications from Fixd to AngelRaise, the hot new angel investing app.

All the other girls from work had been so candid about their side projects with Imogen over drinks. It had been a little ridiculous. Ashley didn't want her new boss to think she was distracted all day by some other passion project. She wasn't distracted all day. She was maybe sometimes distracted a little, but she stayed focused on *Glossy* when she was at *Glossy*. She really loved the job. And she enjoyed working for Imogen Tate. That woman was something else. Eve . . . she had thoughts about Eve. Blergh.

All the lights were out when the doors opened onto the floor of their apartment. Constance and Arnold, her parents, were down in West Palm Beach for the week. Living with your parents wasn't so bad when your parents were never around.

"Yeeeeeep!" Ashley exclaimed to absolutely no one, as she scrolled down through AngelRaise. She'd gotten another $10,000 investment for SomethingOld.com. She shimmied through the apartment, turning on all the lights. She hated being in the dark. Ten thousand dollars would help a lot with the development costs to build the app and website for her side project. SomethingOld was a monthly subscription service, kind of like Netflix, but for clothes—vintage clothes.

Ever since she was allowed to take the 6 train down to the East Village on her own, Ashley had loved nothing more than scouring vintage clothing stores for unique pieces. Her collection spanned more than her two closets in the apartment. By now she had six mini storage units of amazing stuff. But it wasn't for her. SomethingOld would find out a person's taste and their size. It would know a lot about the pieces they already owned in their wardrobe and then, along with Ashley's curatorial eye, it would send subscribers a vintage item every four weeks. It was like having a personal shopper send you a gift every month, except it would be a gift of something crazy and cool from a completely different time.

As she put the leftover half of the pad Thai in the fridge to take to work the next day, Ashley wondered what Imogen would think of SomethingOld.

She stripped off layers of clothes to just boy shorts and a tank top before padding out onto the small terrace behind her bedroom, where she kept her little urban garden. The slight chill in the air felt good after being in the sweaty bar for so long. She'd felt a little silly when Imogen asked about her living arrangements, but come on. This made sense. Her parents had this big old apartment. She liked space. She liked having this little garden. Didn't Imogen's daughter like cooking? Ashley plucked a handful of perky mint leaves to take to the office in the morning.

* * *

Imogen and her husband had long ago fallen into a routine. Alex took off at six thirty to hit the boxing gym most days and a couple mornings a week Imogen's Pilates instructor would come to the house to work out with her. She'd planned to do a light workout today, but Evangeline had canceled at the last minute, citing menstrual cramps. It could be time for a new trainer.

Finding herself alone, Imogen indulged in one of her new dangerous habits. She stood completely naked in front of the full-length mirror on the back of the bathroom door, wiping the condensation away from the glass reflecting her torso. Her middle was softer than she would have liked, but still on the thin side. Skinny fat was what her mother would have called it. She stared at her new tits. She'd never called them that before the surgery, preferring the word "breasts," or even "boobs" with a slight giggle, but now "tits" felt right since these lumps of flesh on her body weren't hers. They were rounder and definitely harder to the touch. She traced the symmetrical vertical scars from the nipples to the base. Something about this daily confrontation balanced her, as long as she didn't let it carry on too long. As usual, she allowed herself only three minutes staring at her body in the bathroom mirror before dressing and starting her day.

An hour later, Imogen strolled quietly through the Four Seasons, enjoying the swish of her beautiful black knee-length crepe Chanel dress and the *click-clack* of her suicidally high black leather Manolo Blahnik pumps.

"I am open-minded and nonjudgmental," she repeated to herself like a mantra before mentally noting Eve's giant dangly earrings and fire-engine-red nails when she spotted her across the lobby. Eve simply had no style. What was that thing Ralph told her once over dinner after the Paris shows? "Style is very personal. It has nothing to do with fashion. Fashion is quick. Style is forever."

Eve's choice of a powder-blue bandage dress showed much too much skin for so early in the day, and Imogen noted the goose pimples dotting the girl's broad shoulders.

Despite the grand lobby there was something intimate and inviting about the Four Seasons. The staff always remembered Imogen's name, and without her having to ask, Frederick, the maître d', brought over an extra-hot skim cappuccino. She had once used him as an extra in a *Glossy* photo shoot and he relished the small bit of fame. Frederick made a small bow to her, revealing a perfect bald circle at the crown of his head. He knew how to make anyone feel like the most important person in a room filled with politicians, software tycoons and big-name designers.

"The queen has returned." He smiled. Imogen enjoyed the flash of intimidation that briefly crossed Eve's features. The girl visibly bristled and immediately launched into work chatter, avoiding the kinds of niceties that people with actual experience in business make sure to go through before getting to the point of any professional meeting.

Eve gesticulated wildly to emphasize her points, violently flinging an arm and knocking a cup of milk from the table. The growing pool of ivory liquid nearly spilled onto Imogen's lap before Frederick deftly swept in with a tea napkin. Eve paused for a moment and stared at Imogen's bare wrist. "Where's your bracelet?"

"What bracelet, Eve?"

"Your Glossy.com bracelet. I left one for you on your desk." Imogen cringed, remembering the slick black rubber band she'd tossed in the waste bin. "That was sweet of you, Eve, but it isn't really my style."

Eve grew apoplectic. "We all wear the bracelet, Imogen. We're a team."

"I don't think that bracelet goes with Chanel, Eve." ("It's black. It goes with everything. And it isn't just a bracelet. It's a FitBoom! It measures all your steps, calories and metabolic rate." Tugging at her own black bracelet, allowing it to snap sharply against her skin to punctuate her annoyance, Eve came in.)

It took only ten minutes for her former assistant to arrive at the pièce de résistance, the reason they were meeting for an expensive breakfast instead of gnawing on hemp-seed granola while staring at computer screens with the other worker bees back in the office.

"I can't get the designers on board without you," Eve admitted sheepishly. "God. You would think they hated the Internet. They hear 'app' and want nothing to do with us. You know these people. You know who we need to work with and you know what to say to get them on board."

It was true that Imogen had the respect and the ear of practically every fashion designer from Manhattan to Milan. Editors in chief enjoyed their real rock star moment in the nineties, before being replaced by Food Network chefs and ultimately tech billionaires and personal trainers as the celebrity careers du jour. Imogen remained beloved inside and out of the industry for one simple reason: she was nice. That was her biggest selling point, and why she was still a little bit famous. Every interview about her began with a variation of the same line: "Imogen Tate seems so perfect that we wish we could hate her but she is just sooooo lovely." Why not be nice? It wasn't really any harder than being mean.

The universe underscored the point about just how valuable Imogen's connections could be when one of the fashion elite, Adrienne Velasquez, breezed by the table, blowing Imogen a kiss and asking after Alex. Adrienne was the fashion director over at *Elle* magazine and she'd recently turned into a huge television star after becoming a judge on a Bravo reality show on which fledgling designers competed to create the most outrageous outfit, typically out of bits of fabric found in trash bins. Adrienne's co-hosts were former supermodel Gretchen Kopf and the head of the Fashion Institute of Technology, Max Marx.

Eve turned bright red.

"You actually know Adrienne Velasquez?" she yelped as Adrienne departed to join Gretchen and Max at a sun-dappled corner table.

"Of course I do," Imogen said, uncertain why Eve was so surprised.

"I just love her. She's my absolutely favorite fashion personality in the entire universe. Oooooo, I never miss an episode of *Project Fashion.* Never! Do you think you can call her back here?" It grew embarrassing as Eve began to do something that resembled hyperventilating. Imogen had to remind herself that the industry was different now. Adrienne was on television. She was a real celebrity. It wasn't Eve's fault that she didn't understand how totally and completely unprofessional it would be to ask for Adrienne's autograph. Adrienne was a fashion director. She had Imogen's old job, for Chrissakes.

Imogen gave Eve a big smile and for a moment enjoyed having the upper hand. "Let's eat for a bit and then say hello on the way out." The rest of breakfast was dominated by talk of Fashion Week logistics. The "action item" for next month, as Eve put it, stabbing at her egg white omelet each time she said the word "action," was to rule online coverage for the shows in New York, Paris, London and Milan. This would be the first year Imogen wouldn't travel for the Europe shows, as apparently Glossy.com had "no budget" for it. Imogen didn't grow up with money, but she had quickly grown quite comfortable around it when she was given the privilege to travel the world for work. She and Bridgett always took rooms next to each other and would throw parties every single night during Fashion Week, all on someone else's dime. It was always someone else's money. She thought Alex would leave her six months into their relationship when he surprised her in Paris only to find a hairstylist giving her a blowout each and every morning in the privacy of her room. It was a lifestyle that was just so easy to slip into, all very fizzy when you were made to feel like a real VIP. Imogen had to work hard when she returned to prove she really was the down-to-earth girl Alex fell in love with. Some days she even had to convince herself.

The next bombshell was that Eve wanted Imogen to throw Glossy .com a launch party at the end of Fashion Week, and Eve needed reassurance that Imogen would invite all of her fabulous friends, making no bones about the fact that she wanted unfettered access to Imogen's contacts.

When the bill came, Eve changed the subject. "Introduce me to Gretchen now," she demanded unceremoniously.

Adrienne was gracious as always when Imogen introduced the stuttering Eve, who immediately asked to take a selfie with the entire table. Gretchen Kopf was rising gracefully from the table to kiss Imogen on the cheek when Eve wrapped her arm around her shoulders and stretched her phone out in front of them.

"Smile!" she ordered Gretchen, Adrienne and Max. The trio was used to this drill and gave their best selfie faces before turning away from Eve and the camera to grab their things from the table.

But Eve wouldn't be deterred. "I'll tag you in that photo, okay? Gretchen, we want you on board for the new *Glossy* app." Eve burst like a bubble of caviar. "And you *have* to come to our party!"

"Now may not be the best time, Eve," Imogen tried to gently place her hand on the small of Eve's back. Gretchen and Max glanced at each other and then at Imogen, not wanting to be rude, but also not wanting to have to awkwardly turn down a business proposition in the midst of a polite breakfast.

"Of course it is. We are launching the new site! Gretchen and Max and Adrienne are perfect. They must be involved." Eve played the role of the recalcitrant child and Gretchen, ever the mediator, smoothed the situation perfectly. She was well practiced in the art of making a fan feel welcome and then turning her attention elsewhere to end their interaction before it became too taxing on her. She smiled and touched them before purring: "I should let you get going" in a way that made you believe she was doing you a favor by dismissing you.

"We will call you, darling," she said in her sexy German accent.

"Let us call you." Imogen whispered a barely audible "thank you" to Gretchen before guiding Eve like a child gently out the exit.

Midtown traffic was dense by nine a.m. as Imogen raised her hand in vain for a taxi with its light on. Eve fumbled on her iPhone to see if Uber would send a car her way. Imogen opened her mouth and then shut it.

A black car sidled up to the curb.

Eve pulled down hard on the end of her dress as she fell into the Town Car. "Aren't you getting in?" Eve tapped her foot impatiently.

"No. I'm not," Imogen replied sternly. Eve barely had time to gather her limbs inside the vehicle before Imogen slammed the car door a bit too firmly for her.

* * *

Ever since she'd arrived in New York the week before college, Eve Morton had wanted to be one of those people who took cabs with abandon, who didn't constantly stare at the meter and think about how many meals the cab fare would add up to. She could count on one hand the number of cabs she took the first year she lived in the city.

Now that she actually made a living wage, better than a living wage, although not nearly anywhere near the absurd salary they were paying Imogen Tate (when did they decide that magazine editors should be paid like brain surgeons?), she enjoyed watching the meter rise and knowing she could afford it. It was something she actually missed when she took one of these sleek black Uber Town Cars and the fare was charged automatically to a credit card on file and no money ever changed hands.

Eve knew better than anyone that Imogen was not tech savvy. Part of her job as Imogen's assistant had been to print out and then reply to all of her emails. Pretty standard assistant stuff back then. Still, she had assumed that her old boss had caught up with technology in the two years she had been away at school. The entire world had caught up by now.

Breakfast went okay, she thought.

The way Imogen handled the Adrienne Velasquez situation was just so completely uncool though. It wasn't as if Eve couldn't make friends with Adrienne on her own if she wanted to. Imogen was so weird about the whole thing. People like Imogen were so precious about their networking, about how and when they would bring you into their circle. Thank god her generation didn't behave like that. Eve loved how connected she felt to all her peers. If she was friends with them on Twitter that was equal to being besties in real life. She didn't discriminate. The old guard of fashion had so many bullshit hierarchies and unspoken rules. It was frustrating.

At least Imogen could be useful (if she went along with the program) in helping navigate some of those barriers. She held the keys to the kingdom for the new *Glossy* app—*if only* she got it just a little bit more.

Eve glanced down at her phone, seeing an email that made her give out a little yelp. It was last-minute, but who cared. This was huge. Eve quickly dashed off an email to Imogen.

From: Eve Morton (EMorton@Glossy.com)
To: Imogen Tate (ITate@Glossy.com)
Subject: DISRUPTTECH!

We have to fly to San Francisco tomorrow afternoon. We got accepted to come to Disrupt Tech conference. Hza. C more here.
👍🔙🐌🎀😊★
www.Disrupttech.com

CHAPTER FOUR

The next evening Imogen pressed her forehead against the cool Plexiglas window in economy class on the plane, looking down at the lights of Manhattan as they curved around the island, twinkling on the dark canvas like jewelry laid out for a fancy party.

Imogen was wearing her layered traveling outfit, perfected over years of shuttling to international shows twice a year—a lightweight long-sleeved gray cashmere T-shirt, black ribbed cardigan, large Hermès gray and black scarf that doubled as a blanket on chilly plane rides and her low-slung Rag & Bone boyfriend jeans. Classic black Ray-Bans pushed her hair off her face. For the past fifteen years plane travel had been a welcome respite from the busyness of life on the ground—a space free of phone calls, text messages, emails and the Internet. She knew all that was changing, but she still clung to the notion of a flight as a few sweet hours of uninterrupted time to indulge in a digital blackout, along with her stash of celebrity trash magazines.

"Didn't you bring your laptop?" Eve asked her right as they reached cruising altitude, snapping her own screen open in a salute.

"No. We're only here for a day," Imogen said, dipping her hand into her bag for her copy of *Us Weekly*.

"The plane has Wi-Fi," Eve said incredulously, as though she couldn't imagine the availability of something as precious as the Internet going unused for a single wasteful second.

"That is so lovely for the plane," Imogen replied, refusing to let a twentysomething antagonize her as she lost herself in a spread of "Hollywood Plastic Surgery Secrets." She paused for a moment. Now could be a good time to try to reconnect with Eve. What sense did it make to start off on a bad foot? She folded her magazine onto her lap and placed a hand on Eve's elbow.

Eve pulled out one of her earbuds with great irritation and let it dangle like a loose thread down her neck.

"What's up?" she asked.

"So, tell me all about business school?" Eve was startled, but once she got going she was more than pleased to talk about what a transformative experience Harvard had been for her.

"If I had stayed at *Glossy* I would be just another lowly associate editor right now," she said seriously. "Now look what I'm doing. I'm literally transforming this company. I mean, B-school was the best decision of my life."

With that Eve turned her attention back to her computer, effectively ending the conversation.

Imogen gazed longingly toward business class. If she'd had more notice she would happily have used her own miles to be in those plush seats where they served actual food that didn't come in rectangular boxes wrapped in plastic.

"Business class is a little ridiculous for a flight this short, don't you think?" Eve snorted with derision as she noticed Imogen's gaze. "I mean, you sit at your desk working for five hours a day. Why can't you be content sitting in this seat? I did the San Fran route back and forth ten times last year."

Imogen turned back to her magazine.

Just after they landed, a little past nine, Eve revealed they would be sharing a room at a Days Inn near the convention center.

"It's like a slumber party," Eve said matter-of-factly in the taxi.

"How many beds are in the room, Eve?"

"One king. We're kind of like a start-up now, Imogen. We need to be on a start-up budget."

"And there is some kind of pullout sofa in the room?" Imogen breathed the words out with false hope.

Eve stopped paying attention to her, focused as she was on taking yet another picture of herself, a copycat of the photographer Ben Watts's famous "Shhhh" pose that all the models were doing. She sucked in her cheekbones and made the international sign for "be quiet" with the edge of her forefinger pressed to her painted lips. The intensity of Eve's gaze was as though Ben Watts actually was on the other side of the smartphone camera lens. Imogen had to admit it was working for her.

"Eve?"

"You know the perfect selfie is all about the eyes, Imogen. People think it's about the smile, but it isn't. It's about getting the eyes just right," Eve said, completely ignoring Imogen's question.

"The bed?" Imogen repeated.

"No. I don't think there is another. No pullout."

Before Imogen could ask anything else their taxi pulled in front of the run-down little motel, a scruffy stray cat scowling into its headlights. Eve hopped out and sashayed into the building and over to the front desk, leaving Imogen to pay the cabbie. The manners of this girl! It was like she was brought up in a barn.

She breathed deep into her belly. The night air was crisp here, refreshing and chillier than back home.

Once inside, she tried to talk to Eve again.

"So we will be sharing the bed?" Imogen asked.

"Of course. Like sisters!" Eve squeezed Imogen's upper arm too hard as she stood at the hotel check-in desk smiling her Cheshire grin at the spotty-faced overnight clerk who just wanted to get back to watching his episode of *Storage Wars*.

Grown-ups who were not engaging in or planning to engage in sexual activity with each other did not share a mattress. Imogen hadn't shared a bed with anyone except for her husband and her children in more than a decade.

"We're not sharing a bed."

Imogen had no say in the matter. To her amazement the hotel was fully booked, as were most of the nicer places around town. This particular tech conference had grown in popularity, due in no small part to last year's appearances by several A-list actors, the ones who had forgone the typical celebrity revenue stream of Japanese cosmetics commercials and cheap clothing lines in favor of investing in technology start-ups.

These accommodations were cheap in every sense of the word. The price for the two of them in that one room was a third of the cost of any Union Square hotels like the Fairmont or Le Méridien.

After three swipes of the faded magnetic strip on the key card they finally entered the small room. Imogen needed sleep.

"Tomorrow is going to be so rad, Imogen," Eve said, sitting next to her in bed, as Imogen struggled to find a comfortable position. "We are going to kill it at this conference." She raised her hand in a high five, and then, thinking better of it, lowered it and stuck out her pinky.

"Let's pinky swear on it. That's how awesome it's going to be." Imogen was at a loss for what to do. She extended her pinky as well, which Eve promptly grasped with her own smallest digit and shook it vigorously up and down.

"I'm bringing pinky swearing back," Eve said, more to the entire shabby room than to Imogen. "Ooo, I should tweet that." Eve spoke out loud to herself as she tapped the words into her keyboard. "Bringin da pinky swear back. Booya!" With that she rolled over and went to sleep.

Imogen was exhausted and jet-lagged, but her mind just wouldn't shut down.

Did I really only come back to work the day before yesterday? She was having trouble processing just how much had changed so quickly. She'd barely even had time to discuss it with Alex in the hour they had seen each other before bed the night before. Her lawyerly husband wanted her to talk to an employment attorney right away.

"You have rights," he told her.

A right to what? She hadn't been fired, hadn't really even been demoted. The situation had merely changed and the ground had shifted from underneath her. She had gotten to say a quick good-bye to the children that morning after she packed her bag and now here she was in San Francisco. This was where Silicon Valley was, wasn't it?

She tossed and turned in the bed, desperate to find a comfortable spot on the scratchy sheets. She felt blindsided—felt like a woman whose husband was having an affair right under her nose, who brought his mistress to dinner parties and called her his protégée. How could she not have known all of this was happening to her magazine?

All of this was because of that damned cancer. The surgery hadn't been easy. Then there were the kids and Alex's new case. Imogen hadn't gone out professionally or socially while she was away, preferring to spend most weekends at their cottage in Sag Harbor. A workaholic for so many years, she'd had to let herself heal. This happened so fast. Eve just finished school in June and came back in July. The site would become an app next week.

Before dawn Imogen woke to the sound of an ice machine dropping its cubes insufficiently into something obviously not meant to contain ice. The frozen water plunked out of the chute into what sounded like a plastic bag. *Plop, squish, plop, squish. Plop, squish.* Eve snored away on the other side of the bed, eyes twitching beneath a purple sequined sleep mask.

Imogen opened one eye and then the other. Light filtered through cheap nylon curtains, revealing a too thick television set bulging off a plywood dresser, a relic of the nineties.

Like me, Imogen thought with a smirk as she briefly flashed back to her last business trip— four days in Italy for the Milan collections the previous February. Those already seemed like the good old days. Back then a shiny black car would collect her from home and deposit her at the airport. She would be ushered into first class and handed a glass of champagne, a warm towel and a soft blanket. The flight attendants knew her name and wished her sweet dreams. She'd sleep for six hours, before being shepherded into a second shiny, fresh-smelling black car upon landing and taken to one of the nicest suites in the Four Seasons. Those rooms were so luxurious she didn't mind sitting through thirty ready-to-wear presentations during the day. If she tried hard enough she could still feel those downy white sheets, adorned with a perfect white orchid accompanied by a small vellum card that simply read in beautiful black handwriting "Love. Tom Ford," a flourished dash through the "Ford."

Back in San Francisco, the ice machine down the hall gave up with a heavy groan followed by the sound of three swift kicks punctuated with an expletive Imogen could hear clearly through the paper-thin walls. Someone was truly unhappy about their inability to chill whatever it was they were drinking at the crack of dawn.

Imogen stretched as she got out of bed, her nose twitching at the smell of paint permeating the room. She spritzed her favorite Jo Malone, Red Roses, to sweeten the air as she opened the closet to search in vain for a hotel robe to take into the bathroom with her, but found only a few wire hangers.

"Dress 'nerd,'" Eve advised her when she emerged from her own shower twenty minutes later, with just a towel wrapped around her waist. Between her left hip and her belly button swam a happy dolphin tattoo, its snout cocked to smile adoringly at Eve's face. A small blush crept over Imogen's cheeks. She was no prude. For years she had watched as models pranced around her in various states of undress. But Eve was not a model and this was no photo shoot. Her perfectly round and pert boobs, the lack of lines betraying evidence of a spray tan, fixed themselves on Imogen, bare and judgmental.

"Let's put on some getting-ready tunes." Eve bounced over to her bed, and, before Imogen could object, Beyoncé's "Drunk in Love" began blaring from a portable purple speaker in the shape of a heart.

This new version of Eve, the one who was no longer her assistant, didn't provide much context. She assumed everyone already knew what she was thinking at any given moment, and so Imogen didn't bother to ask what "dress 'nerd'" even meant. The "nerdiest" she could glean from her limited traveling wardrobe on short notice was a crisp black blazer thrown over a pair of gently distressed faded black boy jeans she had planned to wear on the plane ride back, horn-rimmed eyeglasses, less a function of dressing nerd and more of needing reading glasses. In the scuffed-up bathroom mirror, Imogen thought she was channeling Jenna Lyons as she pulled her wheat-blond hair into a sleek ponytail and added a swipe of Vaseline to her lips. This was the classic "you'll never guess how expensive it costs to look like I am wearing no makeup" look perfected by industry women of a certain age. Imogen had gained a few lines in the places where she showed emotion, but that was what happened unless you were very willing to cut your face open on an increasingly regular basis. Instead, she relied on a trick told to her by her friend Donna Karan years ago at a cocktail party.

"A tight ponytail is an instant facelift," the designer had recommended.

Imogen made it her signature style.

* * *

DISRUPTTECH! was sprawled all over the city, but that morning they traveled to an industrial warehouse space just south of Market Street. Inside, concrete walls were interrupted only by bold signage, fluorescent lights and droopy-faced boys with eyes glued to tablets the size of their sweaty palms. Imogen had never been the oldest person in the room before, and now she felt bad about feeling bad that she was without a doubt the only person as far as the eye could see who remembered the fall of communism. It was a room Imogen felt excluded from the second she walked through the doors. She attempted an internal pep talk. Why did she care that everyone here was so young? Everything—including people, she believed—got better with age. So why did this room of fresh energy make the muscles in her shoulder blades involuntarily tense toward her ears?

Glossy's purpose in coming out here, Eve had explained the night before, was to present the new *Glossy* app to thousands of DISRUPT-TECH! participants. Today Eve would unveil the new product and Imogen would introduce her, which inspired in Imogen a feeling not unlike leaping out of an airplane with a knowingly faulty parachute. This situation was completely out of her control, but she played along and pretended that she, too, wanted to be a disruptor of things, just like everyone else in this brightly lit cell block celebrating technology and the future. Imogen remembered the good old days (not too long ago, mind you) when being disruptive was a bad thing—something toddlers did on planes. When did it become the buzz word for entrepreneurs and newly minted billionaires?

Until the launch of the *Glossy* app, the project was supposed to be spoken about in secret code words. Eve called it Cygnus, named for

the swan constellation, implying that the metamorphosis of a magazine into an app or a website was like turning an ugly duckling into
a beautiful swan. Imogen's job during their demonstration was to
represent the "ugly duckling," the "old guard" of *Glossy*. Her role was
to tell the audience *Glossy*'s creation narrative and forward-thinking
history. *Glossy* had launched in the 1950s, but it was in the sixties that
it really began to shake things up by breaking fashion traditions. It
was the first magazine to put a miniskirt on the cover during the mod
sixties youth quake, then Dick Avedon shot Veruschka in a bikini in
a Paris *hammam* in the seventies. *Glossy* launched the careers of the
eighties supermodels—Linda, Kate, Naomi and Christy.

Now it would be the first fashion magazine to embrace an entirely
digital future. Imogen didn't understand half of what would come
out of Eve's mouth during the second portion of the presentation,
titled:

FASHION 3.0: REAL-TIME RELEVANCE IN FASHION MEDIA

*Entrepreneur and editorial director Eve Morton will analyze the
major technology trends in the fashion industry before unveiling
her disruptive new consumer-commerce interface for* Glossy. *Her
goal is to foster innovation by challenging the status quo of the
traditional magazine advertising model. Eve began her career at*
Glossy *before receiving an MBA from Harvard. Joining her will
be Imogen Tate, current* Glossy *editor in chief.*

Imogen was an afterthought.

Eve was more distracted than usual that morning and hadn't
taken her own advice to "dress 'nerd.'" She wore a skintight black and
cream Hervé Léger dress. She was all legs and breasts. Her lavender
eye shadow matched her shellacked nail polish perfectly.

"I'm playing my part," she said defensively, crossing and uncross-
ing her arms over freckled cleavage. "I am the new guard of fashion tech. You're the old guard of the fashion media. We need to play
that up when we get onstage." Imogen smiled politely. She pulled her
iPhone out of her bag to make a note and show initiative. She kept the

notepad buried deep in the recesses of her Birkin, and wouldn't dare be seen using a pen at this kind of event. It would be the equivalent of rubbing two sticks together to start a fire. She'd only abandoned her trusty BlackBerry right before she got sick and the adjustment felt the same as the switch from a word processor to a PC. No one could fire off an email faster than Imogen could on her BlackBerry's keyboard but she fumbled on the iPhone, and couldn't switch the keyboard from Japanese for two days. The device made urgent sounds, none of them exactly a beep or ring, but more a series of twerps, pings, buzzes and maybe a bark. Being on the West Coast was no help. It was barely light out and she was still hours behind everyone in the office in New York. There were 207 unread emails.

"How do I look in this dress?" Eve asked. This new version of Eve needed a consistent stream of compliments. She kept asking if Imogen liked her dress or her shoes. Her extreme confidence was mixed with an intense insecurity.

"It's nice, Eve."

"Don't you mean hot?"

Imogen yawned. She needed much more than the three hours of sleep she'd gotten the night before.

It was early, but everyone at DISRUPTTECH! looked more exhausted than the hour warranted, maybe more exhausted than Imogen.

"There was a hackathon last night. They've all been awake for twenty-four hours," Eve explained with a roll of her eyes. Imogen didn't want to ask what exactly a hackathon consisted of, but Eve, unprompted, explained.

"There are two types of hackathons. You can come with a preset team, or you can be matched up with people when you arrive. Then there is a prompt. 'You have X number of hours to build something.' Most times it's a twenty-four-hour period, sometimes it's less. The idea is for developers to riff on projects and put out an MVP, a minimum viable product."

Imogen tried to sound interested even though confusion was causing her irritation to swell. "They design a product? They construct something throughout the evening? Is there an exhibit?"

Eve laughed her wide-mouthed cackle that revealed cavities in her back molars and was meant to embarrass Imogen for her ignorance. With every word and gesture, Eve knew how to make Imogen feel like a fool.

"They make an app, or a website, or a new feature on an existing app or website. They build in code. They sit in front of computers all night."

So that was why the room was filled with near-zombies, pulling guarana-based energy drinks out of fridges in the conference's pop-up café. She was dying for a macchiato, but Imogen didn't see a single person drinking coffee. Were they all living post-coffee lives? Was coffee so over?

"Those are just the devs. Most of the biz folks didn't stay up all night. The devs love it, though. It's geek prom. Edward Sharpe and the Magnetic Zeros played for them last night and Bobby Flay came in to barbecue a whole pig at midnight." Eve took pleasure in referring to her fellow techies as nerds, geeks and dweebs. She talked the talk, but even Imogen could see that she didn't walk the walk. Eve was the only one in the room wearing five-inch heels. Eve truly was something all her own. Imogen had opted for understated Reed Krakoff loafers.

At the conference check-in desk Imogen cleared her throat and announced herself with what she hoped was an air of authority. "Imogen Tate, editor in chief of *Glossy*." When no one looked up at her she realized they all had small white earbuds plugged into their laptops, where they watched a video of a moose jumping into a swimming pool with a baby.

After a full minute a doe-eyed girl with straight black hair and severe bangs noticed them standing there.

"Sorry. Badge pickup was yesterday."

Eve interjected, "I called before we took off yesterday to explain to your boss that we would be getting here late. The name is Eve Morton. Check again. You have our badges here." The girl rolled her eyes up to her bangs and rummaged through boxes under the table.

"Oh. Here they are," she said in a flat monotone. "Will you be registering for the Ping-Pong tournament?"

Eve shook her head. "We won't be here long enough. Maybe next year."

"That's a shame. It's going to be really competitive this year," the girl said with a small spark of excitement.

"Ping-Pong tournament?" Imogen whispered under her breath.

"Every company here has two people competing in the DISRUPT Ping-Pong tourney. Shame we will miss it," Eve replied as she looked down at the end of the table, where there were stacks of sticky name labels, the kind you peeled off a slick piece of paper, stacked high. They were blank except for an @ symbol. Imogen tried not to look confused, but bewilderment must have registered on her face. She could feel Eve's impatience.

"It's for your Twitter handle," Eve said, rolling her eyes and elbowing past Imogen as she wrote @GlossyEvie with a bold red Sharpie.

Imogen blinked. "Oh, I'm not on the Twitter just yet. Not all of us have been seduced by the technological revolution." She laughed and received only blank stares. That was the wrong thing to say. "I know I should join, but it still seems a little silly to me," she tried again over the little voice in her head screaming, *"Yes! Twitter is ridiculous! I am right!"* The boys behind the check-in desk were now paying attention to the scene. They cocked their heads to one side as if listening to a foreign tongue.

Eve's mortification played out only in her eyes. "Just put @Glossy—for the site," she said evenly. Then Eve wrote out the tag for Imogen herself as if she were dealing with a small and slightly annoying child.

An excited scrum gathered in the corner of the room around a gentleman in his twenties wearing a zip-up hoodie over a pair of overalls. On his feet he wore dirty Converse sneakers. He had a beaklike nose, acne-scarred cheeks and a single eyebrow that ran in a continuous line across his pronounced forehead.

"That's Reed Baxter, the founder of Buzz," Eve explained. "They treat him like Justin Timberlake here. Rumor has it that he can sleep standing up, knows thirteen languages and lets his hipster fiancée— her name's Meadow Flowers—come and just hang out in the office topless every day, meditating and trying to obtain a higher consciousness while his staff works twenty-four/seven. They're planning a wedding based on *Game of Thrones.* He's awesome."

Eve's exuberance over proximity to emerging power was palpable. "Buzz is the next generation of social messaging. It combines the hundred forty characters of Twitter, the video of Vine, the filtered photos of Instagram and the temporality of Snapchat. Reed made billions off his first company, a tap-based consumer payment platform. We should try to get some face time with him before we get out of here. I would *love* to get him involved with Glossy.com."

Reed Baxter wore a perpetually smug expression on his practically pubescent face. Two striking women, the only people in the room besides Eve who were showing any skin, flanked him on each side. When he stood, they stood. When he sat, they sat.

Imogen had never seen anyone quite like Reed, but she understood him better than Eve did. She knew from experience that all men, no matter their age or IQ, pretty much wanted the same things once they got money and power—sex and attention.

Eve continued to map the room the way a college tour guide would explain to a group of overeager sixteen-year-olds why launching themselves into adulthood should ideally cost them and their parents $100,000 a year.

Some DISRUPTTECH! attendees didn't even look like they were out of college, much less ready for the job market. The crowd was overwhelmingly male, perhaps one woman for every five guys. Jeans and a sweatshirt were the norm. Imogen wasn't the only one in horn-rimmed glasses. It had been a long time since she had been in a room this badly dressed and even in her own jeans she felt wildly out of place. Her iPhone growled. A text from Alex:

>>>> Hang in there. I love you. Try not to commit any acts of violence, real or digital.<<<<

>>>>California is friendlier to first-time offenders, especially 42-year-old mothers of two.<<<<

Imogen fumbled, trying to add a winky face, which accidentally turned into a frowny face before she could hit send.

The room where they were holding panels was still practically a raw space. An LED screen behind the stage glowed green like the monitor of an old computer and blared DISRUPT! Five hundred hard-backed plastic chairs were set up in rows. As the audience shuffled in, many in what looked like pajamas, two young men situated next to her cracked dirty jokes about something called dongles. She watched as one of them clawed at a scab on his right cheek before promptly ushering it into his mouth.

Eve set off in search of a diet Red Bull while Imogen settled into one of the ergonomically unpleasant seats. As Imogen yawned she felt a tap on her shoulder. When she turned she saw the most startling young man. Correction. He wouldn't have been at all startling below Fourteenth Street in Manhattan, but at DISRUPTTECH! he was a complete anomaly. His long black hair was pulled into a top-knot and a unique half-mustache kissed his nose like a baby caterpillar. Imogen wondered if the knot meant he was a practicing Sikh, but then noticed that the sides of his head had quotation marks shaved into them, so probably not. He wore an electric-blue shirt buttoned to his chin and a chubby little tie with a very small button at its tip, its own tiny exclamation point. She looked down and saw his flowing yellow silk pants, which stopped just above his ankles to show off a no-sock look above perfectly handcrafted two-tone Italian white leather brogues. Imogen loved him immediately.

"So sorry for yawning in your face. You must think that I am terribly rude. I'm a little worn out. We arrived late last night." She raised her voice to try to counter the electronic dance music being pumped into the room at a level just above comfortable.

The young man's almond-shaped eyes grew wide as he slapped one hand on his knee in delight. His other hand held a half-eaten breakfast taco. "You live in London?"

He meant her accent. "No, no, New York. I have lived there forever now, more than twenty years. I'm Ameri-lish now . . . Brit-i-can." She made that nationality joke too often because it made people laugh, but only politely.

He nodded his head as if he couldn't comprehend moving any-where twenty years earlier and seemed only mildly disappointed that she didn't currently live in England. Who didn't love a real London accent?

"I *actually* tapped you because I saw you yawn. I have a solution to all your sleep woes," he said. "Are you ready for this?" Imogen nod-ded her head hard, indicating that she was indeed ready, stifling yet another yawn. This was the kind of person Imogen always delighted in meeting in odd corners of the world. She collected them nearly everywhere she went and kept them in her Filofax and on her dinner party invitation list for years, sometimes decades.

"I've got myself on the eight, eight, eight. I break the day into eight-hour blocks." The young man's head moved left and right to an inaudible beat as he explained himself. "Well, actually seven-hour blocks with a flexible three hours. I typically wake up at eleven a.m. I go to the office and have meetings for seven hours straight. Then I transit one hour and use the second hour for socializing or dinner with friends and then I do emails and complete my action items for the next seven hours. I go to sleep at three a.m. and it starts all over again. On weekends I keep to the same schedule but instead of the emails at night I go to clubs. It's highly efficient."

He remembered his social graces only after his explanation. "I'm Rashid, founder of Blast! I'm presenting later." His eyes took in her sleek ponytail, her simple but expensive shoes and her too perfect pos-ture. He gave an almost imperceptible nod that showed he approved of her appearance.

Imogen had to admit that his dedication to this schedule was impressive, even remarkable for a boy who looked no older than twenty. He pronounced Blast! as though she must know exactly what he was talking about, in the way people would say, "I work at Sony" or "Bank of America."

"I'll have to give that a shot." She smiled charmingly, adding: "I love Blast!" *What the hell was Blast!?* It could be anything at all—an app, a website, a company, a foam pillow that warmed your neck at night in accordance with the rising and falling of your body tempera-ture and then recorded your dreams.

"Do you know what Blast! is?"

She *could* fake it, but decided there wasn't really a point. "I have absolutely no clue!"

Rashid rubbed his hands together. "We turn dreams into tech realities. I can build you an app, a website or an entire company from scratch. We're consultants. I like to think of us as the McKinsey of tech . . . in fact, we took a bunch of bros from McKinsey in the past couple of years."

He kept going: "Are you coming to the Awesomest Party Ever tonight?"

"Which party would that be?" Imogen asked, flattered to be invited to a party.

"The Awesomest Party Ever."

"Right, but which party?"

Rashid laughed at her ignorance and their twenty-first-century version of "Who's on First?" "The big party at DISRUPTTECH! that is happening tonight is actually called the Awesomest Party Ever." Eve would have made her feel foolish for her mistake but Rashid seemed to find her lack of understanding about this whole tech conference thing quite charming.

"I don't know if I have been invited."

"You can get in with your conference badge."

"Well, then I'll definitely try to make it. How could I come here and not attend the Awesomest Party Ever?"

"Isn't that just a little bit fun to say?" Rashid smiled, flashing two rows of expensive white teeth.

Imogen had to admit that, though silly, it was sort of fun to say.

Just as she was about to ask a follow-up, Eve reappeared at her side, making it evident she had been eavesdropping. "Making friends, Im! Cute." She flicked her hair and wobbled her breasts. "I don't sleep at all," she boasted to Rashid, as if disrespect for rest somehow lent her a certain distinction. Imogen passed her card back to Rashid and mouthed, "Call me," realizing too late she should have said, "email me," or maybe "tweet me," even though she wasn't sure that was something people ever said.

Eve, naturally, didn't let the moment pass without comment.

"How adorable are you with the business cards? I didn't know anyone used those anymore." She plucked it from Rashid's hand and made a show of examining it like it was an artifact before letting it fall to the floor.

Imogen and Eve's presentation was part of the Start-up Battlefield. They were technically part of a larger corporation, the Robert Mannering media empire, but because Mannering was in the process of spinning off several less profitable assets (mostly magazines) in order to bolster their other businesses (mostly video streaming in China) *Glossy* was allowed to raise money and operate as if it were a start-up.

Start-up Battlefield included thirty companies chosen from hundreds of applicants. After the demonstrations, pitches and tough rounds of questions, the judges—venture capitalists, seasoned entrepreneurs and some tech press—would award the winner a $50,000 check and something called the Disrupt Cup, a trophy made of melted floppy disks.

When Eve explained this aspect to Imogen, she had to stop herself from asking what exactly had happened to the floppy disk. She couldn't remember the last time she had seen one and yet she didn't understand exactly what had replaced it or when. The floppy disk was something she could wrap her head around. It was a tangible thing you could touch and smell, just like the pages of a magazine. The Internet and the tiny computers they worked on these days made less sense to her. You couldn't touch the new Glossy.com—the app or digital magazine or whatever they decided to call it.

Glossy was the fourth presenter in the Battlefield and their talk wasn't allowed to be more than seven minutes long. As the third presenters finished their speech Imogen closed her eyes and took in a few deep breaths through her nose. When she arrived at the podium she felt confident and sure of herself for the first time that morning. This was something she could do. This was where she shined. She had spent years wooing advertisers from the biggest fashion houses in the world. She had hosted cocktail dinners for billionaires and visiting heads of state.

She started off with one of her favorite quotations from Oscar

Wilde—"Fashion is a form of ugliness so intolerable that we have to alter it every six months"—and then made one of her stock jokes: "Mr. Wilde would have to rethink his words knowing that I am allowed to reinvent it every single month."

She usually got a few chuckles from that. Now there were only blank stares. Briefly frazzled, she looked down at her notecards and launched into her explanation of the history of *Glossy*, racking her brain for a way to win this crowd. What did she have in common with them? Who did they care about? Reading rooms was something she typically excelled at.

"I met Steve Jobs a couple of years after he released the first prototype of the iPhone," Imogen started winging it. "He told me that it would change my life. As a late adopter of the technology I wish I had a chance to tell Mr. Jobs that it truly has. Never in my wildest dreams did I imagine I would be so talented at flinging angry birds at feral pigs." It worked. The crowd laughed, all thanks to Alex. He had ad-libbed the joke the night before when she bemoaned having to get onstage at a tech conference: "When in doubt tell them an Angry Birds joke. They love Angry Birds." Thank god she'd married a man who spent time defending millennial repeat offenders.

"Thank you, Imogen," Eve said, walking in front of her, eager to replace her applause. "If Oscar Wilde were alive today he would recognize that we need to reinvent fashion about every six minutes online."

The crowd loved that. More claps followed by hoots and hollers.

Eve pulled out the weighty September issue of *Glossy*, all 768 pages of it.

"This is a lot of paper. A lot of trees," said Eve, who had never once expressed any kind of interest in the environment, with faux earnestness. Imogen saw former vice president Al Gore's head nod in agreement from an offstage Skype feed apparently piped in from Antarctica.

"Reinventing fashion every six minutes is exactly what we intend to do. And we will do it in an entirely eco-friendly way."

With a grand flourish, Eve tossed the magazine into the air behind her, barely missing Imogen's face with its erect spine.

"Next month *Glossy* will be the very first traditional fashion monthly to go completely digital. Stories will update in real time. Want amazing coverage of the Academy Awards' red carpet? We're streaming it, as it happens. Want to see what Kate Middleton wore to the prince's birthday party? We've got you. You have exactly fifty milliseconds to capture someone's attention online. Our content is so good we can get someone in half that. But that isn't what we came here to tell you. That's not exciting. That doesn't disrupt anything. Blogs have been doing that for years."

At the word "disrupt," someone shouted, "Hell yeah!"

Even though Imogen had heard Eve practice this spiel last night, it all still sounded foreign. *Glossy*'s new business model and Eve's brainchild was a grand mission to create a perfect marriage of fashion and beauty editorial plus e-commerce. The site would essentially mirror the pages of the magazine, except all editorial would now be packed with product placement and branded content. As someone lost themselves in the arresting photographs, they were also just one click away from buying the full look.

Some of the content would still be beautifully packaged photo shoots straight from the pages of a magazine. But there were new elements. Lists, lists, lists. The whimsy-loving eighteen- to thirty-year-old demographic devoured them. The site BuzzFeed had first capitalized on that fact, and now everyone was just copying it: 11 FASHION MISTAKES YOU DID NOT KNOW YOU WERE MAKING, 17 JADE SWEATERS THAT WILL CHANGE YOUR LIFE, 13 SHOES WITH CATS ON THEM THAT WILL MAKE HIM PURR!

Millennials, the new target demographic, lived in a tough world. They came of age in the shadow of 9/11. The job market was dismal when they graduated from college and even worse when they came out of grad school. They wanted to consume content that was funny and optimistic and demanded a maximum investment of two minutes. They didn't languidly browse through magazines for hours. They swiped, they liked, they tapped, they shared. Most important, they didn't care if content was branded as long as it made them LOL or ROFL.

The new app would optimize the consumer magazine experience

with a fully integrated shopping platform, allowing the magazine to reap the revenues from an industry it long helped to build and sustain with no real return. Oh sure, fashion brands had always paid money to advertise in the magazine's pages. But that was nothing compared to what they stood to earn from Eve's new plan for one-tap shopping off every item pictured.

The technology had been developed by a friend of Eve's from Harvard Business School. Together they had figured out how to layer fashion editorial over shopping cart code.

Eve asked everyone in the audience to pull out their tablets, an unnecessary overture since most were already on their owners' laps. She asked them to log on to Glossy.beta.test with their last name and the password Cygnus.

"One hundred sixty-seven million people shopped online today. In the next year they will spend one hundred billion more online than they did last year. That's one hundred billion dollars just out there, up for grabs. If you make it super hard for people to shop for your product, you make it super hard for people to buy your product." Imogen was amazed at how many times Eve could use the word "super" in a single breath. "We make it super easy to shop and buy. After you checked into the conference this morning, our engineers created an account for each of you. We deposited a hundred dollars into each account. Now play around with the site."

Glossy.com's new content populated the screen behind Eve.

Everyone clicked on the shoes with cats. Black Chuck Taylors with cat faces, purple boots with tiny cat tails attached to the heels. Hovering over each piece of content was a bright starburst that screamed BUY IT NOW.

Eve grinned.

"BUY IT NOW!" she yelled.

And with one click, two hundred audience members made a purchase.

"Your information is already in the system. We conveyed it to the individual retailer. We know *where* you want it shipped. We know *how* you want it shipped. No need to go off the page. Your receipt will

be emailed to you. You can continue reading now, with the knowledge that your product will be on its way to you within the next eighteen hours."

The crowd was delighted, but Eve really got them with what came
next. This is what had investors salivating.

Eve showed chart upon chart of numbers on the giant screen. The
real cash cow would come after year one of the application's launch,
when they could harness data on when, where, why and how their
customers shopped. The collection, storage, and sorting of that data
would be worth billions to brands.

Eve received a standing ovation. Even Imogen couldn't help but
be impressed by the girl's performance and charisma.

She was excited and terrified all at once. With Eve at the helm
of Cygnus and Cygnus ready to launch into Glossy.com, she didn't
understand what the company needed from her or why they were
even keeping her on board.

Imogen felt small next to Eve, her former assistant who was now a
big bright shining star in this room full of young people who had no
fears about their own futures. Eve was a tech darling.

Imogen kept clapping and smiling. God, she felt so uncomfortable. Wasn't it time to leave already?

* * *

"Teeny Tiny Video, Great Big Impact," "Life's a Breach, Don't Burn
Your Brand" and "Orgasm: The Broadband of Human Connection."
Eve read out the names of the panels she wanted to attend later
that day, scratching her fingernail along the conference schedule on
her tablet. She tapped on a few of the links to read who would be
speaking.

"Blergh! This guy's a douche. That guy is really a douche. Ugh,
who gave him a panel here? Why didn't anyone give me a panel here
over that guy?" she grumbled.

The lanyard attached to Imogen's badge stuck in her hair as she
tried to pull it over her head.

"Keep your badge," Eve snapped, looking up. Her tone was enough to push Imogen over the edge. Rude just didn't work with her. She had been through the terrible twos twice and was not about to go through it a third time.

"The badge was just for today, and I am heading back to the hotel," Imogen said, weary of this constant micromanagement.

"Who cares? . . . The more badges you have on here, the more important you look." Imogen noticed Eve now had a plethora of brightly colored plastic rectangles hanging from her neck in addition to plastic bracelets parading up and down her forearm. She had accumulated them visiting various booths and suites within the conference hub.

"Eve, I'm tired."

"That's lame. You should make the most of being here."

Did she just say "lame"? "I'm exhausted and this isn't really my crowd."

The lack of women at the event was startling. Imogen had never been somewhere so laden with testosterone or with people who looked like they would prefer to be alone in a cool, dark room.

Eve narrowed her eyes and pursed her lips, ready to explain yet again the gravity of being at such an important tech conference. Then she turned her head, distracted. "Oh! There's Jordan Brathman from FashionBomb. We've been emailing about doing a content partnership. I'm going to catch up." With that, Eve gravitated in the direction of someone more important, shoving the double doors back open with both palms, not bothering with a good-bye.

As the doors closed, Imogen breathed a sigh of relief and again tried to tackle the task of removing all badges and name tags from her person.

"Imogen?" She turned to see who could possibly be asking for her. His bright blue shirt was even more dazzling in the sunlight.

"I'm Rashid. We met earlier."

Imogen was surprised by how happy she was to see a familiar face here. "Of course. Hi. Lovely to see you again."

"What are your plans for the rest of the day?" He clasped his hands behind his back and smiled expectantly at her.

"I am trying to figure out where to get a taxi so I can head back to our hotel. We have an early flight in the morning." Even as the words came out of her mouth, the idea of going back to that dingy hotel room grew less and less appealing, even if it did mean a few blissful hours free of Eve.

"That's a shame. I was hoping you would stick around. Have a bit of fun? There is always the Awesomest Party Ever...."

She glanced at her watch and thought about the sound of the ice machine. What did she have to lose?

"I could probably join you for an hour or two. What exactly is there to do here?"

"What isn't there to do here is the better question! My lady, I am going to give you the full DISRUPTTECH! experience." Rashid bent down to one knee. "Are you ready for this?"

Imogen shook her head from side to side. "I don't actually think that I am." The young man handed her what looked like a milk carton.

"Here. First have a box of water."

"Box?" She flipped the rectangle over in her hands.

"Better for the Earth. Entirely made of recyclable biodegradable hemp-based cardboard." The writing on the side of the carton simply read: "I am not a water bottle."

Rashid introduced her to two of his colleagues. AJ, his chief technology officer, was the tallest Asian gentleman Imogen had ever seen in real life. He wore a faded T-shirt with two cartoon frames on the front. In the first box a male stick figure was bent over and in the second he was petting a baby bird. Bubbly writing across the top read: "How to Pick Up Chicks." The chief operating officer of Blast!, Nathan, was a soft-spoken Owen Wilson doppelgänger with tousled hair, tired eyes and a nose that did a jig in the middle that made him look odd and yet handsome.

Over the course of the next three hours they took 3-D selfies at the Netherlands HEARTS Technology tent, where hulking Low Country boys with light hair and light eyes lounged about like attractive furniture. They ate a piece of candy made by the same 3-D printer, though Imogen cowered at actually putting a piece of food in her mouth that was printed right in front of her. It was candy-apple flavored and a little too sweet, but there was something completely delightful about it. They listened to a panel about how the globalization of digital products helped students in war-torn countries use their smartphones to map safe routes to school in the morning. Imogen found it fascinating, even though she needed Rashid to translate half of it. They stood in a long line to take pictures with two famous dwarf cats, one whose tongue lolled lazily out of its mouth and the other who looked perpetually frustrated. They opted against jumping onto the Nest.com moon bounce, but they accepted the free massages in the Cottonelle Toilet Paper of the Future yurt. She grabbed a couple of black and yellow DISRUPTTECH! hoodies for Johnny and Annabel.

"Where are all the girls? Women?" Imogen asked as they walked from the Chevrolet-3M-Esurance Ideas Exchange Pavilion to the Pepsi Bioreactive #MediaFuture Plaza, where a pool party was taking place complete with an open bar, live DJ and a pool full of blow-up orcas. Who wanted to go to a pool party when they were working?

Rashid's topknot bounced up and down as he waved to a guy riding a Segway while wearing a helmet with a video camera attached. "These things can get so bro-tastic. There are some awesome women in tech, but the ratio at these conferences is so skewed, dude."

"And why do I feel like everyone is staring at me? Because I am old enough to be their mum?"

"I actually think it's because they aren't used to seeing a beautiful woman here." He blushed, his cocoa-colored skin turning a dusty rose. "You aren't the oldest person here. This conference *is* young though. You go to TED and you'll see the billionaire version of DISRUPTTECH!, where Sandra Day O'Connor shares a crème brûlée with Nathan Myhrvold while chatting about archaeology, barbecue and the legality of digital permanence."

Imogen considered that for a minute. "Right now I am a beautiful woman who is starving. I wonder if we can get a reservation anywhere in Union Square at the last minute."

"No need." Rashid smiled. "We can go to the Samsung-Blast! Food Truck Court." Before Imogen could protest, Rashid took off around the corner to dart into a vast parking lot resembling a trailer park.

Upon closer inspection, Imogen realized it contained rows and rows of food trucks.

"They come from all over the country for this," Rashid said proudly. "One of my team members came up with the idea."

While standing in line for kimchi fries they were jostled by a large round man wearing an acid-washed denim vest over a turquoise zip-up hoodie, black jeans and pointy black ostrich-skin boots.

Imogen flashed a winning smile at him.

Finally ready to order, Rashid asked her what style of kimchi fry would suit her palate.

"I am afraid to confess this, but I haven't been a fry girl in quite some time," Imogen admitted sheepishly.

"I figured," Rashid began as he looked over the menu to catcalls from the peanut gallery urging him to hurry up. "But come on, YOLO with me a little."

"YOLO?"

"You only live once."

"YOLO." Imogen let the foreign word roll off her tongue. "Okay. I'll take the most straightforward and honest fries they have."

"Good decision. You get too many toppings and things get weird." He turned his attention to the boy behind the counter. "Two regular kimchi fries." Then he tapped a gunmetal-gray plastic bracelet to the side of the cart.

"Do you need cash?" Imogen fumbled for her wallet and pulled out a few bills.

Rashid laughed. "No, we're cool. I just paid."

"You did?"

"Yeah." He held his wrist aloft. "Cashless currency. There is a chip in my wristband that connects to my credit card that pays for everything I do here at the conference."

"Can you use it anywhere in the real world?" Imogen marveled at the simplicity of its smooth surface.

"Not yet. It's in beta. They're testing it here and at a couple of other festivals around the country this year."

* * *

By the end of the night, even though she'd had way more fun than she expected, Imogen was happy to return to an empty hotel room, even one as depressing as theirs.

She put in a quick call to Ashley to check in, and though it had to be close to midnight on the East Coast, the girl said she was still in the office.

"Are you having fun at DISRUPT?" Ashley asked. "I am having the worst FOMO looking at Eve's Instagram. Were you with her in the pool with those big inflatable whales?"

"I wasn't, but I saw those. What did you have? YOLO?" Imogen tried out her new word.

Ashley giggled. "YOLO!" she sang. "No, no, I had FOMO, Fear. Of. Missing. Out. It's like you're looking at all these pictures of your friends and people you know being awesome and doing awesome things on, like, Facebook and Instagram and you get all tense and freak out and you get FOMO because you are not there doing something as awesome as they are. I get it all the time!!"

"That can't be healthy," Imogen said, to which Ashley just sighed. "Don't I know it."

* * *

Sometime, many hours later, hands drumming on Imogen's feet at the bottom of the bed jolted her awake.

"'Rosenbergs, H-bomb, Sugar Ray, Panda moms, Brando, *The King and I* and *The Catcher in the Rye* . . . House on FIRE good-bye! We didn't start the fire, It was always burning/Since the world's been turning. We didn't start the fire.' . . . Sing with me, Imogen!"

Imogen sat up and rubbed her eyes, still blurry with sleep, to see Eve whipping her hair back and forth, hunching her shoulders to a beat that lived in her head of a bastardized version of "We Didn't Start the Fire."

"What's going on, Eve?"

"We took the Karaoke RV back from the Buzz party and Reed Baxter paid an extra thousand dollars to have him drive to Marin and back so we could sing . . ."

"Eve, we have a six a.m. flight. What time is it?"

"Three. Davy Crockett, Peter Pan, Elvis Presley, Disneyland . . . come on, Imogen . . . it's an old song. You have to know it."

She did know it, had actually sung along to it once at the Piano Man's beach house in Sagaponack.

"Ugh. I would like to get an extra half hour of sleep." Trying to focus on Eve's pupils, she couldn't tell if the girl had taken something or was high on herself.

"You're no fun, Imogen." Eve pouted as Imogen rolled over and pulled the thin pillow over her head to drown out her former assistant.

"You're right. I'm no fun, Eve."

CHAPTER FIVE

E ve did not understand why she had to put her laptop away for takeoff. Turning off cell phones and putting away computers on planes were antiquated rules that should have been thrown away when they told people they had to quit smoking.

Eve refused to put away her laptop for takeoff.

"Don't you get how much work I have to do?" she tried to explain to the flight attendant.

"Miss, rules are rules. If you don't comply with the FAA's practices for takeoff I will have to ask you to get off this plane." The woman exhaled, glancing nervously at the tan curtain that separated the coach cabin from first class.

"You'll ask me to get off?" Eve dropped her voice on the final word, offering it as a challenge, clutching her slim MacBook to her chest as she gulped down the last sip of her diet Red Bull. "You're going to ask me to get off the plane? That's ridiculous. That's so ridiculous that I think I should share that. I think I should tweet that out to my huge network of followers from Glossy.com. How do you feel about that?"

Imogen touched her elbow.

"Eve."

She shook Imogen off. The old stewardess seemed to think she was kidding. Or maybe, like Imogen, she didn't even know what Twitter was. She didn't know the power that could come from one little tweet. *I'll show her,* Eve thought. *This will teach her not to fuck with me.*

"I am tweeting right now—@JetEasy Airlines is forcibly trying to take my computer and phone away from me like it is a bomb." *Okay and one more.* "YUP! @JetEasy is acting like I brought a bomb on a plane. They're treating me like a terrorist! I mean!"

That ought to show them.

It didn't take long for the air marshals to remove someone when she tweeted about having a bomb on a plane and made a joke about being a terrorist. It took almost all of Imogen's miles and two hours with Homeland Security to get the two of them on the next flight back to New York City.

Eve was thankfully several rows behind her. Imogen let the roar of the plane's engines drown out the pounding in her head as she pulled out her notebook to make a list of reasons why she should not stay on as the editor in chief of Glossy.com.

1. Not entirely sure how to post something onto a website.
2. Only joined Facebook last year and since then updated status exactly three times.
3. Not doing any of the following: Twitter, Instagram or Pinterest
4. Recently referred to the Internet as the World Wide Web. That isn't right. Right?
5. Buys all books at the Strand Bookstore, not online.
6. Cannot possibly continue to work so closely with a sociopath.

At LaGuardia Airport Eve popped two slim blue Adderall tablets and grabbed a cab straight into work, even though it was past four in the afternoon by the time they landed. Imogen went home. The walls of the old town house squeezed her like a mother who hasn't seen her child in a long while. Her own kids were out with Tilly, and the hubby, as usual, was at work. Imogen fell into the cloud of freshly laundered sheets, let her head sink into the downy pillows and curled herself into the folds of her worn cashmere blanket. Soon she fell into a deep sleep. She never set an alarm.

In her dream, Imogen was in secondary school but she hadn't studied for any of her exams. She didn't even know what her class schedule was or how to go about looking it up. She found herself in an algebra class at a small desk with an exam book in front of her and no idea what test she was about to take. The teacher whirled to face the students from behind the large wooden desk at the front of the room. It was Eve Morton. The bell rang and Imogen woke up.

CHAPTER SIX

SEPTEMBER 2015

The new and improved Glossy.com website and app launched without a hitch. *The Times* business section dubbed it a triumph for Mannering Inc., and Worthington was praised for having an eye for fresh young talent. While all of the press mentioned that Imogen Tate was still at the helm of Glossy.com, it was Eve all the reporters wanted to talk to.

Imogen began studying Eve more carefully. As the weeks passed, Imogen learned that a special schizophrenia characterized Eve's behavior. In meetings she was dynamic and charismatic. One-on-one she was standoffish, cold, even reptilian, but over email and social media she oozed abundant warmth, trying to prove to the recipient and the entire world that she was a good person, fun, fair and aspirational. To that end each week Eve sent an email crowning someone the "Office Prom Queen," an honorary title that, so far as Imogen could tell, came with no clear benefits save for that Thursday morning email filled with effusive praise in the language of middle-school girls, and the one-week possession of a cheap plastic tiara. The title was awarded to the week's best team player, according to Eve. On this particular Thursday that young woman was Amy from the Customer Insight Team.

From: Eve Morton (EMorton@Glossy.com)
To: GlossyStaff@Glossy.com

Hi all,

I couldn't be more excited to crown this week's Prom Queen. HURRAH! This lovely lady has recently rocked it with more than 40 blog posts (Yes, we're counting!). Can we say WINNER! She has really stepped it up with her management of the Bling vertical and she was a gem of a gal organizing this week's three-legged races when we all worked late on Wednesday night. What a doll baby J.

This PQ is hardworking, witty and packs a major punch in her size two frame (zero on a good day—YAY JUICE CLEANSE). Please join me in congratulating our newest and cutest (LOL!) trophy winner . . . Ms. Amy "Pink Undies" Dockson.

GO, Glamour Girls! 👯★👑♥💋✂

Hugs,
Eve

The email came through just an hour after Eve had stood on a table in the middle of the office to berate the staff members who hadn't been using the *Glossy* app in their personal lives.

"It's been brought to my attention that some of you haven't even bothered to download the *Glossy* app," Eve said, her eyes narrowing and her voice oozing disdain. "This is completely unacceptable to me. Everyone needs to be using our product. That's the only way we can make it better and better. If you are one of those people who have refused to install the app or you don't feel like using it when you shop, do yourself a favor and find a job somewhere else." Eve expected applause after her grand statement. Instead, heads bowed and Imogen could see at least three girls furiously downloading the app when they returned to their desks. Eve obviously expected the Prom Queen announcement to make everything rosy again.

Imogen was just trying to assimilate everything in the email when the real-life Eve began hovering over her, devoid of LOLs and hugs. "So I need you live-tweeting Fashion Week starting tomorrow. Can I have Ashley set you up on Twitter? You aren't on it yet, right?"

Imogen was barely on Facebook and had signed onto that only because the kids' school used it for all of their PTA updates (important news about early dismissals, fund-raisers and wear-green-to-school days) and to keep an eye on Annabel now that her daughter was growing more and more distant and mature. The thought of being forced to be witty in just 140 characters made her stomach churn. It was a giant time-suck in an already full day. Imogen didn't exactly hate technology. She just didn't understand it and felt overwhelmed by it. She longed for the days when everyone's eyes weren't glued to a small screen; when you walked into an elevator and smiled at a stranger, or had a conversation with a cabdriver; when your dinner companion didn't spend the meal art-directing an Instagram shoot of the peony centerpiece. Imogen sometimes wondered if people weren't letting social media dictate their entire lives. Did they choose to go to one party over another because it would look better on Instagram? Did they decide to read a story just so they could tweet about it? Have we all become so desperate to share everything that we've stopped enjoying our lives?

"It's good for the brand," Eve said, sensing her reluctance about Twitter. "If you do a bang-up job, you might just get to be the Prom Queen next week."

One could only wish.

This was a fight she wasn't going to win. "I've been meaning to set it up." Imogen smiled. "I'm sure you can teach me a few tricks." As if on cue, Ashley appeared in her doorway, teetering in anticipation of her next step in six-inch heels. One day, Ashley would master the art of walking like a lady in tall shoes. Today would not be that day. When she walked her toes turned in slightly, forcing her knees to kiss each other with every step. Imogen marveled at what a fashion chameleon the girl was. She could be seventies YSL or nineties Versace. One day she channeled a boho Talitha Getty and the next she would be an L.A. surfer chick. She was dedicated. Her perfectly imperfect hair and makeup must take her at least two hours to prep each morning. "Let's do this!" Ashley clasped her hands in excitement. "Twitter time."

Getting Imogen onto Twitter was trickier than they expected. A rabid *Glossy* fan, a drag queen from Saint Paul, Minnesota, who did bear Imogen an uncanny resemblance in full makeup and a blond wig, had hijacked her name, @ImogenTate.

"I'll call Twitter and see if we can deactivate this account," Ashley said right away, blushing as though she were embarrassed for Imogen.

Drag queen @ImogenTate was hilarious, with his strong opinions about fashion, *The Real Housewives of Orange County* and at-home waxing treatments. It would have been much easier to hire him to write all of her tweets during Fashion Week. Imogen did the mental math: airfare from Minnesota, a room at the Soho Grand, a couple of meals here and there. New wig—$5,000 tops and worth every bloody penny.

"Never mind. We need Glossy in there anyway. Eve is @GlossyEvie. I am @GlossyAshley. We can just make you @GlossyImogen." Ashley made a few clicks with the mouse and entered the characters. "@GlossyImogen it is. You're set."

Imogen stared at the screen name and the light blue square with the lonely egg inside.

"We'll need a headshot."

Imogen thumbed through her phone and found a picture of her at an event with Alex a couple of months before her surgery. Her face was a little fuller then, in a healthy way. She had her hair pulled into a "Belle du Jour" ponytail perfectly tucked under a black fur collar.

"Does this work?"

When Ashley scrunched up her nose her foundation created little grooves around her mouth. "Sure, for now. Eve likes the pictures to be a little more candid. She likes to say 'accessible.' See? Here is her picture." The girl pulled up Twitter.com/GlossyEvie to reveal a half-body shot of Eve in her favorite pose, all boobs and teeth, her mouth wide open and head thrown back like a donkey braying for her supper.

Imogen wagered that Eve practiced that pose over and over again, taking picture after picture until she achieved exactly the right shot. There was nothing candid about it.

"I'll work on it," Imogen said. "It won't be a picture just like this one, but I'll find you something fabulous. Just use this as a place-holder for now."

"So tell me what you know about Twitter."

"It's fairly self-explanatory, isn't it? I type and I hit send."

"That's pretty much it. Let's make you a quick bio. What is your title now?"

"It's still editor in chief." Imogen felt her ego crash.

"Okay, so what should we say?"

"Editor in chief of *Glossy*."

"Glossy-dot-com."

"Right, Glossy-dot-com. So what else do I need to say in it?"

"Hmmm, this is mine. . . ." Ashley clicked on her personal Twit-ter profile. "Top of the line, slim face, fair behind. Tweets are all ME! ROFL." Ashley shook her head. "That probably won't work for you. Let's find someone more age appropriate." She bit her lip, thinking, tapping her thumb anxiously on the side of the keyboard. "I've got it! Here is Hillary Clinton's: Wife, mom, lawyer, women & kids advocate, FLOAR, FLOTUS, US Senator, SecState, author, dog owner, hair icon, pantsuit aficionado, glass ceiling cracker, TBD. . . ."

"I can't beat that." Imogen laughed. Hillary Clinton was preparing to run the free world and she still had time to tweet and compose a perfectly droll Twitter bio that made Imogen feel like a slacker. "How about this: 'Editor in chief of Glossy-dot-com, mum, wife, daughter, a lover not a fighter in the mad, mad world of fashion.'"

Ashley cocked her head to one side like a golden retriever thinking about where it has left its favorite ball.

"I like it," she said with her requisite clap. "Since you know what to do, I can just leave you to it. Once you start, you're going to be com-pletely addicted. I already followed everyone here at the magazine for you and we will tweet from our main account telling all of our two million followers to start following you ASAP. *Fun!*"

Alone with her Twitter account, Imogen felt her palms leak sweat.

How hard could it be? You put in a sentence or two and you just hit tweet. What a funny word, "tweet." Every time she heard it she imagined a time traveler from the year 2000 desperately trying to understand all the world's new verbs, like "tweet," "Google," "twerk."

She just put in a line and then. Oh no. That wasn't what she wanted to say at all. No worries, she could go in and edit it. It wasn't clear how to edit a tweet. Were they uneditable? She would just delete and start over. How do you delete? Imogen desperately didn't want to ask Ashley for advice. She couldn't see the old tweet so maybe she had already deleted it. She would try another.

@GlossyImogen: Hello Twitter! Here I am twerking.

@GlossyImogen: Hello Twitty! Here I am tweeting.

@GlossyImogen: That isn't what I wanted to say at all. Twitter not Twitty. Sorry, new followers.

@GlossyImogen: I am new to Twitter. Still figuring it out.

@GlossyImogen: I swear I am not drunk. Just learning.

@GlossyImogen: Bugger. I give up.

Slowly step away from the Twitter. No good could come of continuing this exercise. Twitter would still be here this afternoon and right now she had something like four followers, Ashley, Eve, and two people she didn't know whose photos were still the light blue background with an ominous egg. At least no one saw her epic tweet fail. She would call Massimo after lunch and ask him how to delete the tweets. Massimo was a self-described rock star on Twitter, on a mission to gain more followers than Lady Gaga.

"It's shitty if you don't follow back the guy in the wheelchair," he always said.

The next hour was overtaken by a conference call with the creative director for Carolina Herrera during which Imogen described the evolution of *Glossy* into Glossy.com and how they could get Carolina involved.

"We'll see" came the answer at the end of the call. Imogen had never received so many "We'll see"s in her life. As she hung up the phone, an out-of-breath Ashley ran smack into the spotless glass door to her office, hardly letting it stop her from stumbling inside.

"Stop tweeting."

"Ashley, I stopped tweeting more than forty-five minutes ago. I am still getting the hang of it."

"You're. On. Tech. Blab."

"What is that?"

"TechBlab-dot-com. It's a techie site, gossipy, like Page Six but for people in tech. And your tweets are on it. We have to fix it before Eve sees it."

Imogen typed the name into her browser. What kind of a name was TechBlab anyway? It sounded made up.

She emitted a small gasp. There was her picture, a lovely one of her on the red carpet at some event. With a closer look, she knew exactly what photo it had been cropped from. The larger picture showed her with Steven Spielberg at a benefit for Breast Cancer Awareness in March.

WHEN OLDS TWEET
by Astrid Parkerson

Someone needs to hire a social media manager for Glossy.com's Imogen Tate, 45 (what does she do there these days anyway?). It seems the former editor in chief has tried her hand at tweeting today, but no one explained any of the rules to her. It looks like something my mom would have done . . . four years ago. We're going to assume she's not drunk but you know how the olds like their martinis with lunch. . . .

To start with, she was forty-two, not forty-five.

Ashley was suddenly joined by Alexis from the Public Relations department.

"Imogen, we are so sorry. I have no idea how Astrid Parkerson would even have known to look at your Twitter account, but I assure you we will get to the bottom of it."

Imogen had two options. Act horrified, which she was, or laugh it off.

She rolled her eyes and let out her best, slightly too loud, Joan Crawford full-throated laugh.

"It could have been so much worse. At least I didn't tweet something really embarrassing." She clicked on her Twitter page. "And look how many followers the incident got me." Imogen's follower count was now topping 5,500, which she knew was 500 more than Eve. "I'm a little bit famous on the Internet now. Ashley, sit here with me while I compose a couple of tweets to all my new followers."

Both Ashley and Alexis visibly relaxed. If Imogen didn't think this was a crisis, there was no one reason anyone else should think it was.

@GlossyImogen: Thanks to @TechBlab for all my new followers. Welcome! I hope that I can delight you while I wobble about on here.

@GlossyImogen: I am trying to follow @BlabAstrid's mum. I hear she is an excellent tweeter! I need a mentor.

In the course of the next hour, she was inundated with new followers and retweets. Someone created a hashtag: #GoImogen. She finally understood what all of the fuss over social media was about. This kind of validation was wonderful. She just needed to get a firm handle on how to tweet from her phone and she would be perfectly fine to start live-tweeting from her first fashion show tomorrow morning. She still dreaded the part where she had to seem wonderful and witty in every tweet. It was exhausting.

Hours later, she nearly collided with Eve walking out of the office.

"Easy there on the Twitter, Imogen." Eve smirked. "We can't have the investors thinking our editors are drinking on the job."

"I think the tweeting is going quite well. I'm starting to really enjoy it. Plus, I got nearly ten thousand followers today." Imogen swelled with pride as she noticed Eve balk at the number.

"Try not to embarrass us tomorrow when you tweet from the shows," Eve said. She glanced down at the FitBoom on her wrist. "I think I'll take the stairs. Got to get my ten thousand steps."

Ashley squeezed herself through the elevator doors just as they were closing. She looked anxious, like she needed to tell Imogen something. After the fourth time Ashley glanced sideways at her, made a small sound and then shut her mouth and looked sheepishly away, Imogen prompted her.

"Ashley. Is something the matter?"

"Ohhhhh, I don't know if I should tell you this."

"Just tell me. If it's about my tweeting, I can handle any criticism you lob at me after what I've endured today."

"It's about your Twitter, but not about you. I really shouldn't, but you should know. You're my boss. I'm sorry, Imogen."

The girl looked like she was about to burst into tears. Imogen put on her most motherly look.

"Ashley, please tell me whatever you need to tell me. I promise, whatever it is I won't get mad."

"I'm not worried about you being upset with meeeeeeee." Ashley kept opening and closing her palms as she wiggled her jaw back and forth with a *click, click* sound. "Okay. Here it is. See, I am friends with Astrid from TechBlab. Not friends, exactly. Maybe you could call us frenemies. We were in the same sorority and stuff and I felt so awful when I read her post. She doesn't even know you. I didn't understand why she would be so mean. Anyway, I emailed her to be, like, 'Hey, what the hell?' and she was all, like, 'Hey, I didn't think anyone over there would care what I posted since Eve sent it to me.'"

Imogen didn't grasp the connection at first, but by the time the doors opened to the lobby she realized what had happened. Eve had set out to sabotage her. Eve had planted a nasty item about her on TechBlab. Eve was a backstabbing cow. Imogen could feel the heat rising into her face, but it was important that to Ashley she appear unfazed.

"I am sure Eve thought it would be amazing publicity for us and it was. Look how many Twitter followers I got today. She really is a marketing genius." Ashley looked relieved and pleased that she had come to Imogen with the news.

"So you aren't mad? I thought you might not be mad. You're always so calm and cool, not like Eve." And then realizing she definitely said too much, Ashley dove in for a quick and awkward hug with Imogen and flew out the front doors.

Who the hell was Eve Morton? Imogen still felt a tightening of rage in her chest. Spikes of adrenaline surged through her system. She wanted to call her, scream at her, rip those awful dangly earrings right out of her ears.

Move forward. Breathe.

Breathe. Move forward.

* * *

Imogen's kitchen counter at home was strewn with fruit and veggies. Tilly, the family's nanny and the little sister Imogen always wished she had, held up a hand as Imogen walked in to signal she should pause just outside the room and remain quiet. She was filming Annabel standing behind the counter as her daughter carefully explained the ingredients to make the perfect avocado, kale and mint smoothie. Annabel had her own sense of personal style. She wore a slightly shrunken version of her school's uniform and restyled it with vintage menswear that made her look like a pint-sized Thom Browne model or a Dickensian orphan with an eye for fashion. Imogen loved it.

In just the past year, her daughter had become obsessed with organic smoothie making and insisted on making videos of her "garden smoothie" recipes like a young Alice Waters.

After much begging, cajoling and promising this was the start to an amazing culinary career (was she really only ten?), Alex and Imogen had agreed to let her put her videos up on YouTube. For a year, they tried to enforce screen time limits, something the other mommies at school talked about all the time—an hour a day on the various devices when Annabel wasn't working on homework.

That didn't fly. "This is my passion. It will be my career. What if someone told you that you could only work on your magazine for an hour a day?" her daughter protested. Imogen caved.

To Imogen's surprise the videos were something of a small hit among tweenage girls. Other little girls around the country made different kinds of cooking videos and, as Annabel described it, they all linked to one another. It was a hobby that Imogen couldn't quite wrap her head around, but in the pantheon of things daughters did, making videos of healthy smoothies was harmless enough.

"And that's all-vocado for today, everyone." Her daughter waved cheerily into the camera.

"All-vocado?" Imogen raised an eyebrow and smiled.

So confident on camera, Annabel grew suddenly shy.

"I thought it was funny," she said sheepishly.

Imogen felt guilty for mocking her daughter. "It was cute. I was kidding. I think it's adorable." Annabel rolled her eyes and stalked into the sitting room.

Imogen fell into one of the kitchen chairs.

"She's sensitive today," Tilly said.

Imogen had long ago gotten used to her nanny knowing more about her children's moods than she did. She looked at Tilly quizzically.

"I'm sure it's nothing, but there were some downright nasty comments on Ana's YouTube page this morning."

She had known it was a terrible idea to let her daughter put herself out there on the Internet. Probably some old pervert in a dank basement somewhere was watching and rewatching her daughter make smoothies and then writing something disgusting to get his jollies off.

Tilly shut her down before Imogen could work herself up. "I am sure it's another little girl. It's written in tween-speak. Here, look." Tilly pulled the laptop across the counter to show Imogen. On the top of the screen was her daughter in an apron and a chef's hat, a sunny smile on her face. Tilly scrolled down and clicked on one of the videos so Imogen could look at the comments. All of them *were* written in tween-speak, hybrids of bastardized words mixed with symbols and exclamation marks. The first few were pleasant enough:

U r kewl and kewt! ☺ and make gud smoothies.

We would be friendz if we lived in the same city. You have nice hair.

Make something with mango. Mango munch. Mango munch. I ♥♥♥ mangos.

Then there was this one:

You R Ug-LEE. No smoothie will ev-ur mak you look gud. U r gross.

It was signed: Candy Cool.

Imogen gasped. What the hell? Who spells "ugly" like that?

Tilly just shook her head. "Before you jump to conclusions, remember that little girls are the meanest creatures God put on this planet. They've been bullying one another since the dawn of time and will continue to do it until humanity's dying day. This looks bad because it's written right here for everyone to see, but it's no worse in the long run than little girls passing notes about one another in class."

"I always said I didn't want her on the Internet."

"Come on, Imogen. All the kids are online. This is what they do. They slag off. Ana loves making these smoothie videos. There are a hundred comments that are so sweet and nice. I probably shouldn't show you the other one."

"Show me the other one."

"Bugger."

This one was a picture. It was her daughter's head on the body of a morbidly obese person, one of those people that *Dateline* did specials on when they became too large to fit through their front door. Someone animated the picture to make Annabel's pretty heart-shaped little mouth chomp up and down.

Imogen felt useless. "I should talk to her."

"Not yet. Seriously. She didn't even bring it up to me. I can just tell that she saw it and it raised her hackles. If it happens again, I'll tell you."

Tilly, the voice of reason. Tilly, the one who could seamlessly juggle all of the emotional baggage of this entire family, switched gears and gave Imogen a sympathetic look.

"You've been irritated since you walked in the front door. More Evil Evie? What'd she do now? Drown a sack of kittens in the Lincoln Center fountain?" One of the reasons Imogen loved Tilly was that she was saltier than a curbside pretzel.

"Not just yet."

Tilly reached into the stainless-steel fridge.

"Hold on. You need a glass of wine. You will be less irritated with a glass of wine in your hand."

It was true. Imogen felt her ever-percolating annoyance begin to lighten as she sipped her Sancerre and unloaded it all—the Twitter fiasco, Eve's leak to TechBlab and finally how she found out about it from Ashley, which might have been the most embarrassing part of it all.

"And it will only get worse tomorrow! I am still going to be crap on the Twitter and I am supposed to be live-tweeting throughout all of the shows. I am not spontaneous. I like to think about what I want to say. I've never been good at the spur of the moment. I need to let ideas marinate before they're ready for an audience—an audience on Twitter that now outnumbers Eve's, by the way." The two women exchanged a small high five.

Tilly was pleasantly round all over, with a toothy grin and a smattering of freckles. She unleashed her incongruous fiery Irish temper against Eve for the better part of the next five minutes, using language that would have made a whore blush. The girl slurped at her glass of wine, twirling a piece of her strawberry-blond hair around her little finger, the gears in her head obviously turning.

"Tell me again why you need to be tweeting all day?"

Imogen allowed her lips to linger on the rim of the wineglass as she considered Tilly's question.

"Eve says that it's good for the brand. It breeds intimacy, makes the reader out in Wisconsin feel like she is sitting next to us at the fashion shows." Imogen used some of Eve's words verbatim. "Everything is much more personal these days. I'm sure Eve will want me live-tweeting my selection of knickers in the morning."

"Mmm-hmmmm." Tilly continued to mull. Imogen felt immense gratitude as Tilly poured them each another glass of wine. She swore that Tilly's liver was made of coal. She had, at more than one dinner party, drunk Imogen and Alex right under the table. "I've got it!" Tilly slammed her hand so hard on the granite countertop that Imogen almost cried out in pain on the stonework's behalf.

"You are not a words person. You're visual. That's what makes you such a genius at creating a magazine. You can turn a photo shoot into a movie that just dances off the page."

Imogen smiled at the compliment.

"And what is more intimate than photographs, especially the photographs you take with your wonderful eye?"

"Can I put photographs on Twitter? That seems even more complicated than putting words on Twitter."

"No, no, you're gonna to use Instagram. Have you tried it before? It's wonderful."

Imogen knew a bit about Instagram since Karl Lagerfeld made a huge deal of joining and taking pictures of his imperious white kitten, Choupette, but, like with Twitter, she never bothered to create an account for herself. She didn't get it.

"This is going to be so easy. The brilliant thing about Insta is that you can link it to your Twitter account, so that everything you post there is immediately tweeted. Instagram is a lot easier and you really don't have to worry about the words. You can focus on taking wonderful pictures and just write down your emotional reaction to a piece in the caption. That will go to Twitter and everyone will be happy. Your followers and Glossy.com's readers really will feel like they have been sitting next to you at the show."

Tilly pulled her iPad mini from a cute red patent leather case with gold piping. She opened up the app of the teensy brown camera lens and began typing.

"What do you want your screen name to be?"

"Can it be the same on Instagram and Twitter?"

"Sure thing. That makes it easier."

"Then @GlossyImogen, I suppose," Imogen said, crossing her eyes and making a face. "It makes me sound like a seventies porn star with a particularly good bikini wax. Glossy Imogen, at your service." She did her best Valley Girl accent, making Tilly snort a bit too loudly.

"@GlossyImogen it is. Okay, you're all set. Let me show you how to use it." Tilly was a genius instructor and in fifteen minutes Imogen was using filters and borders. Tilly showed her how to practice first without actually posting anything so as to avoid a repeat of the morning's Twitter debacle. Filters were truly magical things. She adored how "Rise" provided a soft lens over the picture, something that would come in handy when taking close-up shots of anyone over the age of twenty-five. "X-Pro II" made everything feel so vibrant and warm. "Sutro" emphasized the grays and browns in the family cat Coco's face, giving her a positively sinister Cheshire grin.

"You should keep that one," Tilly said, glancing over Imogen's shoulder. "Everyone loves a cat on the Internet."

Everything in "Valencia" looked like it was taken by a Polaroid camera in the eighties. She used it to snap the kids making funny faces, Annabel's tongue hanging lazily out of the side of her mouth and Johnny attempting a headstand. Tilly showed her how she could switch from photo to video and actually produce her own tiny bits of B-roll to add to her Twitter feed. Who knew that her phone could do so much more than text and receive email?

She was hooked. Instagram captured a brighter, more highly produced version of your life. Imogen was pleased with the idea of herself as professional retoucher. Instagram filters were the Botox of the Internet. They made everything Insta-fabulous. She snapped a pic of her shoes. "I love you, shoe!" she captioned it.

Imogen wrapped Tilly in a hug, the two of them giddy from the wine.

"Matilda Preston, can I please make you my mentor for all things related to the Internet from here on out?" Imogen asked. Tilly folded at the waist in a small curtsy.

"You most certainly may, my lady." The four of them, two women and two children, collapsed in a pile of giggles.

"Selfie time!" Annabel yelled.

"What?" Imogen asked. "No. I don't think I should be taking a selfie and then posting it on the Internet. I . . . it's not me." She couldn't get the image of Eve, puckering her lips into the camera for her own close-up, out of her mind.

Annabel made a face. "Come on, Mom. Everyone takes selfies."

"They're so annoying."

Annabel crossed her arms in a fake huff.

Imogen relented. "Fine. One selfie. C'mere and take it with me so I don't feel silly."

Her daughter posed, shoulder forward, teeth showing. Johnny galloped over, carrying the reluctant cat. Imogen held out her arm to steady the camera.

"Okay . . . say *fromage.*"

CHAPTER SEVEN

I mogen felt a bolt of newfound energy as she bounded out of bed the first morning of Fashion Week. The day's schedule was packed, beginning at nine a.m. She perused the bright red Fashion Calendar pages folded into her pale blue Smythson diary in the cab to Lincoln Center, making circles around fifty-seven out of three-hundred-plus events she knew she would attend in the next eight days.

It was starting to feel like fall. Imogen pulled her jacket tighter around her middle and breathed in crisp air, wet leaves and diesel punctuated by something mysterious and sweet, not unlike maple syrup. She took in the scene as she exited the taxi and approached the grand fountain in front of the complex. Photographers hungrily milled about the open space looking for someone famous or elaborately dressed to shoot. Street-style posers skulked behind them, begging to be snapped. If there was a polar opposite to DISRUPTTECH! this was it. In place of soft-bellied men in flannel were statuesque women in stilettos and dark sunglasses.

If you were someone who belonged at Fashion Week, you strode right up the stairs toward the head of security, Max Yablonsky, and his squad, and looked them directly in the eye. Citadel Security was a crew of Queens- and Brooklyn-bred tough guys right out of a story by

Nick Pileggi. Yablonsky knew how to weed out the gate-crashers who kept their eyes down, focused on their iPhones or fumbling in their bags for anything that resembled an invite, but was actually a receipt from the nail salon.

Flanking Yablonsky were the brothers Tom and Mike Carney, a former court officer and former transit police officer, the Rosencrantz and Guildenstern of the entrance to Fashion Week, who would engage in endless banter while on their feet for ten hours at a time.

Max wrapped Imogen in a bear hug so tight she was overwhelmed by his scent of cigars, sweat and Old Spice.

"How's my favorite fashion gal?" he asked. It was a wonderful thing to be referred to as a gal, even by a man old enough to be her father.

"I'm great, Max. How are the kids?" Yablonsky, a high school dropout, had put four kids through Georgetown and Notre Dame as the leading security provider for everything fashion-related in New York City. Imogen adored Max. But she knew mentioning his children was a mistake that could cost her the next fifteen minutes.

"Can I look at the new pictures on my way back out, darling?" She squeezed his arm. "I want to make sure I get a seat."

"Imogen Tate. You know they always have you in the front row." She winked at him and strode past the Carney brothers.

The one thing DISRUPTTECH! and Mercedes-Benz Fashion Week did have in common was the branding. Everywhere you looked there were floor-to-ceiling banners and branded kiosks. There was a MAC pop-up makeup salon. Two new Mercedes S-Class sedans, with models casually draped across their hoods flanking a small bar area serving $17 miniature bottles of Piper Heidsieck champagne and $8 espressos. Bins filled with Smartwaters and teeny-tiny cans of Diet Coke dotted the room. A wall of Samsung Galaxy tablets broadcast the shows in a corner. A second smart wall updated instantly in real time with Instagrams from the shows. *My photos need to be on that wall,* Imogen thought. She was beginning to see things differently.

In the mid-2000s Fashion Week went entirely digital with iPad check-in. Clipboard girls checking invites were replaced by a legion of iPad girls, scrolling through lists of names on their shiny screens. Row after row of Fashion GPS machines allowed you to scan a bar code to receive your seating assignment. Where it used to be a scrum of editors and buyers crowded around a single entryway, now the landscape was as efficient as airline check-in. Imogen strode over to the GPS terminal and expertly scanned her printed bar code for the Senbi Farshid show, glancing around to see who else was in the room as she waited for her confirmation to print. Just coming through the doors in a sea of bodyguards were Olivia Wilde and Jessica Chastain, both in full looks from Marc Jacobs. Sofia Coppola walked slowly by herself behind the movie stars, understated and beautiful as always. As junior reporters mobbed the two starlets, Coppola strode right up to her own GPS and quietly printed her ticket. An even larger crowd stampeded toward the entrance. *Who could that be for?* Imogen wondered. Gwyneth Paltrow perhaps? No, Leandra, the Man Repeller, an Instagram-famous blogger with delicious street style.

A reality star was trailed by a camera crew, her overfilled face bursting with pride that she had arrived at Fashion Week when only a year earlier she had been the bored bride of a celebrity podiatrist in California. Small women with big handbags threw elbows to scuttle in front of Asian men in large black overcoats. Everywhere you looked there was fur, real and faux, despite the temperature hovering above fifty.

Imogen didn't even bother to glance down when her little slip of paper popped excitedly from its slot like a lottery ticket. She knew she would be in the front row, eleventh seat in. All the magazine editors sat in the front row, since it put them within breathing distance of the clothes. Plucking a design off one runway and then pairing it with something from another show and then translating them into a photo shoot for the magazine would set the bar for how these clothes would be worn by women around the world. Photographs of clothes never did them justice. You needed to see how they moved on a model, what the color did under the lights and how the fabric felt to the touch. The attention to detail, even the music that accompanied the models down the runway. All crafted an emotional and visual message. That was how you knew what to include on the pages of a magazine. It was a mysterious and complicated process, one that Imogen believed began in her front-row seat.

Plus, this way the designer could spy on the editors. The black cloth that separated the runway from the staging area was see-through if you pressed your face against it. If an editor didn't smile, a wounded designer would conspiratorially pull ads from her book. Imogen would go backstage afterward to do her obligatory oooohhs and ahhhhhs. Molly Watson was the one who had taught her the importance of going backstage at every single show to congratulate the designer.

"Lord knows you didn't want to sit at their show for three hours," she had told Imogen. "At the very least they need to see your face and know you were there." Most designers were exhausted after a show but would hold court for their loyal subjects. Valentino was the exception. The Italian sat alone, off in a corner, slowly sipping a glass of champagne.

Imogen was caught off guard walking into the Senbi show. Two hands grasped either side of her buttocks and gave them a very firm squeeze. "You saucy minx!" She turned to see Bridgett Hart.

"When did you get in?" Imogen hugged her.

"Three hours ago on the red-eye." Her old friend and roommate, now the most sought-after stylist in Hollywood, had been in Los Angeles for two weeks pulling dresses for a very cool and chic seventeen-year-old starlet who was expected to be nominated for an Academy Award in just a couple of months. Bridgett always developed a kind of bonhomie with her clients. She wasn't just their stylist, she was their girlfriend. "You're seeing the most beautiful, most private and most insecure women in the world completely bare," she once told Imogen. "They need to feel like it's their best friend sitting in the room."

Bridgett looked no worse for the travel. She was a champ at sleeping on planes and Imogen hadn't seen her look at all tired since she discovered thrice-weekly oxygen facials in 1999 and somehow expertly wrote the expense off on her taxes each year. She'd been scouted as a model at seventeen, while living in the suburbs of Toronto. The scout flew her to New York, where she lived with Eileen Ford for her first year before she positively blew up. They'd given her the model nickname Birdie, not because she looked particularly avian, but because shoots made her so nervous she barely ate a thing.

Imogen first met her on a shoot for *Moda* and soon after they moved in together.

Birdie was the first black girl to land both a CoverGirl beauty campaign and a *Vogue* cover. Her body was disarming, featuring curves that Victoria's Secret was always dying to get in their catalog (even though she kept turning them down!). Her green cat eyes loved the camera. But it was her warm wide smile that took over her face and kept getting her gigs. She had hated being a model. Hated the long hours, the overnight flights, the skeevy photographers asking her to fuck them all the time. She confided in Imogen that she never planned to have a career as a celebrity stylist; it had simply become her second act. Years of being photographed had taught her exactly what would and wouldn't work on women's bodies. Soon after she started styling she began booking major campaigns, including Versace, Valentino, Max Mara. The Italians loved her. She was great to look at and talented to boot. Ralph Lauren had begged her to work for him full-time as his creative eye, but for Birdie, one client was never enough of a challenge.

Early on in her career, the chairman of LVMH had pulled her aside to give her some financial advice. She did everything he said and became one of their first shareholders, building herself a small fortune.

Imogen's friend was the embodiment of someone who lived life to the fullest even during its most mundane moments. To this day, Bridgett sent Imogen a postcard every single time she landed in a new city. Bridgett was outspoken and outrageous, which made her a hell of a lot of fun. She was also loyal, sometimes to a fault, particularly when it came to men who didn't deserve her.

"I assume I get the pleasure of sitting next to you?" Imogen said, linking her arm through Bridgett's.

"I wouldn't expect any less." Bridgett grinned. Publicists had been putting the two together in the front row for years now.

"What is your seat, darling?" Imogen asked.

"Twelve A."

"And so I must be eleven A. Brilliant. I can't wait to hear all about Hollywood."

"And I can't wait to hear all about Eve!" The two women laughed at the movie reference like the girls they were when they met twenty years earlier. Imogen had managed to fill her friend in on what was happening in the office in only a few brief emails but emails couldn't possibly tell the whole story.

They easily glided past one of the senior publicists at the entrance to the main hallway. At the entryway to the Main Stage, the runway where all of the major shows were held, a diminutive iPad girl surveyed the crowd with a lazy eye.

"Ticket?" she said in a nasally twang, glancing down at her screen. The two women handed their small passes over. "Ms. Hart, follow me to your seat, twelve A. Ms. Tate, please wait one moment and someone will escort you to VIP Standing."

The words didn't make any sense to Imogen. She had a ticket in the front row and there was nothing at all VIP about standing. She had never stood at a show. And this show of all shows! She was here as a favor. She was just here to support her friend. Imogen was the first editor to put Senbi's collection on a cover model. She had helped to put her on the map.

"Is Senbi playing a hilarious prank? I always sit in seat eleven A, not just for this show, but for all the shows. Please take me to my seat now." Bridgett had assumed Imogen was directly behind her and was now absorbed into the paparazzi flashbulbs.

iPad girl rolled her stubby finger along her screen.

"I believe Orly is in seat eleven A. You know Orly. She has the best of all the fashion blogs—FashGrrrrl-dot-com. Actually. Oh, Orly, HELLLLLLLLO!"

Behind Imogen was the aforementioned Orly. The girl couldn't have been older than twelve. Her chin-length bright blue hair turned out violently at the ends as if the Flying Nun and Ken Kesey had borne a love child. She wore a green cape over an orange Senbi onesie with seven-inch Stella McCartney wedges. She looked wonderful and startling all at once. Frameless glasses with a small camera attached to the right lens perched on her pixie face.

"Love your work," Orly said to Imogen as iPad girl gushed over the diminutive elf, begging her for an autograph. Orly leaned in and kissed the check-in wench's iPad, leaving a bright pink lip mark as a signature, before sashaying to seat 11A.

"Imogen Tate doesn't stand." *Whose voice was that?* Low and husky, vaguely condescending. Eve. How long had she been standing there, watching?

"She can take my front-row seat," Eve said loudly. She repeated herself. "I want to give my front-row seat to Imogen Tate."

She would rather stand than accept help from Eve, who was now breathing heavily onto her neck.

"I do stand now, Eve. I am so excited to stand . . . right now." Imogen straightened up to the full five feet eleven inches she commanded in her heels. "We're all about the consumer and the consumer is in the standing section. I want to be where the readers are. I want to see how they react to the clothes. I'll be backstage with Senbi after the show anyway. I'll see you later."

The girl with the iPad, still recovering from her brush with Orly's greatness, forgot her social graces when dealing with anyone with a VIP Standing ticket. "Move over along the wall. We'll let you in right before the show starts."

As Imogen carefully found her way to the edge of the hallway, a security guard shouted, "Along the wall! Move it along the wall!" *This was what prison would be like; I feel like I'm in* Orange Is the New Black, Imogen thought.

The scrum of VIP Standing ticket holders was a little rougher around the edges than the line of people filing past them. They had more hairs out of place. Their eyeliner was just a little heavier and their designer outfits hung less than expertly on their bodies, announcing the fact that they purchased them at bargain prices at the sample sale rather than at the department store. The guests swooshing past iPad girl didn't just have better clothes than the people in VIP Standing, they had better bone structures.

Imogen ducked her head so that none of the seated ticket holders would see her as she shuffled dutifully toward the wall. The more people that came, the hotter it got in the hallway. Imogen could feel drops of sweat begin to pool at her temples as she picked up on bits and pieces of conversation.

"This is my first show, I am so excited."

"Did you hear about the streaker at the Prabal show?"

"What's going on here?"

"How long will we have to wait?"

"Did you text Alexandra? If she knew we were out here she would lose her shit."

"They're, like, not letting anyone in at all?"

"And you of all people not being let in." Imogen craned her neck but didn't recognize who "you of all people" was.

"Should I eat this pretzel?"

"Is that yogurt on it or chocolate?"

"Chocolate."

"Then no."

A frizzy-haired woman dropped her water bottle on Imogen's toe and furiously apologized just as the iPad girl walked over to tell them they were finally allowed to come in. Imogen's eyes darted immediately to the front row.

Bridgett was sitting opposite Orly, with Jennifer Lawrence, her number-one client, to her left, and Anna Wintour and André Leon Talley on her right. They were just a few seats away from Jessica Chastain and Olivia Wilde. Across from them the front seats were filled with girls Orly's age and maybe five years older, all wearing the same funny glasses and balancing laptops on their knees. At the very end of that row was Eve, wearing the same glasses. Eve's glasses had yellow temples to match her canary cocktail dress. Next to Eve sat Massimo in his wheelchair. He had an appropriately horrified look on his face, which told Imogen exactly what he thought about everything happening in that room.

"Bloggers and YouTube stars," she heard a voice say behind her. Imogen turned her head to see Isobel Harris, a longtime buyer for Barneys. She shifted her bag to her other shoulder to be able to lean over in the sea of standing bodies to give her a hug. God, Isobel must be in her fifties by now, but she looked incredible in a black blazer and gray cigarette pants. Imogen had known Issy since before she met her husband, who was now a famous playwright. Back then he was a waiter at Balthazar, and Isobel, ten years his senior, was in marketing at Chanel. She'd turned around to look at his ass when he brought her another glass of champagne. He caught her and that was it for the two of them.

"We have been usurped, darling. All the designers want those kids in the front row. Look how they did the seating arrangements." Isobel pointed with a perfectly sculpted but polish-free index finger to the row with Anna, André, Bridgett, Jennifer, Jessica and Olivia. "There on the one side you have anyone worth documenting. And on the other you have the documenters. They're all live-streaming this show right onto their sites with their Google Glass."

"What is a Google Glass?" Imogen abandoned the need to act like she had any idea what was going on.

"Those ridiculous glasses they're all wearing. They're called Google Glass . . . not glasses, Glass. They're a smartphone in an eyeglass. They take pictures and videos when you talk to them or tap on their sides. Google gave them to thirty fashion influencers for Fashion Week."

"How do you know all this?"

Isobel shrugged. "It was in *Women's Wear Daily* pretty much all summer," she said, before catching herself and remembering how Imogen had spent her summer. "I'm an idiot. I should have asked you the second I saw you. How are you feeling?"

"I'm wonderful. I really am. I feel great. I do feel a little bit like I am playing catch-up here." It was the first time Imogen had admitted to anyone outside of her inner circle that she didn't have a perfectly capable grasp of what was happening in the industry.

Isobel gave her another hug. The two women were jostled by the other standees, some of whom Imogen recognized as other veteran buyers and fashion journalists, people who would normally have a seat. As the lights blinked, signaling five minutes until showtime, Isobel saw Addison Cao, the wily reporter from the *Women's Wear Daily*'s Eye column, beelining for her.

"Whaaaaaaaaat is Imogen Tate doing in the standing section?" he interrupted, his voice rising a pitch on each word's final syllable.

"You've lost weight," Imogen said, playfully reaching out to tickle Addison's ample midsection. Only a gossip columnist could get away with being so rotund in this industry. No one was judging him or putting pictures of him in the gossip pages.

"I lost seven pounds on a juice cleanse," Addison said, allowing "cleanse" to sound like "clanze" as he smoothed his palms down the front of his pressed trousers.

The two of them proceeded with the stock complaints of Fashion Week that everyone traded at these kinds of things.

"The schedule is too crowded this year."

"Nothing is going to start on time."

"After the shows I am absolutely going to the ashram."

With the niceties out of the way, Imogen leaned in to whisper in Addison's ear, inhaling his scent of body odor and hash browns. "Do you want to know why I am really back here?" she purred. Addison had a definite preference for young Asian men, but everyone liked a little sexy talk right into his ear.

"I do." He breathed heavily.

Imogen launched into the same bullshit she'd made up at the door when she ran into Eve. She said she wanted to see the show from the consumer's perspective, not the editor's. "I've spent fifteen years in that front row. It's gotten dull. Let the Orlys of the world experience it for once in their lives. I want to see what my readers see and my readers are not going to be sitting in the front row." Imogen borrowed some of the talking points from Eve's DISRUPTTECH! talk. "*Glossy* is a multimedia brand that caters directly to the consumer who loves fashion just as much as we do. In this day and age the magazine editor *needs* to look at things from a different perspective." She had no idea if she even meant half the words coming out of her mouth, but they kept coming. Addison had no compunction about using a pen and paper. He furiously scribbled away in his reporter's notebook.

"I just adore you, Imogen Tate." He slammed the notepad shut with the efficiency of a vise. "Can we take a selfie together?" Imogen smiled and nodded, wrapping her arm as far as it would go around

Addison's midsection. He reached his arm into the air to take a photo from above.

"You don't get a double chin if you do it this way," he said.

"Very smart, Addison."

Like everyone else in the room, Imogen readied her iPhone as the house lights went down. If someone were to travel forward in time from just ten years earlier, what would they think seeing all these people doing the exact same thing, the bright faces of their phones leveled in front of them as they ignored reality in favor of their screens? It wasn't too long ago that the unwritten protocol of a fashion show dictated that no cameras were allowed.

"VIP Standing" could have been worse. It was true that from this vantage point she was actually able to photograph the entire runway and the faces of the A-listers along the front row. She began clicking away at the first look. Tilly had taught her all about hashtags, reminding her that it would be important for her to tag @Glossy, the site's main Twitter and Instagram feed, and to use the tags #MercedesBenzFashionWeek and the general catchall #Fashion. Tilly also instructed her to be creative.

"Have fun with a hashtag. Instagram followers love creativity."

And so Imogen created the tag #ScenesFromTheBackRow and took upward of thirty pictures, one for each model who came down the runway. She commented on cut and color, using three different filters that complimented the lighting and the distance, giving the white runway a magical aura. Eve must have been looking at her Twitter feed on her laptop, or perhaps somehow she could see it on the Glass contraption out of the corner of her eye. Imogen could see her craning her neck to try to see where Imogen was standing, but the lights were so bright on the runway the rest of the room was bathed in darkness.

Imogen didn't wait for the last walk-through, when all the models would come out onto the catwalk together and Senbi would take her bows at the end of the stage. Like Theseus winding through the labyrinth, she found her way through "VIP Standing" into "Mediocre Standing" and then into "Shouldn't Even Be Allowed in Here to Stand Standing" and began walking toward the back of the stage, slipping quietly behind a curtain. On the other side, a security guard, one of Max's guys, ran over to examine the breach.

"Ms. Tate. Why didn't you just come through the runway entrance?"

She placed a hand on the small of his back. "Oh, I wanted to avoid the bun fight on the runway. Wanted to try to make it back here first so I could congratulate Senbi."

"Of course, Ms. Tate."

By the time Eve joined the rest of the crowd walking in from the runway, Imogen was chatting and laughing with Senbi, who seemingly had no idea where Imogen had been forced to perch during the presentation. Imogen marveled at the woman's beauty each and every time they met. Genes from Vietnam and Egypt had constructed themselves in such a perfect way, making for almond-shaped eyes and skin the color of cocoa flecked through with gold. Eve glared at the two of them as they examined the inseam of a pair of palazzo pants. Behind them hairdressers and makeup artists furiously prepared models for the next show before placing a black bag over their heads, Abu Ghraib–like, so that the models could be dressed without getting makeup all over the clothes. One hairstylist was determined to build a foot-high elaborate updo fashioned around pieces of netting and held in place by what looked to be an entire bottle of hair spray. Imogen watched as another makeup artist intently sought the perfect smoky eye, first adding a shimmery beige MAC eye shadow and then darker and darker lines for contour before applying a black cream liner along the lash line to finish the look.

Imogen was mid-sentence when she saw Eve elbow one of the bloggers in the ribs to get her to move to the side.

"Is your phone broken?" Eve barked at Imogen.

"Not that I know of, darling." Imogen glanced at her iPhone for the first time in seven minutes. She had six texts from Eve.

>>>>Are you going backstage?<<<<

>>>>I'm going backstage.<<<<

>>>>Should we meet backstage?<<<<

>>>>Are you already backstage?<<<<

>>>>Where the hell are you?<<<<

>>>>How do I get backstage?<<<<

It was as though Eve thought that the texts went directly from her hand into Imogen's brain. She chose to ignore it for the time being.

"Eve, I am not sure if you have had the pleasure, but I would love to introduce you to my dear friend Senbi." "Friend" wasn't a stretch. Senbi and her partner had adopted their first child around the time Johnny was born, and then the two women took water babies classes together.

"Senbi, I am so happy to finally meet you," Eve said. "You're so awesome!" Senbi looked Eve over coolly.

"Your voice is so familiar."

"Eve used to answer my phones," Imogen said, smiling sweetly at Eve.

"I'm the editorial director of Glossy-dot-com now." Eve tried to recover. "Awesome! We would love to have you involved in the new Glossy platform. It's a multimedia applica—" The designer cut her off.

"Imogen told me all about it. If she's in charge, then I'm in." The designer triple-kissed Imogen's cheeks. "I have to go pay homage to the peanut gallery."

Imogen noticed Orly inching her way toward her, that blue helmet of hair bobbing up and down as she walked.

"I loved the hashtag ScenesFromTheBackRow. Genius idea. I regrammed you and linked to your feed from FashGrrrl. That's exactly what I felt like at my first fashion show. You really get it." Orly was suddenly swarmed by other bloggers and Imogen was worried that when their Glasses all got too close to one another a circuit would short and the entire backstage would go up in flames like the prom scene in *Carrie*.

For the rest of the day, no matter her seating assignment (it varied each time from VIP Standing to front row), Imogen found her way into the standing section. Addison kept winking at her. She saw Orly tapping on her temple, live-streaming her live Instagramming. Eve sulked from the front row. Bridgett texted her:

>>>>You are one savvy and sexy bitch<<<<

Imogen wrote back.

>>>>Today I am. Let's see about tomorrow.<<<<

Leaving the tents after the final show, Imogen found herself once again in the company of Addison Cao.

"Imogen, I have a question for you. A friend was whispering in my ear and I am trying to wrap my head around an item for tomorrow. What do you know about Andrew Maxwell and Eve Morton?"

Hearing his name spoken out loud was jarring. Until a year earlier Imogen genuinely thought Andrew Maxwell had disappeared from the face of the Earth and she was content in letting herself believe that was true. Andrew was quite possibly the worst dating decision she had ever made. If only she had been as good at spotting narcissists in her twenties as she was now in her forties, but back then she had merely been dazzled by his confidence, his charm and his habit of dating the most eligible girls in Manhattan. One of those super-preppies, he wore a pink shirt so often that Massimo and Bridgett took to calling him simply "Pink Shirt." Andrew—always Andrew, never Andy—resembled a young Robert Redford with floppy blond hair and a perpetual five o'clock shadow. His parents were newly rich from mortgage investments in the eighties and their Madison Avenue penthouse was filled with painfully expensive but not especially tasteful art. Their money meant he didn't actually need to do anything and so he didn't, except for excessive amounts of cocaine and Imogen for two years. The things young girls will abide by to have an attractive man on their arms are disgusting and Imogen abided by a lot in those days. His broad smile and easy charisma hid his uncertainty about what kind of man he wanted to be when he finally grew up.

She had just moved into a teensy studio of her own on West Fourth Street, a third-floor walk-up with barely enough room for a bed, but spacious French windows that looked down on the tree-lined West Village street.

When he was wooing her, after a late-night encounter at Moomba, Andrew sent ten bouquets a day to the apartment. The two of them flew all over the world on his parents' private jet. He couldn't stand to be apart from her and soon she let him move into her tiny flat. Only a few months into their cohabitation Andrew got fat, grotesquely fat. He had nothing to do during the day, and so while Imogen would go off to work every day as an associate editor, he slept away his hangovers and ordered takeaway from the dodgy Chinese joint down the street with stray cats milling about the cash register. Sometimes she would come home in the middle of the afternoon after a particularly grueling early morning shoot only to find him downstairs watching soap operas with the old Armenian woman in the studio below Imogen.

"You know, you should get to know your neighbors," he slurred at her as he leaned his weight against her, walking back up the stairs. "You're such a snob."

One day Imogen opened the telephone bill to find $1,300 in charges to a 1-900 phone sex line. His parents were these billionaires and here she was living in a tiny flat she could barely afford and he rang up a phone bill more than double her rent. He stumbled in late that night with two black eyes and denied everything. Then he went into the bathroom for twenty minutes, finished up the bag of cocaine in his pocket and confessed to it all. His mother, dripping in jewelry and smelling of bourbon and desperation, picked him up in the morning to ship him off to a fancy rehab out in the Nevada desert. Three months later Imogen met Alex. She answered the door early on a Sunday morning, wearing one of Andrew's old custom-made pink button-down shirts, boxer shorts and stolen white hotel slippers, still licking her battle scars from her bad relationship and nursing a French 75 hangover. *What time is it?* she wondered, first considering the time in New York and then switching to consider the time it was wherever Andrew had been scuttled off to.

A gorgeous man stood there holding out a sheaf of papers. His black hair was a mess of curls just long enough to brush the top of his pugilist's jaw. She was staring too hard, which she realized when a smile touched his slightly chapped but full lips.

"I'm sorry, could you repeat what you just told me?" she asked the handsome stranger. He was there to serve Andrew with court documents. Some bugger Andrew picked a fight with in a bar must have realized he had deep pockets and was suing him for assault and battery.

"He doesn't live here anymore. He's off drying out in the desert."

Alex couldn't leave until he got the documents into Andrew's hands or got a new address where he could be served in person. Imogen invited him in for tea and ran to the bathroom to pull her disheveled bed-head hair into a tight pony, dab on some under-eye concealer, smudge some gloss over her lips and spray mint into her mouth. She couldn't help but smirk as she emerged to find him making himself barely comfortable on her tiny chintz armchair, before she rang Andrew's deranged mother for his forwarding address. In the hour it took for her to return Imogen's call, she learned that this young lawyer was the first child in his family to go to college, and he had followed it up with Yale Law School. He didn't give a shit about clothes and he didn't need to since he kept his six-foot-three-inch physique trim from boxing in his dad's gym on the Lower East Side. Style is much more than a designer name on your back, Imogen observed. He was different from anyone she had dated. Smart as a whip, he believed in equality and democracy, values that drove him to work long nights advocating for the rights of those who couldn't advocate for themselves. He had ambitions to enter politics, but for the time being he was happy where he was, grateful even. He seemed particularly grateful to find himself in Imogen's apartment.

After Imogen located the elusive Andrew and Alex dispatched a courier to the western part of the country, the young lawyer professionally excused himself. Imogen was distraught that he waited nine days to call her for dinner. On that first date they shut down Piadina on West Tenth Street, giggling for hours at a tiny wooden table in the cramped basement filled with cigarette smoke, the smell of roasted garlic and Dean Martin crooning from a speaker hidden behind a bookshelf in the corner. The wax on the candlestick centerpiece burned all the way to the rim of the Chianti bottle it perched in before their night was over.

She noticed he sipped his wine slowly, inhaled just a whiff as he raised his glass and then sloshed it around a little in his mouth so that he could truly enjoy it, so different from Andrew, who drank in large swallows, more interested in the intoxication it produced than the taste. He looked at her while they ate, really stared, his eyes hungry, all over her body, not even hiding the fact that he enjoyed taking in her milky white décolletage, which was maybe too obvious in a low-cut cashmere sweater. For the first time since she'd started dating boys back home as a teenager, her stomach didn't do nervous somersaults. Instead she felt an intense sense of calm with this man. *Here you are,* she thought to herself. It was that simple. *Here you are.*

She held out as long as she could, but a few weeks later they had amazing sex in his tiny studio in the East Village, which was dominated by books and a giant bed. He undressed her slowly and kissed her everywhere. He was the least selfish lover she'd ever had.

Alex was the rare breed of man who got on with your granny as well as your male best friend—the opposite of Andrew. For every designer dinner she was invited to, the publicist would always ask whether Alex was available to accompany her. Imogen was so proud to walk into a room with this towering, handsome man. His casual elegance and the fact that he lived inside an episode of *Law & Order* made him a favorite dinner companion.

It had been easy to let Andrew slip away. There was no Google then, or if there was, Imogen didn't know about it. There was certainly no Facebook. By the time those things became staples in everyone's life, Imogen was a happily married woman. Even socially, she and Andrew rarely crossed paths after that. A year ago she read that he was now a United States congressman and, last she heard, running for the Senate.

She never imagined hearing his name in the same breath as Eve's, but she wasn't willing to give herself away to Addison.

"I'm sure you know more than I do, darling."

"Oh, as usual I don't know too much. I know Eve set her sights on him around July and has been spotted coming out of his apartment building at One Fifth Avenue six times in the past three weeks very early in the morning."

"Lots of people live in that building, Addison."

"Lots of people don't have a private stairwell into the garage."

"How about I do a little investigating for you and you make it worth my while, by doing a teensy item on Glossy-dot-com's fantastic new Instagram campaign: Hashtag ScenesFromTheBackRow?"

"I like the way you negotiate, Tate. I'll text you tomorrow." Addison fancied himself to be J. J. Hunsecker, if Hunsecker's phone at the '21' Club were replaced with a tablet.

Imogen was complete crap at being a source, but Bridgett wasn't.

"I haven't heard anything about Pink Shirt and the Pink Bandage Dress. But I'll ask some of the people who would know," she said when Imogen called her. Bridgett was stuck backstage doing an on-camera interview with *Extra* for the next hour.

But before either of them could assist Addison in his quest for information, Imogen got a Page Six text alert.

>>>>Congressman Andrew Maxwell of the Ninth Congressional District of New York has a new lady love. We hear the 49-year-old politician is dating 26-year-old editorial director for Glossy.com Eve Morton.<<<<

Imogen clicked the link to read more and was rewarded with a picture of Andrew and Eve, her hair pulled into a first lady chignon, his neatly shellacked into a Ken doll helmet. He was in a tux and she wore a floor-length red Badgley Mischka gown.

The new couple stepped out earlier this week at the mayor's residence, Gracie Mansion, for a dinner reception honoring his Royal Highness of Thailand. Maxwell, who won election to Congress two years ago, has been spending time with the young New York–based entrepreneur, who graduated from NYU and then Harvard Business School before returning to New York to launch a digital application at Robert Mannering Corp.

Maxwell and Morton were recently spotted together in the Hamptons, prompting rumors of a relationship. We are told

that despite their 23-year age difference they looked very affectionate and that it was quite clear they were a couple. "They
were holding hands and kissing in corners," one of our spies
tells us about a rendezvous they had in East Hampton over the
summer. Other society spies gushed about how great the pair
looked together. "He is just in such tremendous shape. He's like
a blond John F. Kennedy Jr.," one of them told us. They made
it official in pictures at the other night's event, holding hands
as they posed for photographs. Just an hour after we contacted
them for comment, their photo was erased from the website
of society photographer Billy Farrell only to appear again
moments later. We guess their teams couldn't make up their
mind about how to spin this one, especially since Maxwell
used to date Morton's current *Glossy* colleague Imogen Tate.

Ugh. Why did they have to drag her into it?

Her phone flooded with text messages from Bridgett and then
Massimo.

>>>>Eve and Pink Shirt. Ewwwww<<<<

>>>>Power and sobriety have obviously clouded Pink Shirt's judgment<<<<

And one from Addison.

>>>>We've been scooped.<<<<

That little bitch was stealing her life.

CHAPTER EIGHT

Eve wasn't trying to be difficult, but what the hell had happened at the Senbi show? She had texted Imogen, like, fifty times trying to figure out how to get backstage. Who didn't check their phone? And why was Imogen lurking in the back rows of all the shows like a creepster anyway? What was she up to?

It was five a.m. on the second day of Fashion Week and, as she did every morning before the sun came up, Eve sat up in bed, her devices spread in front of her like a command center, drinking a diet Red Bull. She smiled as she saw that her #SleepyMe Instagram that she snapped before bed had 536 likes. She regrammed it from the official *Glossy* account. The caption read: "How adorbs is our Editorial Director before bed!!" Sweet dreams.

All she wanted was for Imogen to get it. Late last night Eve sent Imogen an email asking if she could please make her a Google Doc with a list of all the designers she was trying to get to work with the *Glossy* app. She actually wrote back and asked what a Google Doc was. *Seriously? Was she kidding?*

Next Eve asked her what her non-*Glossy* email address was and—get this—she doesn't have a Gmail account. She uses a Hotmail address for her personal email. Eve wasn't even born when people stopped using Hotmail.

How did Andrew date that woman for so long? Sure, Imogen Tate was a brilliant fashion editor, but how could someone get so far in her career and be so inept about technology? It literally blew Eve's mind. I mean. Come on.

She knew Imogen was going to assume the worst about Eve and Andrew, assume that they somehow met because of her. Of course, Eve had known all about Andrew and Imogen. She'd done a lot of due diligence on Imogen back in the day, all the best assistants did. She talked to a few reporters, a few old friends, she had read almost every email the woman had ever written. It helped her keep her boss's life organized. And, well, it was also a little fun and juicy. She'd known that Andrew was one of Imogen's exes.

When he first approached her at that Young Friends of Andrew Maxwell fund-raiser at Elspeth Pepper's Hamptons house over the summer, Andrew had no idea that Eve knew Imogen, much less that she used to work for her. It was a party filled with people under the age of thirty who mattered—mostly the children of people who had mattered for longer, except for her. Eve was ready to impress. She wasn't little Evie Morton from Kenosha anymore. She was a Harvard woman now and that meant something. Eve ordered a glass of white wine from the bar, but she wasn't drinking it. She never drank. Hated to be out of control. She threw flirtatious looks Andrew's way as he made the rounds of the room, shaking hands and, at one point, trying to underscore that he, too, was young and hip by doing the lawn mower dance on the makeshift dance floor. When he finished he met Eve's gaze and she playfully stuck her tongue out at him before walking out to the stone terrace overlooking a pristine clay tennis court

"Do you play?" he asked her without introducing himself.

"Not professionally." She turned to face him full-on, standing tall in the new five-inch Christian Louboutin sandals she'd purchased for this very moment. "My golf game's better."

He texted her the next day, inviting her to play eighteen holes.

Eve didn't bother to mention to Andrew that she was gunning for a big new job at *Glossy* until she knew she'd hooked him. It wasn't lying, just omission, and when he brought up that he knew Imogen she played dumb.

Men were stupid.

Andrew was clearly a man who had gotten plenty of women in his heyday, probably more than one at a time. Now he needed a wife. Bachelors made for odd political candidates. It was how rumors of toe-tapping in airport bathrooms began.

Eve clicked on the tab on the *New York Post* to reread the item about her and Andrew. Nearly half a day had passed but she still felt a rush over seeing her name in a gossip column. Then she opened her other email account to delete the "tip" she'd sent over to the junior gossip columnist at the newspaper. "He is just in such tremendous shape. He's like a blond John F. Kennedy Jr." was a nice touch, she thought. Her mom had always been obsessed with looking at pictures of JFK Jr. in *People* magazine.

Now that the press cared about them, where could they go to dinner tonight that would make a splash? Carbone? Michelle Obama and Kim Kardashian were there last night . . . not at the same table, but close enough that they were in the same picture. There were sure to be paparazzi lurking outside tonight.

Perfect.

She grabbed her Kindle to read aloud her quote for the day. From Sun Tzu, *The Art of War:* "Supreme excellence consists of breaking the enemy's resistance without fighting."

* * *

Imogen had less than a week to throw a party and barely any staff to help her do it. She thumbed through the dog-eared file cards in her old Filofax, which now resided deep in a drawer in the kitchen table, where it would be sheltered from any judgmental eyes. The spine of the thing sank low, heavy with two decades of contact information for everyone from Imogen's tailor and cobbler to the chiefs of staff for two former first ladies of the United States, both of whom had sought Imogen's advice when dressing for their inaugural balls. Flicking through the cards was a stroll through her personal and professional lives. In doing so she realized she was a bit of a contact hoarder. When someone passed away, Imogen believed it was bad luck to retire his or her card to the bin. Instead, she merely folded down the right-hand corner. It was an odd quirk she had never admitted out loud or explained to anyone. Day-to-day contacts were of course stored in her phone, like any other member of the twenty-first century, but when she planned parties and events she still preferred to curate a guest list with this old dinosaur.

All right. Eve wanted designers. Imogen knew it would be easy to get her loyal friends in the business to swing by—Carolina, Michael Kors, the Rag & Bone gents—plus a smattering of the young designers, the ones who show up at the opening of an envelope because they want the PR. Naturally, the hot Asian boy designer mafia would be there: Alexander Wang, Prabal, Jason Wu, Thakoon and Peter Som.

Proenza Schouler would be the big get, but Imogen knew better than to even bother. They didn't show up anywhere these days unless they thought it would help land them in Italian *Vogue*. They were simply too cool for anything American. For a second she considered inviting Carolina Herrera, but she knew she also wouldn't bother to show. Instead, she shot off an invite to her inimitable PR girl, Mercedes. No one tweeted parties like Mercedes. The girl was Proust with hashtags.

This was too last-minute. Imogen used to spend six months approving plans for *Glossy*'s annual Women in Fashion event, held without fail the last week of every March. Imogen tried to suppress the thought that Eve was hoping she would fail. Her ideal budget for this kind of thing would be $150,000 for a party and dinner at the Waverly Inn. The cocktail of the night would obviously be the French 75 in vintage cocktail glasses. In her perfect world, Imogen would hire Anthony Todd to do all the flowers and the table settings.

She allowed herself a minute to indulge in the memory of one of the best Fashion Week parties she had ever attended. Paris in 2004. Small. All the best ones are small. The publicist for Mr. Valentino called the guests only a few hours before it was scheduled to start to build a sense of urgency around the whole affair.

"Don't tell anyone," she cautioned in a low and sultry voice over the phone.

It started at eleven p.m. in the intensely glamorous basement of the Ritz hotel, all smoky mirrors and little lamps on low black lacquered tables with mother-of-pearl chairs. Everyone in the room looked extraordinarily sexy, like they'd just pranced off the pages of French *Vogue.* Through the smoke small groups of models shimmied together to too-loud Rolling Stones songs. A few actresses were there, the photographer Bruce Weber, a handful of those straight scuzzy British aristo/modelizer types like Jonny Rothschild and a couple of members of Duran Duran. No one talked to one another. There was no food, but an endless parade of waiters served the yummiest pink champagne from silver trays.

Enough daydreaming.

Eve had budgeted $5,000 for this event (an amount Eve wanted to be very clear that she found to be incredibly generous)—$5,000 for a space, staff, an open bar, passed hors d'oeuvres, entertainment and flowers. For a party for two hundred people, that broke down to $25 a head, which was $5 less per person than she had spent on Annabel's last birthday party at the pottery painting shop on Christopher Street.

"Get a liquor sponsor! Let's have it at your house, it's definitely big enough," Eve snapped when Imogen dared raise a single eyebrow at the budget.

Part of Imogen's compensation package when she started out at Robert Mannering included having the company co-sign the mortgage on the $7 million town house on Jane Street that her family now occupied. Her deal with the devil. Sara Bray, the former creative director of a now-shuttered interior design magazine, and a longtime friend from the children's school, helped Imogen with the interior of the house, a studied mélange of chic combined with comfort and warmth. A custom-mixed eau de Nil paint adorned the walls of the open and airy sitting room that dominated much of the first floor of the town house. Modern art, including a prized but very small Cy Twombly sketch, competed for wall space with Moroccan tapestries Alex haggled for in a night market in Tangier. A large old Victrola with a wide blue horn that Imogen picked up in an antiques shop on Royal Street in New Orleans held court in the corner. They'd kept the original molding and corrugated tin ceilings, but repainted them in an eggshell finish. Books climbed the eastern wall and family photos dotted the mantel of the working fireplace. A mixture of antiques with modern pieces and cozy overstuffed chairs appealed to both Imogen's need for nostalgia and comfort and Alex's adoration of clean and orderly lines. Walnut French doors opened onto a garden filled with handpicked Panton furniture. Wisteria bushes climbed the fence. For parties she added tiny, white magical fairy lights to the branches.

There had once been a spread on it in *The New York Times*'s Styles section, where Imogen posed prettily on the gray velvet chaise in the sitting room, issues of *Glossy* fanned artfully amid *Grazia* and French *Vogue* on the Yves Klein blue pigment coffee table. ("She's in Prada, but don't call this EIC a devil," the caption jested.)

She loved giving parties. In the five years since they signed their formidable mortgage, Imogen had thrown a dozen parties at the house, mostly for the magazine, but occasionally for a friend's birthday and once a fund-raiser for a New York State senator. Half of the events had been a roaring success. The other half simply succeeded by virtue of the fact that guests had arrived and dinner had been served. One truly memorable evening had Imogen arriving thirty minutes late to her very own dinner party after her guests made it through their first course. Sometimes a working mother tried to do it all and sometimes it happened to work out.

Ashley was dispatched to help with securing a liquor sponsor. Each day the girl impressed Imogen anew. She got things done, found elegant solutions, channeled creativity into technology. Imogen smelled a pure talent there, one that reminded her of her younger self—if her younger self had thoughts in 140 characters or fewer.

It was Ashley's idea to use Paperless Post for the last-minute invites and Imogen capitalized on the eleventh-hour nature of the event in her text: "The best-laid plans have nothing on those made with an air of whimsy. Please join Glossy.com's Imogen Tate and Eve Morton for a celebration of Glossy.com at the home of the editor in chief." She convinced her friend Danny, an up-and-coming chef of some regard, the kind who did things with foams and molecules, to help her with the catering for a mere $4,500. Male models, fresh off the bus from Des Moines, would work the room as cater waiters and bartenders for free just to get the chance to mingle with fashion's finest.

She could pull this off.

* * *

All the mommies at school drop-off were desperate to score an invite to Imogen's Fashion Week party.

"It might be the most interesting thing I get to do all year!" Sara, mom to Jack, said to Imogen as the two women walked through Country Village Elementary School's wrought-iron gates and into the secluded green oasis, a daffodil-lined path dotted by protective trees.

Small, with huge black eyes and a short black pixie cut, Sara was a tax attorney who was self-conscious to a fault. Jack had the same eyes and practically the same haircut, on a head that was shaped like a peanut. There were two types of mommies at Imogen's school, the ones who worked, and the "entrepreneurs," the mommies who stayed home but had their financier husbands bankrolling their organic skin-care products or cashmere handbag lines. For a brief spell, once Imogen had a few months of recovery under her belt, she experienced what it was like to be part of the tribe of stay-at-home mommies. For the first few weeks it was glorious. She attempted to cook her way through Jessica Seinfeld's entire cookbook. Growing anxious, by week four, she wondered if she, too, could find success in organic lip balms.

The mom-trepreneurs, always in head-to-toe black spandex (more like a Catwoman costume than something anyone should wear to sweat), had the most fuck-off bodies, from all the spinning they did together. The working moms typically rushed in and out in short order, anxious to get to work on time, but today, with Fashion Week gossip to be discussed, even the working mommies didn't mind lingering. The nannies kept to themselves.

"I am sure it won't be, but you're obviously welcome to come," Imogen said. Sara let out a small yelp of happiness just as Bianca

Wilder, the school's resident Academy Award–winning actress mum, leaned in to join the conversation. Hollywood beautiful, Bianca's eyebrows were perpetually arched in surprise. She possessed the tiniest rosebud-shaped mouth and skin that grew tighter each semester.

"You look like you got some color," Sara commented on Bianca's perfect tan. The woman's hand fluttered upward to touch her cheeks, a look of horror crossing her face. Imogen remembered the days in the nineties when complimenting someone's tan was a good thing. It meant they'd just finished up some fabulous jaunt to St. Barth's. Now tan was an insult.

"I wore a hat when we were in Turks," Bianca said defensively.

"It's just the right amount," Imogen interjected. "Perfect glow."

It had been only three years since Bianca had won her award for playing a paraplegic biologist living with the large apes in the Congo, but Imogen believed that her most accomplished role yet was the one she played at school, when she fancied herself the "normal mom." In the weeks after she won the award, she made a point to come to drop-off looking perfectly disheveled. Whenever someone congratulated her she insisted on saying things like, "Oh, I am so over myself," while rolling her eyes and laughing the way only an Oscar winner could. She would drop her voice next and add: "My real job is being Sophie's mom. I mean, I work in Hollywood, but I don't participate in Hollywood."

Bianca worked hard at cultivating her faux intimacy with the other school moms and had a small army of plain mothers who followed her all over the neighborhood, always offering to do favors for her, like entertain her nanny and children for the weekend when she had to fly to London for the BAFTA Awards or feed her cat three times a day while she was shooting on location in Morea.

The actress pulled her hair into a jaunty ponytail. "How is the job going, doll?" She hugged Imogen gingerly. Bianca shot a *Glossy* cover around this time last year. Imogen hadn't been present at the shoot, but she had heard through the grapevine that the term "diva" would have been a gross understatement to describe Bianca's behavior. Some of the talent wanted to keep a skirt or a pair of earrings they'd worn during a cover shoot. Bianca wanted it all, from the underwear to the diamond studs . . . and she'd wanted the outfit in three more colors.

"It's different being back," Imogen said neutrally. "You know the magazine is now an app, which was a huge change. We have a new editorial director. She's young and ambitious and sometimes a bit of a heavy lift. I had to get on Twitter and that was a disaster."

Kara let out a groan and the other mothers looked at her questioningly.

"Kara, you're great on Twitter," Sara said.

"Oh that isn't me. I hired someone to tweet as me."

Imogen wasn't shocked and she was dying to ask the uncouth question.

"What do you pay this person?"

"We did pay her $120,000 a year," Kara said very matter-of-factly. "Until she up and quit last week. She said she needed to do something more meaningful. I think she tweets for some online dating company now. What's the editorial director like, Imogen? Is she nice?"

Imogen considered her answer. There didn't seem much point in sugarcoating it.

"She can be charming, I'll give her that," Imogen said resolutely. "But no. She isn't nice. She isn't nice at all."

"I can relate to that," Maryanne piped in. Maryanne was a financial advisor who recently left her job with a big bank to enter the start-up world. Her new company, MEVest, was a platform that provided simple wealth management. No matter the season Maryanne was always in a perfectly tailored black pantsuit with her hair in a crisp bob. Wearing dark-rimmed black glasses, she radiated an aura of cool and success. "The CEO of MEVest is a downright little bitch," Maryanne continued. "'Nice' isn't in her vocabulary."

"Did she go to Harvard Business School too?" Imogen laughed.

"No. She's practically right out of college. She started managing other students' money while she was an economics and computer science undergrad at UPenn. I could tell you stories. The sense of entitlement is out of control. She honestly believes that everything out of her mouth is gospel. That she is the smartest person on the planet."

That made Imogen laugh. "What's the deal with these girls? Is it an age thing?"

Sara groaned. "Like the twentysomething we hired at the firm who wanted her own corner office after six months."

Campbell, a cable television executive who rarely indulged in the mommy gossip, chimed in. "We have plenty of those. They believe they deserve six-figure salaries right out of college."

"Maybe it's an age thing. Blame the millennials." Maryanne made air quotes around "millennials." "They say helicopter parents and too much praise turned this generation into monsters. But everyone said the same thing about the slackers of Generation X and I think we turned out okay." Maryanne glanced left and right and then dropped her voice conspiratorially.

"We are not alone."

"What do you mean?" Imogen asked.

"Are you on Facebook?"

Imogen sighed. "Reluctantly."

Kids streamed into the school around them, oblivious to the mom chatter, some still clutching the hands of their own parents, others absorbed in their self-determined packs.

"You have to join this group called TECHBITCH." Maryanne mouthed the bad word since they were surrounded by children.

"What is it?" Imogen asked, intrigued. "What is a tech bitch? Is it a support group?"

"Techbitch is like the verb. Like 'Oh, I have so much to techbitch about.' Well, I guess it's also a noun because a lot of people have a boss who is a total techbitch . . . like mine . . . and yours." Maryanne grinned. "This is an invite-only page on Facebook where people in the tech industry get to vent about their jobs. I think anyone can be invited, but mostly it's women like us who are pretty new to tech and all of a sudden we have these twenty-two-year-old wunderkind CEOs and CTOs and CMOs as bosses—"

"Eve is not my boss," Imogen interrupted, but Maryanne waved her comment away like it didn't matter.

"Whatever. People tell the most amazing stories. One woman went on a business trip to Miami and was forced to share a bed with her company's CEO and CTO to save money. She woke up in the middle of them."

Imogen's hand went up to her mouth. "That happened to me. Eve thought it was totally okay for the two of us to just share a bed. I had to tell her there was nothing normal about it. I personally don't think you should ever see your co-workers in their knickers." The other women looked at her in horror.

"There has been a hilarious thread about CEOs who force their staff to learn coordinated dances and then perform them in the office," Maryanne said matter-of-factly.

"One boss makes everyone wear the same color on Fridays and another one insists on taking selfies with the staff all day long. It's hilarious. You're going to love it."

"Is it anonymous?"

"Yup. It hides who is doing the posting."

The working mommies were all crowded together. Imogen was curious. "How many of you now have a younger boss?" About half of the women raised their hands. Imogen tried another question. "Or how many of you work directly with someone who is techbitchy?"

Everyone's hand went up.

My God. Imogen really had thought she was completely alone. She had no idea this was a thing happening across all industries.

Imogen was intrigued. "How do I join?"

"Oh, I can invite you," Maryanne said. "But be careful, I swear you can spend all day on it."

"Well, I can't wait to take a look this afternoon." Imogen smiled. Unsure exactly how to join a new Facebook group, she made a mental note to pop into the Genius Bar at the Apple Store on Prince Street to see if they would give her a quick tutorial on the way to work. That Genius Bar was her dirty little secret. The boys there knew her by name. Surprisingly, they were never condescending, and always cheerful about helping her learn how to do something new. It was Mike at the Genius Bar, the one with the nose ring and intense eyes who sang easy-listening songs under his breath, who helped her create a Facebook account. He did it while quietly humming Vanessa Williams's "Save the Best for Last" with perfect pitch. She preferred stopping off in the early morning when it was just her and an elegant group of blue-haired older ladies eager to learn the best scrapbooking applications.

Maryanne pulled out her iPhone.

"What is your personal email?"

"Oh, just send it to my *Glossy* account," Imogen said.

Maryanne scoffed. "You definitely don't want this to go to your work email. You know if they ever let you go they can go through everything you write on there." Imogen hadn't known that. She had never paid much mind to which email account she used. Her personal email was all muddled up with her work email. She gave Maryanne her Hotmail address, knowing exactly how uncool Hotmail made her sound. At least Maryanne didn't flinch when she said it.

"I am going to send you an invite to the TECHBITCH page when I get to the office. You're just going to love it."

Sure enough, when she arrived at the office, interspersed with emails promising penis enhancement and announcing new online J.Crew sales, there was an email in her Hotmail from Maryanne. In the text portion of the email was a warning: "I only give myself thirty minutes a day on here. I swear it could eat up all my productivity if I let it. Enjoy!!!!" Imogen felt tingles of excitement, knowing she was about to do something naughty, as she clicked the link to access the password-protected page. She glanced over the shiny top of her Mac's screen and through the glass wall into the main work area to make sure she wasn't being watched. It was an irrational gesture, since no one could see her screen anyhow. She laughed when she arrived at the page. The profile picture was of a woman about her age sitting in front of a computer, pulling at her hair. Her expression showed an equal mix of frustration, anger and desperation. It was exactly how Imogen felt at least ten times a day.

Maryanne was right: everything was anonymous. Imogen could read the posts and the comments, but it never showed who was posting or commenting. Some of the posts were funny, others were sad, some downright bitter. All of them were completely relatable for Imogen.

"Sometimes I feel like a ghost in my office. I have worked in the travel industry for twenty years. I consider myself something of an expert in the field, but at our travel start-up the real rock star is the twenty-three-year-old founder and CEO. People ignore me in meetings and defer to her, despite my years of experience. It stings, but I've started to learn that I need to humble myself. I can't waste my energy being angry every time someone talks over my head or asks her what she thinks about something I know she has no idea about."

"My boss talks to me while she pees."

"Our CMO goes around the office braiding everyone's hair whether they like it or not."

"My twenty-six-year-old CEO rolls her eyes every time I tell her I have to leave early (at seven!) to have dinner with my kids."

"My boss doesn't know who Duran Duran is."

"I don't know the difference between java and JavaScript and I am okay with that."

It was fascinating to peer into the office lives of other people in a similar predicament to hers, to learn she wasn't the only one being tormented by a twentysomething at work. Mixed in with the terrible comments was some sage advice.

"Make sure to tell your millennial employees they are great . . . every single day."

"Don't bother correcting their grammar."

"Don't, under any circumstances, let their parents come to the office."

"Try to avoid calling them on the phone. It scares them."

Imogen was both terrified and exhilarated at the idea of contributing something to this page. She was just worried that she would mess up. What if by some quirk in her privacy settings she was the only one on the whole page who didn't remain anonymous? This could end up like the Twitter debacle all over again. She also wasn't sure what to write. She could talk about how Eve leaked the Twitter stream about her. Was that TECHBITCH-worthy? She could tell them about how she was forced to share a bed or about how Eve insisted on wearing her tiny Hervé dresses everywhere they went while she tried to make Imogen dress more and more like a mom. There was certainly no shortage of things she could write about. Maryanne had been right. Before Imogen knew it, forty-five minutes had passed as she read the comments and daydreamed about contributing her own. She could fall down into this rabbit hole all day long. It was addicting and vindicating. For the first time in a long while, Imogen didn't feel quite so alone. It may have been the first and last time she would ever utter these words, but as she closed the Facebook window she whispered, "God bless the Internet."

CHAPTER NINE

Imogen had $500 to spend on flowers for their big party. A complete party order from L'Olivier would top $5,000. Eve's thoughts on the subject were clear: "Fuck flowers. They won't add to my ROI." Imogen believed flowers could make or break the ambience of a party. The scent elevated the mood and completed a scene. When they first started dating, Alex picked up on her love of fresh flowers right away without her even having to mention anything. Once a week without fail he would bring home the most beautiful arrangements of lilies, hydrangeas and roses, letting her believe all the while that he had been the creative genius behind their construction. Years later she learned he had befriended the owner of a small Koreatown flower shop, charming her with the few phrases he knew in Korean and spending way too big a chunk of his assistant U.S. attorney salary to purchase them each week. Song Lee still owned that shop in what was now a flourishing flower district. Imogen crossed her fingers that Song would be game to help her now.

She headed downtown from Lincoln Center during lunchtime the day before the party, enjoying the twenty-five-block walk, replacing her high-heeled Isabel Marant booties with ballet flats.

Much to her dismay, Song was not there. A beautiful girl with a hint of Song's strong cheekbones, wearing a tight orange tank top over brown leather leggings, tapped away at an iPad behind the cash register.

"Mom went to Korea for a few months to take care of my grandma. She'll be back in October if you're planning, like, a wedding or something," the girl said in perfect English without looking up. It was a marked contrast to Song's charmingly broken language skills. A name tag above her right breast read ELEN.

Imogen smiled. "I'll miss your mom's expert eye. She always knows how to help me stretch a dollar when it comes to decorating for my events, but maybe you could help me. We are throwing a party for Glossy.com tomorrow night."

The girl's eyes widened. "I love *Glossy*!! I just downloaded your new app." Imogen tilted her head in interest. "It's great. I ordered a pair of Charlotte Olympia cat slippers yesterday. BUY IT NOW!" She raised her fist in the air as she shouted out the site's signature tagline.

"Yes, BUY IT NOW." Imogen made a small shake of her own fist in solidarity, and then awkwardly received a fist bump from Elen, which made her feel quite silly.

"I can help you pick some things. You sure are cutting it close, huh? Most fancy companies place their orders months in advance. We're gonna have to work with what we have in the back. How much do ya want to spend?"

Imogen didn't want to say the number. She felt ashamed telling this girl who'd just spent $545 on those Charlotte Olympia cat slippers that she had less than that for flowers for a "fancy" party. So she fibbed.

"The party is pretty low-key . . . small, very intimate guest list. We already did a *huge* flower order last month. I would have ordered it with you, but we had to use one of the company's big vendors. I just need accent flowers now really. I am so embarrassed I didn't think to order them sooner. In fact"—Imogen winked—"I am just going to pay for them in cash out of my own pocket right now so that no one will notice the oversight." She pulled five crisp hundred-dollar bills out of her wallet.

"Your party is tomorrow night?"

"It is!"

"I can help. This is perfect for the leftovers."

"The leftovers?"

"The flower industry is soooo wasteful." Elen rolled her eyes. "We always over-order and we never give flowers to a customer unless they will last for a full week after the day the person buys them. That makes it look like we are selling shoddy flowers. Not good, ya know? So the leftovers are flowers that look great today and will probably be good until, like, next Tuesday. They're just a little older than the new flowers. Sometimes we give them to the deli owners at a good price. A lot of them just get thrown out. Come on. I'll show you."

Elen led Imogen through the narrow store, past the finely organized refrigerators of lilies, orchids, peonies, dahlias, amaryllis, tulips and succulents. They walked through a door so short Imogen slouched to enter the back room, the heart of the shop, the part the customers never got to see. The floor here was cement and covered in a light dusting of sawdust. Off to the right was another glass-doored fridge, this one a little dirtier, a little older, singing a dull hum to the two women.

"There. Those are the leftovers. Go through them. I can give you a great price for whatever you take. I remember you now. Mom talks about you. She says your husband is a real babe." Imogen was still pleased any time someone told her how attractive he or she found Alex. She didn't need the validation. She *knew* her husband was a babe, but it made her feel good that she was the one who'd landed him, even if it was through a weird twist of fate and a drug-addicted ex-boyfriend.

"That he is. I am an incredibly lucky woman." D.I.L.F.—that's what one of the other moms drunkenly said about Alex during a school Christmas party.

Despite its dusty face, the leftover fridge was a treasure trove of beautiful flowers, some with a brown leaf here or a droopy petal there, but mainly still perfectly intact. Imogen sympathized with this lot, whose expiration date came sooner than they expected, before they had a chance to fulfill their destiny walking down the aisle at someone's wedding.

Imogen buried her face in a bunch of magnolias, their heady

vanilla scent sending her back to the very first photo shoot she had done in New Orleans. Molly brought her down there just a few months after she landed in America. Imogen had never seen anything like that city. The smells, the crumbling old mansions in the Garden District, the melting pot of brown, white and black faces, jazz wafting through the trees . . . it was like living in a movie. There was always a party going on. Oh my god . . . and the food. She'd eaten beignets from Café Du Monde every morning. The imaginary smell of the sweet dough with the real magnolias made her want to buy a plane ticket. She took them all from the fridge.

Elen was once again engrossed in her electronic device when Imogen emerged, her arms laden down with the leftovers. The girl surveyed the bunch. "I'll charge you $450 for 'em all, and then give me the remaining $50 and I'll get them where you need them to go." Imogen provided her address and texted Tilly to expect a delivery.

* * *

Eve was sitting on the couch in Imogen's office.

"What are you wearing tomorrow night?" Imogen still felt jarred every time Eve was so casual with her. She knew it was unfair that she felt this way, and with anyone else she would have felt guilty for still thinking of her as her subordinate once they had been promoted to a position like Eve's, but something inside her still expected Eve to address her with the respect she gave during their first two years together. Imogen didn't want her lounging on her couch, her dress creeping high on her thighs, long legs stretched into the middle of the room, her hands behind her head.

"I asked Zac to pull me something from his new collection," Imogen replied, crossing her own legs as she sat down.

"Can I do that too?"

"It might be too late, but I can give him a call."

"Is he coming to the party? I just love him."

"I'm not sure yet."

Eve pouted, pushing her thin lower lip over the even thinner top one.

"Can't you make him come?"

Imogen laughed. "I can't make anyone do anything."

"We can ban him from the site."

"We won't ban one of the best women's designers in the business from our app. How does that benefit us?"

"Is anyone even coming? Jesus, your job is to be fabulous. Are you going to be able to pull this off?" *How much longer can I endure this little brat talking to me like this?*

"The party will go down as a night to remember. It's going to be wonderful, Eve. You're a size two right now, yes? Let me put in a quick call. We'll get a few options over here for you to try on later this afternoon."

* * *

Alex took the kids out to a movie for the night, freeing Imogen to spread her promptly delivered leftover flowers on newspaper she'd laid out around the sitting room. Tilly directed her to look at Pinterest, where the new hipster trend was #DeliFlowers—flower arranging with cheap store-bought stems.

The process of the flower arranging became strangely meditative. Matching color with color and shape with shape and then shape with color energized all of her senses and made Imogen feel creative in a way she hadn't in months. She clutched a bunch of white magnolias with pale pink peonies, lilies of the valley and chamomile in her right hand, using a pair of nail scissors to snip off a few brown leaves before wrapping a black ribbon firmly around the stems. She was adding odd branches and greens to a tall mason jar when her cell phone rang. Holding a wide white ribbon in place with her teeth, she put Massimo on speakerphone.

"Darling, what are you doing?" he purred.

"Making flower arrangements for the party tomorrow night."

"You know you can hire people to do that kind of thing, right?"

"Isn't it more fun to do it this way?" Imogen knew that without telling him Massimo would infer that her getting her hands dirty had something to do with Eve.

"I won't keep you then. Just wanted to say I'll see you at seven tomorrow."

"Oooh, I am so happy you're going to be able to make it. I know there are a million parties tomorrow night."

"But no other party will have Imogen Tate." She laughed at that. "I'll let you go."

"Well, thank you for calling, sweetheart. I'm happy to know that at least one person will be coming."

"Oh, stop it. Priscilla will be wheeling me about, so there will be at least two people there!" Imogen loved him so much. "Oh, and Im. I don't know if you've heard but herbs and weeds are all the rage in flower arranging these days. Just a tip!"

Herbs. What did that mean? What kind of herbs? Weeds?

Imogen wandered into the tiny backyard garden she'd started, then stopped, and started and stopped more than a dozen times. Gardening was something she actually enjoyed, but life consistently got in the way of a real commitment to a green thumb. In the back, by a very small goldfish pond, was Annabel's small plot of neatly planted vegetables, bordered by her herb garden—rosemary, thyme and mint all madly overgrown. She grabbed a bunch of mint and rosemary. *What the hell?* she thought, as she added them to each of the arrangements.

An hour later Imogen was faced with ten centerpieces that made her bloom with pride.

"Better than I could have done." Alex snuck up behind her, wrapped his arm around her middle and kissed her on the shoulder. "Did Song help?"

Imogen shook her head and leaned into her husband. "Song's in Korea! I met her daughter Elen."

"Elen was about twelve years old last time I saw her," her husband said, scratching his head. Imogen laughed.

"It's been too long since you've gotten me flowers then. You must've seen her about six years ago, because she's now a very beautiful young woman and I have no doubt that you would've noticed her."

"I don't notice any beautiful women except my wife." He nuzzled her neck, the daylong growth of his beard scratching her in a way both pleasurable and familiar.

"Where are the kids?"

"Upstairs. I fed them too much popcorn. They're in a food coma, both ready to hit the sack." Alex yawned. "So am I. Joining me?"

"In a little bit. I want to finish up here, if that's all right?"

"Of course." Alex surveyed the flowers again. "That Elen is almost as talented as her mother, the woman who helped me win my wife."

Imogen didn't know why, but she wanted to keep her newfound talent to herself for the time being, make it something that only she knew she was any good at.

"She's a talented girl! I'll be up in just a few minutes. Start reading to the kids and I'll come along soon to finish up."

* * *

Oh, how she missed the days of a glam squad coming into the office to get all the girls—all the editors and advertising reps—ready for a big event together. Hairstylists, manicurists and makeup artists used to descend in a pack on Robert Mannering Corp., turning the office into a giant spa for an entire day before a party.

Now Imogen just asked Allison, her favorite stylist from the salon, to come over and give her a blowout at the house.

"Who's coming tonight?" Annabel perched on the ottoman at the foot of Imogen's bed, her orange backpack at her feet, ready for a night at Suki Abraham's house down the street.

"Whoever was free," Imogen said distractedly, trying not to let the guest list make her too nervous. Ashley had a lengthy list of RSVPs, which flooded in just minutes after the Paperless Post had gone out, all typed out by diligent assistants, but Imogen knew better than anyone that everyone simply RSVP'd for everything during Fashion Week and then scattered where the wind and their Town Cars took them. She never wanted to be early for her own party, but this time she couldn't be too late either.

Imogen had to ignore a barrage of texts from Eve.

>>>>What r u wearing?<<<<

>>>>How shld I do my hair?<<<<

>>>>Whoze coming??<<<<

>>>>Y aren't U ANSWERING MEEEE!!!!! ☹ <<<<

She kissed her daughter good-bye and walked slowly down the stairs, drinking in the room. Her flower arrangements looked pretty and fresh in mason jars.

The front door was open and Ashley was greeting guests on the front stoop. Early evening sunlight streamed in to dapple the attractive crowd, most of them dressed head to toe in black or white, with splashes of vibrant color on a shoe here or jewelry there.

Imogen was lightly brushing her lips across Ashley's cheek to say hello when she heard Eve's voice pipe up behind her, forcing the hairs on her neck to stand at attention. They would have saluted Eve if they'd been able.

"I thought I told you not to spend money on flowers," Eve barked. Ashley, appearing uncomfortable for Imogen, turned her attention back to checking guests off on her miniature iPad.

"I didn't. We got them free." Bald-faced lies were unfortunately the best policy with Eve, who considered the free flowers with a new eye.

"Oh. Well then, they're nice. I like them. When is everyone getting here?" Eve said, as though the already crowded room were completely empty.

The clatter of glassware and idle chatter from clusters of well-dressed guests already filled the intimate space. Trays of hors d'oeuvres were passed: thinly shaved tomatoes topping a dime-sized dollop of milky burrata on Parmesan squares, unnervingly large shrimp next to a silver bowl of cocktail sauce and salmon carpaccio with shaved truffles in bowls just twice the depth of a thimble.

Out of the corner of her eye, Imogen could see Donna Karan, wearing a wonderful black jumpsuit paired with an orange cashmere throw, engaged in a heated discussion with an Oscar-winning actor and his model wife. At the other end of the room Adrienne Velasquez, of *Project Fashion* chatted up an attractive bartender with a slight Mohawk. The model Cara Delevingne held hands with her latest girlfriend in a hushed chat in the corner. Salman Rushdie raised his hand halfway into the air in a finger-wiggling wave to Lily Aldridge and Stacey Bendet of Alice & Olivia. Imogen watched as the actor Alan Cumming, fresh off a new stint on Broadway and wearing a cropped tweed suit in a way few men could—or should, for that matter—crept up behind Alexandra Richards to give her a wet kiss on the cheek. Anjelica Huston and her handsome nephew Jack chatted in a corner.

Bridgett bounced across the room, a ball of excitement, her long legs ensconced in silk harem pants that flapped like wide Technicolor wings.

"I just came up with an idea for my very own app." She lowered her already sultry voice conspiratorially as she spoke to Imogen.

"Tell me all about it, darling. I am sure it's brilliant." Imogen reached over to pluck a small piece of lint off of Bridgett's black cashmere shell.

"Well, I want to create something that can live on their phones that will help my clients choose their outfits every morning. I want them to be able to input everything in their closet and then the app will tell them how to put it together each day to keep their look fresh."

"Aren't you worried it will make what you do irrelevant, darling?" Imogen asked, still convinced that most technology served to make someone somewhere irrelevant.

Bridgett thought on that for a second. "No, I actually don't. They still need me to tell them what to wear and I think it could help me get new clients, ones who don't have the time or the money to see me as often, who live in different parts of the country."

Imogen considered this. It was a fair point. Bridgett putting herself on people's phones would increase her reach from Beverly Hills to Capitol Hill.

"I love everything about it," Imogen said. "I think you should absolutely go for it." And Imogen knew the perfect person for Bridgett to speak with. His signature topknot sprung jovially up into the air as he walked through the door, completely at ease in this room of fashion royalty. He wore a high-waisted Thom Browne three-piece suit in burnt sienna atop a simple white button-down paired with the same flawless loafers he had worn when Imogen first met him at DISRUPTTECH! She grabbed him by the elbow as he strolled past.

"Birdie, I want you to meet Rashid. Rashid is the founder of Blast! I think the two of you have a lot that you could talk about." Rashid kissed her hand as Imogen left the two of them to talk apps.

Paloma Betts, a top buyer for Barneys with feathery ash-blond hair that framed her oval face, tottered over to Imogen in an intricately beaded black crepe minidress.

"Is that DJ who I think it is?" she asked. "She's so hot right now."

The DJ, Chelsea (she went by one name these days), a socialite turned DJ in a camouflage snowsuit, had set up at a small table in the corner underneath an oil painting of Imogen's great-uncle Alfred.

Imogen smiled coyly. "It is." She failed to mention that Chelsea had been Annabel's babysitter just five years ago and was spinning at the party for free.

"You're so hip." Paloma swayed her head to a remix of Pitbull dipping into a Lionel Richie throwback.

I used to be, Imogen thought. "Don't go that far! I just pay attention." Imogen shrugged. "I'll give you all her information." Paloma caught sight of Adrienne's Mohawked bartender and sidled over to order her glass of rosé.

Scattered on tables were gift cards for Glossy.com, each one promising $50 to BUY IT NOW! Next to them were the despised black bracelets.

Imogen felt a warm hand on the small of her exposed spine. Her dress had a high, nun-like collar in the front, with a back that dipped dangerously close to her derriere. Thinking it was Alex, she turned seductively, only to come face-to-face, for the first time in practically a decade, with Andrew Maxwell.

"Immy!" No one called her Immy anymore. The years had been kind to Andrew in the way they always are to wealthy men. A smattering of gray was just beginning to show at his temples, but it suited him. His hair was now sculpted into a perfectly political helmet. His suit was impeccably tailored and the collar of his signature pink shirt immaculately ironed. He surveyed the room.

"Different from that tiny place we used to shack up in, right?" *Did he have to say that so loudly?*

"Andrew, it's wonderful to see you. Thanks for coming."

"How could I ever pass up an opportunity to see the inimitable Imogen Tate in her element?" His teeth were no longer riddled with tobacco stains. Now they shone too brightly, reflecting light of their own back at Imogen. He gave his characteristically easy smile, one that brought wrinkles around his eyes that would have aged a woman but made a man appear rugged.

A sixth sense told her she was being watched.

Sure enough, Eve swooped past, hurling herself into Andrew's arms and planting a boisterous kiss full on his lips. Eve hadn't chosen any of the dresses Imogen had pulled for her. Instead she opted for her standby, another bandage minidress in black and white, her breasts swelling seductively out of the immodestly plunging neckline. How many of these bandage dresses did Eve have? Andrew planted his eyes squarely on her breasts and didn't look away.

"You didn't like any of the dresses we pulled for you, Eve?"

"Too old. Stuffy. Perfect for you. Not for me."

"Well, you look beautiful," Imogen said politely.

"Right?" Eve replied, pivoting on her heel to stroll into the corner of the room, where she huddled with three of her bloggers. Imogen rolled her eyes and began to circulate.

Imogen congratulated Vera Wang on a show very well done that morning before being bounced from guest to guest—the famous ballerina whose name began with an *O* but she could never remember it, the art critic with breath that always smelled like kitty litter, the creative director for Prada. She stopped short in the rear of the room, surprised to see teenage blogger Orly there, sitting quietly on one of Imogen's mid-century white armchairs while she meticulously spread foie gras on a toast point, making sure the creamy pâté reached to the very edge. She added a dollop of grainy Dijon mustard before nibbling at the end. The girl's appearance struck Imogen as fairylike, with her light blue eyes and matching hair, her slightly too large head floating above a slender frame.

She was so close to Annabel's age that Imogen wanted to put her hand on her head and ask the girl if she was having a good time and get her a slice of cake, but before she could approach her, Orly looked up and patted the chair next to her in a way that was wise beyond her years.

"I never know what to do at these things." Her small hands fluttered like wings around her face as she talked.

"I think I am failing you," Imogen replied, making sure to keep her tone as adult as possible so that she didn't come across as condescending. "It's my job as a host to walk you around and introduce you to everyone. No one really knows what to do at these parties. You're not alone."

The girl was so unlike Eve, completely guileless and straightforward. She didn't bother to kiss Imogen's ass because no one had taught her how.

"Walk with me a little." Imogen offered her hand to Orly.

At the heart of the room, Massimo held court with the beautiful it girls. He loved interesting-looking people of both genders. Priscilla perched perfectly on the handle of his chair behind him. Imogen settled herself delicately onto his lap, making sure to shift the majority of her weight into her own legs, but knowing that he loved the attention of having a beautiful woman drape herself across him like this. She kissed him on the lips.

"I have hardly seen you all week." She pretended to glower.

"That's because I still sit in the front row and you lurk all the way in the back like a shifty little commoner taking all those delicious Instagram photos."

"Massimo, meet Orly. I am sure you have heard all about her, but I think she could teach even you a thing or two." Orly's face lit up.

Metal clinked against glass and Imogen saw Eve trying to climb atop a chair. Two waiters rushed over to lift her up, attempting to pull her dress back down as it crept up over her thighs.

"HIIIIIIII!" Eve said to the room. This wasn't planned. The plan was to let people mingle for the better part of an hour, before Imogen and Eve would, *together,* welcome everyone and talk a little bit about the new Glossy.com. It was evident this would be Eve's show, not hers. The three bloggers Eve had been chatting with raced to the front of the room, jabbing elbows at guests. Imogen had taken to calling them the Selfie-razzi, since they were Eve's personal documenters.

"We NEED to get up there," one of them shrieked.

"It's, like, our job," another one said to Cynthia Rowley as she practically shoved the petite designer against the wall. One began tapping the side of her Google Glass. The other two raised their phones up to record and snap Eve, not caring who they blocked behind them.

"So grunge is apparently back at this year's Fashion Week." Eve paused. "Either that or there are a lot more homeless people in Lincoln Center." It was meant to be a joke, but the delivery and the reception crippled it at both ends as murmurs of disapproval hummed through the crowd. Eve continued unaware.

"I want to welcome everyone to this adorable little party we just threw together at the last minute." Eve paused for a second as the star of *Project Fashion* walked into the room. "Heya, Gretchen." She fluttered her hand as the supermodel gave a tight smile and nod.

"You don't know how excited I am to launch Glossy-dot-com. Forget boring old magazines. This is the future." Eve's voice always had a certain authority to it, even when she was standing on top of a chair, but she didn't know how to read a room. She wasn't savvy enough to realize that this crowd loved magazines, had grown up in magazines, was supported by magazines still. But she kept going, doing the same spiel she gave in San Francisco. Imogen could hear the rustling around her crescendo as guests shifted uncomfortably from foot to foot.

"I am so happy that we have so many amazing designers here in the room with us. I want to thank Timo Weiland, Olivier Theyskens, Rebecca Minkoff, Phoebe Philo. Alexander Wang, I'm wearing a pair of your booties right now." Eve pointed at Thakoon. Alexander wasn't at the party. The only thing the two men had at all in common was their Asian heritage.

"My goal is to make fashion exciting again. My goal is to bring all of you"—she spread her arms wide as if she were hugging the room—"into the motherfucking digital age, and I will not rest until I do it." Eve believed that cursing for effect was a sure way to get people's attention. Instead the crowd winced.

"I know what the Internet likes. It likes cats and side boob and beaver shots. We are going to find a way to take advantage of all of those things at Glossy.com to make us *the* destination for millennials to do all of their shopping."

Imogen had never heard the words "beaver shot" spoken out loud. She took a deep breath and waited for Eve to finish before gently pushing herself forward. She placed a hand on Eve's waist to alert the girl she was there and smiled up at her, making a small gesture meant to indicate, "May I?"

"I think Imogen wants to say something to you," she said, visibly disheartened by the lack of enthusiasm for her speech.

Even Imogen, positive often to a fault, couldn't think of a way to spin that terrible speech. She cleared her throat. "Thank you, Eve. Eve is a tech genius. I can't begin to thank her enough for all of her hard work and everything she's teaching me." Imogen knew she had to repair the bad vibe in the room. "We live in a crazy Wild West of a new world. Who would have thought six months ago that my magazine would become an app? If I'd known, maybe I would have extended my vacation." That brought a few titters. "You were invited here tonight because we consider you part of the *Glossy* family and we want to keep you in the loop about all of our future plans. We know that none of you had any shortage of parties to attend this evening, so we are grateful you chose ours. I know how important hashtags are these days. Please send out lots of tweets and Instagrams. We have an inkling of how to make this party go viral, so sit tight for a surprise. Drink up, eat up, thank Danny, your amazing chef, afterward and drink lots of water, because you don't want to be hungover tomorrow." Imogen raised her glass and the crowd applauded briefly before Chelsea drowned them out with the opening chorus of Iggy Azalea's "Fancy." While Imogen spoke, Eve had managed to scurry down from the chair.

The sounds of the party—small talk and nibbling—resumed.

"That's it?" Eve hissed into her ear. "That's all you're going to say? We spent five thousand dollars to make sure these people aren't hungover? We invited them here to get them on board with our app." What exactly had Eve wanted her to say?

"That isn't how business is done in this world, Eve," Imogen hissed back, irritated by Eve's gumption when all she had done was save her neck. "These things take time, patience and schmoozing. I think I know more about how this is done than you do."

"We need them now. We needed them yesterday. You didn't even get the guest list right. I know most of the people here already." Imogen looked around and knew that wasn't true. Eve couldn't have already been introduced to half these people, except possibly when they rang her phone years ago. "I wanted new people at this event and you didn't deliver."

Eve stalked off to the bathroom, leaving Imogen with her mouth agape. While she was talking Alex had joined the crowd at the back of the room. He picked his hand up to wave and then rushed forward when he realized she was upset.

"Great speech. Short and to the point. Let them drink at night and do their business during the day," he reminded her. It was something Carter Worthington had told him years ago at one of their advertiser schmooze fests when Alex, after a few too many margaritas, had asked her boss what exactly was the point of spending so much money on their events.

"I have to deal with Eve." Imogen kissed him quickly and then took off for the bathroom. She heard Eve before she saw her, giant heaving breaths echoing through the hall. Imogen knocked on the door to her own powder room. "Eve, it's Imogen. Can I come in?" She heard the lock unclick.

Eve was covered in a fine layer of sweat. There were no tears on her cheeks, but her face kept contorting in a way that suggested it would prefer to be crying.

"I think I'm having a heart attack," Eve sputtered. Her chest heaved, which caused her entire body to begin shaking.

Imogen grabbed a Kleenex from its tortoiseshell box to wipe off the edge of the sink before she leaned gingerly against it. She had experience with anxiety attacks. You had to wait them out. Back when they lived together in their shoddy little apartment, Bridgett suffered from at least one a week, brought on by anything from a bad day at work to seeing a rat on the subway, before her doctors found the right cocktail of drugs to keep them at bay.

The bathroom was small and cramped. Imogen stood so close to Eve that it would have been easy to touch her. By stretching her arm out just a few inches she could have put a comforting hand on her shoulder, but the very idea of touching Eve now, this new iteration of Eve, made Imogen recoil. She stayed as far away from the girl as the confined space would allow, but still she could hear Eve gnashing her teeth together—a sound like a well-heeled boot crunching over gravel.

Eve's breath came in stilted waves. "They hated me," she moaned, pulling at her curls, yanking them down around her chin and then, like a child, putting the end of one in her mouth to suck on it. "Everyone here hates me. I failed tonight." Imogen was worried the girl was going to hyperventilate. The tears finally came and Eve reached out to hold on to the hem of Imogen's dress the way a drowning man would clutch at a life preserver. Only the mascara on her left eye had smeared. The right remained perfectly intact.

All of the party's previous joy was siphoned away by each word from Eve's mouth. "You need to breathe." Imogen emptied out her glass of champagne and ran cold water into it. "Drink this." She handed her two Xanax. "Take these. Wipe away your tears." Did she sound too motherly?

Eve glared at her through her gasps, her face turning the color of merlot. "You wanted this party to suck, didn't you?"

Imogen's heart sank. Nothing she did was going to help. Eve had the manners of a psychopath. It was in these moments that Eve reminded Imogen of her old dog growing up, a Jack Russell who had been perfectly well behaved in their London flat, but revealed his true colors on a day trip out to Kent. Nutkin forcefully escaped from an open car window, running straight toward a small lamb that had been caught in the barbed wire at the edge of a field, its leg bent at a ninety-degree angle and bleeding. Once Nutkin smelled blood there was no turning back. He was an attack dog cloaked as a city dog. The shepherd's boy got Nutkin with his shotgun shortly after the dog killed the sheep. It was Nutkin's fate. He was born like that. Eve was born like this.

Rage clouded Eve's eyes as she glared up at Imogen. "Why do I even keep you around?"

Dropping her voice, Imogen glared back at the insolent little bitch.

"Watch it, Eve. I wanted this party to be a success just as much as you, and so far it is. You have some of the most powerful people in the fashion industry in that room right now and they are more than happy to speak to you about Glossy-dot-com. If I were you, I wouldn't let that opportunity slip away."

Eve lifted her face and stared dully into space before standing up and turning to the sink. Imogen barely had a second to jump out of the way before the girl vomited next to her. She watched as Eve chugged the glass of water and then threw the Xanax into her mouth.

"Get out. I need a few minutes."

Imogen shook her head in disbelief. "Get yourself together before you come back to the party, please," Imogen said coolly before she slipped sideways back out through the door, brushing against Andrew Maxwell, the only person standing in the small hallway between the sitting room and the backyard.

"Is she all right?"

"As a human being, no. Right now I think she will be fine. You certainly have your hands full, Andrew." He moved his hand toward his head, wanting to run it through his hair, before thinking better of mussing it up and bringing it back down to his pocket.

"She's just a perfectionist, Imogen. She just wants this project to succeed."

Imogen gnawed on her bottom lip. "That isn't what she wants. She wants this project to be all hers." She regretted the words the second that they came out of her mouth, knowing that Eve probably heard them and that if she hadn't, Andrew would most definitely repeat them.

When she emerged from the bathroom, Eve looked worse for the wear. Imogen tried to ignore her as Eve kept to the edges of the party, typing furiously on her phone, stopping only briefly to whisper in the ear of Addison Cao, conspicuous as always in a blue crushed velvet suit, before hopping into a black Uber without saying good-bye.

Soon after Eve left, Imogen's surprise arrived. She was going out on a limb here, but from the little bit she understood about how things went viral on the Internet, she thought she had a shot at making this work. Her friend Ginnifer (one of the mommy gang from school and a longtime volunteer with the ASPCA) arrived right at the stroke of nine with a crate of wiggly, squiggling rescue puppies. It wasn't really her idea. It was Annabel's. The night before, as she had fretted over the party being a disaster, her daughter peeked her head over her iPad.

"Just bring in a bunch of puppies," Annabel said matter-of-factly.

It sounded ridiculous. "Why, darling?"

Her daughter shook her head. "Because . . . the Internet," she said breezily as she walked up to her room.

Of course her daughter was right.

The crowd at the party went wild. So many Instagram videos were taken, phone batteries died. There was a miniature melee to get close to one particularly grumpy-looking little bulldog named Champ. Dog hair covered couture, but no one cared, and nine adorable puppies got homes they never could have dreamed of.

The party went until midnight. Once Eve left it turned into such a good time, the night becoming boisterous and buoyant. Or maybe it was all in Imogen's imagination that everything grew louder and less serious. Furniture was pushed to the side of the room to allow for flailing limbs to catch a beat. The crowd danced like they were in the basement of the Ritz.

Fashion Goes to the Dogs
By Addison Cao, WWD columnist

Fashion went to the dogs last night at the Glossy.com party to celebrate yet another Fashion Week. Returning editor in chief Imogen Tate hobnobbed with fashion royalty old and new, including Donna Karan, Thakoon, Timo Weiland, and Carolina

Herrera, at her gorgeous West Village town house. By the end of the night, no one was paying any attention to the posh set. Seriously! It was all about the puppies. God bless the Internet. It just might be the most Instagrammed party of all of Fashion Week after Tate brought in a crate of adorable adoptables. #Perfection.

Not everyone was delighted. Glossy.com's new editorial director, Eve Morton, slipped out of the bash early. . . .

CHAPTER TEN

OCTOBER 2015

O n a crisp fall Friday night Imogen found herself staring into the ruddy red face of Santa Claus. Ron Hobart, Imogen's psychic and shrink (he was a package deal), bore a remarkable resemblance to Father Christmas. Editors and designers lived and died by him. "The Fashion Psychic" was his nickname. Not a single season passed without Donna and Tom ringing Ron to find the most advantageous date for their runway shows.

What most people didn't know about Ron was that in addition to his knack for predicting successful dates and modeling careers, he held a PhD in clinical psychology from Johns Hopkins and was a licensed therapist. He was also a certified Reiki practitioner, if anyone cared to ask, which Ron hoped that they did.

More than a decade ago, during her first visit with the psychic, he told Imogen she would marry a tall, dark man with a distinctive birthmark. She laughed, convinced at the time she would absolutely marry the towheaded Andrew Maxwell. Six months later she met Alex and discovered a birthmark in the shape of a teddy bear on the back of his left thigh.

The moment Imogen arrived in Ron's office, a steady stream of tears fell down her cheeks. Ron let her cry, alternating between glancing over his half-moon glasses with compassion and quietly reading passages from a worn hardcover of Kahlil Gibran's *The Prophet* as they sat opposite each other in ugly green armchairs atop wall-to-wall shag carpeting. A fake fire crackled in the background. Photographs of Ron with his idols, Deepak Chopra and Oprah, lined the mantel.

Finally calm enough to speak, Imogen caught her therapist up on what was happening with Eve. Their previous sessions had been mostly about wife drama, mommy drama, friend drama. Imogen rarely talked about work.

"What bothers you the most about this situation?" he asked her. Ron's index fingers formed a steeple supporting his chins. "You don't still fantasize about Andrew, do you? About the man Andrew is right now?"

"No." Imogen shook her head in a genuinely violent way that convinced her this was the truth. "But I do fantasize about having other things that Eve has. I fantasize about being relevant again. I fantasize about people asking me to make big decisions and caring about my opinion, the way they care about Eve's." Imogen laughed back a sob. "I feel invisible. I'm the invisible older woman. I walk into a room and no one notices. No one looks up. Then I feel guilty for wishing people noticed me."

"I don't think you're invisible."

"You should come to my office."

"You know what you need to do?"

"Be grateful." Imogen said, curious if she was wandering into a trap. "I am grateful. I have a gratitude journal and everything."

"You sound like Saint Gwyneth Paltrow desperately trying to sound humble."

Imogen tried to swallow her frustration. "I feel like a fucking imposter every single day and I hate that. I'm forty-two, for Chrissakes. I'm too old to feel stupid."

Ron grimaced. "I think you need to weigh what you are getting out of this job with how much you can handle being bullied by a woman, who, as you describe her, is a sociopath."

Ron grew quiet for a minute and rolled his eyes back in his head. His frame began to shake.

"What do you know?" she asked him warily, wishing, not for the first time, that her shrink and her psychic were not the same person.

Ron trembled his fingers, making a show that the cosmos was communicating directly with him. "This is going to get a lot worse before it gets better," he said reluctantly. "A lot of things are going to change."

Imogen sat straight up, her spine a pillar. "What is going to change?"

Ron looked at her woozily. He always claimed that peering into the future exhausted him. "I don't think you will stay in New York. Not full-time anyway. I see you spending time in the South. And there is going to be a wedding."

"Eve and Andrew?"

Ron nodded slowly. "I think so."

"They just met!"

Her therapist shrugged. The universe had spoken to him.

The timer on his iPhone beeped. Their session was over. He rubbed his temples and stretched his arms above his head.

She gazed at the man's chest-length white beard gamboling above his belly, which did quiver, not unlike a bowl full of jelly.

There was one more thing. "Ron, do you tweet?" Imogen asked shyly.

He raised a bushy eyebrow.

"I do indeed."

"Will you follow me?"

CHAPTER ELEVEN

Imogen couldn't ignore a burning sensation close to her left nipple. It came in waves that made her bite down hard on her lip. In a wash of guilt, she didn't want to wake Alex. Had she been taking good enough care of herself over the past few months? Or had she been so focused on Eve and her job that she neglected to pay attention to her recovery? In the days following the surgery, when she pushed everything but healing out of her mind, she fixated on every detail, caring for the surgical drain and getting rid of the fluid every couple of hours. She religiously exercised her arm to keep the muscles strong, but she hadn't done it since she went back to work. The doctors had warned her to stay on top of all these things to prevent an infection. She definitely didn't want to wake Alex and complain.

"Mommy."

"Hey, John-John. Why are you awake so early on a Saturday?"

"I had a nightmare."

She lowered the seat of the loo and sat, lifting him on her lap, which only aggravated the pain in her breast.

"Tell me about the nightmare. Was the witch there?" He nodded his blond curls up and down. "I'll bet she was scary. What did you do?"

"I hides."

"Brave, smart boy. Where did you hide?"

"In a tree!"

"Trees are the best place to hide from witches!" Johnny's frightened face turned proud.

"You know what I want you to do next time that mean and nasty witch pops into your dream, darling?"

"What, Mommy?"

"You don't have to hide. You can stand right up in front of her. Close to her face." Imogen put her face right in front of Johnny's, making him giggle. "And you tell her, 'You don't belong here. I belong here. This is my tree and this is my dream.'"

"You're so smart, Mommy. You're smart and you're so soft." He nuzzled into her, rubbing the lace of her slip against the parts of her chest that hurt, but she balanced the pain with his need to be as close to her as possible.

"I always like to hear that, darling. Do you think you can go back to sleep?" He nodded again, this time his eyes already growing droopy. She bit down hard again on her lower lip as she lifted him up in both of her arms, favoring the right one. He made his small snuffling noises as she laid him in his bed. She peeked into the next room at Annabel. Her daughter had left her laptop on her bed. Imogen brought the machine downstairs instead of going into the bedroom to grab the one she and Alex shared and risk waking him.

When the screen flickered back to life Imogen closed out twelve tabs of instant messages, videos of Siamese cats, Reddit and a fan page for a band composed of three boys with asymmetrical haircuts. Facebook was the last page she closed out. Her daughter was the main reason Imogen forced herself to be on Facebook in the first place, thinking it added a layer of accountability to Annabel's online life to know her mom was (albeit feebly) somewhere on the site too. She loved the photo Annabel had as her profile picture, an adorable shot of her trying to hold both Johnny and Coco on her lap. She didn't want to snoop, never wanted to snoop, but couldn't help but notice that there was a new comment on the page: "WHATz WRONG WITH YOU? Do you Cry when u look in the mirror bc u r so UGLY?"

Imogen physically doubled over as if she had been punched in the gut. Candy Cool again. It didn't sound like anyone's real name, but Imogen did the Google anyway to see if anything came up. Only the Facebook profile appeared, a picture of a smug little brunette with a perfect complexion except for small scar in the shape of a half-moon on the right side of her chin. Bitch. *Did I just call a ten-year-old girl a bitch?*

Despite Tilly's strategy of noninterference, Imogen's immediate instinct was to protect her sweet and friendly daughter from the words, to toss the computer across the room, shut down Facebook or at the very least delete the offensive post. She began clicking with little direction around the comment, wishing there was a very clear button that just said, "Click me and this will be erased forever." Damn it, why wasn't there a button like that? An "erase me from the Internet forever" button.

Imogen tensed with frustration that she was so impotent. Then. Finally. She found an arrow at the top right corner of the comment and clicked a pull-down menu that allowed her to hide the offensive post from the timeline, feeling a small sense of accomplishment. Maybe she *could* protect her daughter from the evils of the Internet.

She refocused. Into Google she typed: Breast cancer AND pain. The top hit was Warning Signs of Breast Cancer. She was already too familiar with the light pink website. Sign eight was "a new pain in one spot that does not go away." It was the same as before. They didn't get all of the cancer. She had known this was a possibility. It was one she dwelled on during the early days after her surgery, worrying about going through this all over again and maybe again after that, living in a constant state of recovery, never being able to fully return to a normal life.

She wanted to scream. She wanted to cry. She cursed herself. She cursed her job. She cursed Alex for not taking the high-paying corporate job he was offered two years ago that would have meant she was no longer the breadwinner of this family, even though she had told him not to. She cursed Worthington for turning her goddamned magazine into an app that she didn't understand. She just stared for a while. Out the window, across the street, she could see a small man walking a very large dog, a Great Dane. Johnny loved Great Danes, had ever since he was small. He referred to them as the ponies of the Wet Billage, which was the way he had pronounced West Village until just last year. She desperately wanted a cigarette and understood the irony of wanting to smoke when she learned she had cancer again, and didn't care. She wondered if she still had packs hidden in the house. When she first quit she used to hide them far back in the freezer just in case she needed one. She knew they weren't in there now. That was a year ago. She'd been good, only bumming a fag here and there at a party after a cocktail or two. She needed to call the doctor. It wasn't even seven a.m. No one would answer before nine. She threw on her favorite worn Lanvin cardigan and walked around the block to Jack's Stir Brew Coffee to stand impatiently in line behind two women in tweed pants debating the benefits of adding lavender to their coffees. The mommies at school had started drinking lavender-infused everything. People will buy anything if they think it's good for them. They will pay extra if it's beautiful. A real lavender moment was happening right now.

Back outside on the street she said a quick hello to Jack, the shop owner, who was sitting on the bench outside the bright red door, *The Times* sprawled across his lap as he sipped on his hardcore Ethiopian brew. Jack was a former banker who had used his parents' money to create more money and then lost most of it in a real estate deal gone wrong. The coffee shop was his second act, which came with a second wife and a new baby.

The smell of coffee wafted through the air, promising the next best thing to nicotine—caffeine. She felt more human already.

"I haven't seen you in ages," Imogen leaned in to kiss his scruffy cheek.

"We haven't gone out since Kip was born."

"You poor love. It gets better, I promise." She must have been wincing.

"Imogen, are you okay?" She held back the tears threatening to spill down her cheeks.

"I'm fine, darling. A bit sleepy. Hoping a bit of your delicious coffee will snap me out of it." He nodded in understanding.

"I can't wait to sleep again." He groaned. "Maybe once he's eighteen?" Imogen laughed and nodded in mock seriousness. They made a small cheers with their respective caffeinated beverages and Imogen headed back toward her house.

Walking through the door, she felt the fire in her breast flare up again. She'd quit the serious painkillers just a week after her surgery. They made her feel woozy and not altogether there, but she couldn't take it any longer. Her arm shook as she reached for the little orange bottle. The tears finally came when she couldn't get the lid off. She swallowed three in quick succession and then lay down next to Alex.

Imogen woke to a light slap across her cheek.

"There you are. I nudged you, I squeezed you, I touched you inappropriately and you wouldn't open your eyes. I was starting to get a little bit worried. Imogen Tate never sleeps past noon."

She stretched her arms over her head and in doing so felt the pinch again, letting out a cry mixed with surprise and pain.

"What's going on, babe?"

She didn't want to keep it to herself any longer.

"The cancer's back," she whispered.

Alex's face switched from cuddly hubby to rapid-fire litigator.

"What? That's not possible."

"It is. I'm in so much pain. It's one of the symptoms. It's one of the ways you know they didn't get it all. I have pain in a new spot, a spot that never hurt before. It feels like it's on fire."

Alex grabbed his glasses off the night table.

"Show me."

"Show you the website that told me this?"

"Show me your breast. Show me where it hurts."

"You're not a doctor." Imogen pulled her sweater tighter across her chest.

Alex sighed. "I just want to try to help. I don't know what else to do. Did you call the doctor yet?"

"No, I took a pill and fell asleep before I could." Imogen grew defensive.

"I'll call her. You stay here." Alex was back to being sweet. She couldn't help but doze again once he left her alone in the bed. Sleep let her leave the pain behind.

"Your oncologist is out at the beach for the weekend for her daughter's birthday. She will come back late tomorrow night and see you first thing on Monday morning. Can you hang on until then?" Alex said when he reappeared.

Imogen nodded and then shook her head.

"Shit! I have to meet with Eve and Lucia van Arpels for breakfast Monday morning." Lucia van Arpels was the best-known women's contemporary designer and the woman single-handedly responsible for the creation of the wrap dress in the seventies and its resurgence in the early 2000s. For sale at more than $400 a piece, the dresses were a staple of every professional woman's closet. She hadn't yet agreed to let Glossy.com sell her pieces and Imogen knew she was stubborn about which retailers—brick-and-mortar and digital—carried her dresses. Imogen thought she could persuade her, had even asked Eve if she could take care of this one on her own, but the girl was adamant about meeting Lucia. She would probably try to take a selfie with her.

"You can't go."

"I can't miss it."

She admired the furrow that cut through Alex's brow as he was working something through in his head. "I'll make you an appointment at eleven," he said. "Go straight from breakfast."

Tilly didn't mind working a few extra shifts through the weekend. Imogen spent the rest of Saturday and Sunday trying not to lift anything or even to move. Both kids were beyond sweet, bringing their iPads into bed to watch movies with her as she drifted in and out of sleep, careful not to lean too hard on her chest.

* * *

Lucia van Arpels arrived everywhere fifteen minutes before she was scheduled to be there so that everyone else had to be there a half hour early if they wanted to beat her to the punch. Arriving first allowed Lucia to scope out the room, choose the best table and then pick the best seat at that table. She preferred to control a situation. Imogen coveted the idea of that kind of control. And so the elegant woman was already on her second cup of coffee when Imogen arrived. High cheekbones made her look more severe than she actually was. Her brown hair all fell to one length and swung expertly atop the neckline of her simple cream cashmere sweater.

Molly Watson had introduced Imogen and Lucia years earlier and the two women had remained friendly ever since, sitting on many of the same boards. Lucia's granddaughter was in school with Johnny. They were trading photos when Eve flounced in the door wearing a bright yellow LvA wrap dress. No one wore the dress of the designer to go meet the designer. Before she sat down Eve snapped her fingers in the air at a passing waiter.

"Can you bring me some lemons for my water?"

At that moment Lucia's phone beeped. She gave an apologetic look as she rose and picked up the device.

"I'm so sorry. I have to take this quickly. We are about to do a major campaign in Japan and they are all about to head home for the day." Imogen nodded.

"That's rude!" Eve said as the waiter delivered a pot of coffee to the table and placed a saucer of limes in front of Eve.

Imogen watched Eve swirl Splenda into her drink. "We all take calls during meals. It's how we live. You of all people know that."

Eve looked at the sliced fruit with disdain. "I asked for lemons. Does that retarded waiter think lemons and limes are the same thing?" Imogen cringed, as Lucia returned to the table.

"Okay, ladies, you have my undivided attention."

First Eve slid a piece of black rubber across the table. The bracelet: "Good, Great, Gorgeous, *GLOSSY.com!*" "So Lucia, I brought this for you. All of the girls in the *Glossy* office wear them." The woman picked it up and turned it over in her hand, squinting at it in confusion.

Next, Eve established her list of bona fides. She prattled on about how she started working for Imogen at *Glossy* (she didn't say "assistant"), went to Harvard for her MBA, graduated at the top of her class. Then she launched into her pitch.

"Allowing us to sell your products will seamlessly integrate magazine content with retail sales. We have a reach of one million eyeballs in a single day, the majority of them high-earning young women."

Eve was charming in her business school way. You could say a lot about the girl, but you could never say that she wasn't smart.

Lucia flagged down a waiter to order a yogurt topped with fruit and a light sprinkling of granola.

"It has so much sugar," she whispered to her tablemates. "Everyone thinks the granola is so healthy, but my nutritionist told me that it's the granola that has been killing me." Imogen ordered the same. Eve just asked for another coffee. She had been on a no-food diet for the past week.

"We've already moved millions of dollars of merchandise," Eve kept on.

Lucia raised her hand. "I'm impressed by your website. I really am. I spent some time on it this weekend. I just don't know if it is the right place to be selling the LvA brand. I don't see the real benefit for us just yet. Dilution of our brand strength is a big concern for me."

Without warning Eve leaned forward importantly and reached her arm across the table. Before Imogen knew what was happening, all five of the girl's bright red talons were covering Lucia's mouth.

"Shush," she said, pressing her fingers into the fashion icon's mouth. Imogen recoiled in horror. A nearby waiter dropped a saucer with coffee. Eve had just shushed Lucia van Arpels in public.

"Lucia." Eve couldn't mask the condescension in her voice. "I have an MBA from Harvard Business School. You need to trust me. I know what is good for your brand better than you do."

Lucia's eyes lit with rage, but she had lived enough lifetimes to know how to handle herself. In a single deft movement she raised her own hand to Eve's and slowly peeled her fingers off her mouth.

"Thank you for enlightening me, Eve." She reached behind her to grab her scarf. "Unfortunately I need to head to another meeting. We'll talk soon." Lucia's gait was even and clipped as she made her way to the door.

Imogen raised her hand in the air to signal the waiter for the check so that she wouldn't have to address what was happening.

"I think she's in," Eve said when Lucia was out of earshot.

Imogen felt her phone buzz with a text. It was Lucia.

>>>>Keep that little brat away from me. I will never do business with her. I don't know how she was raised, but something is very wrong with her.<<<<

"Eve, I don't think it's as simple as that. What you just did was ridiculously rude. You know that, right?"

"What I just did was convince Lucia van Arpels to sell her dresses with us." Eve showed no remorse.

Imogen briefly considered showing the text message to Eve, but thought better of it. Her loyalty now was closer to Lucia than to Eve.

"Eve, I think you just made a huge mistake."

"What do you know anyway, Imogen? You never even look at the website." Eve stood to leave her at the table.

"I'll see you at the office."

"I have another meeting," Imogen said. "I'll be in right after lunch."

Eve shrugged. "Whatever."

CHAPTER TWELVE

The examination table in her doctor's office was surprisingly plush and spa-like. It could have been relaxing if she weren't wearing a paper robe that tied loosely in the front and threatened to open with a sneeze.

Imogen thumbed at Instagram to try to distract herself, feeling a small rush of euphoria at how many likes her previous day's photographs had gotten. She liked a photograph of Bridgett standing in the middle of Seventh Avenue with traffic whizzing by her. God only knew how she had taken that picture. She liked Ashley's #IWoke UpLikeThisSelfie, her eyes even bluer without liner and mascara, her pale hair fanned over half her face.

She liked a photo of Massimo's miniature Yorkie, Ralph. She liked a picture of a woman's bright red nails, her fingers layered in elaborate cocktail rings, holding onto a Céline clutch in the same color. She checked the name on that picture, Aerin2006. The name wasn't familiar, but she didn't know a lot of people in her Instagram feed. She'd asked Tilly to help her find interesting accounts to follow and then left it in her nanny's hands.

She was about to search through the rest of Aerin2006's photos when Dr. Claudia Fong walked quietly into the room. She was an unassuming woman with small glasses and pin-straight long black hair that reached almost to her backside. She shuffled when she walked and murmured when she talked. She was gentle and kind and the best oncologist in Manhattan according to last year's *New York* magazine's Best Doctors issue.

The doctor softly pressed in a circle around Imogen's right nipple.

"The pain is on the left side," Imogen said, too anxiously.

"I know that, Imogen." Claudia smiled, used to anxious patients. "I need to check the healthy one before I check the one you say is bothering you." Imogen nodded and resolved to keep her mouth shut and let the doctor do her job. When she moved to the left side she cautioned, "This may hurt," before launching into her favorite diatribe about why New York continued to be an unsuitable place to live.

"Why do we live in New York, Imogen? Why? I keep asking myself that every single day. Humans aren't meant to live like this and I don't just mean the cold. We work all the time. We never have enough money. We never do those things that allegedly make New York such a great place to live." She put air quotes around the words "great place to live." "I keep telling my husband we should go to Santa Fe. I had an aunt in Santa Fe. Dry heat there."

Imogen nodded supportively even as it began to hurt when the doctor pressed her fingers into the soft tissue around her nipple. Her breast felt like it was clamped in a vise every time the doctor pushed down, which was why Imogen was shocked when Dr. Fong finally smiled, Santa Fe a distant memory for the time being.

"I don't feel anything at all abnormal, Imogen. But I want to do a mammogram just to be sure. Let's get you back into the X-ray room and get one done straightaway so that we can assuage your fears."

That wasn't possible. Imogen knew that her cancer was back. She could feel it, feel it growing inside her and taking back control of her life. The mammogram would prove Dr. Fong wrong.

But it didn't. Sitting in Dr. Fong's office, the inside of her breast illuminated on a flat screen in front of her, even Imogen had to admit that both sides looked like they contained healthy tissue. Dr. Fong traced the edges of the illuminated breasts with a lighted pointer.

"See, here are the implants. You can tell because they are less dense than real tissue. But you still have some of your own tissue right around the nipple and underneath the implants." She pointed to a cloudy mass. "That tissue appears more dense, but it also appears completely healthy. Imogen, I think what you are experiencing is phantom pain."

This made her feel hysterical. "You think I am making this all up?"

Dr. Fong quickly shook her head. "No, I don't think that at all. Phantom pain is actually very real. It's a lousy name. Sometimes it can originate in a patient's head, but it is most often because the nerves are short-circuiting a little bit, as they are getting used to the surgery. They are sending pain messages to the brain when they shouldn't be there. Pain is useful for us. Pain tells us when something is wrong with our bodies. Think of pain as a referee throwing up little red flags all over the place. In this case the pain made a mistake. There is nothing wrong with you, Imogen. I promise."

"What should I do?"

"Try to relax through it. I'll prescribe some more painkillers. I need you to keep up with the exercise of your chest and your arm." Dr. Fong finished taking notes on her tablet and started writing out a prescription. "Keeping those muscles strong will help you heal even faster. Beyond that I can't tell you much else except that I am incredibly pleased with your progress."

Imogen felt relief coupled with annoyance. Phantom pain wasn't something she wanted to say to people. It sounded like something she made up.

"What do I tell Alex?" Dr. Fong could tell that Imogen was displeased with the diagnosis.

"Tell him the truth. Your nerves are getting used to the new tissue and there is a learning curve. You don't ever actually have to say the word 'phantom.'"

Sometimes fake felt so real.

Imogen sank back onto the table and typed out a text to Alex:

>>>>Tests okay. You get to keep me.<<<<

Was it possible the entire scene with Lucia van Arpels hadn't happened, that Imogen had imagined the entire thing? She kept replaying it over and over in her head as she popped into the chemist to fill her prescription and then again on the way to the office—Eve's hand moving in slow motion across the table. The whites of Lucia's eyes expanding as she tried to comprehend what was being done to her. It couldn't have been real. It was too much like a scene out of a movie. But when Imogen glanced down at her phone, there was Lucia's text to her.

Eve was perched on a table in the kitchen regaling the staff about her meeting with Lucia when Imogen walked in to make an espresso.

"And then I just told her, 'I know what is good for your brand.' You should have seen her face."

"Yes, you should have." Imogen wished she weren't still surprised at Eve's nerve, but it managed to blindside her at least twice a day.

"Eve, let's have a chat about this in my office."

Eve popped off the table and did a small dance, biting her bottom lip and shaking her ass.

Imogen had no choice but to show Eve the text. "She won't work with you again, Eve. What you did just made you a techbitch in Lucia van Arpels's world."

The word "bitch" didn't faze her in the least. If anything it ener-gized her. The girl twirled a piece of hair around her finger. "It's not my fault she can't see that we're the future. She needs us."

"No, Eve, right now we need her more than she needs us. We need people like Lucia to want their designs sold with us. Lucia's dresses are the kinds of things our readers will really want to buy."

Eve shrugged. "So call her back. We'll have another meeting."

"She won't take another meeting with you, Eve. That's the point I am trying to make."

"Fine. What do we do?"

Imogen sighed. "Money talks, Eve. We offer to buy two million dollars at wholesale to prove how serious we are about moving her inventory."

Eve scoffed. "Two million dollars is crazy. That's like thirty percent of our new round of investment."

"It's the only way to save this situation with Lucia. And I can tell you another thing, Eve. Lucia doesn't have a big mouth, but her staff does, and unless you want to get us blackballed in this town, we need to find a way to mend this situation."

Eve lifted her eyes and fixed Imogen with a look of utter bewilder-ment.

This was the part of the job that was making Imogen feel ill. When she described what she was doing to Massimo, he referred to it as being paid to open your kimono. Imogen was opening up her network to Eve. No, she was opening up her network to Glossy.com. That was how she had to think of it. She was doing what was best for the company. But at what price? How long could she protect *Glossy*'s reputation from Eve's antics?

"Pay the bitch then." Eve stood. "I didn't do anything wrong. I was assertive in that meeting, Imogen. If I were a man in that meeting Lucia would've called me powerful."

If she'd been a man in that meeting Lucia would have called her abusive, Imogen thought irritably. She had always agreed with the hypothesis that men in powerful positions could be complete bastards and be promoted, while women could be called cows for the smallest offense. Still, even Donald Trump couldn't have gotten away with what Eve did.

"Maybe you should try keeping your hands to yourself in the next meeting, Eve."

* * *

GChat between Eve and Ashley:

GlossyEV: I need to vent for a min. About Imogen. I MEAN SERIOUSLY?

Ash:??

GlossyEV: Why doesn't she understand how to do ANYTHING? I swear something is always wrong with her computer or her phone or her iPad. She swears it is never her. It is always the fault of the technology. I can hear her huffing in her office RIGHT NOW.

Ash: She's getting better.

GlossyEV: It's just cray that someone made it so far in their careers without ever learning how to use any kind of technology. I try to help her. I do. I am a nice person. You know I am a nice person. It's just so frustrating. I can't keep repeating myself. "Tell me my password again, darling," she titters as though it's adorable that she is as forgetful as an Alzheimer's patient.

Ash: *shrug*

GlossyEV: And what about when she talks to the screen like extra loud like a dumb American in Europe for the first time. Just figure it out ALREADY. I don't know how you do it. How r u so nice to her?

Ash: *shrug*

GlossyEV: ROFL

Ash: She's learning. It's getting better.

GlossyEV: Not fast enough.

Eve slipped out of her heels, Louboutin knockoffs she ordered from Korea, to stretch her calves. She rose onto her bare toes and rocked back on her heels a few times.

It was proven that people made decisions quicker when they stood up at work. Sitting at a desk all day made people lazy.

Eve's desk was immaculate except for her devices: a laptop, an iPad mini, an iPhone and a Samsung Android. She craved order. All of the other girls back home had rooms filled with trophies and riding ribbons. Eve kept those things in a pretty little box under her bed. She prided herself on having a room as neat as a hotel suite.

She had been the right amount of assertive with Lucia. It wasn't like she face-palmed her or anything. She'd made an affectionate gesture with her hand, that was all. Imogen needed to quit it with the overreaction.

How much longer did they need Imogen Tate here anyway? It was nice to keep her around for the transition, but was she more trouble than she was worth? She'd just cost them a lot of money. Worthington really liked her, but if Eve could prove that Imogen wasn't a team player for the new Glossy.com maybe he wouldn't want to keep her around anymore. He was a man after her own heart, one who thought in terms of cash instead of emotions. So what if he was a little Handy McGrabberson under the table during their meetings? He could paw at her bare thigh all day for all she cared. Maybe she would invite him out to dinner next week, slip into that low-cut new Alaïa dress she'd ordered (from the site, natch!) and see what he had to say about Imogen's future with the company.

CHAPTER FOURTEEN

NOVEMBER 2015

The Human Resources department for Robert Mannering now mandated that two people be in the room whenever someone was being let go from the company in case the aggrieved party made a scene or later claimed they were fired under unfair circumstances. The decree was handed down after Eve fired three people by text message. For no discernible reason Eve decided that third party would be Ashley Arnsdale, and bearing witness to biweekly executions, as she had come to think of them, had become a part of Ashley's job description that she never talked about with anyone.

Back in the summer of 2009, Ashley had been fired from Old Tyme Ice Cream out in Montauk, where her parents had their summer house.

"You are so good at so many things," Mr. Wilson, the shop's long-time proprietor had said to her. "But you are terrible at scooping ice cream." It was fair and true. Ashley spent most of her time chatting with the customers about the ice cream, rather than serving it to them. Mr. Wilson at least let her go with a week's pay and a kind smile. Eve smiled when she fired people, but it wasn't kind.

"I just don't see how you are useful to this site," Eve said to the young male engineer sitting in front of her in the conference room, well after ten p.m. one night. Weren't there rules about firing someone this late?

"Seriously," Eve continued. "Prove to me that you should keep this job when the rest of your team has worked at least ten more hours than you have in the past three weeks."

Oh jeez. Ashley wanted to hide beneath the big white conference table. Or hug him. Or both. Humans shouldn't treat other humans like this. This was literally the worst.

"I'm here until midnight every night," he countered meekly.

"The rest of your team sleeps here," she said, her lips curling at the end. "You aren't a team player. You don't want to succeed. Plus . . ." Eve paused and made a show of looking at his grimy Converse sneakers and plaid button-down over a faded gray T-shirt with a Stormtrooper on it. He was tall and doughy, with a belly that belied too many nights of Seamless. His eyes were slightly crossed. "I just don't think you are a cultural fit here."

He looked like every other tech dude that Ashley knew. This was their uniform: sneakers, jeans, button-down. Eve just liked saying words like "cultural fit." She learned them in business school. The lingo reminded Ashley of Benji, her college boyfriend who went to Northwestern B-school right after college. That guy was a douche.

There was no correct response to "cultural fit." It wasn't like Eve said, "You dress like a slob or a homeless person." But it was a lie. Eve was trying to outsource all their engineering jobs to the Balkans, an apparent new hotbed of nerd talent. Ashley focused on a moth across the room, desperately beating its wings against the glass wall. *I feel you, buddy,* she thought.

Ashley felt the urge to make a joke to lighten the mood, but she didn't dare. She'd learned six firings ago not to interrupt Eve. When she did, Eve turned on her. It was best to sit as still as possible. There really wasn't a worse person for this job though. Ashley had no poker face. When she knew Eve's attention was directed the other way she would silently mouth, "It's okay," and, "I'm sorry," to the former employees. She'd have to bring this up in therapy tomorrow. She'd been going twice a week since August and had just hit the amount for her deductible, so now she was going three times a week. Free therapy! Woo hoo!

"You're just not good enough to work at Glossy.com," Eve concluded this time and stood, walking out of the room without another word.

The engineer turned his tired eyes to Ashley in disbelief.

"I'll help you clean out your desk," she said before lowering her voice and handing him a slip of paper with her cell phone number on it. "I might have some work for you on a top secret project."

* * *

Imogen worried she might be growing more invisible. She was no fool. Each day that she was still editor in chief could very well be her last. The fashion industry had always been cutthroat. You were only as good as your last collection, your last shoot or your last cover. To call this world judgmental was a grievous understatement. For a long time, Imogen had done all the right things. She'd craft a brilliant cover line she knew would sell. And it would. She would find a young twig of a girl and turn her into the next Kate Moss or connect a talented no-name designer with a massive label to make him or her the next big thing. Along the line the career hadn't been so much a choice as something that was an inescapable part of her character.

What she couldn't deny was that this new world was making her feel like a fucking dummy. Angry and stupid was not exactly a winning combination for an editor in chief. She nodded along to the metrics that the little girls in her office were showing her, but it might as well have been a bird's nest of figures, for all Imogen could untangle them in her head. The rules ceased to exist. A career was no longer linear. Eve proved that, leapfrogging straight from assistant to a number two (maybe a number one).

Each day Eve found new ways to make Imogen feel subordinate. She left Imogen out of meetings and she made big decisions without consulting her, including the hiring of new staff.

Of course, there were some things Imogen loved about this new world. The instant connection to an entirely new group of people through Instagram and Twitter was just as addictive as a jolt of caffeine. The favorites, the likes and the retweets all made her feel a strange sense of validation, which didn't jibe at all with how she felt in real life. In the Insta-filtered world she was bathed in this kind of golden glamour that made everything look perfect, when outside the filter she sometimes had trouble remembering to breathe.

This must have been what workers felt like during the Industrial Revolution. All of a sudden their entire lives were upended. One month they had a small family business making horseshoes or cheese for their neighbors and the next they were forced into a factory to make things for nameless, faceless customers. That was how Imogen felt about the Internet. Sure, she never met most of the readers back when *Glossy* was a magazine, but she felt a connection with them. She *understood* them. She didn't quite get the young women who clicked on "20 Essential Items to Make Pumpkin Picking Chic" or "The 10 Weight Training Tricks You Can Do in Your Car with a Water Bottle." She desperately wanted to understand them, to climb inside their millennial brains and knock around the wires and coils to figure out what made them tick.

A heaviness enveloped Imogen the first thing every morning. Its weight dared her to rise out of the bed against it. No matter how early she woke up, her in-box was buried in emails, most of them composed of abbreviated words and phrases written in a Joycean stream of consciousness from Eve sent at all hours of the night. When you're on top of the world, getting out of bed is such a simple thing. When life makes a wrong turn, just pulling off the covers can be the hardest thing you do all day. *I just want to lie here,* a voice in Imogen's head whispered as she buried her face in her pillow each morning.

Where she had once left the office every night at six, she now found herself having to sneak out to make it home by nine p.m.

On one of those nights Imogen stumbled upon a girl weeping in the elevator.

It could have been any night of the week. The schedule never changed. There was no longer the rhythmic play of the monthly magazine schedule, when it became frenetically busy, then relaxed, before picking up to start all over again. She tried desperately to maintain a small amount of editorial control, at least glancing at things now before they went up on the website, sometimes giving them a hard edit, approving and discarding photos.

She had never been a true line editor, but she had also never seen more errors in her entire life.

"Who is editing these?" she'd asked Eve that morning.

Eve barely looked up from her laptop as she shrugged her bare shoulders. "No one. They go straight on the site. It's the Internet. It can always be fixed."

"You don't think it's sloppy?"

"I think more is better."

The conversation ended there.

It was nonstop. The site was updated twenty-four hours a day, content determined by traffic. If a certain celebrity got engaged then the site could do as many as thirteen related fashion posts on that celebrity's style, her fiancé's style, their future child's style and the obligatory wedding style. Right now they averaged more than one hundred pieces of content a day. All of it ended with the same juvenile tag line: "Make sure you never miss any of our LOL-worthy stuff! Sign up for the *Glossy* newsletter today!"

Leaving at eight felt like a luxury when there was still an army of women inside the office clacking away at their keyboards, nibbling on the sushi platters Eve ordered in for dinner and chugging their cheerfully colored Organic Avenue juices and diet Red Bulls.

Imogen felt guilty about staying and guilty about going home. She never turned the lights out in her office. She would leave a sweater behind on her chair, her computer screen on and the office fully aglow, hoping to create the impression that she could be somewhere else in the building at any given time. At the end of the day she knew she wasn't fooling Eve. Something told her that Eve knew exactly where she was at any given moment. There was probably an app for that.

The girl was already standing at the elevator bank when Imogen arrived. Her perfectly round head hung limp and her shoulders shook. She walked quietly into the elevator once it reached their floor and kept her face to the back wall instead of turning forward. It was only after the doors closed safely behind her that she let loose a wail like an animal being led to the slaughterhouse. She was just a speck of a thing, with hair the shade of honey. She looked vaguely familiar to Imogen, but there were so many new faces in the office these days. They all blended into one another.

Moments like these made Imogen feel validated in still carrying a small embroidered white handkerchief in her purse. She had small bags of Kleenex as well, the kind you purchase in bulk a month after becoming a mother. Imogen tapped the girl quietly on the shoulder and offered up her proper handkerchief. The girl took it without glancing up and wiped mascara down her cheeks before blowing her nose and letting loose another wail straight from the bowels of hell.

"It can't be all that bad." Imogen patted her uncertainly. Why did she say that? She knew exactly how bad it was in that office.

"It is. She's a witch." The girl finally turned her exhausted eyes up at Imogen. "I did everything Eve asked me. I've been working for three days straight. Then I fell asleep at my desk. She told me that only losers need sleep. That was it. That was enough for her. She just fired me. Right in front of everyone. She told me to pack up my things and go home and not bother to come back tomorrow."

Now Imogen recognized the girl as one of the editorial assistants Eve hired to do the typical assistant duties, transcribing, answering phones, setting up market appointments, the things she had done herself just a few years before.

"Why haven't you been home in three days?"

"Didn't you get the memo? She told us we all had to stay to help meet the traffic goals she set for the investors by the end of the month. She set up air mattresses back in the supply closet. We take turns back there, but it was loud. I had a hard time falling asleep."

Now Imogen could see the dark circles beneath the young woman's eyes, giving her the appearance of someone much older.

"I've seen a lot of people besides me get fired," the girl said. "It's sort of like, 'Let's see who lasts the longest.'"

There was nothing Imogen could say. She'd heard whispers of how Eve fired people, but she had never been around to witness it. She'd assumed she did it late at night. Eve was on such a hiring streak that Imogen could barely keep track of who was coming in, and she definitely couldn't keep track of who was going out.

"I'm sorry" was all she could think to say. "No one deserves to be let go like that." Imogen didn't even know if it was legal to let someone go like that. She had fired only three employees in her life and each time she'd had to create a monthlong paper trail of their offenses and had a member of the Human Resources staff present. For a second the girl looked at Imogen with pity in her eyes, as if she believed Imogen could be the next one bawling in an elevator.

There were only a few floors to go. "I don't have any savings. I won't be able to pay my rent next month." It wasn't a plea. The young woman said it as a fact, as if she needed to say it out loud to make sure that the universe knew it was true.

She didn't have anything left to say to Imogen. The girl strode fast onto the street, not bothering to look back. Imogen stepped into the lobby and then pivoted into the elevator, pushed a button and watched it light up for the twenty-seventh floor.

As Imogen stepped back into the office, she saw Eve standing tall in the middle of the room.

"Go!" she yelled. Twelve young women were lined up on opposite sides of the room. Each of them held a silver spoon out in front of her and on top of that was balanced a white egg. When Eve shouted they ran across the room, eggs flying off half the spoons and splattering on the ground. The room was fraught with the anxiety of planned fun, the kind commonly experienced on holidays like New Year's Eve and Halloween. You played, you partied, you danced, you drank, you balanced an egg on a spoon in a midtown office building. You did these things because everyone else was doing them and someone told you this was what you were meant to be doing to have a good time. But the women in the room just looked tired. Imogen knew they would rather be at their desks finishing whatever it was that was still on their to-do lists so they could go home to their own apartments and have fun with their real friends and real families.

"Break time is over." Eve clapped her hands and with that everyone scattered back to their desks, leaving the egg yolks coagulating on the floor.

Eve had noticed Imogen when she walked into the room, but waited until her game was over to acknowledge her. "Hey, Imogen. I thought you had gone home for the night."

"I just popped downstairs for a macchiato."

"Where's the coffee?" Eve countered, smiling knowingly.

"I drank it on the walk back. Could we chat in my office?"

Eve shrugged and trailed behind her. The lights had been turned out and the computer shut down. Imogen knew that wasn't how she had left things just ten minutes earlier.

"Did you turn off my computer?"

"Of course not." Eve rolled her eyes aggressively. "I never come into your office. One of the cleaning ladies must have done it or something."

"Who was that girl you just let go? She was bawling in the elevator."

Eve flicked her hand. "Just an assistant. I let all of them go today."

Imogen wanted to reply slowly to make sure the right words came out of her mouth. "We need assistants. Have you talked to HR about hiring new ones tomorrow?"

"No need. I have a plan. It's going to save us a ton of money so that we can hire new content producers in their place."

Imogen raised her eyebrows, indicating Eve should continue her explanation.

"I'm outsourcing all of the assistant duties offshore. One of my friends from B-school just started the most amazing virtual assistant company. For just five dollars an hour you can farm out all the menial work we have those office assistants doing. We can have them transcribe interviews, make appointments, order office supplies. They'll even order delivery food for you. It's so disruptive. It's genius."

Imogen shook her head. "You know the point of having assistants in the office is to eventually train them up to work on more and more things and then to promote them. I started out as an assistant. You started out as an assistant, remember." Imogen took in a deep breath, catching a whiff of Eve's Miss Dior perfume.

Eve flicked her hand again. "Yes, but we don't need them anymore. That's how things used to get done. I'm creating a new system, Imogen." Now Eve was scowling. "Why can't you accept the changes I am making around here. I brought *Glossy* into the twenty-first century and I want to bring you with me, but you aren't helping me."

"Some of the old systems actually work, Eve. We don't need to throw everything out to start something new just for the hell of it."

Eve continued. "Come on. Let me do my job. I am letting you do yours. Go home and spend time with your kids. I know you weren't getting a macchiato. You just came back up here to lecture me. Point taken. I'll see you tomorrow."

The women were all back at their desks, their headphones on and their fingers flying furiously over their keyboards. Imogen felt stunned, but was reluctant to make a scene. She made her way to the elevator, careful not to put her heel in gooey egg along the way.

CHAPTER FIFTEEN

Imogen arrived home and drew herself a long bath, pouring a glass of wine and trickling a bit of lavender oil into their antique claw-foot tub. She liked her lavender better in her tub than in her coffee. She and Alex discovered the tub at a tiny antiques shop upstate in Phoenicia and spent hours negotiating for it, only to find out that it had a terrible leak once they got it home. They had to have the entire thing resealed and it cost them a small fortune, but Imogen loved it so much she believed it was completely worth all of the trouble. It was deep enough that she didn't have to slouch to slide her entire body beneath the water. She was able to submerge herself up to the middle of her neck in water scalding almost to the point she couldn't stand it.

Annabel was asleep when she got home. Imogen kept thinking back to those comments she'd seen on her daughter's Facebook page. What kind of monster would write that kind of thing to a little girl? She didn't know how to bring it up without looking like she was spying on her daughter, a surefire way, she knew, to make any and all personal conversations end before they even had a chance to begin.

Everything was a mess. Her daughter was being bullied online and she was being bullied at work. She woke each day with a pit in her stomach about the very thought of walking into that office and seeing Eve. Not a morning passed when Eve didn't comment on something Imogen didn't know or had done wrong. She didn't send a document in the right format. Why didn't she understand how to access the photographs they now stored in the cloud and not on the server? You know you don't have to reply all to emails! You know you should reply all to emails more often! Could she tweet more?

There was now a very clear line drawn through the story of her life, Before Eve and After Eve. It should be Before Cancer and After Cancer, but Imogen wasn't certain that the cancer had more of an impact on her well-being than the reappearance of Eve in her life.

We all have tropes that run rampant in our heads. Before Eve, Imogen thought endlessly about being the best editor in chief out there, about beating the competition, about selling more magazines. That little voice told her that *Glossy* could always be better if she just tried harder. Now that little voice changed its tune. Now she was no longer good enough. Now it told her to just give up because she couldn't survive here.

She stretched her leg out, which felt good, and wiggled her toes. Decades of six-inch heels did feet no favors.

The hot water from the faucet falling created a pleasantly thumping crescendo and Imogen indulged in a new fantasy. What if they just left? What if they gave up the wildly expensive mortgage on their town house and the private school tuitions? What if they packed it all up and moved to New Orleans? Taking a large swallow of wine, she remembered how much she fucking loved New Orleans.

What would it cost to live in New Orleans? Maybe a fifth of what it cost them to keep up appearances in New York? She picked up her phone from the little vintage bamboo table she kept by the tub and fumbled with her wet hands for the real estate app, the one Tilly downloaded for her. Careful to keep the device above the water, Imogen pecked in some parameters. New Orleans—Garden District—Bedrooms (4+).

So many options. She shook bits of water off her thumbs so she could scroll down the smooth screen. Then she fell in love.

It was a nineteenth-century historical manse in the Garden District. Peculiar and beautiful, with its all-white exterior and robin's-egg-blue trim, a formidable wrought-iron fence wound lazily around the property. Enlarging the picture allowed a glimpse of a rickety porch swing. The price for this gem was less than 20 percent of what they'd paid for this town house.

Down south, Alex could put up a shingle as a local attorney, fixing DUIs and divorces. The kids could go to public school. She'd find the space to figure out what she wanted to do next, what she could do next. Photography? Interior design? Both fields were different and digital now, but she had an eye. It was the only place in the world besides New York City where she felt like she could thrive as a creative person.

Butterflies fluttered in her belly. She was excited. New Orleans would be new and fresh. A challenge, sure, but a new challenge. Goddamn it. Did everything always have to go in a straight line? Her career could move across a diagonal. What if Alex came home and she just said, "Leave your goddamned job"? She could have choices!

Imogen finished her wine. Why didn't she bring the bottle upstairs?

The phone slipped from her hand onto the bath mat.

You think New York is everything, until it isn't anymore.

She sighed. It really was just a dream. Sure, getting rid of the house and the private school would give them some breathing room, but both Imogen and Alex had aging parents, both with little in the way of retirement savings. Then there was her pile of medical bills, growing all the time, which needed the attention of her jaunty Robert Mannering Corp. insurance plan.

The weight of an entire family cleaved to her shoulders. No matter how much hot water she put in the tub now a chill crept over her and goose pimples prickled the surface of her skin.

CHAPTER SIXTEEN

DECEMBER 2015

An excerpt from "Recess Theory," by Axelrod MacMurray:

We need to be happy in order to be productive. We need to push the boundaries of the workplace and allow adults to tap into their inner child in order to maximize success and innovation. It is important for the adult employee to be given time to be social in an unstructured and creative way during the work day and it is incumbent upon managers to foster this. The focus of the play should not have a goal. Used properly in the workplace, an hour of playtime will ultimately increase your output exponentially.

In 2013, a squat, balding Harvard Business School professor named Axelrod MacMurray (Stanford PhD, Harvard MBA) wrote a book proposing the "Recess Theory." It was based on a proprietary study conducted over several years by Dr. MacMurray himself that proved even adults needed an hour of unstructured "play" to bolster their productivity in other parts of their lives.

After Eve took MacMurray's class in 2014, she very briefly became his most devoted student and sometime late-night companion.

Their fleeting, but apparently playful and productive, time together could have been what inspired Eve to take the whole office on an outing to Spirit Cycle for a spin class. All of the mommies at school swore by Spirit Cycle, this kind of New Agey take on cardio spin that was supposed to unite body and soul. Imogen thought it sounded like bollocks. She'd been a runner in her twenties and through most of her thirties. Mainly she just ate right and did Pilates with her trainer. In the same way that she'd missed the Atkins craze in the early 2000s, spin somehow passed her by.

It would be nice to get out of the office early though. The Spirit Cycle studio was close to her town house and she planned to go home straight after, which significantly lifted her mood as she walked into the dark cycling studio with its bright yellow bikes and inspirational words written on the walls.

Eve strutted into the studio, a vision in Spirit Cycle yellow pants and stringy top, her hair pulled up into a high ponytail on top of her head.

"Yeah, Spirit!!! I love it here. We're gonna get our spirit on." She high-fived the instructor as the other girls from the office climbed onto their bikes. Imogen had taken the funny shoes with the metal clips on the bottom from the front desk and clomped the rest of the way back into the cycling room, but once she found herself on the bike she hadn't a clue how the bloody things worked. She tried angling her foot flat against the pedal, hoping it would quickly clip in. Nothing happened. She made these odd clanging sounds as pedals and shoes around the room mated in satisfying *click-click*s.

The anxiety of not doing it properly just compounded each time her foot slid off the pedal without that requisite *click*.

Ashley planted herself on one side of Imogen in the front row. Eve was on the other. Ashley quietly reached down to guide Imogen's toe into place. *Click.*

The instructor bounced up and down on a podium lit only by candles that smelled like grapefruit.

"Heya, Spirit sisters!" she hollered into a headset mounted on top of her white-girl dreadlocks. Eve leaned in to Imogen to whisper, "The instructor is Angelina Starr. She's, like, a spin goddess."

Angelina Starr? It is obviously a stage name, Imogen thought. *When did spin instructors start warranting stage names?* Angelina Starr was too tanned and too made-up to be breaking a sweat. She wore nothing but a teensy yellow bandeau top and teeny-weeny black Lycra panties.

Eve and the girls in the room who were obviously Spirit regulars chanted back in unison, "Heya, Angelina!"

"Everyone got everything?"

"I would quite like a water." Imogen raised her hand politely, which made Angelina sneer.

"Oh, would you now? Could I get you some skim milk with that? Would you like Splenda too? How about I come over there and braid your hair?" As Imogen's jaw dropped, Angelina just as quickly turned her attention back to the rest of the room.

"Who's ready to get their SPIRIT on?" the instructor yelled.

"We are," they singsonged in a chorus.

Jay-Z's *Black Album* began blasting through hidden speakers as the instructor mounted her bike and began a monologue.

"We're here for us. We're here for one another. No one speaks during this class. We ride together. You are here for you and for your Spirit sisters. We are all one. Before we start riding you are going to write down your Spirit sister's name. She's right next to you. You will write down her name and you will put it in your shoe." A group of employees all wearing matching yellow Spirit shirts walked around the room with small pieces of paper and miniature golf pencils.

Eve scrawled her name in cursive and thrust the small piece of paper at Imogen.

"Put my name in your shoe," she commanded in a voice devoid of emotion.

Was this the stupidest thing Imogen had ever been asked to do?

"And now your Spirit sister's name will give you energy all the way from your feet up to your heart," the instructor continued. "Let's ride. You Spirit warriors in the front row. You owe it to your sisters to set an example. I would rather you slapped my face than slowed down your ride."

What was happening with the temperature in the room? Imogen

suddenly felt much too hot. Buckets of sweat poured down the back of her neck. They had obviously turned the heat up to make you feel like you were working out harder than you actually were. The shoes just felt unstable. She must not be clipped in correctly. Imogen slowed to wiggle her foot out of its cage in an attempt to clip it back in properly, but Angelina Starr began staring a hole straight into her soul.

"The front row must keep the rhythm!" she screamed, obviously to Imogen in particular. "Left. Right. Left. Right."

Pumping her legs to the beat, Imogen wondered why the fuck the spin-mommies at school paid $50 a pop for this. Carefully choreographed movements with your feet strapped to pedals flailing wildly out of control was unnatural, like being tortured. People paid good money to be abused here?

The lights went out. It was pitch-black except for the spooky Salem-like candles in a circle around the instructor.

"Put your right hand on your head!"

"Crunch your tummy!"

"If you yawn, I WILL spit in your face!!!!!!"

"Tuck your booty! Tuck your booty!"

Naturally, Eve was a pro. She bobbed her high ponytail left then right, left then right, tucking and tucking. All the while singing along to the hip-hop songs with the enthusiasm of a Hitler youth.

"You're a better you because you're here!! You're successful!! You're amazing! You are the best you that you can be right here, right now. You love yourself so much. Life is messy! What matters is how we clean it up!!!!" the instructor screamed as Eve pumped both her fists into the air and bellowed, "WOOOOOOOOOO!" This wasn't just a fitness class. It was therapy by way of sweat. You came for the cardio, you stayed for the aphorisms.

Imogen hated it. Near the end of the class her hair was soaked with sweat. Places hurt that shouldn't hurt. She was reminded of the Leonard Cohen lyric, "I ache in the places where I used to play." She'd almost forgotten Eve's name languishing on a piece of paper inside her shoe. Reluctantly, Imogen rose with the rest of the room for one final push toward the finish line.

"Faster. You can see it in the distance. That's your goal. That's why you came here tonight. You are the best version of you right now. Right in this moment."

Imogen pushed harder and harder on the pedals, her legs beginning to move slightly out of control. She could see the finish line in her mind. She raced even faster, no longer paying attention to Eve or Ashley or any of the women in the room.

Click. Her right foot slipped off the pedal. She toppled over to the side. No one missed a beat. Imogen was sandwiched on her bottom in between her bike and Eve's.

After she caught her breath, Imogen looked left and right. Eve's pedal whirred in front of her face like a lawn mower blade.

"Spirit sister . . . help?" Imogen squeaked. And yet her Spirit sister couldn't be bothered to stop until that bike reached the finish line. Eve just kept cycling.

Ashley had sneakily put her headphones on in the class and was completely oblivious to what was happening.

No one would help her. With Eve's legs whirring around it was nearly impossible for Imogen to rise without being maimed. She found herself slithering forward on her stomach toward the podium, where she could finally pull herself up.

As she walked herself to the door and tossed her offensive, faulty shoes in the bin, the class just kept spinning.

CHAPTER SEVENTEEN

Throwback Thursday was one of Imogen's favorite things about Instagram. After Tilly introduced her to the concept of posting a vintage shot once a week she began searching the boxes she kept under her bed for old tear sheets and Polaroids taken backstage at Fashion Weeks and photo shoots over the past twenty years. On Monday she found the perfect picture—a vintage shot, probably twenty years old, of Naomi Campbell, Christy Turlington and Linda Evangelista sipping champagne in a bathtub.

The photograph was worn at its glossy edges, one corner ripped cleanly across. In it, the women are giggling. Naomi is covering her face, an eight-carat diamond on her slender finger, crossing over the top of her lips. Christy is half hidden underneath the other women, only a sliver of her beautifully imperfect face peeking through. Half of the photo is a tangle of long legs, unclear where one body ended and the other began. Imogen had taken the picture in a suite at the Ritz after the couture shows in Paris. It was the perfect moment captured with a Polaroid camera and would have been so much more famous if it had been taken today, but before the Internet only a select few people had ever seen this private moment. Imogen snapped a photo of the old picture with her phone and posted it as she sipped her macchiato at Jack's before heading into the office. "One word: SUPERS.

#ThrowbackThursday." Imogen smiled. She had cracked this whole Insta-shizell game.

"Such a fun Throwback Thursday, Imogen," Natalie, a lovely wisp of a WASP blogger, wearing a cream cable-knit sweater with patches of leather at the elbows on top of teensy black leather leggings and pointy mules, said as she wound her way through the rows of desks.

"Big thanks, darling. I can't tell you how much I adored those girls. That was such a fun day. Pop into my office later and I'll tell you all about it."

"Buzzfeed just reposted it!"

Imogen opened her eyes wide with surprise. "Oh my! Is that a good thing?"

"It's a great thing. I am sure it will be picked up everywhere. So if it's okay with you, I'm going to post it on our website."

"Of course it's okay. Let's make sure we get that traffic." Imogen was almost completely positive that she had used the word "traffic" in the right context there. She held up her hand for a high five. Natalie looked at it in confusion for just a second before earnestly going in for the hand slap. Other members of the team looked up from their previously stony silence and smiled at the interaction. Imogen felt a little lighter than she usually did walking through the office. Today would be a good day.

She could see Eve standing at her desk wearing her Google Glass, her eyes furiously darting between her computer screen and her iPhone. Thankfully she didn't glance up as Imogen walked past, too intent on whatever she was working on. Settled in at her own desk, Imogen checked her Instagram. Her #ThrowbackThursday had 9,872 likes, which was 9,800 more likes than anything else she had ever posted. That Buzzfeed knew what it was doing.

Imogen's phone pinged. Before she even opened it, Imogen could tell it was part of a group text.

It was a collage of four pictures. In one there were two hands clinking champagne glasses. In another a vase of three dozen or so white roses. Then a close-up of an enormous princess-cut diamond ring and in the fourth there were Andrew and Eve kissing, her left hand touching his cheek in a way that made her diamond perfectly catch the light.

Andrew had proposed to Eve. Eve was marrying Andrew. Eve was marrying Imogen's ex-boyfriend. Those three thoughts raced through her head before she had time to process that Eve had just sent a photo collage of her engagement to her entire address book. She heard squeals from a contingent of girls over near Eve's office. Imogen knew she should go over there. The staff would surely judge her if she didn't, but her legs felt like lead. Since the day she met Alex she hadn't given a thought to who Andrew would date after her, except that she pitied the poor girl who came next. Andrew was a man she was sure would never completely change, no matter how successful he became, how high an office he achieved. And yet, it was Andrew she now felt protective of. It wasn't jealousy; it was the nagging feeling that Eve had done this specifically to annoy her. She couldn't let that idea bubble too close to the surface and she most definitely couldn't say it out loud to anyone, since it made her seem incredibly self-important. Perhaps this had nothing to do with her. Eve had a thing for powerful older men and Andrew was exactly that. Andrew liked young, clever women. New York City was filled with both of those kinds of people. Either the universe had played a grand trick on her when it brought this couple together or it had somehow been engineered by Eve to make her feel exactly like this. She shook her head and breathed in through her nose. She had waited too long to go in there and shouldn't wait any longer. Reaching into the mini fridge in her office, Imogen pulled out a bottle of vintage pink Dom Pérignon sent over by Marc Jacobs when she returned to work. About fifteen girls were crowded into Eve's office admiring her ring.

"I told him I wanted a giant diamond," Eve was telling the girls. "It's my insurance policy. He can't back out after getting me a ring like this." Eve laughed the loudest at her own joke.

Imogen stood outside the glass wall and popped the cork, making sure she pointed it away from Eve, despite the dark thoughts lurking in the back of her mind.

"Cheers, darling. It looks like we have something to celebrate."

Eve's look of surprise pleased Imogen. She had not expected her to come over, had expected her to pout. Imogen was so glad she hadn't given her the satisfaction.

"I don't know if we have proper champagne glasses, but I am sure we can find something to toast Eve and Andrew with. And what a lovely collage you made, Eve. I certainly hope you shared that across our social networks." The smile was starting to pain her face, but she managed a joke anyway. "And are our readers able to BUY IT NOW?"

"I did share, Imogen," Eve replied shortly, twisting the ring on her finger. "I somehow doubt that most of our readers could afford a ring like this, but that isn't a bad idea. Maybe I'll put up a few knockoffs." She remained taken aback, as if she expected Imogen to club her with the champagne bottle next. She seemed disappointed, like she wanted Imogen to attack.

"I am going to check the kitchen for some cups." Imogen gave a wink to the crowd. "No one tweet that we are drinking at the office before ten a.m.!"

Four people tweeted that they were drinking champagne at the office before ten a.m., but Imogen didn't pay it any mind. She kept going through the motions of being pleased for Eve.

At noon Eve called everyone into the conference room. She placed both palms down on the conference table and Imogen could tell by the way she kept moving her hand around that she was trying to find the perfect angle to achieve the maximum amount of light glinting off her diamond.

"I want to thank everyone for all of the congratulations this morning," Eve started. "I can't say this was really a surprise. I had been expecting this to happen for a few weeks now. I mean . . . I practically picked this thing out myself. And so I decided to find a way that this wedding can benefit all of us. Andrew and I plan to get married in a month. Literally . . . one month. I mean . . . can you even? 'How is she going to plan a wedding in one month?' is what I know you're thinking. 'Is she crazy?'" Eve twirled her index finger clockwise around her right ear in the universal sign for insanity.

"I assure you I am not nuts. I have a plan. We are going to live-stream my wedding on the *Glossy* site. How cool is that? Everything that the readers see during the wedding will be available for sale on the site, from the bridesmaids' dresses to the guests' dresses and even my dress! They can buy everything right then and there. Can you imagine how cool it will be for a girl sitting at home in Wisconsin looking at her computer screen to feel like she's a part of a fancy black-tie New York City wedding and then be able to buy a version of anything that she sees? I don't want to pat myself on the back, but this is just absolutely genius."

Imogen was trying to think of something to say. It was genius, completely self-aggrandizing, but Imogen had to admit that it was smart—the kind of stunt that would get the app a ton of publicity. Sure, Eve might be criticized by some folks in the media, but this wedding would get her a ton of attention. It was the opposite of what Imogen had wanted on her wedding day.

She and Alex eloped to Morocco and said their actual vows in front of Bridgett and Alex's brother Geno in the most romantic hotel in the world, La Mamounia in Marrakech. She'd never seen a more handsome man than her future husband, wearing a pale blue linen suit she'd borrowed from Ralph, looking like he belonged in a summer fashion campaign. She walked toward him down the aisle in a beautiful foam-white silk bias-cut dress with skinny spaghetti straps, a design by her friend Vera Wang. On her feet she wore super-high silver sandals and her only accessory was a small diamond ring in an antique art deco setting belonging to Grandmother Marretti. The day was heaven on Earth.

But then, to please her mum, Imogen agreed to a second very small, very intimate London church wedding with about forty of her mother's friends and neighbors present in a tiny old Chelsea church with ivy-laced walls and a fantastically jolly vicar.

You could see her mother's house if you craned your neck around the corner.

Imogen was secretly delighted to be able to wear her wedding dress twice. Massimo and Bridgett brought bags and bags of confetti. Her favorite shot of the day was in black and white, confetti everywhere, she and Alex with smiles as wide as the church doors. She didn't need that picture on an Instagram account. It remained clear and in focus in her mind.

Just tea and sandwiches followed. Alex's parents joined them, but the rest of his family had absolutely no interest in making the six-hour flight from Queens to London. The real celebrity of the day was the cake, a meringue with whipped cream, covered in whole strawberries. It was Imogen's dream cake and they spent more on it than they did on the rest of the wedding events combined. For twenty minutes it was the most beautiful cake Imogen had ever seen, five tiers of meringue clouds topped with the ripest strawberries that England had to offer. Everyone oohhhed and ahhhhed over the cake and then turned to take photos of the bride. When they looked back the cake had collapsed inward on itself as if it had been siphoned through a black hole. There was a reason that strawberries don't top meringue cakes. The acid from the fruit makes the entire thing unstable. Though the cake melted into itself before the newlyweds could cut their first slice, it didn't stop them from eating it like soup from bowls.

Smiling at the memory, she saw Eve frown in her direction.

CHAPTER EIGHTEEN

I mogen drank her coffee at her kitchen table and wondered: *Is it normal to stalk someone you don't know on Instagram?* When she gave her a tutorial, Tilly had assured Imogen that she could follow anyone at all, even strangers, preferably strangers.

Aerin2006's Instagram feed was delightful and Imogen couldn't get enough of it. It was also quite clever. When you tapped on one of her pictures, the names of the designers she was wearing appeared as if by magic. *Could just anyone do that?*

Who was this woman behind the well-curated pictures? The account was definitely owned by a woman because half of her posts were her #OOTD, or Outfit of the Day. The photographer always artfully kept her face out of the picture. Most of these were cleverly taken in the back of a taxi on what looked like a ride to work. Imogen also loved the pictures of Aerin2006's beauty products, always laid out on a porcelain bathroom sink. In another shot there were rows and rows of colorful and mouthwatering macarons lined up on a desk at her office, paired with a list of the most delicious flavors you have ever heard of, like Caramel Fleur de Sel, Honey Lavender and Lychee Rose. This was tagged with #ShoppitOffice and #Office Snacks. Google informed Imogen that Shoppit was a relatively new commerce platform trying to compete with Amazon in the high fashion space.

What a refreshing change Aerin2006's Instagram was from the predictable pictures of babies, cats, dogs and bacon that dominated the rest of Imogen's feed. The account was exclusive too. It followed only 97 people in comparison to the 567,000 followers it commanded. Imogen grew intensely excited when she received a notification that Aerin2006 was following her!

She wanted another cup of coffee and considered the Nespresso machine perched on the corner of the granite countertop with a measure of disdain. A well-intentioned gift from Alex to satisfy her morning craving for a macchiato, the machine, apparently the Ferrari of coffeemakers, thwarted her at every attempt, making her feel clumsy and silly. She much preferred her old-fashioned French press, a gift from her mother when she'd gotten her first apartment in New York City and a fail-safe kitchen device for nearly twenty years. This new device came equipped with a cup warmer and a milk frother and six buttons that did something different each time she pushed them.

She pulled out the stained old French press and set the kettle on the stovetop.

While waiting for the water to boil, Imogen commented on one of Aerin2006's photographs of a model hoisting a giant Valentino bag over her head that was juxtaposed with a hockey player hoisting the Stanley Cup high into the air.

"Victory is in the eye of the beholder," Imogen wrote, quite pleased with herself.

She was just finishing up and moving to check her email when Annabel wandered downstairs. It was fifteen minutes earlier than she usually emerged in the morning and she was wearing one of Alex's cable-knit fisherman sweaters over her khaki school pants.

"Does this make me look fat?" she asked. Imogen felt a stab in her stomach hearing her beautiful daughter even say those words out loud. Ever since Annabel was a baby, Imogen had been careful to try to cultivate a positive body image, knowing that her own job as the editor of a magazine about fashion could somehow lead her daughter to doubt her looks. Objectively it was true that Annabel was a beautiful little girl, a replica of Alex. Johnny was the one with the blond curls and fair and delicate features like Imogen's, but Annabel had her husband's dark smoldering looks. She was a healthy size, not stick thin like many of the little girls in her school, but athletic, which was a natural by-product of years of soccer practice and eating well.

"Darling, you look adorable." Annabel winced at the word "adorable." Ten was most definitely too old to be referred to as adorable.

Imogen kept going. She didn't know what else to do. "You look beautiful. Do you want me to braid your hair?" Annabel shook her head, her dark curls moving in waves around her shoulders.

"Are you sure? We can do one of those wonderful wraparound braids, the kind I saw Selena Gomez wearing to her movie premiere last week. I taught myself how to do it from a YouTube video just so I could do it on your hair. I know it will look so pretty on you." Annabel had her arms crossed in front of her still blessedly flat chest and looked at her with skepticism. Imogen could tell the idea of a wraparound braid was incredibly appealing. Maybe now was the time to talk about Candy Cool.

"And is there anything at all you want to talk about?" The girl just shook her head, choosing instead to plop herself in front of Imogen. This was her way of telling her, without telling her, that she did want her hair braided.

Imogen had to stop herself from leaning in to take a whiff of her daughter's head. Ever since they were babies Imogen loved nothing more than smelling Annabel's and Johnny's heads. She thought she would get over it once they no longer had that distinctive new baby smell, but it carried over into their time as toddlers and even now, with Annabel on the cusp of being a teenager. Instead she wound her fingers through Annabel's soft hair, trying to remember what she'd watched on the video the night before. The result was surprisingly good and Imogen asked permission to snap a picture of it for her Instagram.

"I won't put your face in it, I promise."

Annabel's face fell for a second.

"You don't think I am pretty enough to put my face in it?"

"No, sweetie. No, not that at all. I just didn't want to violate your privacy. We can put your face in it." *Who is planting these terrible thoughts in my daughter's head? When had this once confident child become so insecure?*

"No," Annabel replied. "Let's keep my face out of it. Just my pretty hair." Imogen obliged and snapped the photo of the braid winding around the back of her head before helping her daughter get the rest of her things ready for school. As they prepared to head out the door, Imogen smiled when she noticed Aerin2006 liked her braid photo. She left a smiley face emoji in the comments section.

She planned to meet Rashid for coffee before going into the office. He had promised to give her a crash course in traffic. That was specifically what she asked for in the text message she sent him.

>>>>Could you teach me about traffic?<<<<

>>>>U R adorable<<<<

He was already sitting at one of the six tables in Jack's when she arrived, thumbing through something on his iPad, which he quickly stashed away when she walked in, rising to kiss both of her cheeks and then lean in for a hug to top it off. She marveled at his use of color. Today he wore a bright yellow wool overcoat atop a navy sweater, perfectly fitting olive-green flat-front pants that hit right at his ankle and laced black brogues. Did he ever wear socks?

He sat back down. One of the things she liked about Rashid was that he put his electronic devices away during a meeting, giving you his undivided attention, unlike Eve, who behaved as though you were an unwanted distraction keeping her away from her gadgets.

Imogen offered to buy Rashid a macchiato, but he waved her hand away to indicate he had already ordered two for them and that they should be waiting on the counter. Once again she marveled at his efficiency. Sure enough, there they were, two perfectly foam-topped macchiatos just waiting for her to pick them up.

"Rashid, do you know anyone at Shoppit?"

"I do indeed. I went to Stanford with their chief technology officer."

"When, like yesterday?" Imogen teased. Rashid bristled and Imogen remembered it was just as rude to joke about someone being too young as it was to joke about someone being too old.

"Six years ago, thank you very much. Anyway, he is some kind of freak kid genius."

"Isn't that what you are?" Imogen asked.

"No way! Not like this guy. Erik started Stanford when he was fourteen. He stayed there eight years, which is how I got to meet him, but in that time he got a BA and two master's." Imogen, who had never even gone to university, didn't know what to say to that. "Why do you ask?" Rashid's golden eyes looked at her with curiosity.

"I am trying to figure out who someone is who works there. I follow her on Instagram and I like all of her pictures and she likes mine and I am just curious whose pictures I am liking."

Rashid nodded. "Probably Aerin Chang."

"Yes, Aerin2006! That's her. Who is she?"

"She's the CEO over there. And you have good taste. Her Instagram is awesome, isn't it?" Imogen nodded again.

"Is she also, like, ten years old?" She had to stop cracking these jokes.

"I think she graduated in 2006," he replied. Imogen did the mental math. That made her thirty. A thirty-year-old CEO! "Also from Stanford . . . a couple of years before me. She's amazing. The two of you should definitely meet." The idea was creepy to Imogen, starting a friendship online and then moving it offline.

"Maybe you can introduce me one of these days?"

Rashid nodded. "Of course. You'll get along splendidly. She loves fashion, loves designers. She has a real respect for them, not like a lot of these other e-commerce brats." Imogen knew he was talking about Eve. "She has an eye for what works. Now, tell me why you brought me here. Was it really just to help you cyber-stalk Aerin Chang?"

Imogen laughed and shook her head, but that was the main problem with his question. Imogen didn't know exactly what it was that she wanted to know or what she needed from him at all.

She heard the word "traffic" bandied about the office like it was some kind of celebrity. She knew that it meant more people were coming to their website and that was a good thing. What she didn't understand was any of the other things Eve was constantly mentioning in relation to the traffic.

"You do know that people teach entire classes on this, right? Sell books about it?" Rashid had a smart little twinkle in his eye.

Imogen was happy to take his word for it.

"I think what I want to know is, how can I sound like I know what I am talking about in a meeting about the site's performance?"

"Oh, darling, that's easy. Let's talk about increasing your conversion rate."

"My what?"

"Your conversion rate. Conversion is the act of changing visitors on the site and the app into customers. It's the most important of all the traffic components. One thing that I tell my clients, who, by the way, I charge way more than the price of a decent macchiato"—he looked at her with mock anger—"is that the longer they have someone on their site, the more likely they are to sell them things. No one wants to feel like they have wasted their time. They want to buy something. You just need to keep their eyeballs on the screen and then make it really easy for them to check out once you have them hooked."

Imogen was starting to understand. "So that's why BUY IT NOW works so well."

Rashid's topknot wiggled as he nodded his head. "Exactly. It's telling the visitor what to do. People like to be told what to do."

"So what suggestions can I make to get us a better conversation rate?" Imogen asked.

Rashid sighed.

"'Conversion rate,' my dearest, not 'conversation rate.' Imogen, you're actually killing me. But since you handed Bridgett off to me and she has an incredible app idea that just might make Blast! a hell of a lot of money, I am happy to help you pro bono. Here's what I know. Your site actually makes fulfillment, buying, really easy. You store everyone's information. You make everything go through a single process. It's as close to one-click shopping as you are going to get. What you could do better is identifying the fringe consumer, the one who is on the fence about making a purchase. If someone has been on the site for more than three minutes, they are thinking about buying something. How can you give them a nudge?"

Imogen sipped her macchiato, swirling the foam around with her spoon, before lifting it to her mouth, thinking about the kind of nudge that would get her to actually buy something right then and there.

"Ooooo, I have it," she said a little too loudly, causing the couple at the table next to theirs to give her a disapproving stare. "We can have a coupon pop up after they have been on the website for three minutes giving them ten percent off."

Rashid groaned. "Nooooo. I mean, yes. A coupon is a good idea, but just a plain old coupon is boring-sauce. It's like giving someone a blender when they want a Vitamix."

At least she was on the right track.

"Think, Imogen." Rashid stood and stretched his arms skyward, his slender fingers cracking as they spread. "How can you engage your customer? How can you make them see that buying something from your site is something they have to do?"

Seeing. That was it. She remembered Eve in San Francisco opining on how the key to the selfie was all in the eyes.

"We want to see your sale face!" Imogen blurted out. "Your salefie. It's a coupon, but you get it only if you share your best salefie—your excited-about-our-sale face. You share your *Glossy* salefie on Instagram with the hashtag salefie and we send you a coupon. Is that even possible?"

For a minute she thought Rashid might tackle her, he looked so excited.

"That. Is. Perfect."

"Really? It's a made-up word. Is it stupid to make up a word?" Imogen knew *she* thought it was stupid to make up a word.

"The Internet is all one big made-up word," Rashid said. "What do you think Google and Twitter are? They're baby talk. It's all about how you own that baby talk." Rashid snapped his fingers on the word "own."

It made a lot of sense to Imogen. Still she marveled that Rashid could so easily give her something she could go into a meeting with that might just possibly impress Eve and the rest of her team. She stood up to hug him.

"I owe you."

"You don't. You came up with hashtag salefie all on your own. I just gave you a bit of a nudge. You don't owe me at all." He smirked as he meticulously sipped on his macchiato. "In fact, I am going to see if I can buy salefie-dot-com. We may be on to something. I think you have a website or app idea percolating around in that gorgeous head of yours too, and when it's ready, I'll help you build it."

Imogen shook her head. "I don't. I honestly wouldn't even know where to start."

"You will. You know I can make you a million bucks off the smallest of ideas. The best apps are the kind that exploit some kind of inefficiency in the market. Think about Airbnb. What did they do? They found a huge inefficiency of people's second homes not being used or their primary home not being used when they went away on vacation. They decided to help people make money on something they already owned, but didn't know was worth anything. Does that make sense?"

Imogen nodded.

"I really could make an app out of anything? What if I knew someone had an inventory of something perishable that would last for only three more days. Could I try to find a way to pair those things with someone who needed them in the next few days?" she asked, thinking of that refrigerator filled with all the leftover flowers.

"Yes, that's exactly it," Rashid said, rubbing his hands together like two sticks. Imogen enjoyed the way his dimples stayed put, even after his smile faded.

"Think about it." He tapped the side of his head as he rose and carefully replaced his yellow overcoat one arm at a time before whirling out the door and onto his next shift of meetings.

* * *

Imogen had never, ever, heard of a couple using Paperless Post for their wedding.

But sure enough, there it was in her in-box, an emailed invite to the nuptials of Mr. Andrew Maxwell and Miss Eve Morton, taking place on the starry evening of January 15 in the grand ballroom of the Plaza Hotel. Guests were encouraged to visit Glossy.com's website for "recommendations" on what they should wear.

Imogen looked up from her desk to see if everyone in the office had gotten the post at the same time. She assumed they must have, given the fuss Eve had been making about the wedding around the office and the fact that they would be promoting her wedding so heavily on the website. Up and down the rows of computers the young women whispered to one another and pointed at their screens. Imogen could tell they were furiously messaging at the same time. She watched them as they undoubtedly went to the special section of the *Glossy* website—an entire vertical column now labeled "Wedding!"—to find out what Eve wanted them to wear. Imogen was curious herself. How did Eve envision her wedding? She clicked on the tab to find a new page subdivided into four sections: Bride, Bridal Party, Lady Guests, Gentleman Guests. She clicked Bride first. This page contained sixteen different dresses and allowed visitors to vote for their favorite. Eve promised she would take all of the votes into consideration when she was choosing her dress for the actual day. Imogen clicked the back button on the browser and went to "Lady Guests." She shouldn't have been surprised to discover that this section contained an unusual amount of Hervé Léger bandage dresses all in a distinctive palette of various shades of sherbet. *Perfect for a winter wedding,* Imogen thought with the requisite amount of sarcasm.

As the day went on it became clear that Eve did not invite the entire office to the wedding. The hurt was apparent on the faces of the women that Eve had neglected. She had invited her personal favorites, along with the girls Imogen knew Eve found the most impressive, the ones whose parents were prominent on the New York social scene, who had fancy boyfriends or who were particularly attractive. It was easy to pick out who in the office would be attending the event. Even if they despised their boss, the ones who had gotten the invitation couldn't hide a certain smugness, the kind that came just from being included in something you knew others had been excluded from.

"What'd you think?" Eve leaned languidly onto Imogen's desk. As she tucked a red curl behind her ear, Imogen noticed a new set of Frisbee-sized diamond studs, no doubt a gift from Andrew, adorning Eve's lumpy earlobes.

"Think of what?" She assumed Eve meant the wedding invitation, but with Eve it wouldn't be out of the ordinary for her to be referring to an email she had sent five seconds earlier.

"My wedding invitation, silly." Now Imogen knew this would be one of those moments when Eve played like they were two girlfriends instead of work colleagues who despised each other. Imogen had learned it was best to just start playing along. It made it end that much sooner.

"What an ingenious idea to use the Paperless Post, Eve. I never would have thought of that. So eco-friendly of you."

"Wasn't it? You know, that's exactly what I was thinking too. I mean, except the truth is also that we are having the wedding so soon that picking out and then mailing all of the invitations would have just taken up too much time. Plus, I love supporting other tech companies. It makes me feel good." She rubbed her hands on the tops of her arms to show that the feeling was something akin to warmth and fuzziness.

Imogen nodded, dropping her gaze back to her computer, wondering how long she would need to coddle Eve about the wedding invites.

Eve narrowed her eyes and gave Imogen a funny look. "Have you ever gotten another wedding invitation on Paperless Post?"

"I haven't, Eve. It was definitely one of a kind."

This was the right answer.

"Yeah, it was. Although try telling Andrew that. I thought he was going to die when I told him about it. You of all people know how conservative he is."

Imogen nodded that she did know that about him, choosing carefully not to say anything more than that. It was as if Eve was baiting her to say something more, something personal about her long-ago ex-boyfriend that would make this conversation awkward. Imogen decided instead to switch gears.

"Who from the office did you invite?"

"You know, the ones I work with most closely, the ones who have been here the longest. I feel like they should have really earned the right to come to my wedding. Don't you think?"

To this Imogen didn't know whether to agree with Eve or tell her how she really felt, that all of the girls should have, at the very least, been invited to the cocktail hour if they were using this wedding as some kind of de facto Glossy.com event.

"I think it's your wedding and you should have invited whoever you wanted to invite. Have you decided on your dress yet or are you really going to wear what the website votes for?" Imogen had the sense that this aspect of the wedding had been borrowed from a reality television show.

Eve threw her head back and laughed. "Of course I'm not going to wear what they vote on. You know the girls on the website will probably pick the very worst of the dresses. Most of our traffic comes from the middle of the country." Eve stuck her finger down her throat. "We just did that to build engagement. Things that make people vote get them to stay on a site longer and that kind of site stickiness is good for advertisers to see. I'm still narrowing down my options. Some designers are sending a few things over next week. I'll try them on and decide. I don't think I'll choose just one dress though. I was thinking I'd wear at least three on the big night."

"It's your big day. I think you should have as many dresses as you want." Imogen smiled in what she hoped was a motherly way, even though in her head she was vowing that her own daughter would never grow up to be such an entitled brat.

Eve liked that answer.

"How many dresses did you wear at your wedding?"

"Just the one."

Eve considered Imogen's answer for a few seconds.

"Things were different back then. It was a long time ago," Eve said, as though Imogen had been married in 1904 instead of 2004.

Imogen decided it would be best to change the subject since it was clear Eve could talk about her wedding plans forever.

"So I have some ideas for the site," Imogen said carefully.

Now Eve looked bored. "Oh yeah. For photo shoots and those long, lame articles you love and stuff?"

Imogen just kept moving forward.

"No, actually. I wanted to talk to you about our conversion rate and how I think we can convert more readers into customers." Now she had Eve's attention, if she was a bit incredulous.

"Okay," Eve said, obviously choosing her words. "Talk to me." Imogen pulled up the website on her computer, happy that Tilly had made it her homepage. "The average customer will typically buy something after being on the site for three minutes. If they don't buy something after three minutes, they are considering buying but are probably on the fence. I was thinking we could give them a nudge. Make a pop-up to let them know about a sale. *But,* they have to Instagram a picture of their most excited sale face—their salefie—and hashtag it. Then we can give them a discount code."

Imogen had written down exactly what Rashid told her in bullet points in her notebook and reread it at least twenty times. She knew she had gotten it right. After reading it so many times the words coming out of her mouth actually made sense.

Eve tapped at Imogen's keyboard, aimlessly clicking around. Imogen wasn't sure how she would use this information.

"How did you come up with this?"

"It came to me after listening to the women from the Customer Insight Team talk the other day."

"Have you talked to anyone else about it?"

"Not yet. I thought we could discuss it first."

At that Eve leaned in to squeeze her arms around Imogen's shoulder. "What a wonderful idea. And . . . I'll have to talk to the product team . . . but I imagine we can make it happen."

This version of Eve didn't bother Imogen. Watching the girl grow kinetically excited made Imogen understand why some people *did* want to work with Eve. When she was like this, she was smart and creative and easy to cooperate with. The two women sat side by side for a minute, holding on to their moment of collaboration.

"Let me think on this a little more, Imogen," she said, pulling absentmindedly at the diamond stud in her ear. "Don't say anything about it to anyone. But I like it a lot." Imogen allowed her to squeeze her shoulders again, not minding her touch as much as she usually did. Eve was lost in thought as she walked out of the room.

As soon as she was out of her line of sight, Imogen pulled up her iPhone to text Rashid.

>>>>We did it. You are my Prom Queen!<<<<

B y the time Imogen left the office at nine she knew it was so late she would have no chance to see the kids before they got into bed. Alex had warned her he would also be working late every night this week, so Tilly stayed on to lend a hand. Even though he was in the middle of a big case, when her husband disappeared for these long stretches of time Imogen wondered whether she was missing something. Was he actually a spy? She swore he could be a spy.

Imogen asked the cabdriver to let her out a few avenues over from their house so she could nip into Li-Lac, the couture European chocolate shop, to grab a few of her favorite dark chocolate–covered espresso beans. They were her weakness and after a day like this she bloody deserved them. Golden Christmas lights twinkled in the trees along Jane Street. She'd cancelled the family's annual trip to Parrot Cay between Christmas and New Year's, a time when the magazine was traditionally closed.

"The Internet doesn't go on vacation. I'm not even taking a honeymoon!" Eve's voice echoed in her head, as Imogen had reluctantly passed the hotel reservation along to her mum and stepfather.

Coming out of the shop she nearly collided with a tall man in a dark gray overcoat. She knew there was something familiar about him even before she could pull back far enough to see his face.

"Immy!"

"Andrew."

He wasn't drunk. Yet. He had obviously had a drink or probably two. His perfect helmet of hair was now slightly out of place, his smile easy and slightly goofy.

"I just received your wedding invitation," Imogen said.

"My wedding email, you mean?" he replied, a tinge of annoyance in his tone.

"A lot of people use Paperless Post these days, Andrew. I use it for all of the kids' birthday parties. It saves a ton of money."

He scoffed. "Oh, come on, Immy, you know I don't care about the money. Would you ever send an Internet invitation for your wedding? You wouldn't. *You* would never do something like that. You have class."

Recoiling at the nickname, Imogen smartly chose to ignore the binary implication that Eve in turn did not have class. She smiled stiffly.

Most of the time she would be eager to find someone to commiserate with over Eve, but doing so with Eve's fiancé, her ex-boyfriend, felt wrong.

"I saw you on the news for something the other day, didn't I?"

That did the trick. Given a carrot, Andrew preferred to talk about himself over any other subject. He straightened up to his full six foot two.

"You probably did," he said, nodding his head, putting on the mantle of the serious and grave politician. "I've been working so hard to reverse the ban on large sodas in this city. It's against federal laws and infringes on an individual's personal liberty. It's a fight we can win and it's a fight that the voters will really get behind."

Now Imogen remembered that she hadn't seen Andrew on the television news. She'd seen a cartoon version of him in the *New York Post*, his head poking out from a Big Gulp. The bubble coming out of his mouth read "Like me."

She nodded as though she were interested, starting to look past him to indicate she was ready to end the conversation and go home, but Andrew wasn't picking up on her signals.

"Hey! Let's grab a drink."

Imogen shook her head. "Not tonight, Andrew. I'm completely knackered."

"Come on, just one drink. We're in our old stomping grounds. One quick drink to catch up. Please." He lowered his head. "I don't want to go home yet." Imogen wasn't sure if he and Eve were living together now, but she imagined Eve being home might be the reason he didn't want to be there. She could sympathize. And so, against all her better judgment, she agreed.

"Just one drink."

Andrew insisted on going somewhere nostalgic and so he led her downstairs to one of those neighborhood bars in the West Village that are always subterranean, but have the best jukeboxes in the city and cheap beer despite the astronomically expensive rents in the rest of the neighborhood. It was a place they had spent many a late night in their twenties, Imogen drinking and smoking too much, Andrew hitting on waitresses and doing cocaine in the bathroom.

"What are you drinking, Immy?"

"Just a glass of rosé."

"A glass of pink wine for the lady and a double bourbon straight up for me." He flung a hundred-dollar bill down on the bar.

"Keep 'em coming," he said to the tattooed woman with the face of a model and the arms of a bodybuilder behind the bar.

"Andrew, I really can be here for only one drink. I want to see my kids before they go to sleep."

He placed his index finger over her lips. "Shush. Come on, even I know Imogen Tate wouldn't keep her kids awake past nine. We both know they're already in bed." This was obviously a mistake. Imogen resigned herself to the fact that she had agreed to this one drink and so, no matter how awkward it was already making her feel, she would have the drink, deal with twenty minutes of conversation and get out.

Andrew threw back his drink the second it hit the bar and he signaled the bartender for another, the same. Andrew had always drunk quickly, the way alcoholics often did, hating themselves for taking the drink in the first place, but wanting to feel its sweet effects with as little interruption as possible.

"So how is Adam?" Andrew was starting to slur. Imogen took in a breath and examined his profile. What was once a chiseled jaw had softened into something more like papier-mâché.

"Alex, darling. My husband's name is Alex."

"Adam, Alex, same difference really. The guy you married who wasn't me."

What was the point in reminding him that he hadn't proposed to her, nor attempted to contact her after his mother dragged him off to rehab, a rehab that, judging from this evening, hadn't been effective.

"Alex is good. He is working on a big case right now, a Ponzi scheme."

"Oh yeah. Good old Marty!" Andrew slapped his thigh. "My old man had some bucks invested with Marty. Lost a pretty penny when your hubby went after him." Now Andrew was laughing. "I never put my money in those crazy schemes. I like it in real estate, where I know it is working for me, but Dad really got fleeced by Marty." Imogen had forgotten the many layers of animosity Andrew had for his father. "You should have seen the old bastard's face when he found out that Marty got charged. I'll bet he wants to absolutely murder your husband." That made Imogen shift in her seat.

The bartender paused to ask if they wanted another. Andrew was too busy checking his phone to hear so Imogen just shook her head slightly, rolling the stem of her wineglass back and forth between her thumb and her index finger before shifting the subject back to Andrew.

"It's been a long time since I saw your parents. I assume I'll see them at the wedding." Andrew threw back his head to laugh and then did it a second time, taking his drink with him on the next pass, dumping the brown liquor down his throat and then asking for another one. Imogen stared hard at the baby white-yellow hairs on his knuckles as he clutched his glass like a man holding on to a life preserver. She knew that his grip would loosen, become all butterfingery the more booze he went through.

Imogen wanted to place a hand on his arm and tell him to slow down, but she remembered quickly that it wasn't her place to do that anymore. What she needed to do now was finish her own drink and get out of there.

"You'll probably see them there. They don't mind Eve that much. They think she's a little tacky, but they like her credentials. Harvard B-school and all." He drew out the *a* sound in Harvard, pronouncing it "Hahvahd." "The B-school their ne'er-do-well son sure didn't get into. Yeah, they like her enough to show up, I think."

Imogen didn't think they would have liked her enough to show up at their wedding had things ever reached that point between them, but she kept silent.

"She's good for the campaign trail . . . Eve is. She helps a ton with the young voters. Smart young go-getter. Young women like that. Entrepreneur. She courts the girls and the tech industry here, which is becoming a big constituent, my guys tell me." He paused, his eyes now bloodshot and tired looking. "She photographs well. My team wants to get her covered up a little more, but she looks good on camera." Imogen picked up her glass to take a healthy sip, now only a few sips away from being able to politely excuse herself. Andrew was still wound up and going, his Windsor knot slowly coming loose at his Adam's apple.

"But she isn't you, Imogen. She definitely isn't you. There's absolutely nothing cool about her. You were always so cool. Sometimes I think Eve might be a robot. Do you ever think that Eve might be a robot?" He traced the shape of a body with square corners in the air in front of him and looked at her, his eyes longing for her to agree. She let out a laugh, because Andrew wasn't completely wrong. Sometimes she did wonder whether Eve was one of those cyborgs sent from the future to try to fix what was wrong with the present.

She chose her words carefully. "Sometimes I do think she's a little bit mechanical."

"I don't think she has feelings at all." Imogen tipped the rest of her glass of wine into her mouth. Andrew was worked up now, moving his hands around his head in jerky mechanical gestures, doing what appeared to be some kind of robot dance that Imogen vaguely remembered from the eighties.

"I am Eve. I am a robot. I am Eve. I would like to give you a blow job now. Would that be all right with you," he said in a monotone.

No matter how much she despised Eve, everything that came out of Andrew's mouth made her feel sad for both of them.

"I'm not the person you should be saying this to."

He nodded his head and looked at her like a shamed puppy dog, then attempted a chuckle that cracked in an effeminate way in the middle, further shattering the façade of his confidence.

Before she knew what was happening, Andrew was lurching toward her, his breath heady with the smell of bourbon. She couldn't move away before his full lips landed firmly against hers. She wasn't sure if it was shock or flattery, but for the briefest of moments she felt a power rush through her before she snapped back to reality.

"What the hell do you think you're doing, Andrew?"

"What were you doing, Imogen Tate?" He straightened up as though the brief kiss had awoken him from a drunken slumber, and blotted his forehead with the pointy end of his silk tie. "I believe you may have kissed me back."

"And I believe you just took advantage of a friend who wanted to sit here and listen to you talk about your problems."

She stood in disgust, disgust at him and disgust with herself for being so slow in her horrified reaction to the kiss. She picked up her purse.

He pulled on the arm of her coat as she put it on. "Have one more drink with me?"

Imogen shook her head. "I can't, Andrew. And you probably shouldn't have one either. Go home. Get some rest. This can't be good for your campaign. You know that."

"I'll just have one more and then go to bed," he said sheepishly. "I just need one more before I can go there."

Imogen greedily gulped at the frigid air outside. If she were a different kind of woman she would have immediately rung one of her girlfriends and divulged the whole story. Instead she pulled her coat tighter around her body and picked up her pace to get home.

CHAPTER TWENTY

O h, how she missed the days of ten a.m. arrivals. Those days seemed so decadent now. The office was busy, busy, busy when she arrived at eight thirty. She noticed a new addition to the space as she passed the worker-bee rows, a lump of new beanbag chairs thrown haphazardly into the corner of the room. Someone had typed up a sign and taped it to the wall: NAP CORNER. No one appeared to be napping now, but Imogen could make out the imprint of bodies on two of the beanbags, evidence they had been used just the night before.

"Morning, Imogen." Eve waved from her desk, uncharacteristically friendly for first thing in the morning. Imogen raised her eyebrows and waved back, a vise clenching her stomach as she wondered whether Andrew came home and told Eve he had been out drinking with Imogen.

"Good morning. How was your night?" She couldn't bear the uncertainty of not knowing what Eve knew about the night before.

"Oh, I was here until about four a.m.," Eve said, showing no sign of having gotten only three hours sleep. Imogen forced herself to let out a small laugh.

"Did you at least get home for a little sleep?"

Eve shook her head. "No need. I went down to the gym and had a good workout. I showered there. I'll get some sleep tonight if I need it." Eve really was a robot. Relief washed over Imogen.

Eve was oddly ebullient in the morning meeting. As soon as everyone sat down, she smiled widely.

"I had a brilliant idea last night and I am so excited to share it with all of you this morning. I stayed up all night figuring out how to implement this and it's going to be a real turning point for us in terms of sales." Imogen smiled. She felt a jolt of anticipation. Eve was going to talk about Salefie. But did she just say it was her idea?

"So what I am thinking is that once a user has been on the site for three minutes, we will have a pop-up coupon appear on the screen to tell them about our promotion. If they Instagram a selfie with the hashtag Salefie we will give them ten percent off. *Salefie!* It's their sale face. How adorbs is that? I talked to the product team and they stayed up all night implementing this change and I'm so excited to announce that the conversion rate doubled this morning!"

The room clapped. Where was the credit? Imogen wasn't sure what she had expected. Her mouth went dry. She wanted to speak up but wasn't even sure where to begin. This was lower than Eve had ever sunk. As Imogen stood, prepared to confront her once and for all, Eve gave her signature sharp clap, dismissing the meeting.

"Okay, busy day, everyone. Go, go, go, go."

Eve was already clacking down the hallway in her too-high heels by the time Imogen caught up with her.

"Eve!" Imogen yelled out too loudly. Eve spun around, a look of complete and utter innocence on her face, like a mask she had prepared for this very conversation.

"Yes, Imogen?" she said sweetly.

"We need to talk."

"Sure. Your office?"

Eve settled herself on the couch while Imogen closed the door behind her.

"That was my idea."

"What was your idea?" Eve's eyes widened with incredulity.

"Salefie was my idea. I told you that idea before I left last night and you know it."

Eve cocked her head to one side. "Was that you? I could have sworn that it was one of the ideas I wrote down weeks ago. I think it came from a jam session with the Customer Insight Team about how we could get the conversion rate up."

Imogen felt like she was entering a parallel universe.

"We talked about it last night."

Eve kept the confused stare on her face.

"I talk to so many people about so many ideas every single day, Imogen. My job is to make sure that everything is efficiently implemented and this was. I am sure something you said could have contributed to what I came up with." Eve's expression shifted to something nearing pity.

"This is low, Eve. Stealing ideas."

Eve just kept smiling. "All of the ideas belong to everyone, Imogen. We are a team." Imogen had no words left. She could go on for another twenty minutes, but Eve had backed her into a corner.

"I have a meeting," Imogen lied, mustering all of the strength she had left into her voice. "I'll be out of the office for a couple of hours."

Eve had already turned her attention back to her phone.

"No worries, Imogen. All of us will be just fine here without you."

* * *

Imogen squinted unhappily into the dull winter sun. She needed to think.

There was only one person she wanted to speak to and once she walked outside, Imogen pulled out her cell and from memory dialed the number for Molly Watson's Upper East Side apartment. Molly had never owned a cell phone. Her fleet of assistants always knew how to reach her, and if that failed, she had a landline in her apartment with an answering machine she checked religiously every evening.

"No one needs to be able to reach you all the time," Molly once told Imogen in the languid hours of the morning after an eleven-hour photo shoot. "Always be a little inaccessible. Everyone will just want you all the more." How long had it been since she talked to her old boss? Five months at least. She had stopped returning Imogen's calls over the summer.

Someone answered on the third ring. The voice was small and Imogen imagined it must be one of Molly's many minions.

"This is Imogen Tate for Molly Watson," Imogen announced herself.

Silence on the other end.

"Im, it's me, darling."

Molly's voice could command a room of models with egos the size of the Hope Diamond. When she whispered an entire photo shoot went silent in fear they would miss out on something of dire importance. The voice Imogen heard on the other end of the line was limp and spiked with anxiety.

At first Molly hesitated when Imogen said she would love to pop by and catch up before lunchtime, but relented with little protest.

"It's probably a good idea, my darling," she said. "Come straight up. I will tell Isaac you are on your way." Isaac, Molly's doorman, had been manning the white-gloved lobby of 100 East Eighty-Seventh Street for thirty years, ever since Molly bought the three-bedroom apartment with a sweeping terrace and a library with one of the most extensive collections of fashion tomes anywhere in the Americas.

Molly had never married. She would have died if she heard anyone use the term, but she was one of the many, many fashion widows in New York City—women so devoted to the industry that they never put a man ahead of a promotion. Aside from being professionally single, Molly was everything Imogen wanted to be—tough yet fair, demanding but willing to listen with energy that was contagious. But most of all she inspired Imogen to find a job that she absolutely adored.

"Love what you do, darling, otherwise what's the fucking point," she'd told her over and over again.

In the marble-floored lobby, Isaac, wearing his crisp uniform, greeted Imogen by name. His lips contracted as if he wanted to tell her something more before she boarded the elevator to the twelfth floor.

The lift opened to the left, directly into Molly's foyer. Typically overrun with friends, caviar and cigarette smoke, the space now smelled slightly stale, like a book left too long on a shelf. Imogen could hear the din of a television in a room farther into the interior, but couldn't imagine where it was coming from. As long as she had known her, Imogen had never seen Molly watch TV. Lula, Molly's longtime maid and sometime cook, was noticeably absent from the foyer, where Imogen was accustomed to her whisking away coats and shawls and proffering tea, coffee and the odd Xanax to the particularly anxious visitor. Imogen followed the unmistakable voices of Kathie Lee Gifford and Hoda Kotb of the *Today* show. Molly's apartment was an exercise in coziness. Books on subjects ranging from art to fashion to history lined every wall. There were biographies of every great designer of the twentieth century. Custom-printed Colefax and Fowler wallpaper of Victorian roses peeked through between the shelves. Persian rugs were layered one on top of the next but couldn't prevent the wood floor from creaking gently beneath Imogen's heels. A mahogany grandfather clock in the corner had stopped with the hands splayed in opposite directions. Without squinting Imogen couldn't tell if it was stopped at six or twelve thirty. On a wonderful wrought-iron mantelpiece sat old Polaroids from long-ago photo shoots propped against tall white candles. Above those was Imogen's favorite piece in the entire apartment, an original Edward Hopper painting, *High Road*. The oils showed a country thoroughfare sloping gently into a bucolic town. The painting had been on loan to the Whitney for the past eighteen months. Imogen was pleased to see it back. More than a beautiful piece, its title was Molly's mantra: "Always take the high road." Each time Imogen looked at it, she discovered something new. Today she saw it as something aspirational, a road far outside of her urban existence. Far away from Eve.

A massive dark green velvet chesterfield sofa covered in no fewer than twenty cushions occupied the majority of the room. It was whispered that Molly had someone come in to fluff those cushions every afternoon. The schoolteacher's daughter in Imogen always marveled at that. Imagine one person just to fluff your pillows!

Enveloped within those massive cushions was Molly, her eyes affixed to what, judging from the thin plastic still covering the screen, had to be a relatively new very thin and flat television. Imogen shuffled her feet and cleared her throat to grab the woman's attention, causing Molly to swivel her elegant steel-gray ballerina bun around to greet her with an unsure smile. The woman's face was unlined even at seventy, from five decades of religiously avoiding the sun. She was, as ever, dressed all in black, Olatz black silk pajamas so tailored that from afar they could be mistaken for a bespoke pantsuit, crisp, classic and ever so cool. Just a pop of color at her neck, four adjoined strands of red beads on a vintage Chanel Gripoix necklace.

Her posture, once celebrated at Miss Porter's finishing school, remained straight as a pin.

Imogen's gaze traveled to the painting. "You got it back."

"I did," Molly said simply, with a studied admiration of the piece. "The room wasn't entirely complete without it, was it? Is that a silly thing, to believe that a painting can complete a place . . . or a person? Edward Hopper loved to paint. He never made much money from it, but he loved it. He made his money making illustrations for advertisements, did you know that? Despised it, but it paid the bills. This right here, this perfect scene, this is something he truly loved."

"You look wonderful," Imogen said, even though it wasn't exactly true. Molly looked tired. Navy semicircles under her eyes were the only imperfection on an otherwise flawless face. Her smell wafted over Imogen, a mixture of expensive tobacco and Joy by Jean Patou.

"I've been calling you," Imogen said with a sense of urgency she hadn't expected to use.

Molly reached over to place her hand on the younger woman's.

"Shall we smoke a ciggie?" asked the same small voice Imogen had heard on the telephone. Imogen made a small glance at her own breasts, thinking about the cancer, before giving a slight shake of her head, indicating that Molly should smoke alone as she lowered herself down onto the outlandishly large couch. Sitting next to Molly made her feel calmer, gave her a sense that the world could be righted and go back to the way things used to be.

The older woman pulled closer a pale green gold-leafed Limoges ashtray sorely in need of emptying and secured a wearied pack of Dunhills from the folds of the couch. A window was cracked for the smoke to escape and heavy lilac chintz grand curtains shimmied like burlesque dancers in the autumn breeze. Neither woman spoke until

Molly exhaled her first heady pull. They were still in the easy and familiar silence.

Imogen embraced the smoke blowing toward her like a long-lost friend she might never hold again.

"How are you doing, my dear?" Molly asked.

Of course Molly knew what had happened to *Glossy* and she would know that Imogen knew she had been let go from *Moda*. Imogen didn't want to dive right into all of the uncomfortable details, but she couldn't help it. She let it all unload onto Molly: her shock at returning to the magazine, the horror of Eve's brash behavior, the way she lorded over the staff.

"I just don't think I can stand it, Molly. I may need to leave *Glossy* altogether and go to another magazine. *Elle* was calling about a year ago."

She could have kept going, listing various publications that should be offering her a job, but Molly's eyes were drilling into her.

"Keep your job, Imogen," she said tightly. "Keep your job."

"But—" Imogen began.

"It's no longer 1995. It's no longer even 2005. It's 2015 and we are a dying breed in a dying world. I cannot get another job. No one will hire me. I've called everyone. Everyone in this town who owed me so many favors for so many years, favors I never needed to collect. When I needed to collect them, those people stopped returning my calls. I am a dinosaur. I am extinct. You, my darling girl, are merely endangered. You can save yourself. Keep this job. Do what they tell you. Don't end up like me."

Imogen didn't know what to say.

"Who does Eve think she is? Does she think I'll just give in? Does she think I'll just quit?" Imogen's voice wavered.

"She does. It's clear Eve believes editors of our vintage should be put out to pasture like old mares."

Imogen sat there stunned, but still ready to fight.

"What bothers me the most is how she turned on me. This was a girl I mentored. I wanted her to succeed and she double-crossed me and stabbed me in the back."

"She did, darling. That she did. She is an ungrateful little cow."
Molly's eyes dimmed.

"You're a good person, Imogen. You still have your passion."

Molly patted her gently on the knee. "I need to rest." As Molly
rose, Imogen noticed her age for the first time, the slight hunch in
her back, her body recoiling at the idea of movement, as if it hurt to
shift ever so slightly. She shuffled slowly into the adjoining bedroom,
looking over her shoulder a very small bit. "See yourself out, my dear."

And then, as an afterthought, she added quietly: "Good luck."

CHAPTER TWENTY-ONE

Imogen felt a sense of relief when her phone rang and it was the principal of Annabel's school. No parent ever wanted to get that call, but it meant she had an actual reason for not returning to work.

"Ms. Tate, I need you to come to the school immediately" came the stern voice of Ms. Oglethorpe, a woman with the demeanor of a drill sergeant who has just eaten something unpleasant. Ms. Oglethorpe's voice at the other end of the line made Imogen's mind swim with terrible thoughts, the worst of which was that one of Marty McAlwyn's wealthy former clients had finally snapped and come after her children, kidnapping Annabel for a small ransom to replace the money they lost when Alex put their deadbeat benefactor behind bars.

"Is Annabel all right?"

"She's fine. She isn't hurt, I can promise you that, but you will need to come take her home."

"Can you please tell me what is happening with my daughter, Ms. Oglethorpe?" Even as the words left her mouth, Imogen knew she'd learn nothing over the phone. Ms. Oglethorpe delighted in the pageantry of informing parents in person that their offspring had disappointed her.

* * *

Annabel looked small on the generously proportioned chair out-side Ms. Oglethorpe's office. She swung her legs back and forth in a rhythm that looked like it soothed her. Her head was low and she wasn't crying, but when Imogen put a finger beneath her daughter's chin to raise her face, she saw that her eyes were rimmed red.

"I'm sorry, Mommy" were the first words out of her mouth. "I just wanted to know who was doing it. I just needed to know which one of them was saying those terrible things about me." Tears spilled down Annabel's apple-round cheeks. What exactly had her daughter done?

Ms. Oglethorpe, a stern groove whittled between her deeply set eyes, exited her office and cleared her throat.

"Ms. Tate, please come into my office. Miss Marretti will be just fine sitting out here for a while longer."

Imogen felt like a child herself as she eased into a chair opposite Ms. Oglethorpe's imposing mahogany desk.

"I can assure you Annabel is not the kind of little girl who gets into trouble. This has to be some kind of misunderstanding."

Ms. Oglethorpe folded her hands in front of her, the fingers gnarled and red around the knuckles. She dispensed with any nice-ties about Annabel. "First of all, you do know our policy of not allow-ing smartphones in the classrooms. We understand that you parents feel the need to buy them iPhones and iPads and all other 'manner of 'i' things at a younger and younger age each and every year, but we cannot have those things in our classrooms when the teachers are trying to teach. It's an enormous distraction." Imogen nodded. Every single one of Annabel's friends were given a smartphone well before their eighth birthdays. They'd been able to hold out until she was nine. It would come even earlier with Johnny. He already tried to swipe his finger across picture books to turn the page.

"Did you call me down here because Annabel had her phone in the classroom?" Absurd, even for a school like this one.

"No. I just wanted to point out that Annabel had her phone with her when she screamed and threw food at Harper Martin and a table of other young ladies."

Imogen was familiar with Harper Martin's mother. Ella Martin was the socialite fourth wife of the George Martin, the owner of the Brooklyn Nets. If the younger Miss Martin was anything like her entitled mum, Imogen could understand screaming at her, but she still didn't fully understand what would make Annabel lash out like that, unless Harper was the one sending the nasty messages to her daughter.

"Ms. Oglethorpe, I am sure there is an explanation. Did you ask Annabel why she did what she did?"

"I did. She clammed up."

Imogen sighed. "Would you mind giving me some time with my daughter? Would you let me try to figure out what is wrong? There has to be a reasonable explanation."

"I prefer you take her home. She's suspended for today and tomorrow."

Imogen didn't know what to say. Her daughter, suspended from school.

Annabel was suitably cowed when Imogen walked out of the office. She stood and placed her small hand in her mother's, something she had refused to do for a couple of years now. They walked the six blocks back to their house in silence. When they got there, Imogen told Annabel to go upstairs and wash her face and asked her to meet her in the kitchen in fifteen minutes. Her daughter silently obliged. Imogen busied herself putting on the kettle for some tea.

Annabel was wearing pajamas with little penguins dotted all over them when she padded back down the stairs. They made her look much younger than ten.

Imogen gestured to the kitchen table and the English Breakfast tea, her favorite. Her daughter wrapped her small hands around the warm mug and sat down.

"Do you want to tell me what happened?" Annabel nodded. "Go on, then."

"I've been getting these messages." Annabel squirmed uncomfortably. "First they got posted to my Facebook wall and then they came as Facebook messages. Sometimes they are mean comments on my Instagram and my YouTube."

"Can I see them, darling?"

"I erased a lot of them. I didn't want anyone else to see them. But there are still a couple." Annabel pushed her chair back from the table to grab her laptop out of her bright pink backpack. She logged onto the Wi-Fi and then opened up her Facebook page. Sure enough, the messages came from the same girl, "Candy Cool."

There were still four messages in Annabel's in-box. Imogen gasped when she saw what they said.

No boys r ever gonna like u because u have a face like a monkey.

U should ask your fancy mom if she thinks u r fat. I bet she does.

Do u ever look in the mirror and cry?

Hey chubs. U Suck!

Imogen shuddered.

"Why do you think these came from Harper?"

Annabel shrugged.

"Harper and her friends are jerks. They don't like me. They laugh at me. I saw Harper on her phone in the cafeteria. She snuck it. She had my Facebook up on it. They were laughing at it."

Annabel was in tears again. How could Imogen blame her? Imogen understood better than anyone right now what it was like for a bully to push you to your breaking point. She crossed to the other side of the table, picked her daughter up out of her chair and sat down in it herself, pulling Annabel down onto her lap, letting her cry into her breast. Breathing in the scent of her hair, Imogen could feel her heart just breaking for the girl.

"I think we need to let Ms. Oglethorpe know that you think it was Harper who bullied you."

Annabel violently shook her head from side to side.

"You do. You have to tell her."

"I don't know if it was her anymore. When I yelled in the lunch-room she denied it. That's why I threw my smoothie at her."

"Did it hit her?"

Annabel nodded. "In the face." Imogen tried not to smile. There was a certain satisfaction in being of an age where you could settle something by throwing a giant green smoothie in another girl's face.

Her daughter continued. "But she didn't seem to know what I was talking about. At first I just thought she was a good liar, but I don't think that she's that good of a liar at all. Now I don't know if she did it."

"Okay, Annabel. But you know how serious it is to be suspended from school, right? You know how disappointed your dad is going to be?"

Annabel buried her head back in her mother's chest. "I know," came the muffled reply. "Please don't tell him."

"Ana, I have to." Given the talking-to Imogen knew Alex would deliver that night and the stress Annabel had been under, she opted to play the good cop.

"Well, it looks like we are both playing a little bit of hooky today. How about we make the most of it and have a girls' afternoon? I can ask Tilly to keep Johnny for the next few hours."

"What should we do?"

"Why don't we go to the salon and get our hair done like proper ladies?" Annabel had never been much of a girly girl, but she loved having her hair done in elaborate styles. She nodded.

"You'll need to put actual clothes on." Annabel raced up the stairs. Imogen kept staring at the nasty comments on her daughter's Face-book page.

Imogen briefly checked her own email as she clicked off Annabel's Facebook. Six emails from Eve, all asking with escalating urgency where she was. She considered not writing back, but what was the point? Eve would only send more emails.

"I'm taking a personal day, Eve. I'll see you in the office tomor-row." The rest of the emails could wait until the morning. She put the phone away just as Annabel was coming back down the stairs, pajamas replaced by a pair of skinny jeans and a bright purple sweater, her long dark hair pulled into a knot on top of her head.

"You know, Ana, sometimes people are terrible. I wish they weren't, but some people are just jerks." What was the point in lying to her daughter? Annabel nodded and hugged her around her middle, surprising Imogen at how tall she was getting.

"You know you're beautiful, right, honey? Really totally stunning," Imogen said.

Annabel scrunched up her face. "You have to say that, you're my mom."

Imogen kept going. "More important, your character is beautiful. You're a gorgeous person inside and out. I may be your mother, but I don't lie. I've hung around with some of the most famous supermodels in all the world and I can objectively tell you that the most beautiful humans I have ever met are the ones just like you . . . the ones who were genuinely nice, good people."

Annabel laughed. "You sound like Oprah."

Imogen raised her arms into the air and tried to affect her best Oprah voice. "And now everyone's getting a car!" At least she could still make her daughter laugh.

The time to lecture was over. They both needed a little distraction. "Now let's go to the salon and then take loads of selfies and see who calls us ugly after that."

* * *

Bundled up against the cold, Annabel shuffled her feet as she walked along the sidewalk, avoiding the cracks and the tree roots that sometimes burst through the old New York City concrete. It had been a nice day with her mom. A great day actually. Mom really did mean well, but no one's parents actually understood what it was like to be a kid these days. When her mom was her age, the Internet hadn't even been invented yet. Things were different.

Candy Cool might not even be a girl at school. It could be anyone. It could be Green Grrl, who was really, really good at making GIFs and memes and weird graphics and stuff. She'd never met Green Grrl, who was also ten and also lived with her parents. She was in Florida though, not New York. They followed each other and once when Green Grrl first started making YouTube videos about smoothies last year she IM'd Annabel to ask if they could share recipes. But since then she had gotten really competitive and weird with her.

Whatever.

Annabel didn't want to care. But it totally sucked when people posted things about you that everyone could see. The really worst thing about Candy Cool was that every single person at school could see it and they were all laughing at her. She thought about unfriending her or blocking her, but it would be worse if she didn't know what people were saying, right?

Plus it hurt when people said things you already sorta felt yourself. She felt a little chubby. Her whole family, her mom, her dad and Johnny, were thin as wilted arugula. When Annabel was little and had even more baby fat than now she thought she had sprung straight from the belly of her grandma, Mama Marretti, a woman who never met a lasagna she wasn't totally in love with.

Annabel never felt pretty and it was lame to hear her mom say, in her British accent that just wouldn't go away, that Annabel was gorgeous. It came out like "gore-juice" and it just wasn't true. Her eyes were too far apart and her nose was too thin. Her hair did whatever it wanted to with no regard for how it made Annabel feel and most recently she had a colony of pimples break out on her chin.

Her mom was always so put together and pretty. Annabel felt sloppy in comparison, like that character in Charlie Brown who always had a cloud of dirt around him. She loved her mom. She didn't really mind that she wasn't always at home like some of her friends' moms. She always made sure to spend a lot of time with her and Johnny. Plus, her job was cool. Last summer she had bought Annabel a brand-new dress and shoes and surprised her with a visit to the set of Martha Stewart's television show and she made a big deal introducing Annabel to Martha Stewart. Martha Stewart!!! Mom talked all about her YouTube show and garden smoothies like they were some big important thing. Then Annabel got to talk to Martha and was so excited to learn that they both felt the same way about kale—it was great with everything!

Until about a month ago Imogen could watch Annabel's videos only when Annabel pulled them up for her on the computer screen.

Afterward she would absentmindedly wave her hand at the screen and say something like, "Oh, you'll have to show me how to do this one of these days." Then she would say it again the next time they'd watched a video. She'd gotten a lot better lately though. She was picking things up quickly. Annabel heard only bits and pieces about what was happening with her mom's job, but it sounded like it sucked pretty bad. She had a new boss who was a jerk or something. She looked up at Imogen, her perfect blond hair bouncing over the top of her crisp white collar. Too bad her mom couldn't just chuck a big old green smoothie in her boss's face. Annabel decided to say that to her mom. It made her smile.

CHAPTER TWENTY-TWO

The next morning Imogen woke up sick to her stomach, so ill in fact that she considered calling in sick, before reconciling that she just couldn't let Eve get the best of her. She stretched on her back and then rolled over onto all fours on the bed, trying some cat and cow yoga poses, hoping to stretch the knot in her stomach away. When that didn't work she tried the breathing exercises Ron recommended. She breathed in for eight counts, held her breath for ten, then let it out for eight. Each time she held her breath Eve's smirk popped into her mind.

Eve won this round. Imogen had trusted her to play fair. Until yesterday she believed that despite all of Eve's shortcomings, they were actually on the same team. Now she knew that was the furthest thing from the truth.

She rubbed her hand along the indent that had been Alex just an hour earlier. She estimated he was getting maybe four hours of sleep a night. The actual trial was starting next week, which meant his hours might be a little more regular.

Imogen paid less attention to how she dressed these days. For years she had meticulously planned her outfits. Now she threw on whatever had just come back from the dry cleaner. She was still pleased with how she looked in her black pencil skirt, turtleneck and sling-back pumps, but it wasn't the same as taking the time to think about her outfit every single night. She used to feel like she was dressing for success, dressing up for the others in the office. Now she was competing with a bunch of young women in tight dresses and high heels. Most of her colleagues were gone. There was no longer anyone to truly dress up for except herself.

* * *

Something wasn't right in the office. You could always hear a pin drop, but now the mood was actually morose. Eyes were downcast, the typing not as frantic as usual. Eve was nowhere to be found when Imogen walked through the doors at eight thirty. Shortly after she turned on her computer, Ashley knocked on her door.

"Is something going on?" Imogen asked tightly. Ashley nodded her head.

"After you left yesterday some of the investors came by. They sat with Eve for a long time in the conference room. All I gathered was that the site hasn't reached some of the traffic benchmarks it promised for the first couple of months and they were disappointed."

"Were you eavesdropping?" Imogen tried not to sound accusatory. Ashley looked a little like Annabel with her sheepish look.

"Yeah, I can hear everything that happens in the conference room from the kitchen."

"So what happens now?"

"Nothing. We still have plenty of money. It hasn't been that long. They just wanted her to know they weren't as happy as they could be. I think she took it pretty hard."

"Why do you think that?"

"Because she came out and screamed at everyone, told us that none of us were really doing our jobs. Demanded everyone work through the night, put up more content, better content. She was crazy-pants. Then she left around midnight and everyone else has been here pretty much since, taking turns napping in the beanbag chairs."

"Those poor girls. Do we have coffee here?"

"We ran out a few days ago."

Imogen handed Ashley her credit card. "Can you call Starbucks and ask them to deliver enough macchiatos—or coffee or cappuccinos—for the entire staff? Have them bring some snacks too."

"I don't think Starbucks delivers," Ashley said.

"Everywhere delivers if your order is big enough, darling."

Imogen decided that if she was ever going to give this office a pep talk, now was going to be the time. She ran her hand over her hair, smoothing the bits that had sprung wild as she got out of the cab. This was her staff now too. She may not have chosen many of them, but they worked for her and it was her job to take care of them. She clapped her hands together. Barely anyone looked up. Imogen realized they all had their headphones on. Ashley hadn't moved from the spot at her side. She was typing on her iPhone.

"I'm sending them an email to let them know you're going to make an announcement. That will get their attention." Sure enough, as the email pinged through, dozens of heads popped up from their desks.

"Good morning, ladies. I know you're exhausted. And after I talk we are having coffee brought in. Anyone who pulled an all-nighter and feels like they need to get home for some sleep is more than welcome to do so and then spend the rest of the day working from home." Imogen clasped her hands together.

"Each of you has been working so hard for the past three months and all of you deserve to be commended for that."

The women looked at her with their zombie eyes, unused to someone in this office saying nice things about them out loud.

"Seriously. Launching anything is never easy, but you have given it your all and I am proud of each and every single one of you." She finally saw some smiles.

"We still have a lot of work to do. We have goals to meet. I know we'll get there." She heard a few scattered sighs of relief. She looked at Ashley, who gave her a thumbs-up. No one was making a video of her and no one was snapping her picture. None of them had the energy. She didn't know how to close out her announcement, so instead she just gave another clap of her hands. "Let's get back to work for a little while. Have something to eat and then go home if you need to." With that, the women diligently went back to their desks. Imogen went to her office, half expecting Eve to pop out from behind her desk and scream at her for daring to let the staff go early, but Eve was still nowhere to be found.

Many of the young ladies in the office perked up after having the coffee and only two or three girls, who looked like they were in dire need of their beds, actually left to go home, poking their heads into Imogen's office to let her know they could come back that evening.

"Get some rest. Tomorrow is a new day. I'll see you then."

For the first time in a long time, Imogen felt like she was back in charge. With Eve gone people came to her with questions. She answered them to the best of her ability. When she didn't know the answer she asked someone to explain it to her. It ended up being her most productive day since she had returned to the office in August.

Look at her. She was running a website.

Eve walked in around five and looked no worse for the wear. She had obviously gotten enough sleep the night before and judging from the ruddiness in her cheeks she had been at the gym or a Spirit Cycle class before coming into the office.

She glanced around at the few empty desks.

"Where is everyone?" Imogen heard her ask from a half dozen yards away.

One of the remaining girls dared to answer.

"Imogen said it would be all right if some people went home to get some rest."

Everyone expecting some kind of volcanic explosion was disappointed. Eve only walked toward Imogen's office and shut the door.

"We have to fire six more people tomorrow," Eve said flatly.

"What?"

"We need to get rid of about six employees tomorrow."

"I heard you, Eve. Why? Why do you want to get rid of anyone when you have your existing staff working around the clock?" Imogen asked.

"Because I need to double my staff. I need to get rid of the majority of these girls who make more than fifty thousand so I can hire more workers at thirty-five or forty thousand. More workers equals more content, equals more traffic."

"But doesn't it matter if that content isn't good? Some of these women are really good at what they do."

Eve looked at her with a pity that showed she couldn't imagine Imogen would ever understand.

"More is always better."

CHAPTER TWENTY-THREE

Ten hours later, Imogen found herself sipping a double martini with a twist at the little French bistro tucked inside The Jane hotel. After the day she'd had, the drink tasted like magic. They'd dispensed with the requisite discussion of Imogen's shitty job and moved swiftly on to Bridgett's love life. "I'm dating a great guy," Bridgett informed Imogen matter-of-factly.

Imogen could picture him. From years of living together, Imogen knew her friend's type as well as she knew her own. Bridgett went for older, distinguished, rich and successful. These days it seemed like everyone except Imogen was single and dating again. Most of her single friends and the single mommies at drop-off had been dipping their toes into online dating, where they all lied about their age—all of them except for Bridgett, who was incredibly honest about being in her forties and thought the ten-year-old photos or blurry shots on most of their friends' profiles were nothing but false advertising. Another close girlfriend of theirs used a photograph clearly taken fifteen years earlier. When she met her date at the bar, he took one look at her, got up and left. Didn't utter a single word.

Bridgett really didn't look a day over thirty-five, so when they saw her in person men always complimented her on how young and fabulous she looked.

"Why would I lie?" she always cooed. "I'd much rather have someone show up on a first date and ooo and ahhhh and say, 'Wow, you look so young!' I don't want anyone to get buyer's remorse."

Men ate that right up. Her last boyfriend had been the number two at Sony Pictures. Despite the fact that he stood only five foot two, in Los Angeles he could bag just about any woman he wanted. He acted as a sponge for all of Bridgett's neuroses and the crazier she became, the more he was devoted to her. That was until a much younger and apparently even more neurotic actress stole his affection on the set of a $100 million action movie being shot in Dubai. He at least had the courtesy of ending their relationship over Skype, rather than relegating the task to text message or email. "It was nice that he let me see his little face," Bridgett explained at the time.

"Do I know the guy?" Imogen now asked, knowing her friend wanted to draw out the telling of her news for as long as possible.

"You do."

"Is it someone I dated?" She had to ask.

"I don't think so."

"Shall we play a guessing game or do you want to tell me?"

With that Bridgett opened up her cardigan to reveal a soft gray T-shirt with the word BLAST! across the front.

"Oh, that's cute. Did Rashid make that?"

"He did." Bridgett said, her hazel eyes twinkling as she batted Imogen affectionately on the forearm.

"It's adorable. Next time you see him ask him to give me a couple for Annabel and Johnny. Those are cute. Are you guys meeting up to talk about your app soon?"

Bridgett looked at her like she was simple. "Imogen, I am dating Rashid."

She hadn't expected that.

"But I thought he was . . ."

"Gay."

"Yes, gay."

Bridgett grinned and spooned a piece of creamy burrata flecked with dried olives into her mouth. "You of all people should know not to jump straight to conclusions. He's just well-dressed and groomed and articulate. I know it's a stretch, but there are still straight men out there with manners and class."

Imogen estimated their age difference at about fifteen years and she felt doubly guilty that she felt a small bit of judgment about that. Pushing it down, she mustered all of her happiness for her friends. Rashid was amazing. He was brilliant and kind, and that was exactly the kind of man that Bridgett deserved. If Demi Moore, Heidi Klum and Madonna had taught them anything, it was that younger men were terribly attracted to strong, self-reliant older women.

Confident that she had given Imogen enough of a shock, Bridgett began rifling around in Imogen's Birkin.

"What are you doing?"

"Do you mind if I go through your meds?"

"My what?"

"Just let me look at your medication?"

"Here at the table?"

Bridgett glanced around the dim room. "No one interesting is here," she said as she pulled Imogen's small cushioned bag from her purse and began looking at vitamins, supplements and four bottles of pills.

"What are these? Neupogen?"

Imogen grabbed the bottle. "Cancer drug."

"What are these big ones?"

"Vitamins."

Bridgett popped one of the large cylinders into her mouth. "Ooooo, Zoloft. Excellent. I'll take one of these."

"Bridgett!" Now Imogen rolled her eyes and smiled. "You can't just take one Zoloft. It isn't like Xanax."

Her friend waved her hand away.

"Oh, please. I've been taking these since before you knew what a panic attack was. I am going to pick my new prescription up tomorrow. It's fine. I just left my pills at the office. . . . Besides, I am a little nervous about hanging out with you and my new man."

As if they had conjured him just by speaking his name, Rashid appeared at the entrance to Cafe Gitane, resplendent in a red sweater with heather-gray pants. He leaned in to double kiss Imogen's cheeks before brushing his lips seductively across Bridgett's.

"I hope I gave you enough time to let the cat out of the bag, otherwise that kiss is sure to make Imogen really uncomfortable." He settled into the chair next to a flushed Bridgett.

"So Imogen, how is that idea for your app going?"

"I've barely had time to breathe, much less invent a new company."

Rashid laughed. "One of these days you will start thinking about ideas for new companies while you breathe. I can tell it's in you, Imogen." He lowered his voice and gave it a mechanical monotone. "The force is strong with this one."

The two women delivered blank stares.

"Yoda?" he said, giving them a questioning look. "*Star Wars*?"

Bridgett piped up. "I don't think this is an age thing, is it?"

Rashid shook his head. "No, it's a nerd thing."

The word "nerd" caught Imogen's attention, since Eve loved throwing it out there as if "nerd" were somehow synonymous with "tech." She said as much to Rashid, eliciting a grand sigh from him.

"Eve is the opposite of nerd, isn't she?" Bridgett asked.

Imogen just shrugged.

"I never try to pigeonhole exactly what Eve is. It changes every single day."

Rashid wanted to explain. "There are so many smart women working in technology these days. Take Aerin Chang. She's just so fucking brilliant it makes my brain hurt. Half of the coders we have at BLAST! are now women. That's a big deal considering we had just two last year. I love women in tech. But I hate women like Eve in tech. Eve was very obviously the popular girl in college."

Imogen nodded, indicating that he was not wrong.

"You know what most of the guys in tech were doing in high school and college?" Rashid continued. Both women shook their heads.

"We played a lot of tabletop Dungeons and Dragons and we played with computers. Girls like Eve went to Beyoncé concerts and drank wine coolers while we learned code and we built code and we played games and made games, mostly because we didn't have many friends in high school. We had acne. We were short. A lot of us smelled funny. Our parents' suburban basements were our football stadiums. I figured I would always be the odd brown kid. We didn't go into tech because it was cool. We went into tech because it was what we were good at. Now you have women like Eve sweeping in, hopping onto the next hot thing. She isn't in it because she loves what we do. She's there to make money."

He paused. "Which I respect. I love money. But she's condescending to those of us who've been doing this our whole lives."

Imogen got that. Eve was as condescending to her, a person who had been in magazines her entire life, as she was to Rashid, a person who knew more about technology than she could ever hope to. Eve was simply condescending to everyone. It wasn't the tech that made her a bitch. She was just a bitch.

Imogen's phone peeped at her like a baby bird.

"That's a funny alert noise," Rashid commented.

Imogen blushed. "I am still trying to figure out how to make it make a proper sound." Rashid reached across the table and grabbed her phone. He made a few swipes and taps and then returned it to her.

"Now all messages will come with a very dignified and solemn small bell."

"Thank you," she said, taking it back.

"Oh, and it seems that your girl crush might just have a reciprocal girl crush on you?"

Imogen tilted her head in confusion.

"If I am not mistaken, you just got an email from the one and only Aerin Chang." Imogen tried not to look too eager as she opened her mailbox. Sure enough, there was a message at the top from Aerin2006@gmail.com.

From: Aerin Chang (Aerin2006@gmail.com)
To: Imogen Tate (ITate@Glossy.com)
Subject: Fancy a coffee?

Hi Imogen!

I hope you don't think this email is too forward. I'm a big fan of both you and *Glossy*. I've been having a real blast following your

Instagram. I would love to chat with you about *Glossy* and about what we do over at Shoppit. Essentially I just love sitting down to coffee with smart women and I think we have a lot in common. Would you let me buy you a macchiato?

Cheers,
Aerin

She had her at "macchiato." Imogen must have had a goofy grin on her face, because Rashid and Bridgett were smirking at her.

"She wants to have coffee," Imogen explained. "Did you tell her to email me?"

"I didn't," Rashid replied. "I meant to after we talked about her, but I haven't had the chance yet. You go, girl. Go have coffee and then go take a job at Shoppit and stop working for that little witch," Rashid said.

"Um, that isn't at all what she wants to meet about. One, I have no place at all at a start-up. Two, she hardly knows me. Why would she want to hire me? Three, I like my job."

"I could refute all of those points," Bridgett said. "But I won't. I do think you should meet up with her."

"Is it weird that we kind of became friends on Instagram first and now we are meeting up?" Imogen asked.

Bridgett and Rashid shook their heads, practically in tandem.

"That's how everything works these days," Rashid said. "Everyone meets first online." He considered it further. "For a while people were only talking online, but now everyone seems to be jumping on the whole 'in-person' thing, so online friends are becoming offline friends. Everyone wants to hang out IRL—in real life." Even though Bridgett continued to nod, Imogen doubted that her old friend understood any of this much better than she did. Bridgett was simply better at faking it.

"Should I write back now or should I wait a bit?"

Bridgett laughed. "You're not trying to sleep with her. Just write back and make a date. I don't think you need to play coy here."

"You're right. Obviously." Still, she slipped her phone into her purse, wanting to choose the right words to type back later when she was alone. She didn't know why she wanted Aerin Chang to like her.

Imogen gave a long look at her old friend and her new friend. They were an odd couple indeed, but this was New York City and she had most certainly seen odder. What mattered was that they were both happier together than they'd been when they were apart.

"I love you two."

They rose to hug her.

As she walked home, she composed an email to Aerin in her head.

From: Imogen Tate (ITate@Glossy.com)
To: Aerin Chang (Aerin2006@gmail.com)
Subject: Would love to meet up!

Dear Aerin,

Your email wasn't too forward at all. I am just getting my bearings on Instagram, but I do adore everything that you post. I would love to grab a coffee or a drink. Do you want to let me know what works for you next week and we can go from there?

xo,
Imogen

The reply came in no time at all.

From: Aerin Chang (Aerin2006@gmail.com)
To: Imogen Tate (ITate@Glossy.com)
Subject: RE: Would love to meet up!

So excited! I actually have an opening tomorrow afternoon. It's short notice and I'm sure you are busy as hell, but do you have any

interest in coming by the Shoppit office for lunch? We can order in
here. Super casual. Let me know!

xo
Aerin

Why not? Imogen asked herself. Lunch with Aerin Chang at the
Shoppit office sounded delightful. Still, she had butterflies in her
stomach, as if she were going on a first date.

CHAPTER TWENTY-FOUR

This dress is a complete piece of shit!" was the first thing Imogen heard when she walked into the office the next morning.

"Someone get me out of this piece of shit!"

Rounding the corner, Imogen could see that all of the fuss was taking place around three stainless-steel rolling racks of wedding dresses lined up along Eve's desk. Without an ounce of propriety she was slipping them over her matching red lace bra and panties, oblivious to the fact that her brazen nakedness might make anyone within eyeshot a little bit uncomfortable. Imogen glanced at the labels: Vera Wang, Dennis Basso, Pnina Tornai, Reem Acra, Lanvin and Temperley. These were all $10,000-plus dresses, $100k on that rack alone, and Eve treated them like she'd just grabbed them from the discount bin at T.J.Maxx. She wiggled her way out of a Monique Lhuillier mermaid dress and chucked it across the room.

"Nothing is right!" Eve glowered at the rack.

Trying to make her eyes fall anywhere else, Imogen strained not to take in Eve's toned physique—a six-pack of abs, sculpted little triceps like oblong kiwis and not an ounce of cellulite. What must it be like to have that self-confidence? To have no barrier, no apprehension about what anyone else was thinking about you? She wandered over to Eve's tall desk and distracted herself by picking up the only piece of clutter, a toy plastic dinosaur. The long neck meant it was a brontosaurus. Johnny begged for one of these every time she took him to the American Museum of Natural History. It was nice to have something to occupy her hands. She ran her finger along the pebbled plastic surface of the toy.

"Imogen." Eve's snap brought her attention back to the moment. "Which of these dresses do you like?" Walking closer to the racks, Imogen tried not to feel like she was following orders. She feigned an actual interest in pulling them down and examining them.

"Well, Eve," she began slowly. "It depends what look you're going for. When you thought about your wedding when you were a little girl, what did you see? Were you a princess? Were you glamorous? Sexy?" Eve's lower lip protruded from the top one and she bit down a little. Her hands moved up on her hips.

"I loved Kaley Cuoco's wedding dress . . . and the one Chrissy Teigen wore when she married John Legend. Oh, and that bitchy girl from *The Bachelor,* the wedding they had on live television. I loved Pippa at Kate's. I think my style can best be described as 'sexy princess,'" she said, with the determination of an Olympic figure-skating judge.

Imogen briefly imagined shaking the girl and telling her she was the reason brides got such a bad name. Instead, always the editor, she thought quickly, considered the dresses, and ran her hand over the fabrics. She loved wedding dresses, loved the sense of occasion that went into creating them, the beading, the lace, the handiwork. A wedding dress was an event all unto itself, for some women the most important part of the big day, maybe even more important than the groom. "Okay, so I think we want a fuller skirt, but nothing too big, with a strapless top."

Imogen pulled an Alexander McQueen sweetheart ball gown in silk satin with a natural waist and beaded embroidery and presented it to Eve. "Be delicate though, the beading can get caught on nearly anything and the whole thing will unravel at your fingertips." Eve rolled her eyes and clumsily stepped into the dress, her foot coming down on the inside seam. Imogen blocked out the sound of something tearing. Eve yanked it up. The dress caught on her bra and she wailed for Ashley to come behind her to zip her up.

What a gorgeous gown, Imogen thought. Classy and yet sexy at the same time, a dress fit for royalty that showed the right amount of skin.

Eve wrinkled her nose. "Is it too old-fashioned?"

"I think wedding dresses should be a little old-fashioned," Imogen said.

"Of course you think that." Eve gave a rueful laugh. "I like this one. Let's add it to the maybes." She reached behind her, cocking her arm at a painful-looking angle to yank the zipper down and let the dress fall to the floor.

"Eve, be careful," Imogen warned.

"If I mess it up they'll send over another one. We're getting them so much press for this wedding." Eve stepped out of the dress, leaving it in a crumpled heap and knocking her hip into the corner of her desk. Rubbing the bruise, she scowled at the piece of furniture as if it purposely tried to trip her. She walked to the corner, her perfect ass swaying with each step, and pulled on a tight black skirt and low-cut sweater. "Did I tell you that I think we nailed down *Martha Stewart Weddings* magazine?"

Imogen shook her head. "You didn't."

"Yeah, I met one of the editors at Spirit Cycle last night and invited her to come to the wedding. You know she will write about it if I invite her. It will make her feel all special. It *is* expected to be like the wedding of the year."

That was not entirely accurate, but Imogen was sure it would be a well-attended event.

"I'm happy for you." As the words came out of her mouth, Imogen remembered some advice Molly gave to her in her late twenties before she got married. Her mentor had been incredibly intuitive and never needed to ask any questions to know exactly what was going on in any of her employees' lives. There was a stretch, when Imogen was dating Andrew, when six of her friends became engaged and Imogen thought she was never going to find that particular happy ending. Molly, sensing her ennui during a lunch at La Grenouille, said to her: "It's best to be happy for all the weddings . . . all the engage-ments, all the babies, all the job promotions. You must try to be truly happy for these things."

Small talk wasn't ever easy with Eve, but Imogen thought she might as well give it a shot.

"Is your dad walking you down the aisle at the wedding?"

"My dad is dead," Eve said evenly and then, as if realizing she may have been too flip, added, "He passed away last fall while I was at B-school. Heart attack during the last football game of the season."

What could she say? With anyone else Imogen would have apolo-gized profusely, maybe hugged her. Eve had already whipped out her phone, perhaps as an emotional shield, and was snapping pictures of the racks of dresses and posting them on Twitter.

"I'm so sorry," Imogen said.

"It's okay. He went out doing what he loved best." For a second, her steely resolve wavered. "He'd be proud of me right now though. He always wanted me to be in charge of something."

Eve quickly shifted gears. "We can check the dress off the list," she said as she walked back over to her desk while Ashley stooped to pick up the remaining dresses off the floor, doing her best to smooth out wrinkles in the satin and organza before returning them to the rack and rolling them into another corner of the office.

"Eve, I have a lunch meeting today," Imogen began.

"Sounds good. Have you met the new staffers?"

Imogen hadn't. Twelve new women arrived in the office that morning to replace the six they let go the day before.

"Not yet, but I'll make some time this afternoon."

"Good. The amount of content we are producing is already up. Traffic is up. It was a good move. My decision was definitely the right one." Eve paused for a second.

"This city is hard." Eve swallowed impatiently. "Not everyone is cut out for it."

"Sometimes you have to give people chances."

"Isn't that what I gave them? When they got the job here?"

Imogen decided to change the subject again. "So, after my lunch why don't we go over the details for the big winter fashion photo shoot?"

The winter fashion photo shoot was something of a coup for Imogen. She knew Eve hated spending money, especially on photo shoots, but showcasing designers in innovative ways was still something that mattered to Imogen. It was the heart of *Glossy*. Her own employees had been her inspiration for this shoot. She would feature young women working in tech wearing amazing designers. They would use a few models, but mostly real women, on the subway on their iPads, walking around town in Google Glass, on a conference call while going for a jog and sitting with their laptops all over the city. It would be gorgeous and empowering all at once and Imogen had exactly the photographer for the job. Her good friend Alice Hobbs was perfect for this. A fellow Brit, Alice was raised in both London and Switzerland. She understood women, captured their inner strength. She'd taken a two-year hiatus from fashion in the 2000s to shoot tribal women in Namibia, publishing her first book of photographs, titled *Brave*. Alice wasn't cheap, but Imogen knew she was worth every penny and she somehow managed to convince Eve that she was the way to go. Eve was reluctant to spend money on things that mattered to Imogen, but she was loose with Glossy.com's cash when it came to things that mattered to her.

Ashley let it slip that Eve was paying $10,000 and $20,000 to a handful of celebrity starlets to compel them to show up to her wedding and be photographed for just half an hour. She was also in negotiations to have her idol, the pop singer Clarice, serenade her as she walked down the aisle.

Eve shrugged. "Whatever. It's just a photo shoot. I would be just as happy with someone taking pics on their iPhone. It might even be better, right? More raw! Maybe we should think about that?"

"We already put Alice on contract, remember?"

"Well. Next time. Let's see how much extra traffic we get from having 'the famous Alice Hobbs,' as you call her, taking pictures instead of, like, 'Intern Number Two.'" And then as an aside, more to herself than to anyone else in the room, Eve muttered, "We should get some more interns in here. One more thing . . . let's talk about creating some holiday GIFs."

"You're so right," Imogen said. "I've been so busy I forgot all about the holiday gift guide. I think we should think out of the box this year. We can still do some of the traditional mom gifts, dad gifts, boss gifts, but let's get a little wild. Gifts for your gay best friend, gifts for the office frenemy. We could have a lot of fun with it."

Why was Eve laughing? She guffawed so hard a small snort came out of her mouth.

"GIFs, Imogen. I want to create some viral GIFs, you know, those moving pictures Buzzfeed is always doing . . . gift guides. You crack me up. Can I tweet that? I'm going to tweet that." Imogen felt like a fucking idiot and began backing toward her own office, not noticing the plastic brontosaurus still in her hand until Eve shouted to her.

"Hey, give that back to me." Flustered, Imogen looked down at her hands.

"I'm so used to grabbing these toys when the kids leave them around. I wasn't paying attention." She twisted it around as she tried to return it to its rightful place on the desk. On the side she hadn't looked at, very clearly written with a thick black marker, was her name, IMOGEN, in neat all-cap letters. Why was her name on this plastic toy?

Eve noticed her confusion and for a moment she may have been at a loss for words. The moment, however, was brief. And she picked up the brontosaurus.

"I named it Imogen." She held it aloft in one hand and made it do a little jig. "Because you're our office dinosaur." Eve's lips turned up at the corners in a cruel smile. How was Imogen meant to respond? There was no shame in Eve's face. She kept her eyes locked on Imogen's.

Laugh it off. I have to laugh this off.

"I've always thought of myself as more like the T. rex than a bronto," Imogen said, walking away from Eve's desk.

* * *

Eve didn't want anyone walking her down the aisle. This was *her* day. If he'd been around her dad surely would have stolen the spotlight. He always did. It sucked being the unwanted daughter of the most popular man in town.

Big John Morton had passed his willful stubbornness along to his daughter as surely as he passed on his lumpy earlobes and wide mouth. The man was the most successful failure in Kenosha, Wisconsin. That was Dad—the high school football coach with the best record in the state who had never been invited to move up the ladder because of an attitude problem so severe, no one in the upper echelon of academia wanted to work with him. It was no secret that Big John wanted a boy and he hadn't even tried to mask his disappointment over Eve. It got worse around the house after Eve's mom died. Their similar facial structure and red curls made Big John cringe when he saw his daughter, who he regularly referred to as "just the girl," instead of by her name, despite her best efforts to do all the things a boy child could do.

The girls at Ronald Reagan Memorial Elementary had been cruel to her. Her father had insisted on buying her asexual clothing, striped rugby shirts and baggy khaki shorts. He cut her hair off like a boy's.

Finally, in junior high she rebelled through fashion, dressing as girly as possible, growing out her hair and overdoing it with eye shadow, lipstick and mascara. Boys started to like her and when boys liked you other little girls liked you too, or at least they pretended they did.

Making the varsity swim team in high school and getting a 4.0 still didn't make up for her lack of a Y chromosome. Harvard was the first thing that made her dad proud. Now he was gone. Eve knew she was supposed to feel more, but at the funeral she had a hard time projecting the emotions people wanted to see. She'd almost stayed out East, but then she'd always be known as the girl who skipped her dad's funeral, and that would look like hell all over Facebook.

She'd gone and seen all the losers who didn't think there was a life to live outside of Wisconsin. They really should have been more impressed with everything she had achieved in New York and then in Cambridge. But no one even mentioned Harvard or *Glossy*. It was like they didn't follow her at all. Still, she had invited a group of them to her wedding. That way they would at least post pictures so people back in town would have to see that Eve Morton (soon-to-be Maxwell) was Winning-At-Life.

* * *

The girl who Imogen had seen crying in the elevator had looked broken, but harmless, which was why it surprised Imogen when she saw the email from her that afternoon. It wasn't addressed to her, but to Eve. Imogen was copied, not blindly, along with twenty other *Glossy* employees and journalists from outlets all over the city, ranging from newspapers including the *Post,* the New York *Daily News* and the snarky *Observer* to websites like Gawker, BuzzFeed, TechBlab and the Daily Beast. The email criticized the way that Eve treated her while she worked there and systematically fired her.

From: Leslie Dawkins (Leslie.Dawkins@LeslieDawkins.com)
To: Eve Morton (EMorton@Glossy.com)

Hi, Eve,

You might not remember me. You hired me two months ago as an assistant producer for Glossy.com. Last night you abruptly fired me. No explanation given. I had been working for days on end. I was tired, but I didn't let that stop me from doing my job.

You enjoyed firing me. You smiled the whole time.

I know that I have what it takes to succeed at this job. I have a dual degree in computer science and English from UPenn. This job was MADE for me. You need bright young women like me in that office. Right now you are breeding a staff of robots, there just to do your bidding.

It's not normal to force your staffers to be your friends. It's not normal to make us all stay late and play games. It was weird that you made us all play Truth or Dare.

We're not sisters. We're not family.

I wanted to be your employee.

You made the wrong decision. I hope that my voice can speak for all the young women you have laid off.

You can't treat people like they are disposable.

You can't make people work 24 hours a day.

You can't call us dumb and retarded and lazy and expect us to want to work for you.

You can't shush someone when they ask you why they are being let go after they have worked their ass off for you.

I don't want to work for you anymore, but I did want to give you a piece of my mind about how poorly you are leading Glossy.com. I am fine with burning this bridge down all the way to the ashes because it is a bridge I never want to cross again.

I deserve to have a last word.

Leslie Dawkins

Imogen felt a surge of embarrassment for the young woman. Was she drunk when she wrote the email?

"What is this?" she messaged Ashley, copying and pasting the text.

Ashley replied with a frowny face emoji. She appeared in Imogen's office a minute later, sighing and looking less perky than usual.

"I'm surprised this hasn't happened yet. It's like a kind of a trend these days. When people get fired or they don't get a job, they shoot off these public rants. I'm sure it will get picked up on a website soon."

Imogen was horrified. Wouldn't someone want to bury something like this, move on quietly? Ashley correctly read Imogen's expression.

"My people overshare. I'm sure you've figured that out," Ashley said, referring, Imogen assumed, to millennials as "her people," not Upper East Side WASPs, who traditionally did not overshare. Imogen nodded, indicating she should go on. "People actually end up getting job offers from other places after they do something like this. It's ballsy, but it can end up working in someone's favor."

"How so?"

"Some start-ups want to hire people who aren't afraid to put themselves out there. It's kind of like blasting your résumé out to a million people. You're bound to hit someone who is hiring."

"But it *is* humiliating," Imogen countered.

"Humiliation is relative these days. Maybe it is, maybe it isn't. All she said was that Eve was a crappy boss and that was why she was let go. There are worse things that can happen to you on the Internet."

"So what do we do?"

"Oh, we ignore it. If anyone calls for comment we say that we don't discuss current or former employees. These things have a life cycle of about twenty-four hours . . . even if they get picked up by another website," Ashley said casually.

"Damn. I'm late for my lunch." Imogen stood and grabbed her cashmere camel coat. "I hope people just delete this. Maybe no one will forward it or repost it? It's silly."

* * *

That morning, Imogen had scoured her closet for the perfect outfit to wear to Shoppit for lunch, finally settling on a copper-colored Chloé pencil skirt with a Peter Pilotto embroidered top paired with an oxblood Kensington Mulberry bag and Vera Wang black suede pumps. Chic and conservative without being stuffy or, as Eve would so kindly put it, "old-fashioned." She ran a brush through her hair sitting at her desk, happy she'd had the roots touched up over the weekend. She swore the gray began creeping in faster over just the past six months. Gray made some women look sophisticated. Imogen didn't think she would be one of those women. She would be a blonde until they shut the lid of her coffin.

Shoppit had offices in a loft space downtown. Rashid informed her that the company had plans to move at the start of the new year into a new space in Williamsburg, Brooklyn, carved out of the old Domino Sugar Factory. For now, they had half of a building on Greenwich Street. Reception for Shoppit was on the ground floor.

"Hi, Imogen," a perky Asian girl with an egg-shaped head and large red glasses said as she walked through the door.

"Hello," Imogen replied with what must have been a look of utter surprise. *Do we know each other?* The girl giggled.

"We take people off guard sometimes when we just blurt out their name," she said. "It isn't magic or anything. Your name is in our system to go see Aerin and it has an image of you that we pulled from Google. We just think it's nice to greet guests by name when we have the time." She lowered her voice. "It creeps some people out though."

Imogen moved back half a step as she laughed along with her. "It definitely creeped me out a little bit."

"Do you mind signing in on the screen there?" She motioned to a sleek white tablet on the desk in front of her. "It will print out your badge for you. It already has your name and stuff, but it wants to take a picture of your ID. Just hold your license under the little red light." Imogen pulled out her New York State driver's license and held it under the blinking red dot. A name badge slid out of the side of the tablet. The girl handed Imogen a small gray piece of plastic no bigger than her thumb that looked like the kind of key fob she used to enter the gym in the Robert Mannering Corp. building.

"This will tell you where to go. It makes noise and vibrates a little. Do you want a water for your walk?" The girl gestured toward a refrigerator stacked with individual boxes of water similar to the one Rashid had given her at DISRUPTTECH!

Imogen *was* a little bit freaked out as she ran her thumb over the smooth plastic shape, especially when the small gray object spoke to her with a perfect Oxford British accent. "Please proceed to the right elevator bank. You will be going to floor number four." Behind the desk, the girl's eyebrows bobbed in delight at the technology.

"These are new. They're programmed to know who you're seeing and how to get you there. It also knows where you are. It has a GPS so it lets us know if you go anywhere you aren't supposed to go. It will open any doors along the way. I just think they are the coolest."

"The coolest." Imogen nodded.

She walked to the right elevator bank and held the device up to her face. It looked entirely unremarkable, just a piece of plastic with three small holes on one side that must have been a speaker. Once she was in the elevator it politely reminded her to push the button for four. At the fourth floor she entered a brightly colored lobby-like space with a couple of low-sitting couches, but no reception area. The walls were covered in scribbled marker and there were glass doors to the left and to the right.

"Please travel through the set of doors to your right."

Imogen did as she was told. The voice was soft, just loud enough that she could keep it in her hand and have her arm resting alongside her body and still hear it, but not so loud that it could be heard by anyone more than two feet away from her. As she approached the glass doors she heard a small beep and the click of a door unlocking, undoubtedly the magic of her little toy.

"Please proceed straight."

Open and airy with battered concrete floors, the Shoppit offices confirmed every urban legend about start-up work spaces Imogen had ever heard. Eager young people sat at rows and rows of desks, not unlike the ones at Glossy.com, but also on couches and in beanbag chairs. Some stood at their desks, like Eve. Others took it a step further and appeared to be walking on treadmills right at their desks. In a completely clichéd moment someone zipped by on a scooter. No one paid Imogen much mind as she strolled among them. At the end of the floor was a wall of glass offices. "Turn right," her device told her as she was about to reach the wall. She walked past four offices and was advised to stop as she came to the one at the corner.

"You have arrived," it informed her. The words felt heavy.

Imogen looked up to see Aerin Chang sitting on a chair in the far right corner of the office. The back of the chair leaned against the glass, making it look as though she could topple, at any moment, into the river down below. The girl's smile was bright and welcoming as she gestured to the table and a platter of macarons and then beckoned Imogen through the door. She stood and walked over, leaning in for a hug and then laughing.

"I feel like I know you after looking at all your Instagrams and that made me feel like we should hug, but then I remembered we had never met in person." Imogen laughed too, realizing that she felt exactly the same way.

"I can't even look at your Instagram. I get so jealous," Aerin said.

"No. Yours! So jealous." Imogen laughed back.

Aerin had a look of studied indifference. She wore a casual pair of waxed leggings with a graphic T-shirt and an Isabel Marant leather jacket with a pair of to-die-for high-heeled studded boots. Sitting on her shoulder-length black hair was a Rag & Bone fedora. She was petite. Despite her four-inch heels she barely reached Imogen's shoulder. An amazing art deco emerald ring adorned the middle finger of her left hand. Her ring finger was bare except for a thin tan line.

"I asked my assistant to stop by our macaron stand before you got here. I remembered that you liked my post about them." Aerin fished a crumpled piece of paper out of her pocket. "She wrote down the flavors: Lemon Meringue, Pistachio Dream, Mocha Raspberry Frappé." Imogen leaned over to grab a pale yellow cookie.

"That one is Lemon Meringue." Aerin clapped her hands in delight.

Imogen bit into the cookie and sweetness tap-danced over her tongue as she felt all of the tension about this meeting melt through to the beautiful wood floor.

"These came from your macaron stand?" Imogen said, confused.

"Yes. Isn't that wild? We have an actual macaron shop right here in the Shoppit offices. We have nine floors in total with all sorts of amenities. The macarons aren't free but they are very, very cheap. The barbecue joint and the taco stand are free, as are the cafeterias . . . obviously. We have a hair salon that does five-dollar shaves and ten-dollar haircuts. There is an arcade on the second floor and a gym in the solarium on the roof. We're getting a noodle shop soon. Everyone is really excited about the noodle shop."

It was like Main Street, U.S.A., in Disney World.

"Sit, sit," Aerin said. "I'm happy you came by. I asked someone to grab us salads from the chopped salad bar in the cafeteria. We stole a chef from Facebook recently! He's sooooo good. But we can go out if you want."

Imogen shook her head. "I'd love to stay here."

Aerin settled into the chair opposite her. "Good, good." She tapped out a quick email on her iPhone. "The food should be up in a few minutes."

"So, I have to ask you." Imogen cleared her throat. "Why did you want to meet me?"

"I knew my invite was strange." Aerin buried her head in her palms. "I feel like a weirdo." Imogen could tell that Aerin didn't really feel like a weirdo. She exuded a calm confidence in everything that she did. Her brown eyes were steady in their assessment of Imogen.

"I love meeting new people." Imogen flicked her hand downward to underscore the point. "In fact, my friend Rashid had meant to introduce the two of us. He just hadn't gotten around to it yet."

"Rashid from Blast!?" Aerin's eyes widened. "He rocks. He is like a weird super genius with the absolute best taste in clothes."

"He said the same thing about you."

"Noooooo." Aerin waved her hand back and forth as if sweeping the compliment away. "He is the genius. He can take the smallest idea and turn it into a multibillion-dollar company. I swear it."

Imogen glanced around. "It looks like you're already running your own multibillion-dollar company."

"Not billion . . . just yet."

Aerin was at ease with herself in a way not many women were. She was humble, but didn't shrink from the compliments. She sat taller when she began talking about her company, telling Imogen about how she started out as the fourth employee at Shoppit when they were working out of a buddy's apartment in Long Island City, Queens.

"I grew up in the suburbs of Saint Louis, where fashion meant the Gap. Don't get me wrong. I *love* the Gap, but I wish I'd had a few other options. I don't just mean expensive stuff either. I wish I could have browsed the stalls in Chinatown, finding two-dollar sandals, or the table vendors in SoHo selling ten-dollar necklaces. That's what Shoppit is all about. We are trying to create a truly global fashion marketplace that will benefit big brands and small brands and kids in Missouri who just want to accessorize. Fashion is an industry that builds walls up and my personality is the opposite of that. I am all about breaking those walls down. Fashion is a lifestyle now. For centuries fashion was inaccessible."

Imogen knew Aerin was dumbing things down for her, but she was still impressed. She loved that the woman didn't once mention traffic or revenue or data. She talked about a creative concept and the love of that concept. That was what *Glossy* was to Imogen in the early days. It was a way to showcase the very best of fashion to people who didn't get to live in that world day in and day out. Imogen said as much to Aerin.

"I knew we had that in common," Aerin replied.

"But don't you ever worry that we are giving too much away on social media? When you show so much of your personal life?" Imogen asked, and she didn't regret the bold question when it came out of her mouth.

Aerin chewed thoughtfully on a macaron. "Designers used to be these mythical people. Who was Coco Chanel? I don't really know what she was like. Until a few years ago people didn't really know who Karl Lagerfeld was when he went home at night. And now he is on Instagram posting pictures of his cat and you have Prabal on there posting pictures of himself at the gym and what he is doing on vacation. People don't want myths anymore. They want to buy products from real people and I think social media helps these mythical figures become real people," the younger woman replied, just as an attractive man in a bright green checked shirt walked in with two trays filled with salads, veggies and lemonade.

"Chuck, this is Imogen Tate."

"Hi, Imogen." Chuck smiled at her.

"Chuck is one of our data scientists . . . and an impromptu chopped salad deliverer."

"So pleased to meet you, Chuck. I have no idea what a data scientist does," Imogen said with complete honesty.

"Some days I don't either."

They laughed easily.

"Chuck is a statistics guru is what he is. Do you want to join us?" Aerin asked him with a genuine sincerity.

He shook his head. "Too much work to do. But I'll catch you guys later. Bye, Imogen." He winked.

"He is so sweet."

"And really good at his job," Aerin said, pulling a plate of salad onto her lap. "Do you mind that we are just eating here, picnic style? I'm sure you're used to really fancy lunches."

"I've been having a lot less fancy lunches lately. This is nice."

Both women chewed for a moment.

"I meant it when I said I really just wanted to meet you in person," Aerin said after she swallowed a few bits of kale. "I've loved *Glossy* since I was a kid."

"I'm glad we're doing this," Imogen said.

"I saw the email that Leslie Dawkins sent to Eve," Aerin said. She'd been having such a pleasant time, it took Imogen a minute to remember both Leslie Dawkins's name and the letter.

"How? She sent it about twenty minutes before I got here."

"It was up on TechBlab five minutes before you walked in. I'm not going to ask you about it or what it is like to work there right now. I can imagine. I know women like Eve. But I also know a lot of young people in this industry who aren't a damn thing like her who would die to get to work with someone like you."

Imogen sighed. "I have a pretty steep learning curve with tech." She thought a second before she added her dirty little secret. "I've become a regular at the Apple Genius Bar."

Aerin's smile was warm. "Then you would love our Shoppit 'Walk Up Windows.' We have help bars right here. You can walk up to them any time of day or night and they'll help you with pretty much anything technology related."

The woman took a second to scoop a bit of salad into her mouth. "You know this is new to pretty much everyone. Ten years ago none of this existed. Five years ago ninety percent of it didn't exist. A lot of what we are working with right now in tech just happened five minutes ago. New industries appear and disappear at a dizzying rate. We're all adapting every single day."

Imogen had never thought about it like that; she'd been too focused on her own pity party about how left behind she felt.

"Can I tell you a secret?" Aerin lowered her voice and Imogen nodded. "Humans built the Internet but they don't really understand it. Even I didn't really believe this whole tech thing was going to take off. My parents thought I was crazy. Why didn't I go into banking or, better yet, go to law school? Why didn't I get a job at a magazine, one like yours? In the beginning, when I was jumping from start-up to start-up, I still had no idea any of this would work out. I took the LSAT and the GMAT and the MCAT and planned an exit strategy every single year. I only stopped doing that two years ago. I know this is here to stay and I feel good about what I am doing."

Imogen smiled and grabbed another macaron. She felt good here with Aerin.

That good feeling began to dissipate when Aerin asked: "What don't you like about your site?"

She wanted to trust this girl. Aerin Chang's question rang sincere. She had none of Eve's naked ambition—at least, she didn't wear it the same way that Eve did. She was smart, but not calculating.

Before she knew what she was doing, Imogen let loose everything that drove her insane about the *Glossy* website: the mistakes, the juvenile content, the obsession with traffic, the way photos and videos were thrown into stories like an afterthought, the cheap design, her inability to do photo shoots that made the clothes leap off the screen.

Aerin nodded, never taking her eyes off Imogen to check her phone or to signal to an assistant. She just listened.

When she finished, Imogen felt like a weight had been lifted from her shoulders.

Aerin said, "You have to love a brand a lot to give it the right refresh. I just think Glossy.com could be so much better. I think that the idea of blending commerce and editorial online is brilliant. I think it can be done in really smart and gorgeous ways. I don't know if Glossy.com has done that." She paused again. "Let me know if I am overstepping with my criticism."

Imogen gave her head a small shake.

"I would be lying if I didn't admit to having it in the back of my head that maybe we could find some way to work together."

"How do you mean?"

Aerin moved her plate back to the low table between the chairs and leaned over, putting her elbows on top of her knees.

"I don't know yet. Maybe a partnership. Maybe something more. I know Shoppit is lacking a clear editorial direction. We need creative eyes. We need to work with more people who know fashion, who love fashion. I'm just not sure what a position would look like yet. I think maybe this is my way of asking whether you would ever even consider leaving *Glossy.*"

Could she know that Imogen considered leaving *Glossy* at least twice a day—once when she woke up in the morning and once when she went to bed at night?

"I am going to be blunt," Aerin continued. "Would you ever consider coming to work somewhere like Shoppit? Probably not, right? You must think we're all a bunch of nerds."

Aerin must have sensed that Imogen didn't know what to say. "You don't need to answer me now. I just wanted to plant the seed in your head."

There was a part of Imogen that wanted to jump up and scream, *Yes! Take me away from the hell I am stuck in every day!* Then there was the part of her who, despite everything that had gone on, was protective of her magazine and wanted to see it through, couldn't abandon her loyalty to *Glossy.*

"I appreciate your offer so much. I know it must seem like things are dire over at *Glossy* from that email, but it isn't all that bad. I love my magazine." Imogen hoped she wasn't letting too much emotion creep into her voice. "I want to see it do well, even if that means it lives online. I need to stick with it for now, if that makes sense, but I cannot tell you how flattered I am." Imogen thought about Molly. Maybe there was a place at Shoppit for Molly? She thought about the brontosaurus toy on Eve's desk. "Seriously, I know that there aren't a lot of people like you looking for people like me and I want us to be friends and keep talking, if that's possible."

"That's exactly what I want too. Now, will you help me finish these macarons?" Aerin paused. "I should also let you know, since you haven't been online since you got here, that another email leaked to TechBlab besides Leslie's."

Imogen froze. Was it something she had written?

Aerin stood and grabbed a slick black iPad off her desk. She typed in a web address. It was an email that Eve had sent to one of the Bangladeshi assistants from the outsourcing company Zourced.

From: Eve Morton (EMorton@Glossy.com)
To: Rupa Chary (RChary@Zourced.in)

Dear Rupa,

How is my favorite Bangladeshi assistant? Can you put all of the wedding guests into a spreadsheet organized by their dress size? Most of the girls I invited to the wedding will be a size two or four. They will look good in pictures.

We have made one exception for a size six. Her husband is a very well-known television broadcaster. I think she has a gluten allergy, so it really isn't her fault.

I am also inviting the Gray Hair, my old boss Imogen, and we need to keep her out of the way at the wedding, so please make sure to send me her seating assignment as soon as that is ready.

One last thing. Could you send an email out to all of the women reminding them that UNDER NO CIRCUMSTANCE can they wear black to the wedding. I need this day to POP!

I hope it isn't too hot over there!

E.

Imogen's hand fluttered to her hair.

"She thinks I'm ancient," Imogen said.

"It isn't about your hair," Aerin replied without missing a beat. Imogen had forgotten she was being watched.

"'Gray Hair' is like a title. It's a noun. Tech investors use it. Any good VC worth their salt . . ." Aerin slowed down. "Any good venture capitalist worth their salt won't just fund a bunch of kids or a kid with a good tech idea. Kids have a million ideas a day. The investors make them bring in a 'Gray Hair,' someone with a history in whatever industry they are in who can keep the kids in line. You might be the Gray Hair for *Glossy*." Aerin looked at her apologetically. Imogen was partially relieved that the nickname had nothing to do with a poor dye job.

"Do you have Gray Hairs here at Shoppit?" she asked.

At that Aerin laughed. "We have purple hairs. Our investors are so conservative that we have a whole squadron of industry vets here. If you came to us you would be considered a toddler."

That brought a small smile back to Imogen's face.

"Who leaks all this stuff to TechBlab anyway?"

"Everyone. I never put anything on email anymore unless I pause for a second and think about whether I want the president of the United States to read it . . . or my dad."

Imogen sighed.

"That is no way to live."

"But it keeps us honest." Aerin reached out her hand to shake Imogen's. "We'll meet again?" Imogen grasped her hand back. Her palm was soft and the handshake firm, but not aggressive.

"We will. And in the meantime we still have Instagram."

"That we do," Aerin replied. "That we do."

Imogen felt energized walking back to the office. Aerin Chang wanted to work with her! She may be a Gray Hair, but still, someone as young and hip as Aerin, at a company like Shoppit, thought she had potential in tech. She was halfway down the block when she realized she hadn't returned her slick little navigator. She rubbed her thumb across it before dropping it in her bag to keep as a souvenir.

* * *

After the kids were sleeping in their beds that night, Imogen ran through the myriad emails she missed during the day.

The Hobbs photo shoot was all set with a seven a.m. call time at the Four Seasons in the morning.

Ashley helped her produce the shoot with six models, including Coco Rocha, Carolyn Murphy and Hilary Rhoda. She had also asked Rashid to help her choose four up-and-coming women in the tech industry, young founders and CEOs, to use as real-person models. The designers were all classic American names ranging from Michael Kors to Marc Jacobs to Lucia to Donna Karan and Calvin Klein. When the shoot was finished all of the photographs would be translated to the BUY IT NOW paradigm, but Imogen loved the concept of the shoot so much that that didn't even bother her. She was eager to capture the young power CEOs wearing fashion-forward techie accessories like Google Glass and bags with Bluetooth technology and sensory mood jewelry while working on their tablets. They'd have GoPros mounted on their purses during the entire shoot. That was Ashley's idea. They'd use that video for behind-the-scenes footage from the shoot. What Eve had said about taking pictures with an iPhone had stuck in Imogen's head through the night until finally it clicked—Alice *could* do the shoot with an iPhone. Why not take this creative, free application, Instagram, and add the exquisite eye of Alice to tell this story. She'd heard through the grapevine that Mario Testino was considering a shoot like this for *Número*. It was a way to be creative and cheap.

Convinced that the photo shoot actually might go her way, Imogen allowed herself to log on to the TECHBITCH Facebook page. It was becoming a guilty pleasure and she tried not to visit every single day, but the comments made her laugh so hard.

My boss asked that no one look him directly in the eye.

My supervisor emails me nonstop through the weekend, starting at 6 am on Saturday.

I've ordered dinner on Seamless at the office every night for 45 straight days.

I signed up for Codecademy! Who's the techbitch now!

Within minutes there were three responses to that post.

You go girl!

I am doing it and it's awesome. Learning JavaScript now! I am like a JavaScript ninja.

It will change your life.

Love it.

Imogen yawned. She could stay up for only five more minutes tops. She typed in "www.codecademy.com." She had expected a lot of fancy bells and whistles, but the site was unassuming and simple.

"Learn to code interactively for free. People all over the world are using Codecademy." There was an option to build projects, join a community or show off your profile to others. It wasn't nearly as frightening as Imogen had imagined. She clicked the button to sign up, entering her first and last names, her email (Gmail!) and a password. She always used the same password, which she also knew was the epitome of foolishness in the age of identity theft. It was Johnny-Annabel1234. She made a mental note to change it one of these days. The next screen gave her the option to sign up for her first course, HTML & CSS, abbreviations that had no immediate association in Imogen's brain. She allowed her thoughts to wander for a moment on what they could possibly mean. Haute Taupe Milled Leather, Cerulean Summer Sandals . . . Imogen giggled at her silliness, yawned and decided she would learn what they really meant tomorrow or perhaps later in the week.

An ad for Shoppit appeared on the side of her screen. Imogen clicked it. The site was well organized by type of item and it looked as if it sold absolutely everything anyone in the world would ever want to buy. Imogen clicked over to the website's fashion section. It was simple and utilitarian, lacking a sexiness that Imogen craved when looking at fashion content. Aerin was right, her site could use some glitter.

Imogen wondered: *What if Shoppit did the opposite of* Glossy? *What if it turned a commerce site into a magazine instead of the other way around? Was that crazy? Was anything crazy anymore?*

She pulled a notepad from the nightstand drawer and began drawing mock pages.

Aerin was serious about importing high and low into the Shoppit website. There actually was a whole section of the site devoted to street jewelry sold by vendors on Prince Street in SoHo.

What if they created a magazine that built stories around those items? They could interview the artisans and tell their story. What if they paired the jewelry with gorgeous clothes? Wouldn't that inspire someone to BUY IT NOW? She began copying her notes into a document on her laptop.

She could do that for Shoppit. She should be doing it for *Glossy*. She went to sleep right after she closed the computer.

CHAPTER TWENTY-FIVE

As promised, the location van for the photo shoot, really a rickety mobile trailer for hair, makeup and catering, was parked in front of the Four Seasons at seven a.m.

Ashley sauntered up the steps of the van at 6:59, her hair pulled into a high ponytail at the crown of her head and cascading down the sides of her cheeks in large curls.

"Am I late?" Wearing Adidas original sneakers, torn-up Rag & Bone jeans and a perfectly crisp white tuxedo shirt, the girl glanced down at her phone, and, seeing the time, smiled with a sense of pride. "Nope. I am a minute early," she said as she sipped from a large Starbucks cup with "Ash" scrawled in cursive on the side. She thrust a second Starbucks into Imogen's hand. "Macchiato, skim milk." Imogen noticed Ashley had one bare ear and that the other was adorned by a huge sculptural jeweled cluster from Marni. It wouldn't have worked on anyone else.

Grateful for the caffeine, Imogen recoiled at hearing the whoop of a siren outside. Probably an ambulance or a fire truck, but a second and third whoop made her stick her head outside the trailer door just as two police officers raised a hand to knock.

"Hello, gentlemen." Imogen beamed at them through gritted teeth.

"Hello, ma'am. We need to see the permit you have for this vehicle."

"Of course. Absolutely no problem. Hold on one quick second." She moved inside the door and lowered her voice.

"Ashley, do you have a copy of the permit for the van?" Ashley's blank stare answered the question for her. "You did remember to get us a permit for the van to park here, didn't you?"

Ashley's head moved back and forth. "Eve said she was taking care of it." Ashley's body tightened into a defensive posture. She slowly raised the Starbucks cup to her mouth to take a sip.

"There were so many details. I booked the models and the hair and the makeup and then Eve wanted new hair and makeup. She wanted Allison Gandolfo from John Barrett at Bergdorf and she was hard to get in touch with and then I booked this van and I called the Four Seasons and Eve said to let her take care of the—"

Imogen cut her off. "So we have no permit?"

"I'll email her. She hasn't sent me any details about one though." Ashley moaned. "I could have missed an email. I'm also trying to tweet and Facebook and Tumbl and Pin and Gram around the clock!" It was no wonder to Imogen that Ashley had a hard time being wonderful at being either an assistant or a social media manager. She was stretched so thin she had no time to master either one and instead was forced to operate at half capacity for each of the jobs. Imogen drew in a deep breath. She'd never done what she was about to do and honestly had no idea if she could pull it off.

After a second of searching, Ashley shook her head.

"She never sent one."

Imogen opened the doors.

"Officers, can I invite you in for some coffee?"

"Ma'am, we really just need to see that permit."

"I am so rude. Can I introduce myself? I'm Imogen Marretti." She used her married name, but spoke in her most proper British accent. "Have we met before? You look so familiar. Maybe at the policeman's ball. My husband, Alex, works in the U.S. Attorney's office and he loves you gentlemen so, so much. He raves about all of the hard work you do. Come on in and let me get you a coffee while I work on finding that permit." The two police officers followed her up the trailer steps and pulled out chairs at the small dingy table in the back.

"We know your husband, ma'am," the first officer, a handsome guy in his late twenties, said. His name badge read OFFICER CORTEZ. "Good guy, that Alex Marretti. He put away a coupla drug dealers I brought in last year."

"I didn't know his wife worked in the movies though," the other one, burly with a bald head, black bushy eyebrows and the jawline of an ox, replied as though he were the most hilarious man in the room. The burly one had no idea that the fly on his pants was down, Imogen noted with a small degree of satisfaction. She waited until no one else was looking and then winked at him and touched the zipper of her own pants. He gave her a grateful smile.

"How adorable are you? I'm not in the movies. I'm a magazine editor. Hold on just one second and let me work on finding you that permit." She went back to Ashley. "Go to that little bakery down the street and get us a box of doughnuts." The girl wrinkled her nose at the mention of trans fats and processed sugars, but complied without saying a word.

Imogen made the motions as though she were looking through her laptop for a very specific email or document. She was actually composing an email to Eve asking if she had the permit for the trailer to be parked there.

"I'm sure I'll be able to find it in just a moment," she said over the top of her screen. "I'm so, so sorry to make you handsome men wait like this. I know how busy the city keeps you guys. This is my first shoot back. I don't know if Alex shared this with his work colleagues, but I was out on medical leave for a few months and I am really just getting my sea legs back." Imogen despised playing a damsel in distress, but with a certain breed of man, it was the one role that could get you exactly what you wanted. She hated the next word even more, but lowered her voice, "Cancer."

"I'm so sorry to hear that, ma'am."

"Please call me Imogen." She paused and then let a stricken look cross her face. "I am so stupid," she cried. "I can't believe I did this. I just cannot believe it."

Cortez looked up and cocked his head in a question.

Imogen continued, "We asked for a permit for the wrong day."

The bald one shook his head a little, but Cortez's eyes implored him.

"We don't normally do this, Imogen, but we could maybe let that permit slide."

Imogen had never expected it to work.

Cortez placed a hand over hers.

"You're under a lot of stress." Cortez tried again. "Seriously. We want to help. Your husband helps us keep the bad guys off the street every single day. How about we put some police tape around this here trailer and no one will bother you for the rest of the day."

Imogen reached over and hugged the man.

"Also, Officer? Would you mind terribly not telling Alex about this? I would be so embarrassed if he knew I wasn't able to hold it together at work like this. I don't want him to worry about me."

Just then Ashley returned with a box of pastries. No sooner had she placed the box on the table than a chubby hand reached in and raised one to his lips, stopping just before he took a bite.

"What is this?" He looked at the baked good with the confusion of a basset hound given lettuce.

"It's a donnoli," Ashley declared. "Half doughnut. Half cannoli. It's like the new Cronut or something." She was proud to have found such a gourmet delicacy in midtown. The officer just shook his head.

"Well, I'll be," he said and took a bite, frosting catching in his bristly mustache.

Cortez rolled his eyes slightly at his partner and nodded to Imogen. "Today is our little secret." Men loved feeling complicit in a secret with a beautiful woman.

The police officers ambled down the steps and began wrapping the trailer in police tape as though it were a crime scene. Imogen texted her husband.

>>>>Asst. forgot permit. Had to cry and drop your name with the police. Hope is ok.<<<<

>>>>Use what you got. Get 'em gorgeous.<<<<

An email arrived from Eve a couple of seconds later with just one line: "Isn't getting a permit for YOUR photo shoot YOUR job?"

Thankfully everyone else was about twenty minutes late for the shoot. Coco and Hilary miraculously arrived at the exact same time, both clean-faced with freshly washed hair, blank canvases ready to be painted.

"Okay, Ashley, now tell me about this makeup change that Eve asked for?" Imogen turned to her assistant, who was busily tweeting something. "I thought we lined up Pat McGrath." Ashley barely looked up as she replied.

"Eve wanted someone cheaper so she booked makeup herself."

Imogen tried not to show how livid she was. "Do you know who it is?"

"Someone she ended up getting for free."

"Ashley, please pay attention. We need to make sure this shoot goes off without a hitch. It's your job to pay attention right now."

"It's also my job to tweet." Imogen could tell the girl regretted the words the second they left her mouth. "I'm sorry," Ashley said. "I'm a little overwhelmed."

Move forward, Imogen thought. *Breathe.* At least the hair and makeup people were here, unlike the permit.

Both Hilary and Coco were hungry, but most definitely not for donnolis.

"Do you have any gluten-free breakfast bars?" Coco asked.

Hilary chimed in, "Can I get a protein shake?"

Imogen looked at Ashley, who shrugged and held up her hands. She would need to figure out catering too.

This time Ashley didn't need to be told anything before she left the trailer in search of an organic grocery store at the same time Imogen realized that no one had thought to bring a steamer for the clothes— all now crinkled from transit.

Alice arrived right on time at nine thirty, her tiny frame swathed in what looked like four layers of cardigans and cashmere wraps in varying shades of gray.

"I can't believe I am actually going to shoot this on my phone," she said incredulously. "I'm excited. But nervous." It was the most small talk Imogen had ever heard come out of Alice Hobbs's mouth. Fashion photographers were notoriously bad communicators, at least out loud. They were somehow always able to convey a grand vision for their photographs through one-word grunts, hand gestures and small tap dances, but conversation was simply not their forte.

"I think you will be as genius shooting with an iPhone as you are with a twenty-thousand-dollar camera." Imogen smiled. "Please excuse me for one second while I check on something."

She texted Tilly to find a way to bring her steamer from home.

Hair and makeup were rolling along fine, not perfectly, but fine. Imogen stepped in for a beat to show one of the stylists exactly how to do a wraparound braid on Hilary. She wanted Coco done up like Rita Hayworth in the strapless gown from *Gilda,* all large loose curls and pushed up breasts. She would hold an e-cigarette instead of the real thing and lean seductively against the wall wearing Google Glass.

The pair of stylists stared at her blankly when she mentioned Rita Hayworth. Ashley walked through the trailer, carrying the steamer.

"Ashley, you know who Rita Hayworth was, right?"

"Of course I do. All my style icons are dead . . . or over fifty." Ashley often talked in tweets, small clips of sound bites with abbreviated words. Imogen pulled a photograph up on her phone.

* * *

The next five hours were a frenzy of activity as more models arrived, along with the CEO of MeVest, the biz dev woman from Blast!, a woman who'd pioneered a pair of high-tech yoga pants that wicked away sweat and odor and never needed to be washed. They all had their hair and makeup done and cycled in and out of the restaurant for the photos. Imogen had hired two freelance stylists to be on hand to dress the women. Both pros, they carried out their tasks without a hitch. Once Tilly arrived with the steamer, Imogen gave Ashley a lesson on how to remove all creases and wrinkles from the clothes. Was she really doing this?

"This is a lot of work," Ashley said, holding the steamer lazily in her left hand as the water dripped onto the trailer's floor.

"You're my assistant, Ashley. This is your job. Do you know

the kinds of things I used to do as an assistant? The very first creative director at the very first magazine I worked at threw a Stuart Weitzman shoe at my face because he hated how I steamed something. It nicked my eye." It was Imogen's version of an "I walked four miles uphill to school in the snow" story, but she told it to Ashley anyway. "When I was an assistant at *Moda* I got to the shoots two hours early to prep all of the clothes."

"I can help, darling," Imogen heard a Southern drawl and turned to see a well-dressed brassy blonde, pillowy all over her body. Paula Deen in very, very expensive clothes.

"Moooooom." Ashley's fair skin tinged red as the bottom of a Louboutin. "I told you to just hang out and be quiet."

"Ashley," Imogen said with a small smile. "Do you want to introduce me?"

Obviously embarrassed, Ashley murmured, "Imogen, meet my mom, Constance. Constance, this is my *boss,* Imogen Tate. I'm so sorry about this, Imogen. My mom loves Alice's work and she just wanted to come hang out."

"I came to help out," the older woman interjected. "I know how busy you girls are. Let me do some dirty work. What can I do?" She looked like she had never done an ounce of dirty work in her life, but she took the steamer right out of Imogen's hand and got to work.

Constance was obviously a woman of means and from the tidbits Ashley had revealed, a woman without a career of her own. "She is, like, obsessed with my job," Ashley had once told Imogen. "She lives vicariously through me."

Imogen moved on to the next fire that needed to be put out.

Mina Ekwensi, a Nigerian model who had just come on the scene a few months earlier, had freakishly large feet, yet another thing that Ashley had not bothered to account for.

"It's fine," Mina told Imogen as she squeezed her size-eleven foot into a size-nine shoe. "Sometimes we suffer for our art." Imogen watched in frustration as the model hobbled to the restaurant's entrance.

Imogen hardly had a moment to sit down and collect her thoughts before the entire thing was over. At four p.m., Alice walked out of the restaurant, triumphant, iPhone held over her head. She beamed at Imogen.

"It might be some of my best work. And on a phone, no less." She looked down at the phone and up at Imogen. "Thanks for letting me do this."

There was no way Alice could have seen the bike messenger whirring down the sidewalk. He wasn't supposed to be there, but the trailer, the one with no permit with the yellow police tape wound around it, was blocking the bike lane. It was that bit of the afternoon, about an hour before the glass towers began spewing people onto the streets, where the sidewalks were less crowded than the road. The messenger was in a hurry. Imogen barely saw him until it was too late.

The tires screeched as he braked before causing a true collision, but his wheel still caught Alice square in the thigh, forcing the small woman to the ground. They say the brain slows down when terrible things happen. Imogen saw the phone's entire arc through the air before it landed on the sidewalk, bounced twice and fell squarely in the gutter, which was filled with motor oil and rancid water. It was submerged in seconds.

"Noooooooooo," Imogen shouted, diving for the puddle, splashing the grime all over her black cashmere turtleneck. She picked up the device and poked at it, aware that she now had a small audience staring at her as she knelt on the dirty New York City sidewalk. The screen was shattered, but she thought it might still turn on. She hit the power button. The phone whirred and lights flickered. Like an old dog, wanting nothing more than to please its master one last time, it made a valiant attempt to boot up for her. She silently willed it to work, promising to alleviate all manner of venial sins from her life if some higher power would just let this phone turn on so that Alice's photos could be downloaded. But just as Imogen promised to stop saying "fuck" in front of the children and eating dark chocolate–covered espresso beans, the phone gave its last whimper and drowned right there in her hands.

Crying wouldn't do any good. More than $100,000 had been lost in that puddle. Imogen couldn't even look up at Alice, who, although shaken, appeared to be fine.

"You're okay? Right?" Imogen asked.

The woman nodded.

"And you only used one phone for the shoot?" Imogen asked, still staring at the dark screen.

"Yeah."

Imogen struggled to maintain a poker face as she rose and then walked straight into the trailer, where she locked the door. Leaving decorum on the sidewalk Imogen hurled herself onto the trailer's small couch facedown and pounded her fists onto the plastic wall.

God, she was falling apart. When had she ever really done this? Fallen apart? Never . . . the answer was never.

When the doctors first found her lump, Imogen had ignored them for six days. For nearly a week she didn't tell anyone, just kept going about her business. She knew the second that she admitted something was wrong everything would change forever. She had been right. Now she wanted to cry, but the moment felt too small for tears.

What the fuck had her life come to? She'd paid her bloody dues. She had steamed clothes. She had scrubbed studio floors. She had booked models and gotten permits for fifteen bloody years. Those fifteen years meant she didn't have to do those things anymore. She'd worked her ass off so that she could happily sit at a desk and say yes and no and have lunches and make deals and never have to get down on her knees on a sidewalk and stick her hand into a disgusting puddle. She couldn't do it anymore. She didn't want to do this anymore. Eve had won. She had broken her. This is what it had taken, a photo shoot quite literally gone down to shit. Something like this had happened to her only once before, ten years ago. She had been doing a shoot on the Staten Island Ferry with Pamela Hansen. They had the boat for two hours and had to pay the city an exorbitant fee just for that. Ten years wasn't so long ago, but still the professionals then preferred film. They shot at a breakneck pace, congratulating themselves on a job well done by popping a bottle of Dom Pérignon once they reached land at the Whitehall Terminal. Only after they were all slightly tipsy did they realize the camera had not been loaded with film. Thankfully, they had the money to shoot again the next day. Now that wasn't an option.

Imogen didn't hear the knocking at the door, didn't realize Ashley was on the floor next to her until she touched her shoulder. She flinched at the touch.

"Is anyone else in here with you?" Imogen whispered.

"No. The door is locked."

"How'd you get in?"

"I had the other trailer key."

"Did anyone else see me?"

"No. I was careful."

Imogen still didn't want to look up.

When she finally spoke again, Ashley's voice was calm and authoritative in a way that Imogen hadn't heard it before.

"I think I can fix this," she said.

"Did you get the phone to turn on?"

Imogen turned to the side and propped herself up on an elbow, not entirely ready to pull herself all the way into a sitting position just yet. "Alice's phone is completely donesky. But there's another phone," Ashley said.

Imogen was ready to lie back down. "No, there isn't. Alice only shot with one phone. She just told me."

"Yeah, Alice did. But did you meet Alice's assistant Mack?"

Imogen vaguely remembered a fabulous young gay dressed all in black from his leggings to his eyeliner, trailing behind Alice with an armful of lighting equipment. He was tall and lean and looked like he needed to be coaxed into fresh clothes each morning.

"I didn't meet him," Imogen said.

"He's great. We talked a little when he helped me finish steaming. Anyway, he was behind Alice the whole time she was shooting. He had his own phone. I think he was taking his own pictures."

That made Imogen sit up.

"We have backup photos?"

"We might have backup photos."

Mack was a reluctant hero who knew better than to outshine his boss and mentor. God bless industries that had a very clear pecking order. Ashley managed to pry the phone from his hands.

Imogen could tell it was good from Ashley's face as she swiped through the photographs. She walked over to look over her assistant's shoulder.

They weren't Alice Hobbs photographs, but they were damn close. Mack hadn't just shot behind Alice. He had worked the room, finding angles that even Alice hadn't thought of. At one point he climbed up above the models, shooting them being shot in a moment that was so meta Imogen fell completely in love with it.

To her credit, Alice behaved as though Mack's pictures were a gift from heaven. She wasn't so easily ruffled, but Imogen could tell her ego was suffering a small blow.

"He is very talented," she said to Imogen. "He's been with me three years. I got him right out of Pratt. I bet I lose him now." Imogen took a look at Mack, still sitting in the corner waiting for his instructions.

"You haven't lost him yet, but you should sure as hell promote him."

Imogen walked over to him and wrapped him in a huge hug.

"Mack, you saved the day." The young man showed the start of a smile in a lopsided and handsome way, only the left corner of his mouth rising toward his cheekbone.

"You like them?"

"Like them? I love them. I would have loved them even if we hadn't lost Alice's photographs. You, my dear, are a true artistic talent. You're one to watch!"

His grin reached from Madison to Fifth Avenue.

Ashley came up from behind and threw her arms around the two of them.

"Do we need to go back to the office?"

"We do."

"Mack, we will be in touch with you and Alice."

"Of course, ma'am," Mack said, straightening his curved shoulders a little. "Thanks, ma'am"—Imogen still flinched a little at the word "ma'am."

"Ashley, why don't you Uber us a car," Imogen said. "Actually, no. I think I can do it myself. I can Uber."

CHAPTER TWENTY-SIX

Snow days in New York can be magical or hell on Earth. Every time a storm hits, the city is surprised anew and, without fail, more than two inches of accumulation stymies city services, delays schools and halts traffic in its tracks.

Winter Storm Zeus was all anyone could talk about as Ashley and Imogen were leaving the office later that night. Would the mayor call off school the night before or would they have to wait until the morning? Predictions varied depending on the meteorologist. The Weather Channel promised Manhattan would be buried beneath a foot of snow, whereas CNN reported a mere light dusting, nothing really to worry about.

Sixteen inches of powder blanketed the city by six thirty a.m. and it showed no signs of stopping. Parked cars perched like igloos on the sides of the street with nowhere to go. When Imogen opened her eyes, Johnny was already sitting cross-legged on the foot of her bed.

"No school?" he said, his blond curls spilling over onto his thick eyelashes.

"What's it look like outside, little man?" Imogen said, pulling him into her body.

"Gimme your phone," the little boy demanded. Imogen grasped toward the nightstand to retrieve it. He padded over to the window and expertly opened up the camera to take a picture, then padded back to climb up closer to her head. Alex let out a grand snore into his pillow next to them.

"See, no school," Johnny said pointing at the piles of white coating their street.

Imogen nodded in agreement. "Yes, no school. Probably no work either." She checked her email. Nothing new. No word on whether the offices would be closed, but last time a snowstorm like this had hit, three years ago, Robert Mannering Corp. closed their entire office for three days. At the end of the day, it was up to her. She didn't want employees out in this kind of mess, rushing to get in, possibly driving in hazardous conditions or getting stuck in a crippled public transit system. They worked online now. Wasn't the beauty of the Internet supposed to be that anyone could work from anywhere? After she and Ashley returned to the office the night before they had gone through all of Mack's pictures and agreed they would make an amazing feature, but it wasn't set to run for a few weeks. They had time.

Imogen sat up in bed and straightened her back against the headboard, pulling Johnny into her lap.

From: Imogen Tate (ITate@Glossy.com)
To: GlossyStaff@Glossy.com
Subject: Snow Day

The gods have decided to grant us a snow day. Work from home today. Obviously check in with your direct supervisors ASAP and make sure that you are meeting all of your regular deadlines, but right now it's safer for everyone to stay put.

Keep warm and dry.

xx
Imogen

Alex let out a groan when she nudged him. Johnny ruffled his father's hair.

"Daaaaaaaady, is time to wake up!" their son's voice boomed.

Imogen leaned in to brush her lips against Alex's scratchy cheek. "You might want to check in to see if the courts are going to be open today." Her husband moaned a little again and then rolled right on top of Johnny, unleashing a torrent of tickles that made the little boy wail with laughter. He expertly and modestly wrapped the sheet around his middle like a toga as he strode over to the window.

"Nothing in this city is going to be open today," Alex remarked.

Johnny leaped up and down.

"We should make pancakes." His tiny cheeks flushed with excitement. "We should definitely make some chocolate chip pancakes!!!"

"Beignets," Imogen said, feeling inspired and having a sudden, mouthwatering urge for the comforting, powdered sugar–coated New Orleans–style doughnut. "I'll make us some beignets." Her husband glanced at her with a healthy dose of skepticism, but smartly kept his mouth shut.

There was no way Tilly could make it downtown from her apartment on the Upper West Side. The snow continued to blow in drifts down Jane Street and up against the front door. Imogen could see some resolute neighbors, the ones with the kinds of jobs where a snow day would never be an option, bundled against the ice and the wind, fighting for each footstep as they slogged to reach the subway. No plows had reached the West Village and not even the most dogged taxi would make it down the road.

A few emails trickled in over the next six hours, but nothing earth-shattering. It seemed that everyone had taken her advice to have a lazy day. The content producers could obviously still post from home. It was nice to be able to give the girls a break.

Leaving Alex to do his own work remotely for a few hours, Imogen walked the kids over to Washington Square Park, where a giant snowball fight was in progress. At the far end of the park some older kids had built some of the biggest snowmen that Imogen had ever seen. Still, the snow was coming down so hard, both of her children lasted only thirty minutes outside before they begged to go back into their warm house for hot chocolate.

For a moment, walking home, with one child's hand in each of hers, Imogen was lost in the contentment of it all, dreaming about her life as a stay-at-home mom. She quickly dismissed the notion. This was nothing like what her life would be like. If she didn't work, both of her kids would be in school all day and she would be bored silly.

Snowflakes caught in her eyelashes, giving everything a fine layer of shimmery sequins. A deliveryman passed them on foot, his head hung low, his weatherproof poncho flapping in the wind as he dangled six bags, three in each hand, like the scales of justice. His gait was at least twice as fast as theirs, determined to reach his destination while the food was still warm. It reminded Imogen that some people didn't have a choice about going to work and that it was a blessing to be able to work from home when it was like this outside.

As the kids changed, Imogen signed into the TECHBITCH page.

My boss has an MBA, but no real work experience. Sometimes I think he was actually created in a lab . . . like a cyborg.

The other day we got $50 million in funding and the next morning pictures turned up on the Internet of our CEO rolling around naked in the money. I can barely pay my rent.

Does anyone post things about their jobs on Glassdoor.com?

I LOVE Glassdoor almost as much as I love this site!!!!!

What is Glassdoor.com? Imogen clicked the link. It looked like a place where companies could post help wanted ads for jobs. As she poked around she saw that employees could also post reviews of the places that they worked. She entered *Glossy* into the search box. Nothing appeared. Then she entered Glossy.com. The rating system was based on stars. Out of five stars Glossy.com received an average of two, with twenty-five reviews. The first one Imogen read gave it only one star. The headline was: *When Mean Girls Grow Up, They Work Here.*

> **Pros**—*Lovely location in midtown Manhattan in the very fancy Robert Mannering Corp. office tower*
> *Healthy snacks provided (also some not-so-healthy snacks ☺)*

Cons—*Crazy hours*
Very cliquey, like high school
Does not act like a publishing company
*Editorial director frowns if you eat the "unhealthy" snacks
and makes you go to Spirit Cycle with her. Someone was fired
for not going to Spirit Cycle with her. I mean SERIOUSLY!?????
Who wants to go to Spirit Cycle with their boss?*

*It's hard to get work done when the girl next to you is crying
all the time.*

Horrible office morale.

*Advice to Senior Management—Management needs to learn
to treat people like human beings. We aren't your worker drones.
Maybe don't go on a juice cleanse if it makes you so mean you
fire people.*

*No, I would not recommend this company to a friend—I'm
not optimistic about the outlook for this company.*

And another one: *A Lady Techie's Worst NIGHTMARE*

Pros—*As if!*
Wait, sorry. There are good places to eat lunch by the office.

Cons—*There's absolutely no innovation in the technology
here. It's all about mimicking website designs and functionality
from other websites.*

*The tech team is looking to jump ship. Someone in manage-
ment (why hide it on here, the Editorial Director) actually told
me I could benefit from a juice cleanse, then she started calling
me the Tubby Techie . . . to my face.*

*The same Editorial Director is always asking the product
team (ME) for people's passwords so she can fuck with their
email, their accounts, their documents and their social media.
SHE LIKES TO PLAY GOD! She is terrifying. When I said no, she
said she would fire me. I think she got someone else to do it.*

*Advice to Senior Management—STOP SENDING US SEXY
SELFIES OF YOURSELF. YOU KNOW WHO YOUR ARE. Also, it's*

bad for the company when you're in the press for all the wrong reasons. Keep your personal life personal—not in the public spotlight—although you pretend you don't like it . . . it's obvious you do.

One more: *THE JOB from HELLLLL!!!!!*

Pros—*Maybe I'll get hired by* Vogue *after this? Working with Imogen Tate is wonderful.*

Cons—*My boss is making her staff be in her wedding because she has no friends. It is so awkward. Too bad Imogen Tate won't be working there much longer.*

Advice to Senior Management—Please just let us do our jobs. PLEASE!!!! Can someone help me get a contact at Vogue?

The other reviews were more of the same. One mentioned Eve specifically, calling her the Cruella de Vil of e-Commerce. "We are all her puppies, expected to sit, stay and shit at her bidding."

Imogen wouldn't be there much longer? What the hell. What did that disgruntled employee know? Who was that disgruntled employee anyway? For a second Imogen wondered if it could possibly be Ashley.

Her iPhone began vibrating on the tabletop with a blocked number.

"What the hell, Imogen?" spat a livid woman's voice on the other end of the line.

"I'm sorry. To whom am I speaking?"

"It's Alice." *Why was Alice Hobbs screaming at me?*

"Alice, darling. Wonderful to hear from you. What on Earth is wrong?"

"I know we lost the photographs I took on my phone for you yesterday and I am delighted that my assistant saved the day, but putting his pictures on the website for the shoot without crediting me when I spent weeks with you planning the concept, directing the shoot and setting up the majority of the photos that you used is just shitty. It's really shitty. Beyond getting the credit . . . I wasn't even given a heads-up that anything would go online today. I assumed I would have some say in the photo selection process and the retouching and post-production. What kind of an operation are you running over there?"

Imogen scrambled for some device that would get her on the Internet. She tried pantomiming that she needed a laptop to Alex and the kids over on the couch, but they raised their hands in confusion and then just waved at her. Finally she spotted an iPad lying on the floor and grabbed it. Out of juice.

"Alice, darling. Please hold on just one second."

Imogen ran downstairs to grab the laptop, which took its sweet time whirring to life.

Imogen could hear Alice release a long sigh from the other end of the phone. "I thought that we had a certain level of both trust and professional courtesy. I've never, in all of my work with magazines, with websites, with commercial brands, been blindsided like this." *Why was it taking the website so long to load?*

"Imogen, are you there?"

"I'm right here, Alice."

Imogen gasped. Oh shit. Alice was right. Who posted the pictures? There it was, the main splashy story on the first page of Glossy.com.

IT'S TECH, BITCH! screamed the headline. "Photos taken by Mack Schwartz," read the byline. It was really just a gallery of the photos overlaid with the BUY IT NOW! graphics. That wasn't what they had planned. The whole point of doing the shoot was to turn it into a beautifully laid out aspirational spread. These weren't even retouched.

Imogen clicked through.

"You could have given me some kind of warning."

"Alice, I'm so sorry. This is a mistake. I never approved any of this. I swear to you, I never would have done this without talking to you. Let me get to the bottom of this?"

"You're supposed to be the editor in chief. That's why I signed on to do this project in the first place. You think I agree to work with every blogger on the street? If you don't have control over this, what do you have control over?"

Imogen went to interrupt her, but realized she didn't have an answer.

"I'm sorry, Alice."

"Kill it. Issue a correction. Make sure my check is in the mail and make it out to me and not my assistant." The phone went dead. Imogen tried to figure out what to do next. Who was posting these pictures? Who had access to them? Ashley had them. She wouldn't have posted them without speaking to her.

Who was in the office anyway?

She dialed Ashley. As the phone rang Imogen sank down onto the hardwood floor of the downstairs family room. They renovated this basement two years earlier and it was now the most lived-in room in the whole house besides the kitchen. Imogen gazed over at the bookshelves stuffed with children's books, young adult books and family photos.

After five rings it went to Ashley's voicemail. "Heya. It's Ash. Are you seriously leaving me a message right now? You're so old-school. Text me if ya want to hear back from me."

Imogen stood and began pacing across the sitting room, trying to work out what to do. Should she just log on and try her hand at removing the photos from the site altogether? Alex, finally finished with his own work, called out to her: "Babe, are you in for a game of Monopoly?"

"Start without me."

She was about to dial Eve when her phone rang. Ashley's photo popped up on the phone. A selfie, her blue eyes wide and head cocked slightly to the side. How did that get there? Ashley must have programmed it herself.

"Hi, Ashley. I was just trying you."

The girl's voice was muffled, as though she were holding her hand over the mouthpiece.

"I saw. That's why I am calling you back. What's up?"

"Where are you? I can barely hear you. Can you talk louder?"

"I'm at Eve's with everyone else."

"With who else?"

"With the whole office."

"What are you talking about?"

"Eve told us that we all had to come to her place to work from there because of the snow."

"I didn't hear about that."

"She told us not to say anything to you. She said you probably had to take care of your kids so it wasn't worth it for us to bother you."

"How did you all get there? Everything is shut down today."

"Most of us walked. Sabine's dad has a big SUV, so he let her take that out and she picked up some people on the Upper East Side, but they ran into a snowbank so they got here real late."

Imogen didn't know what to say. There was no way that Eve was being kind and giving her a snow day with her children. She wanted to make a fool of her for not being there working with everyone else.

"I emailed the staff this morning. Did you get it?"

"Eve wrote back to all of us two minutes after you did and told us to ignore it and find a way to her apartment. She said"—Ashley let her voice slip into Eve's nasally one—"we can't let productivity slip just because of a few flurries."

Furious didn't begin to describe the way Imogen was feeling, but she tried to shelve it for a few minutes to get to the bottom of what happened with the photo shoot.

"Ashley, why is the photo shoot online?"

The girl's voice rose a little before she caught herself and realized she was meant to be whispering. "Ugh. Yeah. I know it sucks. Eve made me post it this morning."

"What?"

"Eve said we needed original content up today since everyone on the East Coast is stuck home in the snow. We are running snow-day specials and getting heaps of people to buy from it. That's good at least, right?"

"I organized that shoot. I was meant to have editorial approval. Alice wanted to retouch the photos. It was in her contract. They weren't ready to be published."

Now Ashley sounded confused and slightly defensive. "Eve gave us approval. The two of you are, like, the same, right? If she tells us we can do something, then it's okay."

"Ashley, we are not at all the same. I worked hard on that shoot. You know that. You worked hard with me and the way it looks on the site is not what we planned. My relationship—and Glossy.com's— with Alice is now over."

"Shit. Imogen, I need to go. Eve is screaming about something." She lowered her voice even more. "She says we are going to have a snowed-in pajama party here. I don't think she's letting any of us go home . . . not that we could get home if we wanted to . . ."

The line went dead.

What good would it do to email Eve now? The entire office was there, probably sprawled across the floor of her one-bedroom apartment. Imogen would look foolish calling over there now.

She stared at the phone.

Too embarrassed to call Bridgett or Massimo, she scrolled down through her contacts and finally landed on *R*. She'd never made an emergency call to Ron before. It rang through to voice mail. What was the protocol for this? Did she leave a message? When did people just stop picking up their phones?

Still sitting cross-legged on the floor, Imogen received a text from the therapist.

>>>>Hold on. I'm going to Skype you.<<<<

She paused before writing back.

>>>>Ok.<<<<

He replied with a smiley face emoticon. Skype therapy? Of course. Why not?

She added a smiley face to show she wasn't in truly dire straits. People in truly dire situations didn't use emoticons.

Her cell phone flashed. She accepted the call and her therapist's beard loomed large on the screen.

"Imogen? What did you want to talk about?" It was the first time she'd tried to use the video function on her phone. She didn't know where to put the device. Farther away looked better, so she stretched her arm as far from her body as it would go. Ron had no such compunction about how he appeared. She could see directly up both his nostrils.

"I'm so sorry, Ron. You must think I'm a complete nut for calling you like this."

"Imogen. My business is nuts."

"Fair point." She laughed. "It's just . . . I'm at a breaking point. I don't know how much longer I can take her games and bullshit, Ron."

"What did Eve do now?"

"It sounds so stupid to explain it. It sounds like some juvenile middle school prank, but that's what my life has come to." She went on to tell Ron all about the snow day and how Eve had the whole staff, except her, over at her house.

Ron paused for a moment before replying very diplomatically, "Do you think there was any chance, any chance at all, that Eve actually thought, 'Hey, Imogen has two kids at home, maybe she does need the day off . . . maybe I don't need to bother her.'"

That couldn't be true. If it had been, Eve wouldn't have made the decision unilaterally. She would have offered Imogen the chance to work with the rest of the team or to stay home with her kids. Eve had the staff come to her house and left Imogen out specifically to undermine her. Eve was a clever girl who knew exactly what she was doing when she posted that photo shoot. She knew it would ruin Imogen's relationship with Alice. Eve had dealt with enough Alice Hobbs photo shoots when she had been Imogen's assistant to know what the photographer was like.

Ron's arm must have been getting tired because the screen was starting to waver and fall. Imogen could see a giant patch of his white skin.

"Jesus, Ron, are you wearing clothes?"

"No, Imogen. I'm not. I'm upstate at this wonderful naked retreat. It's incredibly freeing. I actually think it's something you could possibly benefit from."

"Are you mad, Ron? I don't want to go to a naked retreat. Keep the phone at eye level, please."

"Of course. Sorry about that," Ron continued. "You need to make a choice. Is this what you really want to be doing? You're a woman who loves a challenge. You want to win, but you're also a woman getting over cancer and a mom with two young kids and a wife to a husband with an incredibly stressful job. Do you want to kill yourself every day working with this girl you hate?"

She thought about it. Right now, the future of magazines was like a road that ended at a sheer cliff with a drop so steep Imogen couldn't see to the bottom. But she believed she had no discernible skills outside of putting a magazine together.

"Ron, are you saying this to me as my shrink or my psychic? Because if you know, like you actually know, something important about my future, now would be the time to tell me."

"I'm saying it to you as a friend. I am taking off my shrink hat and my psychic hat. Evaluate if this job is still worth it to you. Do you need it?"

Imogen's voice grew small. "I'm scared."

"Scared of what?"

"Scared that no one will ever call again. Scared I'm over."

"I can't tell you what to do, Imogen, but I will ask you this: Do you want every day to be like this?"

She grew quiet again.

"Life is funny, you know. It isn't a running text. It has chapters. You might have a very different ending than the one you imagined."

"I know. I need to think."

"Okay. You know you can Skype me anytime. I'm here for you." *With no clothes on,* Imogen thought.

"I know, Ron."

She made an air kiss at the screen to say good-bye and sank into the cushions of the couch and into the silence. A vase full of deli roses purchased earlier in the week by Tilly and Annabel sat on the low coffee table in front of her. About four days old, the peach roses were beginning to brown around the edges and wilt in the middle. Without thinking about it, Imogen held up her phone to snap a picture.

Imogen posted it to Instagram. Why should you only post happy things to social media? Where was the Instagram for the sadness? "Dying rose" was her caption.

The Monopoly game was in progress when she returned, but she didn't have it in her to play.

"I'm going to have to lie down for a disco nap before dinner." Annabel had hotels on both Boardwalk and Park Place. Johnny controlled all four of the railroads. They were so intent the three of them barely raised their heads.

She lay on the bed on her back, trying to employ all of Ron's meditation tricks. Sending awareness down to her toes and imagining them relaxing. Moving all the way up her legs. She tried to let her thoughts float away on a cloud. Tried counting backward from one hundred. Tried breathing in for ten seconds and out for twelve. The hamster wheel in her mind kept turning.

She wasn't sure how long she did the relaxation exercises before she actually fell asleep. She must have rolled from her back onto her side because she didn't wake up until she felt Alex curling behind her.

"Is it time for dinner?"

"Not yet. The kids went back out to play in the snow for an hour or so."

Her body remained rigid and tense. Alex moved his hand up to her neck to rub away the tension.

"Baby, what's wrong? What were all those phone calls? What did the Wicked Witch of the Lower East Side do now?"

That made Imogen smile just a little. They had started calling Eve the Wicked Witch of the Lower East Side when a mutual friend informed them she moved into the luxury high-rise above the Whole Foods on Houston Street between Bowery and Chrystie. Facebook founder Mark Zuckerberg supposedly kept a loft there, which is what made Eve so keen on it in the first place. Eve loved little more than proximity to fame.

"Eve demanded that the staff come to work at her house today and didn't tell me about it." Every time the words came out of her mouth, Imogen felt more and more immature. Thankfully her husband chose to take the matter seriously.

"Have you spoken to anyone about this? Have you talked to HR? Have you gone to Worthington? Her behavior is out of hand."

"What can I say to them? Eve ordered everyone over to her house except for me. Come on, Alex. I'm not that petty."

"Not just that . . . even though I think there are serious legal issues involved when a boss forces their employees to come to their home. I am talking about the firings, the verbal abuse in the office. All of it. Someone else besides you needs to step in and deal with it."

Imogen didn't want to talk to Worthington about it. Doing that would be admitting defeat.

She rolled over to face him.

"I have to." Her husband put both of his hands on her cheeks.

"Why do you have to?"

Oh god, was he really going to make her say it? It was demeaning for her to say it. She loved him so much that she hated throwing this in his face.

Alex just knew. "You don't need to be the breadwinner, Im."

"I do."

"You don't."

She squeezed her eyes shut in frustration at her idealistic husband.

"Open your eyes, Imogen." She couldn't. "I'm serious. Open them," he said.

"There are twenty things we can change, not tomorrow, but things we can change about how we live so that you don't need to make your big-time editor salary anymore. We can sell this house and move into an apartment . . . like everyone else in this city. I can go work at a big law firm. The kids can go to public school. We could move somewhere else entirely. We aren't stuck. We're well-educated people with great careers behind us. Nothing is more important to me than this family. We'll find a way to make our lives work whether you have this job or not."

Imogen didn't know what to say. She knew Alex would support her, but she certainly hadn't expected this.

They had good intentions to make love that night. And yet, once again, exhaustion, physical and emotional, overcame them both and, as usual, they chose delirious sleep over married sex.

* * *

Ashley learned fairly early on working for Eve that there was a direct correlation between how many flattering Instagram photos you posted of her and how much she liked you. And so, Ashley made it a best practice to post at least two well-filtered shots of her boss each and every day, always with flattering hashtags (#HauteBoss, #CuteorCutest?). This made her immune to much of Eve's regular ire. Eve's better side was her right and so during the snow day she posted pics of Eve from the right making guacamole in her sweats and pretending to meditate on her snowy balcony, her legs crossed in the snow, thumb and forefinger purposefully balanced on her knees.

"Pissed" wasn't the right word; she just felt like she was being used as a pawn in Eve's grudge match against Imogen and that was the worst. She got shitty service at Eve's creepy apartment. Saying she needed privacy, Eve reluctantly pointed her toward a full bathroom off her bedroom, which was all white on white, like a room in a mental hospital, and it immediately became clear why Eve hadn't been letting the women into the room.

The bathroom was small but clean and the stark white of the walls made the yellow Post-it notes stuck all around the bathroom surface stick out all the more. Written in Eve's measured hand were reminders, most obviously meant for her to read to herself in the mornings: "Be nice." "Say thank you." "Be polite." "Remember to smile." "Make eye contact." They were instructions for how a sociopath should behave to seem human. Beneath them, in hot pink lipstick, cursive letters read: "You deserve everything!"

CHAPTER TWENTY-SEVEN

From: Eve Morton (EMorton@Glossy.com)
To: Auditions@Ted.com

To Whom It May Concern,

I am writing to you to express my interest in giving a TED talk at this year's annual TED Conference. I LOVE your series and have listened to it since I was an MBA candidate at Harvard Business School.

I currently run one of the most influential fashion brands in the world, Glossy.com, formerly *Glossy* magazine. I have been snowed in with my staff for the past twenty-four hours, during which I had a brain spark I had to share with you.

Here is what I am proposing: I want to give a talk at your conference entitled, "Adapt or Die." Catchy title, right? I think this talk has the opportunity to trump Tony Robbins's talk on why we do what we do or Steve Jobs's talk on how to live life.

My concept stems from my personal experience. I am currently working in an environment with people who are two generations older. Their ability to grasp the very basics of technology, the future of business and their desperation to cling to the old tenets of our industry will be their demise. It is positively Darwinian in its simplicity. I think I may be the first person to make this connection. ADAPT OR DIE IN THE WORKPLACE. These dinosaurs have been told the asteroid is coming and still they keep going about life as usual. It is as if they don't fear the extinction. Meanwhile, my generation is coming in hard and fast, ready to take over.

I am telling you. This talk will kill. IT WILL ABSOLUTELY KILL! I would love the chance to discuss this with you more. Please feel free to reach me on this email.

Have a Good, Great, Gorgeous, GLOSSY! Day!!!
Eve Morton, Editorial Director, Glossy.com

From: Amy Tennant (Aten@ted.com)
To: Eve Morton (EMorton@Glossy.com)

Dear Ms. Morton,

Thank you for your submission to TED. As you can imagine, we receive thousands of applications for TED talks each week. At this time, we will not be able to accommodate your request for a talk. And, while we rarely comment on the proposals that we receive due to the fact that we here at TED truly believe that creativity and innovation manifests in a variety of ways, I did want to send a note to let you know that this talk would be offensive and go against the very ethics of TED, which strives to be inclusive rather than exclusive. As a proud woman of 53 years old, I believe this is an idea best kept to yourself.

Warm Regards,
Amy Tennant, Director of Talent Curation, TED

* * *

A magical army of plows and salt trucks did their work overnight, making Imogen's morning commute surprisingly smooth.

She'd succumbed to her husband's advice and was scheduled to meet with Worthington at eleven a.m. She wouldn't be catty. She'd present the facts. Her employees were dropping like flies. *Glossy*'s reputation in the industry was going down the tubes. Eve abused the designers. They didn't want to work with them anymore. Morale at the office was at an all-time low, no matter how many spin classes they did or how many jugglers or international DJs she brought in.

Imogen wasn't nervous. A weight lifted the night before and she was ready for whatever Worthington threw at her. If he told her to get the hell out of his office, that Eve was good for business, she would walk out and feel confident that she didn't need to come back.

She was even unfazed when Eve walked into Imogen's office and flounced onto her couch first thing that morning, crossing the legs of her pristine orange Juicy Couture track pants. She wore a plain white T-shirt with bold black writing: DON'T WORRY, BE YONCÉ. All Imogen wanted was to go through her customary morning routine, check her emails and run through the schedule of stories for the site.

"Where were you yesterday?" Eve asked archly. What a witch.

"I was at home."

"Why weren't you at my place?" Eve volleyed back.

"I didn't know anyone was at your apartment until late yesterday. No one told me."

"That's not true," Eve countered. Imogen could tell Eve was having a difficult time suppressing a smile. "I emailed you first thing in the morning and I texted."

"I never got an email or a text from you, Eve."

"You probably missed them," she said.

That was the thing about technology these days. You could blame a text or an email disappearing on spam or a faulty connection. It was never anyone's fault.

"You never sent me an email or a text, Eve."

"I most certainly did. It's weird you didn't get it. Anyway, we had a really productive day. You should have been there."

"How late did the girls stay?"

"Oh, they slept over. We had a slumber party. Everyone camped out on the floor. We baked frozen gluten-free pizza. We danced. We came up with a whole choreographed routine to Beyoncé's 'Crazy in Love.' Want to see?" Before Imogen could say that she had no interest at all in seeing the coordinated dance routine, Eve crossed to her side of the desk. She held her phone horizontally and hit play.

It was very clear, from the looks on the staffers' faces, that no fun was being had. This could have been filmed in Guantánamo. There was Eve, front and center, belting out the lyrics, feet hip-width apart, bouncing her fists next to her waist before her hips went left and then right and her arms crossed in front of her chest. The other girls followed along, aware they were being filmed, not happy about it. One would think Eve would notice their lack of enthusiasm when she flipped her hair around her head and turned to shake her ass for the camera, but she was just too into it.

"Is that not the most amazing thing you have ever seen?" Eve grinned with pride. "I think we should put it on the site."

"I don't think so," Imogen said, pushing Eve's phone away so she could look at her own computer screen.

Refusing to be ignored, Eve perched on top of Imogen's desk, kicking the wood with her sneakers.

"What did ya think of Mack's shoot?"

"You mean Alice's shoot."

"No, Mack was the one who took the pictures. And you know what that proves? It proves we don't need to pay someone like Alice a small fortune."

If Imogen hadn't been there, hadn't seen Alice get knocked over and drop that phone with her own two eyes, she would swear that Eve had found some way to sabotage that phone and Alice and the entire photo shoot.

"We got lucky, Eve."

"No. Mack was just younger and smarter and quicker. Alice is a dying breed that's about to go extinct." *Same as me, right, Eve?* Imogen thought. She didn't say anything out loud. Eve began kicking the desk harder. *Thud, thud, thud, thud.*

"Anyway, you should have come yesterday. It's bad for morale when you don't show up for these things."

"Eve, like I said, I definitely wasn't told anything about it. You can swear that you sent me an email. I don't think you did. I didn't get a text from you. More than that, I told the staff to stay home. They could have worked from home. Most of New York City worked from home yesterday. There was no reason for them to come to your house and learn a ridiculous coordinated dance to Beyoncé."

Eve's eyes narrowed to slits.

Imogen looked through the glass wall and out onto the main floor. No one out there looked like a happy member of any team. They looked exhausted, bedraggled, like people who hadn't slept in their own beds. She could tell some of them were dressed in Eve's clothes—so many Juicy tracksuits and oddly fitting Hervé dresses.

"This isn't camaraderie, Eve. This is a forced labor camp."

"*You* don't get it. You're never going to succeed in tech, Imogen. You don't get it. It's about building communities, about building a team. There isn't room for people like you here, for lone wolves!" Eve underscored her point by raising her head to an imaginary moon, letting loose a howl and pivoting on her rubber sole to stalk out of the room. Six months ago the exchange would have shaken Imogen to her core. Now she took it in stride. She logged on to the TECHBITCH page and wrote a comment.

"My techbitch just forced the entire office to learn a coordinated dance to Beyoncé's 'Crazy in Love.' Then she howled like a wolf pup."

Within minutes she had six smiley faces, four LOLs, four ROFLs and a gif of a delighted rhesus monkey hopping up and down.

She felt a swell of love from these fellow victims, or rather survivors, of techbitches the world over.

At quarter till she pulled out a compact to check her makeup and ran a comb through her hair. *God, I look tired.*

The desk for Worthington's two assistants stood empty and for a moment Imogen wondered if, influenced by Eve, the publisher fired them in favor of an army of Outzourced assistants overseas. But no, they were merely inside Worthington's office, both typing away on MacBooks, busy, and still homely.

"Imogen Tate," Worthington's voice boomed, his elaborate comb-over rising above his prominent brow. Only after she sat down in one of the chairs opposite his desk did she notice brown cardboard boxes lining the back wall. Worthington wasn't in his regular suit. He wore Nantucket Red chinos below a well-cut blazer with a jaunty matching red pocket square.

"Redecorating?" she asked. "I'll make a couple of calls if you want to switch designers."

He chortled and slapped his thigh. "Remember the days of putting the interior decorators on the company dime? Ahhhh, we had some fun, didn't we? No, I'm not redecorating. Moving."

The hairs on the back of Imogen's neck curled as she wondered if times had gotten so bad that Robert Mannering Corp. would need to sell their building and relocate somewhere cheaper—like New Jersey. She shuddered.

"Where are we going?"

"Not we, Imogen, just me. I'm happy you called this meeting. I wanted to talk to you in person before I made the announcement to the entire magazine group. I'm leaving Robert Mannering Corp."

For a brief moment Imogen wanted to make a joke about Eve taking Worthington's job next but she bit down on her tongue.

"Where are you going? Why did you quit?"

"I didn't quit. Took a buyout. They're about to be offered to all us old dogs, all the senior management. The company wants young blood in here. They want cheap blood in here. I hung on as long as I could. I hired people like Eve, but I know I'm not what they want."

Imogen was speechless, but surprised to realize she was not as surprised as she should have been.

"What will you do?"

"Going to Thailand for a month or two. The women there." He whistled loudly. "They do things that you probably can't even imagine. I mean. Of course, the wife will be joining me, but you never know. . . ." He wiggled his eyebrows up and down as Imogen forced her face to remain completely neutral.

"Sounds like a wonderful trip. But you can't just go on permanent vacation. Can you?"

Worthington joined Imogen on the couch, jauntily crossing one stubby leg over the other, his thigh touching hers in a way that made her skin crawl. "They aren't getting off scot-free here. I'm getting an excellent compensation package that will pay my many alimony payments for at least the next year. I could teach. I'm still on the board at the business school at Columbia. I have so much wisdom to impart," he said very earnestly, his face about three inches from Imogen's, his breath smelling of cigars and Altoids.

"I'll get rid of the apartment in the city, or rent it out, go out to the beach, spend time with my kids. This isn't ideal. I would have run these magazines until they ran me into the grave, but our directors don't want magazines anymore, at least not the kind I made. Everything is changing and I don't know if I want to keep up with it."

It was the most human she had ever seen her boss.

"When are you telling everyone?"

"I'll make the announcement this afternoon. The board is going to meet to decide who else they want to offer a small golden parachute to, so to speak."

"What kinds of people are getting the offer?"

"I think they'll make the offer to anyone who makes in the mid–six figures, anyone whose salary they don't think they can justify in this new world of publishing. We can offer you one too, Imogen. But you don't have to take it."

"Don't I?"

"No." He shook his head. "I've seen you adapt more over the past few months than I have over the past ten years. You're starting to get it."

"Then why would I get offered the buyout?"

He sighed. "Your salary is high and you're over forty. Ageism is alive and well. It's just sugarcoated with lovely going-away presents. Think about it. Like I said, you're doing a great job. You have what it takes to keep running that website, but you could also take the opportunity to try something new."

"I don't want a buyout right now," Imogen blurted out with a conviction she hadn't known she felt.

"So be it. I'll let the powers that be know you have spoken. So what did you come up here to talk to me about?"

Imogen thought for a moment. Why bring up Eve now? The point was moot. *Worthington won't even be her boss much longer.* Someone more Eve-like would likely take his place.

It took a minute to sink in, but Worthington had given her high praise, had said she'd adapted. It was true. She'd learned more about tech in the past three months than she'd learned during the ten prior years. It wasn't without pain and sacrifice, but staying in her job was a possibility if she wanted it. But knowing that she could take a buyout and start doing something totally new was an intriguing proposition.

"What will happen to *Glossy*? Will *Glossy* still be *Glossy*?"

"I imagine that *Glossy* will continue to exist in some shape or form forever. It's a great brand, a household brand. Women know *Glossy*. They trust *Glossy*. But between us, the website isn't doing as well as Eve had projected. There is talk . . . no I shouldn't even bring this up right now."

"Come on, Carter." She rarely used his first name. "Tell me."

"Why not? You'll find out sooner or later. There's talk of selling off Glossy.com to a tech company, one that knows a little better what they are doing, one that can deliver on all of the things that Eve promised—traffic, sales, data collection. The girl came up with a genius concept, but I don't know how she's doing on the implementation side. And she's killing the morale of that office."

Of course Worthington knew what was happening downstairs. You didn't get to his level by being oblivious. She didn't know how he did it, but her boss must have eyes and ears on that floor. If he knew about her progress, then he knew about Eve's inadequacies.

"Robert Mannering Corp. created *Glossy*. They would just sell it that easily?"

"It isn't a child, Imogen. It's a business. Like I said, it's a strong brand. If they can get a good payday from a sale, the board will take it."

It was a lot to take in. Not that she had always seen eye to eye with Worthington. In fact, she'd had some of the bigger blowups of her professional life with him, but she respected him as a businessman in a sea of creative people, the man who had to make the tough decisions because his staff often had their heads in the clouds.

Imogen looked at his moon-faced assistants, both of whom were staring at their boss with adoring gazes.

"What do the two of you plan to do?"

The shorter one smiled widely. Imogen felt badly that she had never bothered to take a second to learn their names.

"Our start-up just got funded!"

The taller one piped in, "Mr. Worthington was nice enough to introduce us to his friends who work in venture capital and we just got our first round of funding."

Imogen both did and didn't want to ask what the girls' company was all about. She didn't have to, because Worthington chimed in with pride.

"Tess and Marni came up with a brilliant idea." The women beamed. "They are disrupting the way people wait for restaurants. They've built an app called LineDodge where users can input how long the wait is at any restaurant in the world so that you never get caught in a line."

The taller one added, "It then crowdsources reviews off Yelp to tell you the next best rated restaurant with that cuisine with no line."

"I invested some pocket change in it," their boss admitted.

The shorter one shrugged. "We rented a co-working space at WeWork and we're incorporated. It's awesome."

Rashid was right, anyone with a dream these days could go start a company.

"Who would buy Glossy.com?" Imogen asked, switching gears for a minute.

Worthington scratched his head.

"It's all early-stage talks. Most of those never go anywhere. But I know there was a Chinese company interested. Plus, the folks over at that e-commerce company Shoppit have been by a few times to talk about it."

Imogen felt a shiver run down her spine.

"Shoppit? Did you meet with Aerin Chang?"

"Chang. That is exactly who we met with. Smart whippersnapper, that one. Loves magazines. Loves you too. Had great things to say about you."

Why didn't Aerin Chang tell her she was looking to buy her website? That was a huge deal. Was their meeting all a calculated game to find out more about the business? Imogen felt used.

"When did Shoppit come here?"

"A couple of weeks ago. The board thought it was a little crazy, but hell, if they end up getting two hundred fifty million dollars for the old product, I don't think they care what that little Korean girl does with it."

Aerin was seriously considering buying *Glossy*. More and more their meeting seemed like an attempt to pump information out of Imogen, especially when Aerin asked her what she didn't like about her magazine. It should have been so obvious. It wasn't the start to a friendship, it was corporate espionage.

Did this mean that Aerin was no better than Eve?

She walked over to Worthington, prepared to shake his hand and then at the last minute leaned in for a hug instead. The man seemed surprised, but he soon embraced her back, sniffing at her neck a little too long.

"We had a good run of it, kiddo," he whispered in her ear. "Think about taking the buyout. Leave the *Glossy* Imogen Tate behind and become a new Imogen Tate. Write a novel, open a bakery. Start a second act. This is New York City. If you don't reinvent yourself, you get left behind."

"I think that might be the most true thing that has ever come out of your mouth, Carter."

"Plus," he said, winking suggestively, "I won't be your boss anymore."

Imogen smiled and patted him on the shoulder. It was hard to be angry at a dirty old man. "No, you won't be."

The assistants, both furiously typing away at their MacBooks, now commanded a new air of respect. Imogen gave them a grin and a small salute as she walked out, making promises to Worthington about getting together with the kids and the spouses, maybe out at the beach next summer.

Riding the elevator back to her office, she considered her options. She could call Aerin and tell her she knew. What would she even say?

How dare you invite me to your office and share macarons with me and then not tell me you wanted to buy my magazine?

Her phone vibrated in her pocket. Deep in thought and vaguely clumsy, Imogen fumbled for it. Ashley.

>>>>Your daughter is at the office.<<<<

It was hardly noon, lunchtime at Country Village Elementary.

Imogen was out of breath by the time she made it to *Glossy*'s floor. Quiet as ever, there was just the gentle *tap, tap* of manicured nails on keyboards. Her eyes scanned the room.

Eve's tall desk stood empty.

They were in Imogen's office. Eve and her daughter were in her office.

This time it was Annabel in her desk chair, laughing, as Eve perched precariously on the side of the desk. Imogen smoothed her hand over her ponytail and wiped her index fingers under her eyes to remove any traces of stray mascara.

"Annabel Tate Marretti, what in god's name do you think you are doing here?"

At the authority in her voice, both Eve and Annabel were startled to attention.

"Mom." Her daughter looked up, chagrined. "I came to see you." There was something so honest and so innocent in her eyes. She saw something guilty lurking in Eve's as she turned to face her.

"Please leave me alone with my daughter, Eve."

Eve let out a hollow laugh. "What's the big deal? She just came to see you."

"Let us be, Eve."

Imogen felt Eve's roll of her eyes and as she turned saw Eve try to lock eyes with her daughter for a conspiratorial stare. For her part, Annabel wasn't having any of it. She kept her eyes on the floor.

"Why aren't you in school? How did you get here?"

"I wanted to see you," Annabel said. Now tears streamed down both her cheeks. She let Imogen hug her. *Keep your shit together,* Imogen said to herself. Her daughter's words were barely audible through her hiccupping cries. "She's so mean. Candy Cool is so mean. She sent this out to my whole school." Annabel held her iPhone out at arm's length like it contained a disease.

Another picture of her daughter. This one superimposed on an obese woman on a mock cover of *Glossy* magazine under the headline EVEN MY MOM THINKS I'M UGLY. The post had 345 likes and 57 shares.

Candy Cool was a cunt.

Her daughter's eyes begged for compassion. Gone was the strong, confident young woman who threw organic produce into a Vitamix on a YouTube channel watched by thousands of other preteens. She was a scared little girl who needed her mother.

"Darling, do you still think that Candy is Harper Martin?"

Annabel shook her head from side to side.

"No. Harper is the worst, but she can barely use a computer. She couldn't make these."

"Do you have any idea who is?"

"No. Harper is like the meanest girl in the class but she isn't this mean. The message posted after this was even worse."

"What did it say?"

"She said, 'Your mom thinks you are ugly because you don't look like her.'"

It took all of Imogen's strength not to scream out loud right then and there. Instead she softened her voice all the more.

"You know I don't think that, right?"

Annabel didn't nod. Instead she looked away.

"Sometimes I think you wish that I were as pretty as you."

"Annabel. Stop it. You aren't as pretty as me. You're prettier than me. You're beautiful. Do you know what I would give to have this gorgeous curly head of hair like yours or your perfect olive skin? I have this terrible pasty white skin that turns red the second I go into the sun. You're the most beautiful little girl I've ever seen. I don't know who this bully is. We'll find out. I promise."

She would let Alex play bad cop. She had to get her daughter out of here.

"Let's go home."

Annabel allowed Imogen to hold her hand as they walked out of the office.

Eve looked pointedly at them as they left, a smile lingering at her lips that Imogen just couldn't interpret.

* * *

Once Imogen assured her daughter there was no truth to anything this bully said about their relationship, Annabel panicked that her parents would take away her YouTube channel.

"I love it. You can't take it away. It's my most favorite thing in the world."

"Annabel. I don't want you putting yourself out there like this right now. You're so young."

"Everyone does it! You put yourself out there on Instagram. You put yourself out there with the magazine. This is my thing. Please let me have my thing. The people who watch my videos are my friends. Maybe I don't know them in real life, but they're my friends and I need friends. It isn't like you and Dad are ever around."

It stung because it was true. Neither of them was home anymore. How could she punish her daughter when she was accusing her of being an absentee parent? Where were her priorities these days? With a stupid fashion magazine or with her child?

She opted to leave things be, and stroked Annabel's head as she fell asleep.

It wasn't until she had the kids in bed that Imogen remembered her talk with Worthington, which now seemed like a lifetime away.

"Worthington is leaving Robert Mannering Corp.," she said to Alex, with less urgency than she had earlier imagined telling him.

"What?" he said, sitting up straighter in the bed.

"He took a buyout. He said they're offering one to a lot of senior management to get salaries down."

"What is he going to do?"

Imogen laughed at the absurdity of what her boss had told her. "He is going to Thailand. He says he might teach."

"He'll go crazy within two weeks without a company to run."

"I know. I'm sure someone will snap him up. He said I could take a buyout."

"Oh yeah? What do you think they would offer?"

"About a year's salary."

Alex whistled. "I wouldn't laugh at that."

"I know," Imogen said quietly.

"Would you take it?"

"Here's the other thing. They might sell *Glossy*."

"To who? The Chinese?"

"Maybe," Imogen replied. "But also maybe to Shoppit. Do you remember that girl, Aerin Chang, I told you about? The one I met when I went to the Shoppit office." Even though Alex nodded Imogen was pretty sure he didn't have any clue exactly which woman she was talking about.

"I think she may have just been pretending to be friendly with me so she could get information about buying my magazine." Alex groaned.

"She sounds like another Eve."

"I don't want to think that. I really didn't get that impression from her." Imogen grew defensive about Aerin's motivations.

"I don't know, baby. All I know is that I am glad I never have to do business with any of these twentysomething millennial women. They're fierce." Alex sighed.

"Should I talk to her? Email her? What if she buys the magazine? What if I have two Eves bossing me around?"

"Then would you take the buyout?"

Now it was Imogen's turn to sigh. "I can't even wrap my head around that."

CHAPTER TWENTY-EIGHT

JANUARY 2016

Ashley did not want to get on a scale in front of the entire office. This was humiliating.

"A hundred twenty pounds. Look at you, girlfriend. Gold stars all around. You've lost fifteen pounds." Eve clapped as Perry stepped off the scale in front of Ashley, who reluctantly took her place to be weighed.

She squeezed her eyes closed as she felt Eve pinch her hard on her hip. "Oooo, you gained five pounds. Maybe just juice for you." Eve snickered before looking her up and down again. "You were prettier when you first started working here." She turned to the next girl in line. Ashley hadn't felt so humiliated since rushing Kappa Theta, when the older sisters stripped the pledges to their underwear and drew circles around their fat bits. The weigh-in was ostensibly part of the "*Glossy* Body Challenge," a three-week juice cleanse/boot camp program to "kick-start a new you after the New Year."

"It's really just to make sure everyone is a size zero at her wedding. She wants everyone there to look completely ano!" Ashley grumbled to Imogen from the confines of her office, where the two of them hid after her humiliating weigh-in. Imogen didn't have to participate in the boot camp or the cleansing. Eve, at least, granted her immunity from that.

"Do you know what she sent a bunch of us this weekend?" Ashley fumbled on her phone to find the picture Eve had texted her on Sunday. It was a frontal shot, taken before a mirror, of Eve in a bra and panties, her stomach concave, her thighs twiglike, with the caption "WEDDING READY BITCHES! Let this be your THIN-spiration!"

Imogen rolled her eyes at the picture. "Tell her you think it was inappropriate." A smile played on Imogen's lips. She knew Ashley would never say something like that to Eve.

"Maybe I will." She crossed her legs and played with the little gold anchor on the chain around her neck, dipping it in and out of her mouth and letting her teeth brush against the metal. "I'm working on being meaner. It's one of my New Year's resolutions. Be more mean!"

Now Imogen laughed. "Please don't do that. How about 'Be more assertive,' or 'Stand up for yourself.'"

Outside the glass walls, Ashley could see the content producers quietly stuffing *Glossy* discount cards into white gift bags for Eve's big day, tying the tops of the paper bags with giant red bows.

"Maybe I'll get the stomach flu tonight and I won't be able to go to the wedding," Ashley said, making a faux vomiting noise and then instantly regretting it. Thankfully, Imogen laughed.

"She'd dock your pay."

"That's not even funny, because it's true." Ashley wanted to tell Imogen her good news. Would she be excited for her? Would she think it was silly? Ashley watched Imogen as she typed on the shiny MacBook Air. Gone was the near-constant frustration that furrowed her boss's brow just a couple of months ago when she sat in front of the same computer.

Ashley wouldn't quit work—not yet. A $100,000 investment wasn't really enough to do that. She needed to hire a product manager, engineers, and a business development person. She needed to build her product before she could think about doing SomethingOld as her full-time gig. Besides, Imogen still needed her.

"So, I have something fun to tell you," Ashley said, feeling like a little girl bringing home a straight-A report card to her mom.

"What, darling?"

"I kind of have this company that I have been thinking of starting. Well, no, I started it. It's totally real. And we reached our fund-raising goal. I raised one hundred thousand dollars for it."

Imogen closed the computer and placed her elbows on top of it, placing her chin in her hands.

"That's wonderful. Tell me all about it."

CHAPTER TWENTY-NINE

Tilly was out of breath when she burst into the kitchen the morning of the big *Glossy* wedding.

"Did you run here from the Upper West Side, Til?" Imogen expertly flipped over a buckwheat-and-banana pancake on the griddle.

"Just from the shop on the corner. I'm out of shape. Sue me. Have you seen the cover of the *Post*?"

"Not yet. We've been crazy this morning getting ready for Eve's wedding."

"I don't know if there's gonna be a wedding!" Tilly cackled, doing a brief Irish jig.

"Don't be silly. Every reporter and socialite east of the Hudson River is going to be at the Plaza this afternoon."

"Not if the groom is involved in a big-ass sex scandal." Tilly plunked the Saturday *New York Post* down on the counter. Andrew's picture was on the right side of the cover, a look of shock on his face, as though he had been ambushed coming out of his apartment.

Imogen felt the quick, joyful sensation that accompanied the promise of gossip about one's enemies.

On the left side of the tabloid was a picture of a pretty blond woman in lingerie. The headline blared: SHIVER ME TINDERS!

"What does that even mean? Did you read it yet?"

Tilly gulped down the glass of water Imogen had placed on the counter.

"Andrew has been sexting this girl here on the cover for the past six months. Her name is Bree-Ann. From Queens. Just turned eighteen . . . last week. Long story short, he was sexting with an underage girl that he met on Tinder."

Imogen opened the paper. The story was as salacious as Tilly promised.

Apparently, a source hacked Andrew's phone, got into his Tinder account and gave it to the *Post*.

"Look at these text messages," Imogen said, reading down the page in disbelief.

"Sexts. They call them sexts."

"Whatever."

>>>>I want you to punish me. I'm a bad, bad boy.<<<<

>>>>How bad are you?<<<<

>>>>SO bad you'll need to spank me and tell me I've been naughty.<<<<

>>>>What else do you want me to do to you?<<<<

>>>>I want you to dress up like my mommy and put a *****
in my ****<<<<

Imogen slammed the paper closed.

"I can't read any more."

Tilly had tears streaming down her face. Her shoulders shook with silent laughter.

"When you dated Andrew, did he ever ask you to dress up like his mommy and put a blank in his blank?"

"He most certainly did not." Imogen thought back for a moment. He *had* asked her to spank him once when he came home particularly drunk, but that had been the extent of their rough sex play.

"So the wedding must be off." She reopened the newspaper.

"It doesn't say anything about whether it's on or off. It says no comment from Eve and Andrew."

Imogen ran into the sitting room to grab her iPhone from where it was charging. Nothing from Eve.

As she went to dial Ashley's number she saw that the girl was already calling her. Both disposed with pleasantries and hellos and instead blurted out at the same time:

"Did you see the newspaper?" Imogen said.

"Did you get the Google Alert?" Ashley said.

"No— Yes. I mean— Yes, I saw the story." Imogen asked, "Have you talked to her?"

"No, she isn't answering her phone."

"There can't possibly still be a wedding."

"There can't be! But ohhhhhhhh, it will be so embarrassing."

For a moment Imogen felt sorry for Eve.

"Wait, I just got a text. Hold on . . . Wow. I mean *wow*."

"What? What did it say?"

"It's from Perry. Says the wedding is on. Get to the Plaza ASAP."

Imogen heard a beep on her end of the line and looked at her own screen.

"I just got a text too."

"From who?"

"Addison Cao. It says, 'TELL ME EVERYTHING!'"

* * *

"What kind of girl walks down the aisle with a guy who was on the cover of the *New York Post* for asking a seventeen-year-old girl to spank him?" Bridgett mused as she grabbed a glass of champagne from a passing waiter inside the Grand Ballroom of the Plaza Hotel.

A police barricade surrounded the main entrance of the Plaza, blocking off Grand Army Plaza and, ironically, the Pulitzer Fountain, to keep the scrum of photographers and reporters (the few who hadn't been invited to the wedding) at bay. Bridgett, Imogen and a reluctant Alex managed to avoid the mess outside by slipping into a back entrance.

"Why hasn't he been arrested yet?" Bridgett asked about Andrew, lowering her voice into a conspiratorial whisper. "Do you think he paid off the cops?"

"I don't think they have enough evidence yet," Imogen said. "The girl is eighteen now and no one can prove that this is definitely Andrew's phone."

"Do you think she'll actually walk down the aisle?" Bridgett asked as the two women glided into the hotel's imposing lobby. Only Bridgett would wear white to someone else's wedding, dismissing the tradition of "bridal color" as patriarchal, then promising there was nothing else in her closet save for the ivory Lanvin sheath dress. Against all instructions, Imogen wore a simple black Jason Wu gown.

If the scene inside the landmark luxury hotel was any indication, Eve was determined the show would go on.

No one had spotted the bride, but she was all anyone could talk about. Imogen and Bridgett barely wanted to chat with each other when eavesdropping on all of the other guests was so satisfying. *Glossy* girls wound their way through the room, shooting live video with their Google Glass of all the guests in their wedding finery . . . all available to BUY IT NOW! The whine of a string quartet floated through the air, underscored by the rustle of elegant (and brightly colored!) dresses.

Standing at the bar in the Terrace Room, Imogen surveyed this prewedding reception. She'd always found the Plaza a little bit vanilla. It was so Eve. It never moved her. Light glinted off the Charles Winston crystal chandeliers, casting shadows across the playful Renaissance frescoes painted on the ceiling. Even the decor gave a wink and a smile, as if it was in on the joke of this wedding. No expense had been spared. Rather, Andrew's trust fund had spared no expense. The high-top tables were covered in pearl-edged linens. Gigantic lilies filled oversized crystal vases in the centers. Eve had planned for an hour of cocktails before the ceremony in order to maximize the impact of hosting the live event on the *Glossy* website. Imogen couldn't complain about that. She'd always liked the idea of guests getting a little squishy before having to sit down to watch the vows. It felt almost British in the midst of this all-too-American wedding.

Across the room, Imogen saw Aerin Chang chatting with a group of handsome young Asian men in tuxedos. Looking gorgeous in a bias-cut navy silk gown that revealed a petite and compact figure, slashed across by a white cashmere wrap, Aerin raised a hand to wave excitedly as she caught sight of Imogen looking her way. Large gold knots adorned her tiny ears. She listened to an impassioned speech from a gentleman to her right, glancing past him and over to Imogen before politely excusing herself.

"Birdie, darling, will you go look after my husband for a bit? Make sure he doesn't get too tipsy on his afternoon off work," Imogen said to Bridgett as she cut across the room. Alex glanced at her warily to warn her that he didn't want to be left for too long. She smooched the air between them. At least he'd come.

Imogen leaned in to kiss Aerin on both cheeks. "I didn't know you'd be here," she said carefully. She paused for a moment and then decided this was not the best venue to pump Aerin for information about the magazine deal.

"I think Eve invited half of New York." Aerin giggled conspiratorially.

"But are the two of you friends?" She had to ask.

Aerin shook her head. "No. We have some friends in common, so I know her socially, but I definitely wouldn't call us friends. I'm so glad to see you here though. I was about to email you anyway to see if we could have another lunch." Aerin dropped her voice and looked around. "Do you have any inside scoop?"

On what? The sale? The wedding?

"None." Imogen threw up her hands.

Aerin mirrored the gesture. "Me neither, but it feels like the right thing to ask here, right? I mean, I get it. It's hard to call off a wedding. Easy to end an engagement, but once the guests have booked their plane tickets and everything is paid for, you just walk down that aisle no matter what."

"That's true." Bridgett had once called off an engagement to a shipping mogul twice her age six months before her wedding and then thrown herself a wild party with two hundred of her closest friends at the Hôtel du Cap-Eden-Roc in the South of France because the down payment for the reception was nonrefundable. The ex-fiancé obviously was not invited.

"Are you enjoying yourself so far?" Imogen asked.

Aerin smiled and sighed out the side of her mouth. "To be honest it feels good to get dressed up and talk to men I don't work with. I've been enduring a wicked divorce for the past six months."

Imogen didn't know what to say, so she said the first thing that popped into her mind. "I'm sorry. I had no idea. Of course. I don't know you very well. But. How can I say this? Your life looks so perfect on Instagram."

"Everything looks better on Instagram, doesn't it?" Aerin said. "Isn't that what all that is for . . . the version of ourselves we wish we felt like all the time. I have to say, yours looks even more perfect. I look at your Instagram and I think you must be the most put-together woman in the world."

"I'm not," Imogen admitted, more to herself than to Aerin Chang.

"I had"—the young woman paused—"a feeling . . . we should talk soon. There's something I really need to tell you." *I am sure there is,* Imogen thought.

Imogen politely kissed the woman on the cheek one more time and excused herself to sit next to Alex for the ceremony, picking up bits and pieces of conversation along the way, all of it speculating about whether Eve would walk down the aisle or not.

The chatter continued right up until the lights flashed and a bell dinged, indicating that guests should take their seats. The show was about to begin. Imogen's husband put an affectionate hand on her thigh. Bridgett lazily texted Rashid #SEXYSELFIE. Imogen scanned the rows of white lacquered chairs before the lights dimmed. The slimmer half of the *Glossy* staff was scattered about the room, all clutching the arms of equally picture-perfect dates, some boyfriends, some obviously gay besties who wouldn't miss the opportunity to get a front-row seat to the biggest scandal of the year. Andrew's terrible mother sat in the front row, her face frozen in an over-Botoxed look of perpetual concern. There were a smattering of lower-level fashion designers mixed in with a dash of socialites old and young.

Imogen felt a whirring above her head. Looking up, she dug her nails into Alex's arm. He glanced upward and whispered, "We're under attack." Then he added, "They're drone cameras."

"They're what?"

"Drone video cameras," Alex repeated.

All eyes turned upward. Guests pointed and yelped in disbelief tinged with fear.

"Like what the army uses?" Imogen asked her husband with suspicion.

"Exactly," her unflappable husband replied, obviously impressed. He pulled out his own phone to take a picture. "Do you think I can take video in here?" Alex wasn't even bothering to whisper anymore. No one was.

"I think it's mandatory at an event like this," Imogen replied. She added reluctantly: "Don't forget to tag at-Glossy."

But of course Eve wouldn't let a little sex scandal or the whir of robotic photographers steal her wedding thunder. Today was all about her. This was being live-streamed to the world, and damn it, she was the star.

Someone flipped a switch and the room plunged into darkness. Confused, the drones stayed in place as a spotlight hit the mahogany doors at the start of the aisle. Except it wasn't an aisle, not in the traditional sense. No, Eve would walk down a bright red carpet. Pachelbel's Canon played as Eve appeared, basking in the lamp's glow and the attention of an entire room. For a moment, even Imogen sucked in her breath at how beautiful Eve looked there in the spotlight, her shoulders and décolletage shimmering, her hair pulled into the perfect side chignon and the dress sweeping down over her narrow hips, the train trailing ever so slightly out the door.

As the lights came back up and Eve confidently took her first step down the aisle, the room erupted in chaos. Drones buzzed busily overhead. Phones replaced faces, held aloft to capture the moment to be posted on Twitter, Facebook, Keek and Instagram, all hashtagged, as decreed in the program, #GlossyWedding. Through it all, Eve remained laser-focused on the front of the room with a smile that appeared painted across her face with a bold red lipstick.

Sweat poured visibly down the sides of Andrew's neck as Eve

advanced. He looked more like he had when he and Imogen dated. His face, puffy and shiny, no doubt from the liquid courage it took for him to face the next few hours, was frozen in a look of terror. Imogen imagined the riot act Eve had read him that morning. She was surprised actually that *he* hadn't fled, but the pull of his public life and the embarrassment he would face leaving town was too much for his fragile ego. *What a plonker,* she thought. His face twitched as he stood there; Imogen recognized it as a sure giveaway that Andrew had indulged in another of his old vices, cocaine, probably just before the ceremony. He shuddered as Eve approached.

Eve was halfway down the aisle when the music stopped, mid-note. *This is it,* Imogen thought. *This is where she leaves him. This is where she walks out.* And for a moment, she had a new respect for Eve, even if she had choreographed a very public exit.

But no.

Pop music began blaring from hidden speakers. *What was this song?* It was familiar, but Imogen couldn't quite place it. From seats lining the aisle, *Glossy* staffers, all in bright pink dresses (and frightfully skinny), rose and formed a circle around Eve. There they stood, feet hip-width apart, swinging their hips left and then right and crossing their arms in front of their chests just as the chorus swelled: "Looking so crazy in love's/Got me looking, got me looking so crazy in love."

Of course, Beyoncé. It was the choreographed dance the girls had learned at Eve's apartment during the snow day. Like they were part of the act, the drones swirled over their heads to the beat. The Internet would not miss a second of this artfully plotted spontaneous moment. Eve feigned shock, as though she couldn't believe her staffers would bequeath her with such a performance on her wedding day. She even rolled her eyes slightly to the ceiling as she smirked to enhance the idea that she thought this might be a little bit silly, but Imogen knew, without having to ask Ashley, who wiggled her bottom in the aisle with a look of horror on her face, that this show had been directed by Eve, down to the very last tasteful twerk.

The girls took Eve all the way to Andrew. His mother desperately fanned herself with a bright pink wedding program. Fainting was not entirely out of the question.

The ceremony itself was brief and nondenominational. Imogen caught Eve pinch Andrew under his rib cage to compel him to remain standing. Just as the Second Circuit Court of Appeals judge presiding over the wedding prepared to announce the couple to the audience, Eve shot her hand toward him, her palm appearing flat in front of his face. *Not again,* Imogen thought.

"Just a second," Eve said, pulling an iPhone out from somewhere within the taffeta folds of her gown. "I need to update my Facebook status." She punched in a few buttons and raised the phone over her head like a trophy. "It's not official until it's Facebook official," she shouted to the room. "And while I'm at it," she added, "let me find something to wear to the after-party."

Oh no. Even in this moment Eve was going to perform a publicity stunt.

She pretended to murmur to herself, but Eve had a microphone on so her words were broadcast loud and clear to the entire room.

"I want something short, something white, something Tadashi. What should I do? I think I will BUY IT NOW!" And as she hit the button, a twentysomething man in a pristine tuxedo, a man who looked like a much more suitable mate for Eve than the rheumy-eyed addict standing next to her, walked through the grand double doors to deliver a white box tied beautifully with a satin bow the size of a Volkswagen.

"Looks like I have my after-party dress." Eve giggled to the crowd, who applauded the moment, if not the woman.

Afterward, there was no formal receiving line. Andrew slunk off to the bar, while Eve insisted on taking selfies with the starlets she had paid a total of more than $100,000 to show up. Waiters circulated with champagne, white wine and light-colored appetizers. Eve mandated all of the food served at the wedding be anemic so that nothing colorful could spill on her dress.

Eve had invited several of her ex-boyfriends, some much older and others her age, fratty-looking banker types partial to pocket squares and whimsical ties from Vineyard Vines. They huddled in packs around the room, eyeing Andrew's friends from Dalton, similar save for twenty years, twenty extra pounds and a couple of divorces.

Dinner tables were artfully arranged around a dance floor in the adjacent formal dining room. A band, one that was fairly well known among hipster yuppies in gentrifying Brooklyn, was setting up on the stage.

Before they needed to sit for the five-course dinner, Imogen wove her way through the crowd to join the small queue for the restroom. The women in front of her surely knew Eve from back home in Wisconsin. They were dressed in black tie, but not as polished as the rest of the crowd. Their hair was just a touch bigger, their nails too garish, the dresses about five years out of date. All three of them wore gold bands on their left ring fingers. From their conversation it was clear that these three women hadn't kept in close touch with Eve.

"Erin . . . are you glad that we came?"

"I'm glad that Eve sent us free airplane tickets to come see New York City for the weekend!" The women chuckled and high-fived one another.

"She sure looks different." The girl nodded over to Eve, who had her arm slung around the waist of the redheaded star of a teenage vampire television series. The photographer was ordered to take one more picture.

"I'll bet she doesn't act any different. I'll bet she's still mean as a cat with his tail stuck in a door."

The smaller and chubbier of the three piped up to defend Eve. "Come now, girls. She isn't all that bad. Remember how much fun we had on the prom committee?"

"Remember how Eve rigged the ballot to make herself prom queen?" said the larger of the women. "Now look at all of this. Looks like she rigged herself a marriage." She spread her arms wide to encompass the enormity of the room before lowering her voice. "Even if it sounds like she's marrying kind of a scumbag, Candy Cool strikes again."

Imogen was jerked out of her reverie.

Candy Cool. It rolled off that girl's tongue like a proper name. Like an old friend. Like someone that she knew. Imogen felt a chill just hearing the name spoken out loud, this name of someone who had been torturing her daughter. She thought she must have misheard, because what would three married women from the middle of the country know about a teenage bully?

The small one slapped her thigh, emitting a snort.

"Oh, I had forgotten all about Candy Cool."

Imogen needed to know if she was hearing these women correctly. It was a possibility that she didn't understand their thick Midwestern accents.

Imogen tapped the bigger woman on the shoulder. "Pardon me? But I couldn't help but hear you talking about someone named Candy Cool. How do you know her? Who is she?"

"Who is Candy Cool?" The two women to her right looked at Imogen with skepticism, but the one she tapped enjoyed an audience.

"You already know her. You're at her wedding."

"I'm not sure I understand."

"Eve used to use the name Candy Cool for all of her screen names in high school, like instant messenger and chat and stuff. She was stupid though. She hacked into the school's voting system to try to make herself prom queen, but she didn't do it right. She got caught because all of the ballots cast for her were from a person named Candy Cool instead of other students." This group of women, all of whom looked so much older than Eve, perhaps because they had already been married and grown up in their small town, collapsed into laughter, tears running down their cheeks at the memory of Eve getting in trouble. In a burst of clarity, Imogen's insides turned to ice.

Eve was Candy Cool. Eve was the one harassing her daughter, her daughter who was nothing but an innocent little girl. She remembered some of the terrible things that had been written on Annabel's Facebook page: "You'll never be as pretty as your mom." "You're an ugly little pig and everyone thinks so." "I don't know how you can stand looking in the mirror every day."

She tried to keep calm, but for an instant everything in the room stopped moving. Everything made horrible sense. Thoughts sliced manically through her mind. A few months ago Imogen never would have thought such a thing was possible, a grown woman bullying and verbally abusing a child. Knowing what she knew about Eve now, she knew without a doubt that it was true.

"What a story, girls. I bet you have so many more of them to tell about Eve, but I need to track down my husband before this party gets started." Imogen managed to extricate herself from the small scrum.

As she walked off, Imogen pulled out her phone to send her daughter a text.

>>>>I just want you to know I love you very much.<<<<

A reply came through instantly. She swore the phone was actually glued to Annabel's hand.

>>>>Awww ... I know mom ☺ <<<<

* * *

Eve couldn't figure out how to get out of her wedding dress. The girls from the office had helped fasten the more than one hundred teensy tiny buttons up the back, but now she had to pee and she couldn't get the thing undone. She'd thought she could do it herself, but now here she was in the gilded bathroom off the Grand Ballroom, stuck inside her dress with a very full bladder.

"I can't believe she married him." "What a gold digger." "How could she walk down that aisle?"

Eve heard each and every thing people were saying about her. Could hear the soft cluck of their tongues hitting the roofs of their mouths to stop their gossip as soon as Eve drew near. As she approached, they morphed into gushing sycophants, congratulating her and telling her what a beautiful bride she made.

Bitches.

Reaching her hand behind her, she nearly grasped the top button. If only she could start there, the other buttons might come undone quite easily. She nearly had it, but the satin slid through her fingers.

They all wanted to know why she walked down the aisle. Why didn't she walk away when she saw the *New York Post* this morning? They wanted to know if she knew. They all wondered how much she knew. Of course she knew. She knew what she was getting into with Andrew from the very beginning. Christ, he asked her to dress up like a schoolgirl on their third date and spank him with his Sigma Chi fraternity paddle. She had heard it all and the truth was, she didn't give a shit. Eve didn't see any point in calling off the wedding. To the contrary, getting married in this city was the same as getting a job promotion. You busted your ass to get it done and then you used it to help you get to the next step, whether that next step was having a baby, getting a better apartment, increasing your social status or putting yourself in a better position for marriage number two. This marriage was an alliance. Look at Hillary. Look at Huma. Look at Silda. Eve could handle a lot. Besides, the wedding was the perfect exposure for Glossy.com. They were under a microscope right now. The sharks were circling. Something big was about to happen. Aerin Chang had come to the wedding. That had to mean something.

Andrew was just her starter husband, the one who would catapult her to another level in New York society and business (the same thing, really). Name recognition mattered with investors and she knew she would be courting a lot of those. They'd get a divorce eventually (no kids for sure . . . she had already made sure of that). She could remarry again in her early thirties, probably someone else in tech. When *that* wedding was written up in *The New York Times* they would describe it as the adorable coupling of "two tech darlings."

Maybe she could pull the dress up from the bottom. The material was very snug around her thighs, but maybe if she crossed her legs in just the right way.

The sound of expensive fabric tearing echoed through the marble bathroom. *Sonofabitch.*

* * *

Half blind with rage, Imogen sliced her way through the crowd. All around her guests continued their lighthearted gossip. Imogen watched the crowd move her as if she were in a dream. Her husband and best friend finally came into focus across the room.

"I heard some scoop," Bridgett said, pulling Imogen in between them and handing her a glass of pink champagne. Imogen took a sip but it tasted sour.

Bridgett continued. "I heard from one of Eve's Harvard B-school friends that she didn't even flinch when she saw the story in the *Post*. She took it in stride, said the show must go on and ordered Andrew to deny, deny, deny to the media so she could have her picture-perfect wedding. How sick is that?"

"I can do you one sicker." Imogen's face must have been drained completely of color.

"Baby, what's wrong?" Alex reached out a hand to steady her.

"She's the devil. The actual devil. She's so much worse than I ever thought."

Everything in Imogen's body, everything that made her a mother, wanted to find Eve and rip her limb from limb for what she had done to her daughter.

"We need to get the hell out of here right now."

* * *

When Imogen told them what Eve had done Alex wanted to call the authorities and Bridgett wanted to call Page Six. Imogen vacillated between never wanting to see Eve's face again and wanting to smash it with something heavy. She volleyed between the options through-out the next several hours.

Alex went to the office and his mom, "Mama Marretti," packed up both of her grandchildren for a weekend in Queens and so Imogen found herself alone in the house on Sunday morning, stewing, plotting, pissed off. Her computer crashed just as she was about to compose a scathing email to TechBlab, exposing Eve for everything she had done.

"Crap!" she cursed to the empty house, jabbing her index finger at the power button to coax it to reboot. A million windows popped up to let her know things hadn't been properly shut down. Word document after Word document that had been hanging out in the background of her computer popped up. Recovered. Recovered. Recovered!!!

What was this? ShoppitMag.doc [Recovered].

Imogen hadn't thought about that at all over the holidays—the ideas she had for a Shoppit magazine after her meeting with Aerin. She must not have saved the document properly. These were good. She probably should have spent more time fleshing them out, but there were nuggets of something in here. Imogen heaved a sigh and carried the laptop over to the kitchen table. She could now balance a laptop on her palm as expertly as the women in her office. *What would be the harm in adding a little gloss to this proposal?*

For the next six hours, that's what she did. It took her mind off Eve and vengeance and *Glossy* and a buyout. Before she knew it, Imogen had a twenty-page manifesto. This is what a digital magazine should look like. It was interactive. It was user-friendly. It inspired the reader with words, pictures, videos and social media. It didn't bash them over the head with BUY IT NOW captions, it merely intrigued them, encouraging them to mindfully consider making a purchase.

She featured real women in the clothes, women of all shapes and sizes and colors. They'd do behind-the-scenes videos of all of their shoots. She could do stop-frame videos of designers actually making the clothes. She'd let the designers take over Shoppit's Instagram and Twitter. She'd let regular readers take over too. They really could make fashion democratic. She pored over old magazines. By midnight the kitchen table was covered with tear sheets, photographs and pages of scribbled ideas—some of them lousy, but some of them quite good. Really good. Imogen hadn't felt this kind of jittery thrill of creativity in years. She drew out pictures of the pages in pencil and then snapped them with her iPhone before copying them into a document on the computer—a Google Doc!

But what now? *Screw it.* Imogen was just going to bite the bullet and send it to Aerin Chang. Time to put herself out there. Before she could talk herself out of it, she attached her memo in an email to Aerin and hit send.

Her fingers wobbled over her phone as she debated whether to call Bridgett or Massimo to tell them what she had done when an email popped up in her in-box.

From: Robert Mannering (RMannering@ManneringCorp.com)
To: Imogen Tate (ITate@Glossy.com)

Dear Imogen,

Please attend an all-hands meeting tomorrow morning at 10 a.m.

Sincerely,
Robert Mannering Jr.

No one had seen the absentee chief executive of the company in the flesh for at least three years, not since he'd married an airline heiress and taken up amateur surfing on her private heart-shaped island off the coast of the Seychelles.

Had he been around when Worthington took the buyout? Imogen hadn't seen him.

Was this when she got offered the buyout? Tomorrow at ten a.m.? Was this how her career in magazines would end?

Imogen fell asleep wondering if she cared.

* * *

The next morning, all the way to the office, Imogen replayed over and over in her head what she would say to Eve. She would confront her with everything she knew and then she would submit her resignation to Robert Mannering Jr., or he would fire her. Either way, with Eve she would get the last word.

Imogen rushed toward the elevator right as the doors were closing. A delicate ivory hand reached out to hold the doors open for her. Aerin Chang looked up, startled to see that it was Imogen walking into the elevator. The Shoppit CEO tucked both sides of her dark hair behind her tiny ears.

"What are you doing here?" Imogen said. "Did you get the email I sent last night?"

Aerin paused. "I did. I was about to email you back, but things got so rushed this morning." Imogen realized that the girl didn't answer her first question.

"Why are you here?" Imogen repeated it.

It was obvious that Aerin was trying to choose her words carefully.

"I have a meeting here with Rob Mannering." Aerin's face was blank.

With a startling clarity, Imogen realized the reason Aerin was there.

"Is this about the *Glossy* sale?"

The elevator doors opened onto a nondescript floor beneath the *Glossy* offices, a floor that housed Sales, Accounting and Human Resources. Aerin began to step out of the elevator.

"Imogen. I can't talk about it right this second. I want to talk about it with you. I want to talk to you about your email last night. I want to talk to you about everything."

The doors closed on her words and Imogen continued up another three floors.

Imogen had never doubted her own judgment of character, at least not until Eve came back. Eve made her question her ability to read people and their motivations. She'd had such a good feeling about Aerin Chang from the moment she started following her on Instagram, and it was only solidified when they met in person. She seemed so genuine. In hindsight, Eve had never been genuine, just eager, and her eagerness masked the naked ambition that was revealed once she was in a position with a modicum of power.

Mannering had sold *Glossy* to Shoppit. Imogen knew it. That was the meeting.

Maybe they weren't going to fire her. She knew Aerin Chang wanted to work with her. But still, could she stomach working with Eve for a single day more? She would endure the same torture from that horrible girl no matter who owned the company. The sale was a good thing for *Glossy*. Of that, Imogen was sure. Aerin was a solid executive with a great head on her shoulders and an incredible eye. But Ron had been right. She needed to make a choice. She wanted Eve out of her life. She would congratulate Aerin on the sale and take the buyout.

Imogen scanned the office, looking for Eve, wanting to confront her before the big meeting. She needed to get it over with.

Her anger surfaced as, across the room, she saw the girl applying a fresh coat of bright red lipstick and pouting at herself into her iPhone camera. Around her neck, the very same shade as her lips, was the red Hermès scarf Imogen gave her two years earlier when she left for business school.

Breathe. She had to remember to breathe.

Ashley cut her off before she could reach Eve.

"I need your help." She was more frantic than usual.

"Ashley, can we talk about it in a little bit?"

"No. I need you now." She pulled Imogen into her office. "The commenters on the site got nasty after Eve's wedding. I don't want to talk to her about it. Because you know. It was her wedding, but I need you to help me shut it down."

"I have no idea how to even start doing that."

"Me neither. It's sooooo bad."

Imogen didn't bother to ask Ashley what "sooooo bad" meant. She took a look for herself.

That is the saddest white girl dance to Beyoncé I have ever seen. Those girls look like they'd rather be in prison!

Could the entire wedding party be any thinner? Gross!

I see a toddler in the corner. Did the groom bring a date?

DESPERATE!

I don't want to BUY ANY of this NOW. I want to forget I saw it.

The bride scares me ... STEPFORD!

Imogen glanced down at her watch. She had ten minutes. "Let me make a quick phone call and see what I can do." As she sank into her chair, she thought about doing nothing at all. Let them skewer Eve for the witch she was. She deserved it. Let the *Glossy* site be covered in hate mail. She'd be gone in a couple of hours anyway.

But she couldn't. This was her magazine, until someone told her it wasn't. She had pride.

Rashid answered on the first ring.

"Hello, beautiful."

"Can you help me with something a bit technical?"

"Of course."

"I need to shut off the comments on all blog posts about Eve's wedding."

He considered for a second. "What CMS are you using?"

Imogen surprised herself that she knew the answer to that question right off the bat.

"It's based on WordPress."

"Oh, easy then. Go into the back end of the system and click on the posts that are getting the comments." Imogen did as she was told. "There should be a drop-down box that will let you see all of the options. You can just hide comments."

It was so simple. Yet this was something Imogen never could have done three months earlier. She breathed a sigh of relief that it was something she could do now. She switched off the comments and pushed her chair back from her desk.

"Rashid . . . one more thing? How hard is it to hack into someone's Twitter account?"

"For a regular person?"

"For you?"

"Easy. Unethical, but easy. You want into Eve's account?"

"I might."

"Anything for you, Imogen." The plan wasn't fully formed yet. She had to go to this meeting. Then she would deal with Eve and Candy Cool.

Eve had already vacated her corner. Deliberately, Imogen walked over to Ashley.

"Thank you," she whispered in her ear.

"For what?" Ashley's wide eyes were confused.

"For everything since I've been back. I can't tell you how much I appreciate it."

The girl blushed. "That's my job. I'm here to help."

"I know you are, darling. But you're here to do more than that too. Make sure that people appreciate that." Tears threatened to smear Ashley's perfectly smudged smoky eye.

Imogen leaned in to hug her.

"Mr. Worthington was right," Ashley said into Imogen's shoulder.

"About what?"

"When he was leaving he told me to try to spend as much time with you as I could. He said I should try to be more like you when I grow up."

Imogen smiled at her old boss's compliment.

"I think you are quite grown-up already."

Imogen's phone pinged with an incoming email.

From: Eve Morton (EMorton@Glossy.com)
To: GlossyStaff@Glossy.com

Please join me in the conference room in an hour to celebrate my big promotion with me. We also have a HUGE announcement about the magazine!!!! We're about to be BIG-TIME LADIES!

It's a Good, Great, Gorgeous, GLOSSY! Day!!!
Eve

* * *

The ecru walls of the hallway leading to the large executive conference room were lined with enlarged magazine covers throughout the history of Robert Mannering Corp. There was *Sporting, Chic, Business Watch, Beautiful Homes, Yacht Enthusiast* and, finally, *Glossy.* Early issues of the fashion magazine had beautifully illustrated covers of prettily coifed twentysomething housewives in tea-length dresses and hats. Then came the photographs, growing edgier and sexier as the years went on. So much more skin. Just steps before the doors to the conference room the covers stopped. They were out of room. It made Imogen laugh. *How do you put a website on a wall?*

Inside the bright and airy meeting room, Robert Mannering's eleven gray-haired board members congregated around the mahogany table, furiously typing away on BlackBerrys. Bridgett liked to joke that it was executives in their sixties who were keeping BlackBerry in business. Imogen glanced longingly at their easy-to-type-on keyboards. The room had floor-to-ceiling windows on two walls and on a clear day the view stretched out to Coney Island and the Atlantic Ocean beyond it.

Aerin Chang sat at one end of the table. Robert Mannering Jr. at the other. Unfortunately, the only empty seat at the table was right next to Eve, who wore a smug smile on her wide face. She had no doubt this was her moment to shine.

Imogen kept a proud expression on her own face as she walked toward the empty executive-style high-backed leather chair. Lowering herself into it, she felt something prick her derriere. She glanced down, trying not to betray anything to the room, to see Eve's plastic dinosaur on her chair.

"Rarrrr," Eve mouthed, her lips red and swollen with collagen. Raising her lacquered blue nails like claws, she was more reptilian than the toy.

Did anyone else see that?

Two could play at that game. Imogen put the plastic animal on the table in front of her. She was older than Eve. So what? She owned it. Eve's immaturity was comical at this point. Imogen placed her hand on her knee to keep her leg from bouncing up and down.

As she sat, Aerin stood, appearing cool and in control in a skinny Thom Browne pantsuit with just the faintest pinstripes. She tucked her hair behind her ears and sucked in a deep breath before smiling directly at Imogen.

"Imogen, I'm so happy you made it. I wasn't going to start until you got here."

Mannering Jr. stood too then. His face was sunburned, as though they'd pulled him, reluctantly, into the boardroom from the beach. He looked lazily over at Imogen. "Heya, Imogen. Good to see you." One by one, the board members turned their eyes away from their phones when Robert began talking.

"First, I know that I don't need to say this, but I will anyway," the chief executive said, tugging at his tie uncomfortably like it was a collar someone fastened too tightly. "What I'm about to tell you must remain in this room and completely confidential until we make a statement to the press." Everyone made a big show of turning off their devices.

Eve stared only at Imogen, who could see her stroking the red scarf out of the corner of her eye.

"I want to thank everyone in this room for being so discreet as we worked on what I'm so happy to announce is the biggest sale Robert Mannering has ever completed. I don't need to mince words here. We have sold the brand-new *Glossy* platform to emerging Internet giant Shoppit for the price of two hundred ninety million dollars."

Mannering smiled and nodded like a pageant queen while his audience made a show of polite golf claps.

With that, he sank back into his chair. His work was finished and the check was probably already in the bank.

A lithe young man with jet-black hair, Mannering's assistant perhaps, in a fine black suit and glasses that covered too much of his face, glided into the room with a silver tray of fresh doughnuts.

"They're still warm," he told the assembled crowd, as if they were the kind of people who regularly consumed these kinds of snacks in meetings. Their warm doughy scent kissed Imogen's nostrils, reminding her of Café Du Monde. New Orleans could still be an option. It hadn't gone anywhere.

Aerin smiled expertly and took control of the meeting. "Thank you for having me here. I know that this might not seem like a traditional media acquisition to you. I've had my eye on this for a while now. I'd been thinking about it even before Eve Morton changed the format of *Glossy*." She left her seat and strolled around the room, forcing the board to swivel their heads to face her as she walked along the wall of windows, the wide expanse of Manhattan at her feet.

"I'm a fan of magazines." Aerin threw up her hands. "Love 'em.

Most of you know that. I love print magazines. I love digital magazines too."

She walked toward a shelf in the corner that displayed copies of all the Mannering publications and pulled the very last copy of *Glossy* they'd printed. Aerin ran her hand over the shiny cover.

"They can live together. My vision is to integrate *Glossy*'s incredible voice across all of Shoppit's platforms. I want our editorial to come to life online the way it does in a magazine." She paused and took another step, now directly across the table from Imogen.

"Additionally, I want to bring *Glossy* back to print. We probably won't do twelve times a year right off the bat, but we will produce a beautifully edited print magazine four months out of the year as a companion to the editorial on Shoppit's site. For women, the print experience is very unique. We shouldn't do the same thing in digital we do in print. Keeping it separate but equal will keep things fresh."

It hadn't been what Imogen was expecting to hear by a long shot. *Glossy back in print?* She knew that Aerin had chosen to stand in that exact spot so that she could see Imogen's expression when she revealed her plan. Imogen tilted her head to the side and made a small curtsy with her hand to tell Aerin it was all right to continue. Eve cleared her throat, her mouth twitching, and she made a noise as if she wanted to interrupt, but Aerin plowed forward.

"And now I want to introduce the team that I've painstakingly chosen to lead this huge endeavor for my company. We're taking a very large and very expensive gamble on this and I need to have the very best people working with me."

Eve grew taller in her chair next to Imogen, looking sideways at her, smirking. Shoppit was a tech company. Of course Eve would have a major role, perhaps even one above Imogen. That was the reason Imogen knew she couldn't possibly stay on. It would be hard to tell Aerin that they wouldn't be working together.

Aerin gestured to the middle of the table, where there was a plain manila envelope. "Imogen, we have an offer for you in there. I would love if you would look it over before I keep talking?" *What was this?* As Imogen reached across the tabletop to pick up the envelope, Eve's eyes darted around, looking for a second envelope.

Imogen slid a nail beneath the metal prongs and pulled out a stack of contracts with an offer letter on the top. She could see Aerin Chang's signature, bold and curvy on the bottom of the page.

This couldn't be right.

"Imogen Tate, we would be thrilled to offer you the position of artistic director of Shoppit. When the board asked for my opinion on this I told them that there is no other person in the industry with your eye and the respect of your peers. If you accept, you'll be leading the charge on a new generation of *Glossy* and overseeing the launch of all our other editorial properties and our portfolio of platforms."

Eve's and Imogen's jaws dropped in unison. If they were in a cartoon, steam would have blown out of Eve's ears.

Nothing but professional, Aerin didn't let the temperature of the room faze her.

"Eve Morton will be working directly underneath Imogen Tate. She will be given the title of deputy editor." Aerin looked over at Eve. Did she expect her to be pleased by the news? Deputy editor was still a big job. It was a huge job for someone who'd been an assistant less than three years earlier. But no one knew better than Imogen that it wasn't big enough for Eve. A vein throbbed at Eve's temple as Aerin clicked a button in her hand so that a slide appeared on a screen behind her.

It was one of the pages Imogen sent through the night before.

"The new *Glossy* is about fashion and the real woman. Designers no longer live in their ivory towers, and fashion magazines can't either," Aerin asserted. "The new *Glossy* will be completely interactive. The reader can enjoy it anywhere. In print, on their phone, on their tablet or on their computer. Imogen Tate is the woman who will help us make the magazine of the future."

Making a noise between a grunt and a snort, Eve pushed her seat back from the table. She paused for just a moment and stared down at Imogen, then, without a word, stalked out of the room.

Aerin continued on to name a team of new business development folks from Shoppit who would be working to bring native advertising to the digital version of *Glossy*. She then turned to Imogen.

"Imogen, I trust you can build a staff of top-notch editorial folks to get us back up and running. I'm sure you have some people already in mind." She smiled warmly at her. Imogen tried to smile back. She hadn't expected any of this.

She nodded. "I do."

"Great." Aerin looked over at another woman dressed all in black. "Sara will prepare a press release to go out this afternoon."

Aerin sat, signaling that the meeting was through, but rose again as Imogen got out of her seat. The two women drifted into the corner of the room and out of earshot, as the other executives filed out, patting themselves on the back to celebrate what the sale would do for the company's plummeting stock price.

Imogen wanted to hug Aerin but extended her hand instead.

"I underestimated you. When I heard that Shoppit was going to buy this magazine, I thought that I was done for. I'm sorry."

"Don't be sorry. I wish I could have been up front with you about this sale from the very beginning."

Imogen shook her head. "I understand. I really do. What *was* our meeting all about?"

Aerin smiled. "I wanted to know if you were really the Imogen Tate I imagined. I wanted to know if you were up for a challenge and for this kind of job."

Imogen nodded. "I have a lot to learn, but I am."

"It's fine. We'll teach you. And you will teach us how to run a magazine. I should let you know about one of the perks of working for a technology company."

"The macarons?" Imogen said, raising an eyebrow.

"Nope. The technology. We make it easy for you to work from almost anywhere. We have people who do their jobs pretty much all over the world."

She wanted the job. But she needed to be very up front with Aerin. "I won't work with Eve."

For a minute, Imogen thought she saw Aerin turn a slight shade of red.

"I agree with you. Mannering thought we had to offer her something but I knew she would never take the deputy job. If it comes down to having to choose between you or her, I choose you."

"I appreciate that."

"Do you want me to talk to her?"

"I'd prefer to handle it."

Imogen could hear her phone buzzing on the table. "I hate to be rude, but could we pick up this discussion this afternoon? I need to take care of something downstairs."

Even as she played out terrible things she wanted to do to Eve, a sense of calm crept over her. It was the calmest she had felt in a long time, the calmest she had felt since she learned about the cancer and definitely the calmest she had felt since coming back to work.

She had a text from Rashid.

>>>>Mission accomplished. I'm in Eve's Twitter. Give me more instructions.<<<<

Things changed, but she could alter her original plan. She thought for a second and typed a few lines back to him, telling him exactly what she needed him to do.

When Imogen arrived downstairs, Eve was standing at her desk, her headset nested in her curls, furiously shouting to someone on the other end.

Standing in the door to her office, Imogen called out to her.

"Eve. Get in my office. Now."

Her tone finally alerted the girl that it was time to listen to authority. Eve murmured into the mouthpiece of her headset before removing it from her head altogether. She walked slowly to Imogen's office.

Imogen sat in her desk chair, the one Eve had twirled so capriciously in just months earlier.

Eve strode in, reeking of insolence. Imogen took a deep look at the girl. Her shoulders were thrown back, turning her body into a parenthesis. Her eyes narrowed into mean slits. One of her eyebrows arched slightly more than the other, giving her a perpetually sinister look.

"That's bullshit what happened up there," Eve spat, digging the heels of her hands into the edge of Imogen's desk and leaning over it like a cobra ready to strike.

Eve unleashed her tirade. "What the hell do you know about running a website? Nothing. I should be the one in charge over at Shoppit. You didn't even go to college. I went to fucking Harvard!"

Imogen stood tall and raised her hand to cut her off.

"Shut your mouth for once, Eve." God, she would love to place her own hand over Eve's mouth and shush her. "Sit down," Imogen commanded, before she continued. Again, Eve did as she was told. Still glaring at Imogen, she perched on the edge of the couch.

"I am going to say this exactly once and after I say it, I never want to see you again. You're nothing but a nasty, jealous bully. I know that you're Candy Cool, Eve. I know that you have been harassing my daughter. You're a sick and evil bitch, and I don't know if you will ever recover from that. I think you sold your soul a long time ago. I think that's the reason you walked down the aisle to marry a man you don't love. I know you came back to *Glossy* to take my job, not to work with me. But you're nothing but a cheap knockoff."

"I don't have to listen to this." Eve bared her teeth at Imogen, crossing her arms in front of her chest. Fury raged in her eyes and again Imogen was reminded of Nutkin. This time, she wouldn't allow Eve the opportunity to slaughter any more lambs.

"You don't. But you will," Imogen said.

Eve believed she was invincible, that she would never be caught. Imogen imagined she had felt the exact same way up until the moment that she was found out for tampering with those prom queen ballots so long ago.

"You are an evil genius, Eve. You're smarter than me in so many ways. You understand tech in a way that I never will. But you forced me to learn. For that, I suppose I have to be grateful. No. I am grateful. I'll have a second act now. And you will too . . . but not at *Glossy* and not in New York City. You will never work in the fashion industry again, Eve. I don't want you as my deputy and I don't want you in this business. Go to Silicon Valley. Go to Silicon Beach. Create a Silicon something of your own back in Wisconsin. I don't care. Plenty of people would die to hire you on the other side of the country. I never want to see your face on this coast again. Stay away from me, stay away from my family and stay the hell away from my magazine."

Eve's jaw nearly touched the floor.

In an instant, her expression changed into that of a little girl being chastised by her mother. She slumped back into the couch and rounded her shoulders. Her voice was quieter. "I only did it to upset you. I didn't mean to hurt Annabel. It was just a way to hurt you." Imogen held up her hand again. She didn't want to hear it. Any of it. Of course Eve would think of some excuse for torturing a ten-year-old girl.

Imogen remained silent.

Eve was defensive, almost frightened. "So what are you going to do now? Are you going to go out there and expose me? Tell everyone what I did?"

Eve's phone pinged with an alert. "What the fuck?"

Imogen smiled. "What, Eve?"

"I didn't tweet that!"

Imogen glanced at the Twitter feed on her own computer.

@GlossyEve: A fond farewell to @Glossy and #NYC. I'm about to embark on a new adventure. C'est la vie!

Rashid worked fast. Now that it was tweeted to the world, there was no going back.

Eve's eyes narrowed. "I didn't tweet that," she said again through gritted teeth.

Imogen feigned surprise. "Well, then. I wonder who did."

She rose and walked over to her office door to pull it open, gesturing for Eve to stand and walk out.

Eve repeated herself as she inched out of the office. "Are you going to tell everyone what I did?"

"No, Eve. No, I'm not going to tell everyone what you did. It isn't all about you, Eve."

Who Said Magazines Were Dead?

Shoppit Shakes Up Fashion Industry with Unveiling of New Glossy *Magazine (YES, A MAGAZINE!)*

By Addison Cao
August 1, 2016

And they said it couldn't be done! The e-commerce newbie Shoppit unveiled their first issue of *Glossy* magazine this week after acquiring the editorial brand for a hefty price tag in January.

The first cover featured the stunning supermodel Chanel Iman, wearing Google Glass and a Balenciaga gown. The new magazine is expected to publish four times a year while the website updates daily with editorial, photo and video content. Artistic Director Imogen Tate said she expects the margins on the new product to exceed expectations in the first quarter.

"We still have the traditional advertisers that have always been loyal to print, but we are able to do incredible things online with native advertising and by driving traffic to our retail partners at Shoppit," Ms. Tate told us at the wedding of the baby-faced tech mogul Rashid Davis to super celebrity stylist Bridgett Hart, who is seven months pregnant. The extravagant affair took place on Richard Branson's private Necker Island.

The magazine had a bumpy road over the past twelve months. While under the ownership of Robert Mannering Corp., *Glossy* was shuttered and turned into a website and an app, run mostly by Editorial Director Eve Morton, who was notoriously wicked to her staff. Ms. Morton left the company after its acquisition by Shoppit and is currently working underneath (ha!) Buzz CEO Reed Baxter as his director of external sales. Ms. Morton recently split from incarcerated Congressman Andrew "I've Been Naughty" Maxwell. A little birdie told us Eve may be the reason Baxter and Meadow Flowers called off their *Game of Thrones*–themed nuptials last month.

Ms. Tate's former assistant and *Glossy* community manager Ashley Arnsdale (you know, the one whose outfits always end up on the street-style blogs looking GORGEOUS) is reportedly working on a top-secret project for Shoppit involving vintage clothing.

Following her toast at the reception for Ms. Hart and Mr. Davis, Imogen Tate told us she welcomes this new age of digital-print partnership.

"The world isn't ready to abandon print," she said, raising her champagne glass into the air. Adding, with a laugh, "Plus, the Internet allows me to work remotely half the time, which is a bonus." Ms. Tate and her family are currently splitting their time between an apartment in TriBeCa and a home they are renovating in the Garden District of New Orleans.

Ms. Tate will be giving a TED Talk next month titled "Don't Call Me a Dinosaur: Embracing a New Era."

Sitting on her wraparound porch, a balmy summer breeze smelling of magnolias, Imogen Tate read the story with a satisfied smile and clicked her laptop shut.

ACKNOWLEDGMENTS

From Lucy to Jo: Thank you, Jo Piazza, for showing me how to work my iPad and being a complete joy to work with and for being a great friend and Fit Bitch who inspires me constantly.

From Jo to Lucy: Thank you, dear Imogen . . . I mean Lucy, for all of your wonderful ideas, your limitless creativity, your contagious passion and your inspiring use of emoji.

We have an entire village of incredible people to thank for helping take this book from a nugget of an idea to the store shelves. Thank you, Luke "Gamechanger!" Janklow, for seeing the vision before anyone else did. Thank you, Alexandra Machinist, for being the best damn superagent a first-time author could have hoped for. We could not have done this without our incredibly talented editor, the constant optimist, Jennifer Jackson. Your liner notes are one of our favorite things to Instagram. Will Heyward deserves a halo and a cocktail for dealing with all of our handwritten edits. We are so lucky to have Maxine Hitchcock and the whole Penguin team in the United Kingdom on our side. You make us feel like rock stars even when we are having a bad hair day.

Thank you, Francesco Clark, for always making us want to be better.

Neither of us could have made this writing partnership happen without the constant support of Chloe, the greatest, most tech-savvy nanny on the planet (and the inspiration for the inimitable Tilly).

Plum Sykes, Tom Sykes, Alice Sykes, Valerie Sykes, Fred Sykes, Josh Sykes, Alastair and Annalisa Rellie, Jemima Rellie, Katie Dance, Lucasta and Kevin Cummings, we would not be writing these acknowledgments without you. Euan Rellie, you win two awards: best husband and best book promoter ever.

The support of The Li.st cannot be quantified. You helped us both believe that we have a future in this brave new world of technology.

Thank you to all of our supportive friends, mentors and inspirations (both online and in real life):

Maxi Sloss, Sandra Ellis, Charlotte Clark, Sara Costello, Claude Kaplan, Lenore and Sean Mahoney, Gin Boswick, Podo, Lucy Guinness, Kara Liotte, Ben Widdicombe, Colleen Curtis, Glynnis MacNicol, Allison Gandolfo, Leah Chernikoff, Tracy Taylor, Toby Young, Amanda Foreman, Mary Alice Stephenson, Amanda Ross, Ann Caruso, Lloyd Nathan, Betsy Rhodes, Donald Robertson, Jennifer Sharp, Mary Shanahan, Paul Cavaco, Paula Froelich, Jaclyn Boschetti, Pamela Fiori, Glenda Bailey, Rachel Sklar, Bob Morris, Hailey Lustig, Jane Friedman, Natalie Massenet, Tristan Skylar, Dee Poku, Patrick Demarchelier, Pamela Henson, Oberto Gili, Ted Gibson, Cynthia Rowley, Christian Louboutin, Vera Wang, Michael Davies, Thom Browne, Bart Baldwin, Zac Posen and Grace Chang.

Thank you to Flybarre and our trainer (yes, we share one) Emily Cook Harris for the exercise highs that kept us going on countless yummy brunches together at Café Cluny.